TOUCHED BY MAGIC

As if he were the lodestone and she the element called to its bidding, Nick leaned toward him. She nuzzled her cheek against his hand. "It isn't the mud." Her voice was a whisper. "It's the . . . the . . ."

"And it can't possibly be the fact that I'm injured." Gowan traced a pattern of swirls over Nick's back and she heard his velvety laugh close to her ear. "If I didn't know better, I'd venture to guess that you had something to do with the whole, mad scheme. You are just cheeky enough, I think. And far too clever for your own good. Did you think fifteen stout lads from Beddgelert could accomplish what Peder could not?"

The last thing Nick needed was a reminder of her perfidy. She swallowed her shame and opened her eyes, but she did not dare meet his. "I—"

He did not give her the chance to confess her sins. Gowan grazed a kiss over Nick's eyes, forcing her words to vanish and her eyes to close again.

"I don't want to hear it." Like the delicate touch of a feather, his statement brushed her skin. "I don't want to hear your reasons . . ." He kissed the very tip of her nose. "Or your complaints . . ." He skimmed his mouth to her ear and traced its shape with the tip of his tongue. ". . . Or your arguments."

His hand at the back of her head, he spread his fingers through her hair. He pressed his forehead to hers and though Nick could not see him clearly so close, she knew he was smiling.

"I don't want you to say anything, Nick. I only want you to let me kiss you."

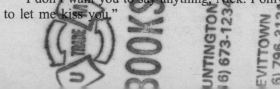

Touched By Magic

Constance Laux

ZEBRA BOOKS
KENSINGTON PUBLISHING CORP.

For Leslie Wey,
friend and cheerleader

ZEBRA BOOKS are published by

Kensington Publishing Corp.
850 Third Avenue
New York, NY 10022

First Printing: July, 1996
10 9 8 7 6 5 4 3 2 1

Printed in the United States of America

One

"Fair is foul."

Her voice hushed, each word drawn out like the careful phrases of a chant, Tildy Rhys bent low over the bubbling cauldron and sprinkled the surface of the liquid in it with heather. She whisked a strand of smoke-colored hair from in front of her eyes and breathed deep, watching as the potion bubbled and the steam rose, redolent with the scents of root and leaf.

"Foul is fair."

Leaning across her, Belle Rhys intoned her part of the charm. She stirred the pot with a birch branch, three times around sunwise, then back the other way, and when she was done, she drew the branch from the pot and made the sign of the cross over the brew with it.

"Hover through the fog . . ."

It was Clea's turn. The webwork of fine lines on her face flushed with the light of the fire, her voice trembling with the excitement of the moment, she stepped around her sisters and added bat wing to the whole.

The potion popped and spit and somewhere outside the walls of the cottage, a dark cloud scuttled across the sky, shrouding the afternoon sun.

Clea's eyes went wide. Her mouth open, she stared out the window at the dark shadow.

As always, Belle would not so easily betray her emotions. Her head was perfectly high and straight, the coil of silvery hair around it glinting like metal in what was left of the afternoon light. Belle's shoulders were as rigid as her head, but Tildy could not fail but notice that she clutched the birch branch so close, her knuckles were white.

More clouds piled up over the sun and Tildy's breath caught in her throat. As much as she told herself she must concentrate on the spell and not allow herself to think of anything else, she could not silence the voice inside her head. The one that wondered. The one that was amazed. The voice inside her that said for once, their magic was actually going to work!

Holding fast to her excitement, Tildy cleared her throat. She took a deep breath, steadying herself, ready to finish the incantation.

"Hover through the fog . . ." she repeated, finding her place in the spell. "Hover through the fog and filthy hair."

Belle sighed. Her shoulders sagged. She rolled her eyes toward the bundles of herbs and flowers hanging to dry at the ceiling. "Air," she said.

"What?" Distracted, Tildy blinked. She swept a loose strand of hair from her face and turned to her elder sister. "What did you say?"

Belle clicked her tongue. "Air," she repeated, and how anyone could make a single word sound so cross was beyond Tildy's ken. "It is air, Tildy. It is 'Hover through the fog and filthy air.' " Shaking her head with dismay, she went over to the table. There was a book open on it and Belle pulled her spectacles out of the pocket of her gown and perched them on the end of her nose. She peered down at the book. "See. Here." She pointed. " 'Macbeth,' Act I, Scene I. 'Hover through the fog and filthy air.' "

Tildy shook her head, trying to arrange her thoughts. The action only succeeded at further disarranging her hair. It escaped from its pins, tumbling over her shoulders in gray disarray. "Are you sure?" she asked.

She joined Belle at the table, squinting at the book, trying to bring the pages into focus, and when she finally did and clearly saw that she was in fact wrong, she tossed her head, dismissing both Macbeth and Mr. Shakespeare completely. "I had got it by heart. I know I did. I repeated it all last night before falling asleep and again this morning on waking." She squeezed her eyes shut and hurriedly recited the verse, as if proving that she really had done her best to commit it to memory. "Fair is foul and foul is fair. Hover through the fog and filthy—"

"Air." Belle finished for her. She punctuated the word with a one-fingered stab into the book. "It is air, Tildy, admit your mistake. If you would pay more mind to—"

"More mind!" Tildy rose up on the balls of her feet. She was considerably shorter than Belle and as round as her sister was tall and lean. Her own stature had never been such as to limit her tenacity, just as her sister's had never been so much as to intimidate her. "It would be far easier to remember one of the usual spells," she insisted, echoing an argument she had put to her sister more than once these past days. "You know it yourself. Why you insisted on something so . . . so . . ." Tildy searched for the right word and finally finding it, she shook her shoulders as if to demonstrate what she thought of Belle's plan. ". . . So bookish is over my head. One of our own charms would have worked just as well."

Belle squeezed her lips into a tight line. "We've been through it all, have we not? We cannot take the chance. Not this time."

"Well, I don't understand why—"

"Belle! Tildy!" As was usual, Clea had been so silent through their discussion, that Tildy nearly forgot she was there. She turned to see her younger sister still standing in front of the hearth, and if she looked excited before, now she looked ecstatic.

Clea's cheeks were the color of summer apples. Her eyes were open wide like those of a startled animal. With one trembling hand, she pointed to the cauldron. "Belle! Tildy! Hurry!"

Both Belle and Tildy scrambled to the hearth. Tildy may have been the plumper of the two, but she could move like the wind when she put her mind to it. She got to the fire a second before her sister and she might have given Belle a triumphant look if her attention had not been caught by what was happening in the cauldron.

"Look!" This time, it seemed not even Belle could hide her excitement. Behind her, Tildy heard Belle's breathless voice. It was clear that Belle was as awestruck as Clea, as astonished as Tildy herself.

As one, they stared into the cauldron. The brew was at a boil and it churned and bubbled, sending the bits and pieces of what they'd added to it rolling to the top, then plunging them again to the bottom. Traces of heather mixed with specks of bat wing. Borage and lavender, mugwort and black snakeroot, all blended and mingled. They combined. They coalesced. And they formed a picture.

Her heart banging against her ribs, Tildy grabbed for Belle's hand. Belle took hold of Clea. Together, they watched as the picture solidified, so clear, even Clea could see it.

"His hair is the color of chestnuts." As the picture got clearer and clearer, Tildy inventoried the features. "Yes. See there! Hair a rich, brown color. That is a good sign, is it not? He has a well-shaped face, too. I can see as much. And a firm jaw. His eyes . . ." She leaned nearer for a better look. "Brown as nuts in autumn." Just as quickly, she straightened, casting a worried look at her sisters. "But they are not very pleasant eyes, are they?"

Belle dismissed the observation with a slight lift of her shoulders. "What matters his eyes?" she asked, looking down into the brew through her spectacles. "There's a determined mouth and a chin that's sturdy enough. It's a fine face."

"It's a handsome face." Clea's voice was hopeful. She reached one hand toward the cauldron. As soon as she did, the picture dissolved, rolling back into itself.

"It will be fine, Tildy." With Belle between them, Clea was not near enough to touch Tildy's sleeve. She caught her eye instead, giving her sister the type of look she usually reserved for children or the sick. "You'll see. The eyes of a man do not matter nearly as much as—"

Clea's words were interrupted by another sound, one that made them all jump.

It was the wind, and it wailed through the cottage like the mournful whistle of a train engine.

Clea ran her tongue over her lips. Belle's shoulders went back. Tildy cast a glance toward the open doorway. "It seems not to matter at all now," she said. "We'll find out soon enough. He's here."

Gowan Alexander Payne, thirteenth Earl of Welshpool, stepped from the train at the station in Beddgelert. He shoved a hat over his chestnut hair and one hand up to shield his brown eyes from the afternoon sun, he looked around.

The town was as peaceful as an abbey and as clean as one of the surgeries at St. Bart's. The cobbled streets reminded him of those he'd seen in the medieval walled cities on the Continent. They glimmered like silver in the afternoon sun. Each stone cottage along the main road had its own garden, the flowers just beginning to bloom in the cool spring air.

Gowan watched as a group of children, rosy-cheeked and laughing, scrambled down the center of the town's main street where in the distance, a single cart pulled by oxen rumbled past a church that was as neat as a pin.

Against an awe-inspiring backdrop of green mountains and glimmering rivers, it was like a dream. After the tumult and grime of London, it was as picture-perfect as a painting in a fairy story.

It was quaint. It was romantic.

It was awful.

"Damn Wales." Wishing for nothing right now so much as a lungful of pungent city air, Gowan mumbled and shook his head as if to clear it. He turned to the sturdy lad loading his baggage onto a cart. "It is the same year here as it is in the rest of the world, isn't it?" he asked, only half in jest. "Eighteen hundred and eighty-six?"

The boy was wearing a cap of rough-spun wool and he dragged it from his head and ran his fingers through a thatch of straw-colored hair. He screwed his eyes nearly shut, seriously considering the question.

Gowan had hoped for more, a smile from the boy at least or a hearty laugh if he was lucky. He got neither and his mood plummeted from merely cynical to utterly morose. "Damn Wales," he mumbled again.

"M'lord?" The lad tugged at his forelock. "You were wantin' somethin' else, m'lord?"

"Wanting to be out of this godforsaken place," Gowan answered under his breath. Recognizing that he'd get nothing further from the slow-witted lad, he offered the boy as much of a smile as he could manage and a shilling for his labor. While the boy was still staring down at the coin as if it were the grandest portion of a pirate hoard, someone at Gowan's back cleared his throat.

He turned to find the stationmaster, hat in hand. "Beggin' your pardon, m'lord," the man said. Turning his military looking hat around and about, he shot Gowan a hesitant look from beneath black, bushy brows. "If there's anythin' else we can be doing for you . . ."

Gowan was tempted to tell him.

He didn't. But only because he suspected the locals weren't ready to hear what he had to say about either their country or his ill fortune at finding himself in it.

Instead, he drew in a bracing breath of mountain air. He coughed. "You can tell me the way to Rhyd Ddu," he said, his tongue moving awkwardly over the unfamiliar syllables. "And to the Lodge beyond."

At the mere mention of the place, the stationmaster winced as if he'd been slapped. The color drained from his face. "Rhyd Ddu? Are you sure it's something you're wantin' to do, m'lord?"

"Yes, dammit." Gowan scowled at the man. "Rhyd Ddu. I own property there. A place called the Lodge."

"Yes, m'lord." Remembering himself, the stationmaster gave Gowan the kind of groveling half-bow that, not three weeks ago, he had found such good fun. "You'll be excusin' me, m'lord, for questionin' you but . . . Rhyd Ddu? Are you certain?"

"Of course, I'm certain." Gowan's store of patience had been sorely tried on the long journey. It was clearly depleted and just as clearly, he was not prepared to face either the stationmaster or himself with the fact that he was tired, miserable, and far more desperate than he would have anyone know. His mind made up, his resolve firm if not fervent, he headed down the platform. "Show me the road and I'll be on my way."

The stationmaster did not look thoroughly convinced. He shrugged resignedly, as if the vagaries of the aristocracy were too much for any mere man to comprehend. He glanced at the sturdy horse saddled and ready to go next to the baggage cart. "We knew you was comin' and we got things ready for you. You can take the horse and—"

"And I'd just as soon walk, thank you." Gowan hurried past the animal. Safely on the far side of the platform from it, he turned back to the man. "If you'll tell me the way."

Surrendering to what he would obviously never understand, the stationmaster pointed one gnarled hand over the rise of the nearest mountain. "Up over," he said matter-offactly. "There's a track that lies along the river. It's no more than three miles."

"Three miles." What was left of Gowan's resolve withered at the edges. One glance at the horse brought it back again in full force. "It's a fine, sunny afternoon. Why not walk?" Even he wasn't sure if he was trying to convince the stationmaster or himself. "You'll have the baggage there?"

"Aye, m'lord." The stationmaster clapped his hat back on his head. "We'll send it along."

Gowan didn't wait any more. He turned and headed the way the stationmaster had pointed, all the while cursing himself and the mercurial fates that had brought him to the back of beyond. He was halfway to the path when a cloud scuttled across the sun.

Gowan shivered and pulled his collar up against the sudden chill. "Damn Wales," he grumbled.

"Smoke of fire and wind of change. Bring on the wind, the cold, the rain."

Repeating the words of power along with her sisters, Tildy dared to open one eye and look around. Like one of the ancient standing stones that stood, unmoving, watching over the moors, Belle was seated at the head of the table. As was intended for the weatherworking, her eyes were shut tight. Her arms were laid upon the table, her fingers linked with her sisters', closing a circle around a burning white candle, Belle to Clea, Clea to Tildy, Tildy to Belle.

Tildy knew she, too, should concentrate. She would have to if this was to work. It would be a good bit easier if she could forget the eyes of the man whose likeness they had seen in the potion.

Hard eyes. That's what they were. The eyes of a man who did not laugh nearly as much as he should. The eyes of a man who, though he undoubtedly had women aplenty, neither understood nor cared to learn the meaning of love.

The thought did little to soothe Tildy's worries, and even less to calm her nerves. The eye closest to Belle still shut fast, the other still open, she looked across the table at Clea. Through the heated air that flickered around the candle flame, she saw that Clea's eyes were wide open, and Tildy wondered if she was having the same misgivings about what they were doing.

She did not have the opportunity to find out.

Somehow Belle found them out.

"Really, Tildy." Belle's eyes flew open. She yanked her hands away and pulled them into her lap. "How can we continue if you insist on interrupting?"

Tildy didn't answer. She couldn't, not truthfully, and she was loath to cause trouble for Clea. Instead, she glanced out the window. The sun was shining again, the few clouds they'd seen earlier had vanished on the breeze. Tildy's shoulders sagged along with her spirits. "In any event, it isn't working. We lit the candle. We repeated the chant. And not a trace of rain."

Even Belle could not disagree this time. She scowled. "We did say the chant. And we did light the candle."

"Yes," Clea added. "But did we sprinkle the bayberry?"

"Bayberry?" As one, Belle and Tildy asked the question. They looked at each other before they turned their collective gazes on their sister.

Clea had been charged with assembling the supplies for this spell as Tildy had done for the first. She chewed her lower lip, her face suddenly red from the tip of her chin to the roots of her hair. "I do believe," she said very quietly, "that I've quite forgotten the bayberry."

Belle rolled her eyes, an action she had perfected into an art form from years of practice. Tildy sighed. They waited as Clea pulled herself from her chair and shuffled to the back of the house where the cabinet with their store of herbs and plants was kept. She returned carrying a small clay pot covered over with cloth.

"Bayberry. I had it out and ready to go." She held the pot out to them, squaring her slender shoulders as she did. "You might have reminded me."

"We are always reminding you," Belle began, and Tildy knew if she did not interrupt, they would be further delayed.

"No matter now. And no time to argue. He'll be up the track and through the village before we're ever done."

As Tildy hoped, that was enough to goad them to action.

Belle snatched the pot from Clea's hand. She sprinkled some of the dried bayberry onto her palm and from there, dusted it over the candle flame. When it hit, the fire soared and sparked and the room filled with a scent like the mountains in winter.

The sisters linked hands, their expressions mirroring each other, excitement and anticipation mingled with a touch of fear. They began again.

"Smoke of fire and wind of change. Bring on the wind, the cold, the rain. Hear us now and answer soon. Before the rising of the moon."

They waited.

Belle tightened her grip. Clea cleared her throat. Tildy held her breath.

Nothing happened.

This time, even Belle sighed. She was about to rise out of her chair when Tildy felt something, like lightning coursing through her body, sizzling over her hands and up her arms. "Wait!" She clutched Belle's hand, pulling her back down. "One more time."

Belle knew enough not to question her. She nodded her agreement. Clea reached out her hand.

"Smoke of fire and wind of change."

A shiver ran up Tildy's spine.

"Bring on the wind, the cold, the rain."

A gust of wind blew over the intricate design of linking

circles chalked upon the doorstep. It guttered the candle, sending weird shadows dancing up the walls. It woke the cat from its place in front of the hearth and the animal hissed and spat, letting them know what it thought of having its slumber disturbed.

"Hear us now and answer soon."

Thunder rumbled high up in the mountains.

"Before the rising of the moon."

Rain spattered the windows.

"It's working." Tildy looked across the table to find Clea shifting nervously in her seat. "Belle! Tildy! Do you see? It's working!"

"Quiet, Clea." Belle shot the admonition at her along with a silencing look. "We must concentrate. All of us."

"Concentrate." Tildy echoed the word. As was always the case when she stared into one of the charm candles, her head felt giddy. Her voice sounded detached, as if it was coming from some place outside her body. "Concentrate on the weatherworking. Concentrate on the air outside. On the rain clouds above the mountains and the winds that blow them through the pass."

"Concentrate. Yes. Concentrate." Clea shuffled her feet. She squeezed Tildy's hand.

"Concentrate. Yes."

Tildy wasn't sure which one of them spoke this time. It didn't matter. Her mind drifted and the words echoed in it, surging through her along with the power.

"Concentrate. Yes. Concentrate on him."

A gust of wind whipped Gowan's coat around his knees, knifing through the expensive fabric, cutting him to the bone. He shivered and swore mightily, not concerned that anyone would hear. How could they? He was in the middle of nowhere, more than slightly lost and even more than a little aggravated.

"Three miles. It seems more like three hundred." Gowan trudged on up the path that had been climbing steadily since he departed from Beddgelert. He'd left the river behind more than a quarter hour ago and something told him that wasn't a good sign. He was surrounded by trees and in the gathering gloom caused by the lateness of the hour and the clouds that were piling up against the face of the nearest mountain, it was getting harder and harder to see his way.

With nothing else to consider more than how miserable he was, he let his thoughts wander to those who could read the weather, wishing he was one of them. The clouds above him spoke rain. Even he knew that. The question was, how soon? And would he make it as far as the Lodge before it started coming down?

The weather was not usually a point of contention or even conversation back in London, Gowan noted, bending to avoid a low-hanging branch. It rained back home. Incessantly. And when it did, a man who had sense stayed indoors where it was reasonably warm and commonly dry. It was always good to have an expensive bottle of brandy on hand for just such an occasion, and even better if there was a woman—young, passionate, and reasonably pretty—who was willing to pass the time in a way that would leave them both satisfied and smiling.

Gowan was not of the type who sighed incessantly, but he found himself doing it now. He longed for the comforts of a fire, a bottle, and a woman. He wished, not for the first time, that the thing he had originally seen as a piece of good luck of unprecedented proportions would have steered far clear of him and what had been, until just recently, a quiet, well-ordered life.

"Well ordered, indeed." Gowan grumbled, remembering the chaos of the last few weeks. It had all started well enough, with the news that he had come into a title he had never thought to inherit.

"I'm the earl of Welshpool, dammit!" Gowan called to

the vast emptiness around him, his words echoing back from the ancient mountains, mocking him. "I'm meant to be warm and comfortable. It's my due. I'm meant to be wealthy beyond my wildest dreams. I'm not meant to be turning tail and hiding."

But that was exactly what he was doing.

Another blast of wind cut through Gowan like the touch of icy fingers and he clutched his coat tighter around himself, listening as thunder rumbled like the thoughts that were pounding through his head.

He was running. Running from all of them. And perhaps from himself, from the anger that built in him even now when he thought back to all that had happened.

Becoming the earl was an incredible piece of good fortune. Or so he thought at the time. It was promising enough to make Gowan leave his prosperous medical practice in Harley Street and allowed him to fulfill a goal that he thought, until then, to be nothing more than a pipe dream. Suddenly, he was a country gentleman, with the leisure to hunt and fish to his heart's content. He was a wealthy man. A powerful man. A peer of the realm.

There were countless dinner invitations those first, heady weeks and lavish parties hosted by new friends who had been, until then, not even passing acquaintances. There was wine, and song, and my God, how many women, throwing themselves at his feet and at his title.

It did not take long for the dream to sour.

Gowan learned soon enough that his esteemed relative and benefactor, the twelfth Earl of Welshpool, had owed money to every man and his brother.

He owed greengrocers for foodstuffs, and tailors for clothing. He owed jewelers for the gifts he gave his mistresses, breeders for the horses he raised and raced. He owed taxes on his estates and taxes on his income.

"And what should have been the best thing that ever happened to me turned into the worst." Gowan kicked a loose pebble from his path.

Gowan soon found that a title wasn't the only thing he'd inherited. In addition to the old earl's debts, he'd acquired his creditors, and not all of them were gentlemen.

Even now, the thought made Gowan uneasy. He had heard of men like those who called at his home that evening not two weeks ago, but he'd certainly never met any of them. Coarse men they were, of the lowest kind, and they were not averse to letting Gowan know what would happen to him if they were ignored. It seemed that while the old earl would never stoop to be seen in public with such men, he had a great deal of private dealings with them.

"Gambling debts." Gowan groaned. The old earl owed gambling debts that mounted to the ceiling and totalled many times more than the income that could ever be gotten from his lands.

Because of entailments, it was impossible to sell the family estate to raise the money. Because most of what was valuable was already in the moneylenders' shops along the river, it was futile to try to pawn the silver, or the paintings, or the other family heirlooms. All that was left was the Lodge, a country property that had been in the family for generations.

Gowan stepped over a fallen tree that lay across the path. Wales might be the last damnable place on earth he ever expected to find himself, but it was the only place left for him to go.

The gloomy thoughts swirling through his mind, blocking out all else. Gowan flinched when the first raindrop hit and trickled down the back of his neck.

"Damn!" He wiped a second raindrop from his cheek with the back of one hand. "What the hell else can happen to me today?"

* * *

Clea could barely sit still from the excitement. She wiggled in her seat like a child at church services on a Sunday morning. Tildy paid her no mind. She was to keep the book during this part of the spell, referring to it if need be and helping Belle with the words should she forget them. It was enough to think about and at least it helped her forget the vision of the man she'd seen in the cauldron. She had no time for Clea.

"Three times around the flame," she said, pushing every other thought out of her head. She pointed to the snow-white eagle feather Belle held above the candle, then to the small leather-bound book that lay open on her lap. "That's what it says. Three times around the flame."

"I know that." Belle took her eyes off the candle long enough to dart Tildy a look. "Three times around." She moved the feather rightward.

"Once around the candle flame. Once again, around again." Belle's deep voice was hushed and hollow. "Three times round and round you go. Come the clouds and make it snow."

This time, they did not have to wait for the spell to work. It took hold immediately and before any of them knew it, the air was filled with snowflakes. Snowflakes that lighted in their hair and danced on their eyelashes. Snowflakes that coated the floor and settled on the tabletop.

"Belle!" It was Tildy's turn to roll her eyes. "Outdoors, Belle. Outdoors. You were supposed to make it snow outdoors!"

Belle's eyes grew nearly as wide as Clea's were. Without even bothering to put her spectacles on, she grabbed the book from Tildy and read through the spell again.

"Hurry, Belle." Clea dashed her arm across the table, swiping at the snow that was quickly piling there. "It's coming faster."

"I am hurrying." Even Belle's imperturbable calm could not hold up in the face of the magical snow. She darted a desperate look at the snowflakes that flew all about and another at her sisters for help.

"Perhaps it is not the spell itself that's wrong, but something you did," Tildy suggested, wiping a snowflake from the tip of her nose. "Three times around. That's what it says. Perhaps you might try the other way?"

If there was one thing Belle hated, it was admitting that Tildy might actually be right. Ever. Rather than be faced with the horrifying prospect, she hurried through the spell again.

"Once around the candle flame. Once again, around again." This time, Belle moved the feather in the opposite direction. "Three times round and round you go. Come the clouds and make it snow."

The snow stopped. At least inside.

All three sisters leapt from their chairs and went to the window. They pressed their noses to the glass, watching in awe as sky and air and ground blended one into the other until all they could see was one endless blanket of white.

"That will teach me for asking myself what else could happen." The dirt track that Gowan was following had long ago turned to mud. With a change in the wind and a sudden, unexpected sharpness in the air, the mud had quickly become slippery.

He went down on one knee in the muck and rainwater soaked through the legs of his trousers. Pulling himself up against the nearest tree, Gowan trudged on.

It was impossible to see the sun through the heavy blanket of clouds, but as far as he could tell, he'd been walking for well more than an hour. With any luck, Rhyd Ddu should be in sight any time now, and if he decided not to go to the Lodge beyond, there must at least be an inn where he could spend the night.

The thought cheered Gowan. But not for long.

With a cry like a banshee's wail, the wind whipped

around the summit of the highest mountain peak and came back at him the other way. Something soft and cold struck Gowan's face and he pulled to a stop.

"Snow? In April?" He did not wait long to consider the unlikely possibility. The snow fell fast and hard until it looked like the kind of false snow he'd seen in the theater, feathers dropped from high up over the stage. Already, the ground was coated, and behind him he could barely see the footprints he'd left only moments before. The air around him shivered with snow, as much as he was shivering inside his woolen coat.

As if to remind him of the precariousness of the situation, another burst of wind caught Gowan in the face. He sucked in a breath, fighting its power, and turned his back to the wind. As if it had hands and a will of its own, it pushed him from behind, nudging him off the path, further and further into the woods.

That's when he saw the light.

Gowan narrowed his eyes and peered into the growing darkness. The light was there one second, gone the next, and the peculiar combination of flashing light and swirling snow made it difficult to gauge either distance or direction.

"There! Again!" His spirits rose when he saw another flash. But no sooner had it come than it was gone. A blast of icy wind cut through Gowan's wet clothing and he wrapped his arms around himself, stumbling on through the gathering darkness.

"A farmhouse." He whispered the words like a prayer and kept it in the front of his mind. Like a light left burning in the nursery to chase away a child's fears, he let it guide him through the dark.

There was nothing for another ten minutes or so, nothing other than snow and more snow. Then Gowan saw it again, a flash in the distance, this time from his right. He turned that way. The snow was even deeper here than on the path.

It came up over his ankles, stealing over the tops of his boots, chilling him to the bone.

Another ten minutes went by. By that time, his ears were frozen. His face was numb. His feet were blocks of ice. And even then, the snow did not stop. It came down like no snow he'd ever seen, so fast and furious that before he ever saw the light flash at him again, it was already piled halfway up his calves.

Peering into the darkness, Gowan passed one hand over his eyes, fighting to bring the swirling snow and white landscape into focus. It was no use, and the realization did little to comfort him. As a physician, he knew what to expect. He recognized the signs.

His vision was already blurred. There was no feeling in his fingers or feet. He knew it would take little time for his blood to slow and less time even than that for his skin to cool dangerously. He didn't want to think about what would happen next.

As if in answer to his prayer, he saw the light again. This time it did not flicker and die. It burned strong and steady, not two hundred yards ahead of him.

Each step slower and more painful than the last, Gowan hauled himself toward the light and the cottage he could just make out through the swirling snow. There must be someone about if there was a light burning, he told himself. There must be a fire.

He hardly remembered any more.

Another blast of wind froze his wet clothes right on his body just as Gowan pulled himself into the clearing in front of the cottage.

He saw the door open, saw the puddle of yellow light that flowed from inside, lighting the doorstep and the intricate pattern of intersecting circles that someone had chalked on it.

It was the last thing he remembered before he collapsed.

* * *

Belle, Clea, and Tildy were already out of the door before Gowan ever hit the ground.

Running to his side, Clea sucked in a breath of surprise and relief. Belle nodded her satisfaction. Tildy eyed him as if he were some wild creature she had never thought to see so close, and nudged him with the toe of her boot.

He never moved.

"Well, it looks as if we've done it," she said, glancing from the man to her sisters. "For good or ill, the die is cast. We've got him!"

Two

Gowan wasn't certain what woke him.

It may have been the peculiar smells that tickled his nose. He caught the fragrance of perfume one second, an aroma of the kind that emanated from a fine cook's kitchen the next. He breathed deep and let his mind wander and another scent wafted by, one that put him in mind of the greens he'd sprinkled in the rabbit hutch that stood in one corner of the garden when he was a child.

Or perhaps it was the warmth that nudged him awake, the delicious heat that filled him from head to toe, seeping like sunshine through his body, melting every last inch of him that had been frozen out in the snow.

Or it may have been the voices.

With limbs as heavy as if they'd been laden with weights, and too exhausted to open his eyes, he lay perfectly still, listening as the sounds penetrated his consciousness.

They were voices, sure enough, women's voices, and from what he could tell, there were three of them. He was lying on his back and they must have been standing directly above him for their words fell down on him like a gentle rain. The women whispered, each in turn, trying not to wake him.

Gowan allowed himself the luxury of doing absolutely nothing more than relishing the softness beneath him that must surely have been a featherbed and enjoying the warmth atop him that could have been nothing but a wooly blanket. Comforted by the sound of human voices, he lay back and listened. His brain as muzzy as his body was relaxed, it took him awhile to realize something was not quite right.

He searched his mind for what it might be, and cursed himself for his dull wits when it took him a full minute to work it out.

The three women were speaking right enough. They very well may have been speaking about or even to him. But he couldn't understand them—not a word—and for a moment, panic welled up in him along with the horrifying thought that the cold had done some permanent injury to his ears or to his mind.

As far as he could tell, the rest of him was undamaged. At least his nerve endings were. He clearly felt someone poke his arm from one side while from the other, someone else bent low over the bed, as if to make certain he was still breathing.

"Cysgu fel daear," he heard one of the voices say.

"Diolch byth," another replied.

Welsh.

The answer to the mystery came to Gowan in a flash. Relieved, he let a lazy, self-satisfied smile play its way around his mouth. He opened his eyes. The first thing he saw was the sloping ceiling, not two feet above his head, as if he was in a room up under the eaves. The next thing he saw was the women.

"You're speaking Welsh," he said, looking from one of them to the next, "and I can't—"

As one, the women gasped and took a step away from the bed. They peered down at him as if he were some creature the likes of which they'd never seen before.

Gowan's words trailed away as he allowed his gaze to roam over the women. He'd been right, there were three of them and they were standing on either side of the bed, one on his right, two more on the left. He took some small comfort in the fact that he thought them just as peculiar as they obviously thought him.

"Damn." Gowan breathed the word in wonder. He'd never seen anything like them in his life.

With the trained eye of a physician, Gowan tried his best to gauge their ages. That was usually easy enough. He could study the gnarled knuckles on hands, the wrinkles on a face, the stoop of shoulders and deduce a person's years. This time, however, it was not so simple a task.

Each of the women had hair of varying shades of gray. The tallest—the one on the right—had a severe coil of it pinned close to her head. It was the color of gunmetal, and after only one look, Gowan knew beyond a doubt that the style and color were perfectly suited to the woman's personality. She stood as straight as a pikestaff, staring down at him through her spectacles. She looked nothing if not wholly satisfied, though about what, Gowan could not imagine.

Setting the thought aside, he turned his attention to the two women standing on his left. The plumpest of the two was also the most pleasant looking. She had the kind of complexion city women pray for. Her face was rose-hued and though she was as wrinkled as a well-used blanket, it was obvious from the lines that spread from the corners of her eyes that she laughed heartily and often.

She was not laughing now. As if she could see right through him, she narrowed her eyes and studied Gowan. If he was a superstitious man and given to fancies, he might say she was reading his mind.

That did little to reassure him.

Neither did the face of the third woman. She didn't look as dour as the first, or as suspicious as the second. She looked nervous, as if she expected him to leap from the bed and attack at any moment. Even as he watched, she smoothed one hand through her hair. Along with a dapple of silver, there was still some color in it, the exact shade of brown as a churchmouse.

Like chalk and cheese, the women were as different from

each other as night from day. Different hair. Vastly different bodies. Different personalities, as far as Gowan could see.

But their eyes . . .

He sucked in a breath and looked again from one to the next.

Their eyes were all the same. They were not young eyes and though none of these ladies could possibly be less than sixty, neither were they old.

Sixty or six hundred? It was impossible to say when he was looking into their eyes. They were ageless, like the mountains, and as gray as the mist he suspected sometimes wreathed the forest in fairy's breath.

It was obvious they were sisters.

"Do you speak English?" He tried giving them the kind of smile he'd always used to flatter those London dowagers who were his patients. "I'd like to know where I am and what happened. I can't tell you how grateful I am that you found me. Deucedly uncomfortable out there, don't you know."

The smile may have worked in London. It didn't work here.

The women simply stared, their odd gray eyes piercing right through him. As if in response to some signal he neither heard nor saw, they moved away from the bed in perfect form, like soldiers on parade. Before Gowan had a chance to say another thing, they filed out of the room and snapped the door shut behind them.

"Wait!" he called out, his voice gruff from sleep and from the effects of the bitter cold. When he got no response, he bolted out of bed. His eyes went wide when the blankets fell away. The chilly air slapped against his bare skin and he realized he was naked. "Oh, bloody hell!"

Even though the door was already closed, the women gone, Gowan scrambled back to the bed and reached for the blanket, wrapping it around himself like a towel in a Turkish bath. He called to the sisters beyond the door, "What the devil have you done with my trousers?"

* * *

This time, it wasn't smells or warmth or even voices that woke Gowan from a deep sleep.

It was a touch. A touch as soft as silk, as velvety as the brush of a woman's hair against his bare skin.

It caressed his face, skimming his closed eyelids, grazing his cheek. It brushed his chin. It slipped down his neck and over his body, playing its way through the fine mat of hair on his chest.

If this was one of those dreams that come to a man when he is in that strange state halfway between sleep and wakefulness, it was a remarkably real one. And as delectable as it was vivid. The last thing Gowan wanted was to interrupt it.

Enjoying the way his senses responded to every delicate stroke, he relaxed for the first time in weeks. Before he knew it, he was smiling. He burrowed his shoulders farther into the featherbed and stretched his legs beneath the blanket that was tangled down around his waist.

His mind still foggy from a sleep so deep it seemed unnatural, he didn't move, not even when the touch became more insistent. It glided down to his abdomen and back up to his chest, tickling its way over the spot on his belly that had always been so sensitive and so vulnerable to a woman's touch.

That was sufficient to make Gowan's smile grow wider and to allow certain other, even more sensitive parts of his body to respond. A delicious warmth curled through him, and he heard a noise that could only have come from him, a small noise of contentment from deep in his throat, like a purr.

Trying to settle himself more comfortably, Gowan shifted his weight. It wasn't much, but it was enough of a movement to make the dream vanish. Something sharp bit into his flesh. Something else scraped across his skin, drawing blood.

Gowan's eyes popped open. There was a sleek black cat sitting square upon his chest. Clearly annoyed at having its play disturbed, it eyed him with distaste and raised one paw, ready to strike again.

"Jesus!" Startled, Gowan sat up like a shot and batted the creature away.

It snarled and hissed and bolted off the bed, but not before it struck again. Gowan was left with a scratch on his arm to match the one on his chest.

"Damn!" Shaking the sting from his arm, Gown scrambled from the bed, determined to corner the hellish creature and put it from the room.

Crawling on his hands and knees, he peered under the bed and used his most cajoling voice, the one he generally saved for his wealthiest patients. "Here kitty, kitty."

When that didn't work, he tried again. "Here, little kitty. Come here!"

There was no sign of the cat.

Frustrated, Gowan hopped to his feet. Ready to explore the rest of the room, he came around to the other side of the bed. "Come here, you fiendish beast!" he snarled. "Once I get my hands on your scrawny little neck, I'll—"

Gowan's words died on his lips at the same time he froze in place.

The cat was nowhere to be found, but from where he stood, he could see that there was a small window set into the eaves on other side of the room. In front of it, he saw a rocking chair, a rough sort of thing that looked to be made of branches and twigs. And in the rocking chair was a woman.

At least he thought it was a woman.

With the sun pouring into the room like melted butter and dust motes dancing in the air, it was difficult to tell if she was real or simply an apparition, a creature of light and shadow no more solid than a dream.

If he was a betting man, he would have guessed it to be the latter.

Even though she was seated, he could tell she was small and slight, like one of the fairy folk he had read about in stories. She looked much as he imagined a fairy would look, too, with hair as black as midnight and skin the color of cream. She had eyes that reminded Gowan of a cat's, pointed at the corners.

Her lips were full though not unattractively so, her brows were dark and he saw them drop as she studied him as intently as he was studying her. The light fell over her shoulder caressing her from behind. It cast her face in shadow, but even so, he could tell her cheeks were touched with color and her eyes were as gray as the face of the mountain he caught a glimpse of outside the window.

She didn't say a word, but met his eyes boldly, the way a woman does if she has known a man all his life. Or the way she might, Gowan knew from experience, when she had just recently met him and some unerring bit of her intuition told her that they would be intimate before long.

The thought was enough to unnerve him even further and he stood there, unable to speak and glad of it. Even if he could, he was certain he would not know what to say.

If it wasn't for a breeze that blew through the open window and ruffled its way over his body like cold fingers, he might never have recovered at all. The breeze reminded him that he was in the land of the living, not in some fairy bower where time mattered little and reality even less. It reminded him that he was face to face with a stranger—and a pretty one at that—and that it was rude to stand here doing and saying nothing.

The breeze sailed by him again.

This time, it reminded him that he was naked.

Gowan's surprise disappeared in a rush of mortification. He looked down at his exposed body. He looked up at the woman. He looked over at the bed and before another second could pass, he made a wild grab for the bedclothes.

"Jesus!" he swore, wrapping himself up in the white blanket, head to toe. "You startled me!"

For what seemed far too long a time, the woman never moved, and he was beginning to wonder if she was, indeed, a figment of his overactive imagination. But finally she shook her head. Her hair hung down around her shoulders and the movement made it glimmer like onyx in the sunlight. "You invoke the name of the Savior a good deal, sir," she said, her "R's" trilled like a Scotsman's, her syllables clipped in the peculiar way the Welsh have of speaking, as if they were biting the words in two. "Are you a churcher, then?"

Hop-stepping over to the bed and perching himself on the edge of it, Gowan snorted. "Churcher, indeed," he grumbled, hiding his embarrassment beneath a healthy dose of outrage. "I wouldn't need to swear at all if things weren't so damnably odd here. Where did that infernal cat come from?" He glanced around the room. "And where has it gone?"

With an elegant little lift of her shoulders, the woman shrugged. "Cat goes where she will. You will not find her anywhere about. Not unless she wants to be found."

That did little to exonerate the ungodly animal in Gowan's opinion, and even less to make him forget his aggravation. Or his embarrassment. His wounded pride hurt nearly as much as the place on his arm where the cat had scratched him, and because he could not ease one, he fixed his mind on the other.

Through the blanket, he gingerly fingered his arm. "The cat goes where it will. That may be true, but did it have to come into my bed? It's dangerous to have a creature like that roaming about freely. That animal's a menace." He lifted the blanket a fraction of an inch and peeked down at his chest. "The beastly thing nearly sliced me in half."

The woman laughed. The sound was as ethereal as fairy

bells, but it did little to allay his sour mood. "In half? Are you certain?" She dared him to repeat the lie. In one fluid movement, she rose from the chair and came to the bed. She reached one hand out to the place where Gowan held the blanket close around him. "Let me see what she has done to you."

"Let you see? Don't be absurd." He clutched the blanket tighter and glared at her. "I'd wager you've seen enough already. Besides, it isn't anything that can't be handled with proper treatment. Soap and water and a dab of iodine and—"

The woman wasn't listening. Before he ever finished, she turned and headed across the room and Gowan's tirade dissolved into the silence.

There was a cabinet against one wall and he watched as she rummaged through the shelves, moving bottles and jars, small potted plants and an amazing assortment of odd-colored candles. With a small cry of triumph, she found what she was looking for. She came back at him, holding out a green glass bottle.

"Take the blanket away," she said, talking to him as one might to a frightened child. She pulled the stopper and poured something thick and oily looking onto her fingers. She set the bottle down on the bedside table and held out her hand to him. "It will not sting but a bit when I rub it on."

Gowan leaned forward and drew in a breath. His nose wrinkled, and if he was skeptical before, now he was utterly suspicious. "It smells like old socks." He inhaled again and frowned. "There's no way on earth that can be therapeutic. No doubt it's brimming with bacteria. Where did you get that awful brew? And what is it?"

"It is St. John's wort, if you must know, and—"

"And iodine would be much safer, thank you very much." He scooted back on the bed, out of her reach and downwind of the foul concoction. "I'll tend to it myself once I've caught up with my trunks and found my medical bag."

The woman's dark brows shot up in surprise. "That explains it, then," she said. "You're a physician, are you?"

"Yes. Well . . . I was." Gowan wasn't about to explain the convoluted situation. He shrugged off the whole thing with a motion meant to show just how little it meant to him, and prayed she would not notice how much it did. "I sold my practice only a short time ago," he said by way of explanation. "My practice in Harley Street."

At the mere mention of the name, he had expected her to be impressed, as so many women in London had always been. This woman wasn't. She stood there with her hand still out, her face as stern as nails, waiting for him to relinquish his hold on the blanket.

Not certain if she'd misheard or perhaps if she simply did not understand, he spoke louder and more slowly this time. "Harley Street. It's in London. And if you have not heard tell of it in this backward place, it is the most prestigious medical address in the civilized world. There are specialists there of all types. Why, I myself—"

"You, yourself, no doubt, dosed rich women who were not really ill with powders and tonics that did not really work." The woman's face clouded over. Her eyes grew hard as granite. "I have heard of such as you."

"Is that so?" Gowan couldn't help himself. The woman's attitude was enough to boil his blood. He sat up a little straighter. "And are you one of those who think the rich are never ill? That it is some special privilege of the lower classes?"

"Aye, the rich get sick right enough. But it is not the same sick as everyone else, is it? It is a headache. Or the vapors." Groaning, the woman laid the back of one hand against her brow and closed her eyes. As reluctant as Gowan was to admit it, he had to confess it was a perfect imitation of the women he'd seen over the years. Countless women they were. Women who were desperate for attention and willing to use any means to get it, even if it meant spending a good deal of their husbands' money on overpriced medical specialists.

He'd seen the physicians, as well. Hell, he was one of them. He knew just how to click his tongue and shake his head. He knew exactly how to offer a bit of much-needed attention along with the overpriced analeptics he prescribed, the ones designed to relieve not only his patients' symptoms, but their pocketbooks, as well.

Odd, the thought had never bothered him before. He had lived with it all these years and it never once disturbed his sleep or gave him the kind of pang of conscience he felt right now under this woman's unwavering gaze.

"You are wasting your time," she snapped at him. "And you are squandering your God-given talents."

Whatever misgivings Gowan might have been feeling dissolved beneath a healthy dose of anger. He let go of the blanket long enough to point an accusatory finger at the woman. "And you . . . You are annoying me, madam. What right have you to—"

"Ah! There you have it!" Quick as a streak, the woman made her move. She pushed the blanket aside and grabbed Gowan's hand. He was tempted to swear again, but she never allowed him the time. In spite of her size, she had the grip of a wrestler. She wound her fingers through his and firmly refused to let go. With her other hand, she stroked the noxious potion over the scratch on Gowan's arm.

She was right, it stung like the dickens, and Gowan sucked in a sharp breath and held it as a feeling like fire raced up his arm. But the sting didn't last long. After the first stroke, the fire tapered off to a nearly bearable heat. After the second, it changed, unaccountably, to a marvelous, penetrating warmth.

Gowan let go a breath that came out sounding like a sigh. Had he been asked for the medical rationale behind the whole thing, he would have been at a loss. He knew that the wound no longer hurt and that it was not nearly as angry-looking now as it was when the woman first began her ministrations. He was certain it could not have had anything to do with the foul tonic. Peculiar potions made from woodland plants would never replace modern medicines. Not in a thousand years.

But that left only one explanation as to why both he and the wound suddenly felt so much better.

The realization scampered across Gowan's skin like the chicken-flesh that prickled over his arms and legs. It ignited a heat in his gut that was not nearly as comfortable as the warmth in his arm.

If it was not the medication that was making him feel this way, it must have been the woman.

Gowan turned the thought over in his head, studying it from every angle. Perhaps it was her nearness that unnerved him so. Perhaps it was her touch. Perhaps it was the warmth that seemed to emanate from her fingers, as natural as the sunshine through the casement. He was still considering all the delicious possibilities when the woman stepped back.

"Now for the other," she said, flicking her finger toward his chest. "Knowing Cat, that one is by far the worst."

Gowan's first thought was to refuse. He was not an invalid, after all, in spite of the fact that the wretched cat had tried to make him one. He could reach over to the bedside table and get the green glass bottle just as easily as the woman could. He could rub the potion onto his own chest just as well as she could ever do it for him.

Or could he?

A wicked imp of a notion tickled Gowan's brain and put him in mind of a splendid plan, one that would get her back, at least in part, for the trick she'd played on him. It would serve her right for luring him into an argument just so she could take advantage of him and anoint him with her strange tonic. It would soothe his pride and she owed him that, too, he decided, for surprising him in his birthday suit and having the temerity not to seem at least as embarrassed as he was by it all.

A slow smile brightening his expression, Gowan propped his hands on either side of him, letting the blanket fall away to reveal all of his torso down to his waist.

"Very well," he agreed readily enough and if his sudden change of heart and his willingness to cooperate was any surprise to her, she did not show it. Without a word, she went over to the bedside table and wrung out a cloth in a bowl of water. She brought it back to the bed along with the green glass bottle.

Gowan waited while she studied the abrasion that went from his clavicle nearly to his ribcage. He leaned back, allowing her a better look at the wound while he himself took a better look at the woman, and because he was seated and she was standing directly in front of him, he had a perfect view of all her choicest parts.

He allowed his gaze to skim from her hips to her waist and from there, up even further, finally stopping at her breasts.

They were small and round and even through the coarse fabric of her modest gown, he could tell she was not bound up underneath with the type of barbarous corsets and stays that city women wore. Her body didn't move beneath her clothing as if she'd been tinned like a sardine. It moved as a woman's body is meant to move, each motion pressing her dress closer to her, emphasizing every curve.

The first touch of the cold, wet cloth on Gowan's skin made him wince, pulling him out of his thoughts. It was probably just as well, he decided. Though he had meant to trap her with this blatant and quite brazen display of flesh and disconcert her as she'd disconcerted him, it seemed she was not distracted in the least. She went on about her business without a flinch or a flutter while Gowan's imagination was well on its way to running away with him. He could not help but think that his body would not take long to follow behind.

Still . . .

The woman slowly stroked the cloth down his chest, giving extra attention to the place above his heart where the fiendish cat had cut the deepest. In spite of himself, Gowan tipped his head back, his eyes half closed, his breath suddenly coming far quicker than was either right or reasonable.

Still, he thought with the sort of clear-mindedness that always came to him when he was feeling pleasantly aroused and utterly content, he could not help but wonder what it might be like to touch her as she was touching him. To stroke his fingers over her as she was stroking him. To fit his hands around her waist and pull her onto his lap.

He would have followed the impulse to whatever place it might lead if he hadn't heard her click her tongue. He opened his eyes to find her with as sober an expression on her face as any he'd ever seen.

"What?" Gowan looked from the woman down to the wound. "What is it?"

" 'Tis far more serious than I imagined," she said, shaking her head. Her steady gray gaze went from his face down to where, he hoped, the blanket covered any signs of his arousal. "St. John's wort will not be nearly enough to remedy what is wrong with you. Nay! Don't," she added, when he tried to sit up. "Don't move."

The woman went back to the cabinet and whatever she was looking for, she found it quickly. This time when she came back, it was with a brown glass bottle in her hands.

"This should fix it," she said. She unstoppered the bottle and, smiling the kind of smile a cat might give a mouse right before it pounces, she poured all of its contents directly into Gowan's lap.

"Blast!" Gowan bolted from the bed. The St. John's wort

stung like fire. This liquid, whatever it was, was as cold as ice. It cooled his ardor as quickly as it chilled his flesh.

Gowan scampered to the other side of the room, and with his back on the woman, turned the blanket about so that the wet portion of it was down around his feet. At the least, it was enough to prevent any further discomfort to his private parts. It did little to repair what damage had already been done. With the kind of absolute certainty that could only be ascribed to the fact that he was angry beyond measure, he decided that portion of his body would never be warm again.

Clutching the blanket close around him, he turned to find the woman regarding him levelly. Her expression was still as solemn as could be, but there was a hint of amusement in her eyes. "Is that better?" she asked innocently enough.

Gowan crossed the room, dragging the blanket behind him. Being careful to keep a safe distance between them, he glared at the woman. "What kind of place is this? First that wretched cat tries to kill me, then you."

This time, the woman allowed a small smile to tip the corners of her mouth. It lightened her expression and added a maddeningly irresistible sparkle to her eyes. "If I wanted you dead," she said, "I would have done it days ago. You were burning with fever. Do you remember? You would have been a gone goose, Doctor," she emphasized the word, "if not for my med'cines."

"Fever?" Something in the word banished Gowan's anger and put him in mind of the last time he'd woken, and all that he'd seen then came rushing back to him. "That explains it," he said almost to himself. "The three women. The sisters. I must have been burning with fever. I was hallucinating."

The woman neither agreed nor disagreed. She tilted her head to one side, considering what he'd said. "Delusions, is that what you think?" She straightened and looked at the door, as if listening to some sound beyond his hearing. "Something tells me you'll find out soon enough."

Three

"Oh, dear." Belle sat back on her heels and shook her head sadly. "Things are not going well."

"Let me see."

"No, let me."

In spite of her ample shape and the fact that she was carrying an armload of their guest's clothing, or perhaps because of it, Tildy managed to maneuver her way in front of Clea. She wedged herself between Belle and the door and before either of her sisters had time to react, she was already on her knees, peering through the keyhole.

"I do wish he'd take away the blanket again," Tildy said, in part because it was true and in part because she knew the comment would shock her sisters.

She was right. Behind her, she heard them suck in breaths of astonishment. "Don't be so priggish." Though she glanced to both sides, Tildy kept a firm hold on the doorknob so she could not be displaced. "You know you agree with me. Both of you. Though neither of you would ever confess it. You have to admit," she added, turning back to the keyhole and watching the young earl lean back on the bed, "it is quite an interesting angle from which to observe a naked man."

"Really, Tildy!" Tildy didn't have to look to know that Belle shivered with revulsion. Her frosty statement was accompanied by a decided chilling of the air. "That is the least of our problems. We must be less concerned with our own preferences and more concerned with what Nick—"

"Oh, no! Not the agnus castus!" As soon as Tildy saw Nick with the brown glass bottle in her hands, she knew what was about to happen. Reluctant to watch and just as reluctant to miss what would clearly be a triumph of sorts, however small, for Nick, she squeezed her eyes half shut. Her breath tight in her throat, she saw Nick dangle her hand and the open bottle over the young man's lap. She watched as Nick tipped the bottle at just the right angle and she cringed as the clear liquid spilled over the rim. She held her breath, and waited for the inevitable.

"Blast!"

The earl's curse rumbled through the house like thunder, so loud and ominous, even Tildy winced and leaned back from the door. She looked from Belle to Clea. "You're quite right," she said. "Things are not going well."

Belle was still on her knees at Tildy's side and with the help of the wall, she pulled herself to her feet. She offered Tildy a hand and hauled her up.

"We cannot let things get so out of hand," Belle said with a stern look at the door.

Like an army, well practiced and equally well prepared, they sprang into action. Not one hour ago, they had discussed all the possibilities. Though the likelihood of out and out hostility between Nick and the young man had never entered their minds, they were prepared for it, as they were for everything else.

At a signal from Belle, Clea hurried downstairs.

Tildy straightened Gowan's clothing, smoothing it over her arm. Belle squared her shoulders. They glanced at the door before they glanced at each other. They nodded and together, they went into the room.

Nick was not surprised to see them. She'd known all the while that the sisters were outside the door, snooping at the keyhole. She only wondered that they had the temerity to pretend they didn't know she knew. They skidded to a stop just inside the doorway and looked at each other and at her in wonder, pretending to be innocently astonished and astonishingly innocent.

"Nicolette!" Tildy was much the better actress of the two. She took the lead, coming at Nick wide-eyed. "We had no idea you were here. I see you've met our guest." She turned to beam a smile at the young stranger and Nick looked that way, too.

The man's face had blanched the moment he caught sight of Belle and Tildy, and he looked pale and shaken still. He'd all but convinced himself they were creatures of his fevered imagination and now, face to face with them, he hardly knew what to say. He stood there all bundled up, no doubt still uncomfortable from the drenching Nick had given his blanket, his privates, and his passion.

Nick offered him a small, triumphant smile. "My aunts," she explained, inclining her head in their direction. "Belle and Tildy. There's one gone missing, but I expect she will be here soon enough. She is not one to overlook something so exciting as this."

"Three." The young man nodded slowly, as if working through the whole thing in his head. "Then I didn't dream them?"

Tildy bustled over to the man, smiling that earnest sort of smile that made her so endearing, even at times like this when Nick would much rather stay annoyed at her. "Dream?" She laughed. " 'Twould be difficult to dream up three such as us."

Belle saw her chance and stepped in. "Or someone as lovely as our sweet niece." She turned and motioned in Nick's direction. She had an odd kind of inflection in her voice that reminded Nick of the time her aunts had introduced her to the bishop when he passed through Rhyd Ddu. "You have obviously met our wonderful girl."

The man sneered in Nick's direction. Nick sneered back.

This time, it was the aunts who blanched.

And that was enough to convince Nick something was afoot.

Trying to work her way through the riddle, she went over to the bedside table. She gathered up the bottle of St. John's wort and the cloth she'd used to cleanse the man's wound. Taking them back to the cabinet, she watched her aunts carefully out of the corner of her eye.

They bustled around the stranger like bees around a fresh bouquet of spring flowers, proudly showing off how well they'd dried, pressed, and brushed his clothing, and if Nick was not wary before, she would have been now. She had never seen the aunts act this way, not around any man. She wondered at the whole thing while she busied herself straightening the objects on the cabinet shelves. There was a small mirror set in among the bottles and pots, and in it, she watched the reflection of all that was going on behind her.

The young man seemed overwhelmed by the aunts, as well he might be. Tildy twittered around him like a bemused songbird. Belle let down her formidable guard enough to offer him a winsome smile or two. They circled like vultures, coming at him from both sides.

The man retreated one step, then another. When he came to the place where the ceiling sloped, he whacked his head, and wincing, he looked over at Nick as if for deliverance.

She met his eyes resolutely.

"Just what you deserve." Even though she said it below her breath, she deliberately spoke in Welsh so that even if he should chance to hear, he would not have any idea what she was saying. "That is what you get for treating me the way you did. And for making me feel the things I did."

Like a thief, the thought crept up on Nick. It snatched the breath from her throat and left her pale and shaken. As annoyed by her reaction to the man as she was by the man

himself, she looked beyo
to his.

His chestnut hair was thick
well-polished wood once he was
of his adventure in the forest was w
his forehead, brushing close against his
tures that were a bit too stern and eyes th
aunts around him like predators closing fo
not as wary as they were worn-out.

Even with a three-day growth of beard, she cou
was a fine looking face, all slants and angles. It was a
match for his body.

Nick did not have to think upon it so very much to picture how he'd looked before he'd swaddled himself in the creamy white blanket. If she lived to be as old as the aunts, she would never forget the expression on his face when he came around from the other side of the bed and saw her, or those few seconds before when he stood, unaware and unsuspecting, his defenses cast aside as certainly as his clothing.

He was not a pleasant man.

Nick's brows dropped low over her eyes at the thought.

He threatened poor Cat and he was not at all friendly. Yet the sight of his naked body glistening in the morning sunlight tugged at her insides far more than was right, or reasonable, or wise.

It was not such a curious thing, she thought, instinctively defending herself against the sensations aroused by the memory.

What woman of sound body and reasonably healthy mind could help but be beguiled by the sight of him?

She thought about the manner in which his muscles played beneath skin that was not nearly as pallid as she might have expected from a city dweller and an Englishman at that. She remembered how broad his shoulders were and how large and capable his hands. She recalled the flat plane

his chest,
his own,
st, downy

elt through
, her blood
ses. At the
her ribs.
hat was for
his charms.
much as to
ust as potent
y. Yet for all
red the signs
of his barely controlled passion and he'd looked directly at her as no man had ever done before, as if promising that this bit of temptation was nothing but the promise of more to come, and that, more than she'd ever dreamed possible.

The thought nearly upended Nick, and she batted it aside. He was not for her, she reminded herself in no uncertain terms.

No man was.

Her heart as firm as her resolution, she loosened her hold on the cabinet shelf and made up her mind to put an end to whatever it was the aunts were up to. Whatever they were about, they best be done with it, she decided. And with the young man. Nick could not even begin to fathom their interest in him, but she knew one thing: She would be better for seeing the last of him.

She turned in time to see Belle and Tildy each take hold of one end of the blanket. Their backs to it and to the man, they held it up so that he could conceal himself behind it to don his clothing. Belle, ready to prove herself as much in charge as ever, filled the awkward silence with conversation. "I am not aware of how well you two have gotten to know each other," she began amiably.

Nick wrinkled her nose. "I know he curses a great deal."

Belle ignored the comment. She glanced an apology at the blanket as if the man behind it could see her. "If you have not been formally introduced . . ."

The man poked his head out from behind the blanket. His voice was infinitely more pleasant than the look he shot at Nick. "You'll excuse me if I don't shake your hand," he said, before he ducked behind the blanket again. "I've learned from experience, it isn't safe to get too close."

Belle laughed self-consciously and continued as if he'd said nothing at all. "This is our dear Nicolette."

Nick pulled a face. All her life she'd loathed the formality of the name. She would not stand upon ceremony, not even with this man. "It's Nick," she said.

Again, the man looked out from behind the blanket. "A fitting name for one so diabolic."

Nick grunted.

The aunts groaned.

It was Tildy's turn to try and smooth things over. She darted a seemingly accidental glance behind the blanket and when she looked forward again, it was obvious she hadn't seen nearly what she wished to see. Her face fell like a badly cooked pudding. "And you, sir?" she asked, barely keeping the disappointment from her voice. "You haven't told us your name."

"My name is Gowan." His trousers and stockings on, his shirt nearly done up except for the last pearl stud at the throat, Gowan came around from the back of the blanket. "Gowan Payne. I was headed for Rhyd Ddu when I got lost in that terrible snowstorm."

"Snowstorm?" Try as she might, Nick could no longer hide her indifference. Listening as her own astonished question ricocheted off the walls of the little room, she looked from one aunt to the other.

Belle was as stone-faced as ever. Tildy hopped from foot to foot in front of Gowan, one finger up to her lips to signal him to be silent.

It was a sure sign of her guilt.

Nick knew from experience that Belle's resolve would not crack easily. She'd have much the better chance with Tildy. She took a step toward her middle aunt. "And what snowstorm would that be?" she asked. "For you know I was further up the mountain looking in on Mai Davies and never did I see so much as a snowflake."

"Yet it did snow here." Gowan sat on the edge of the bed and slipped on his boots. He looked up long enough for Nick to see that his chin was rigid, his jaw set, as if he was prepared for an argument. "I know snow when I see it."

Again, Tildy tried to silence him, and when again he ignored her pantomime, she changed her strategy. Quickly, she pulled her finger away from her lips and brought it up to her temples. She looked over at Nick and lowered her voice. "Fever," she said, rapping her brow. "Burning up, the poor boy was. He must have imagined the whole thing in his pitiful, heated brain. Snow, indeed! At this time of the year?"

"Yes. Snow." Gowan hopped to his feet, looking at Tildy as if she was the one out of her head. "And I didn't imagine it. Ask them in Beddgelert. I wasn't nearly out of the village when the rain began."

"Rain." Nick repeated the word. An idea was beginning to form in her brain though the why of it all was still as foreign to her as this Englishman's queer accent. Side-stepping her way around Tildy, she strolled over to him. "And did the rain come out of nowhere?" she asked.

Gowan shrugged. "Where else does rain come out of? It rained. That's all I know. One minute it was sunny, the next, it was raining. And the next after that," he added with a sharp look at Tildy, "it was snowing. And I didn't imagine it. It was the damnedest thing I've ever seen. It came on so fast and so furiously. It was as if the whole thing was . . ." He cocked his head, searching for the right word, ". . . magic."

Whatever suspicions Nick had were confirmed. She turned to her aunts, giving them a look that said none of it had escaped her notice. She might have asked them to explain themselves if Clea hadn't chosen that exact moment to walk in.

Oblivious as ever to the currents of emotion flowing between the people in the room, Clea bustled past, merry as May and chattering to herself. She was carrying a tea tray.

"Here you go, sir." She scuttled over to the bedside table and set down the tray. "A bit of bread and butter for you. And a nice, hot cup of tea."

She held the steaming cup up under Gowan's nose and he breathed in deep, suddenly looking very hungry indeed.

Her thin face pinched with concern, Clea waited like an anxious mother to see if he would take the cup. When he did, she let go a tiny sigh, and when he drained it, she nodded solicitously, both at Gowan and at her sisters. "There you go," she said, her lashes fluttering as they always did when she was excited. "Drink it down. There's more in the pot where that came from."

Gowan handed her the empty cup and turned his attention toward the bread and butter. Tildy hurried forward to join the touching little scene. She cut a slice from the newly baked loaf. Belle stood ready with the crock of butter. While Gowan dug in ravenously, Clea poured him another cup of tea.

Nick folded her arms across her chest and settled her weight against one foot. It was as fine a display of compassion toward a stranger as any she'd ever seen, a true example of charity at work.

And so unlike her aunts as to confound her completely.

"You've had a bit of a fever, you know," Tildy purred. "And there's nothing better for fever than food."

"I'll hazard that's what they say even in your fine city of London," Belle added. "The physicians, that is. I'm sure even they know there is nothing better for fever than food. And tea."

Nick let go a sigh of frustration. If they insisted on fawning so over the man, she had little choice but to rectify their opinion of him. She knew what men of modern medicine thought of those like her and her aunts who practiced the old arts, and the aunts may as well know it from the start. "He knows all about what doctors do and don't do in London," Nick told them, barely controlling the bite of her words. "He himself is a physician."

Nick had meant the statement only as a gentle warning. She did not expect the reaction she got.

Belle's face went white as chalk. Clea's lower lip trembled.

"What!" Tildy was so horrified, both her chins quivered. Her eyes as big as copper pennies, she stared at Gowan. "You mean we've got the wrong man? You're not the earl?"

"The earl?"

Nick's outraged exclamation nearly drowned out the collective gasps of the aunts.

Belle sent a look in Tildy's direction—one so withering, it made Tildy swallow her words.

Clea looked at Tildy, then at Nick. She braced herself, as if she expected an onslaught of her niece's famous temper. "Oh, no!" she groaned, wringing her hands. "Now you've gone and told her."

Nick did not need any further evidence of her aunts' duplicity. The pieces of the puzzle fell into place and she rounded on them, her voice sharp with outrage. "The earl? The Earl of Welshpool? Here?" A feeling much akin to panic gripped her, like a claw on her stomach. Anger tightened around her throat. Surprise mingled with outrage, disgust mixed with the hollow feeling that came from the realization that she had been utterly betrayed. She stared at her aunts, fighting to organize the thoughts in her head and finding the more she tried to force them into order, the more scattered they became.

She looked at Belle who refused to move a muscle. She looked at Clea. Her lower lip was suddenly quaking as violently as her hands. She looked at Tildy who at least had the good sense to refuse to meet her eyes.

She gaped at Gowan and pointed. "Him?"

Gowan threw his hands in the air. "Me. Yes, I'm the earl. I was a physician. I never thought to inherit, you see. The twelfth earl was my uncle and he had sons of his own. When both the earl and his sons were killed in a boating accident, I became earl. I sold my practice when I inherited the title."

As one, the aunts let go of the breaths they were holding.

"I cannot imagine why it matters so very much," Gowan grumbled. He glanced around at them all, and if Clea was insensible to the flow of emotion in a room, it was obvious this man was not. His gaze missed nothing, not the aunts' momentary agitation or their ultimate relief, and certainly not Nick's reaction to it all. One corner of his mouth lifted in an expression that was as much a challenge as a smile. "I suppose it's too much to hope that it's some sort of great honor to have the earl in your home?"

"Honor!" Nick's voice shot up in direct proportion to her temper. She balled her hands into fists.

Tildy did not wait to see what might happen next. She snatched the cup out of Gowan's hand and tossed it onto the tray just as Clea lifted it from the table. Belle was already at the door. She held it open while her sisters scurried out ahead of her and following them, she clicked it shut behind her.

Silence settled in the little room, a silence so heavy, Nick was sure she could reach out and touch it. She closed her eyes, trying to control the racing of her heart. She drew in a deep breath, then another, fighting to contain the anger that threatened to destroy her composure completely.

There was little to be gained from panic, she told herself sensibly, just as there would be little benefit gotten from displaying the anger that was even now eating away at her insides.

Another deep breath made it possible for her to control the tears that threatened to eclipse even her anger. Another one after that gave her the courage to open her eyes. She found Gowan standing where she'd left him, his handsome face screwed up in an expression of utter bewilderment that might, at any other time, have cheered her no end.

"What the devil was that all about?" He ran one hand through his hair. "Are they always that . . . that odd? And why did they take away my meal? I wasn't nearly done. I'm famished. I never realized it. Not until—"

"How do you feel?" One step at a time, Nick approached him, carefully advancing as one might on a wild animal. "Is your vision clear? You don't feel a rush of heat, do you?" She laid her hand on Gowan's forehead.

He brushed her away and moved back a step, eyeing her with the same sort of confused expression he'd given the aunts before they paraded from the room. "I feel hungry, that's how I feel. What kind of place is this? I thought you and that cat were the only fiendish things here. Now I find that everyone is."

Nick could not be distracted so easily from what needed to be done. She took another step, closing the small space between them. "Are you certain you're feeling well?"

Gowan sighed and sat down on the bed. "As well as can be expected in this house of bedlamites."

Any other time, Nick may have risen to the challenge in his voice and joined, readily and quite happily, in a spirited discussion of why he was so very wrong. Now, her only concern was for him and for what her aunts might have done to him. And to her.

She sat down on the bed next to him. "What did it taste like?" she asked.

Gowan looked at her uncertainly. "The bread and butter?"

"Not the bread and butter. The tea. What did the tea taste like?"

It took a minute for Gowan to decide, and Nick thought she might scream for the waiting. He screwed his eyes shut, trying to recall the flavor. "It tasted like . . . like tea."

"Tea. Like the tea you have at home at your fancy Harley Street practice? Fine Indian tea?"

"Not precisely." She saw him run his tongue over his teeth. "Not as choice. More like a country cousin. Naturally, I assumed that—"

"You must forgive me. I have to know what it was, you see," Nick interrupted him, trying to explain, and even as the words left her lips, she knew they were no explanation at all. Before she could talk herself out of doing what needed to be done, she brought her face up to his.

Startled, Gowan leaned back.

Nick didn't let that stop her. She leaned nearer.

This time, Gowan didn't move. He might not know what she was doing, but it was clear that whatever it was, he was beginning to enjoy it. His arms straight, he braced himself against the bed and refused to retreat another inch. He met her gaze head-on, daring her to get closer, and a slow smile tickled at the corners of his mouth.

Nick would have liked nothing better than to ignore the smile, just as she would have liked to pretend she hadn't noticed the sudden flash of amusement in his eyes. She would have preferred to disregard the way the morning sunlight that streamed through the window added coppery highlights to his hair and his beard. She would have liked to pretend that none of it affected her.

If only her pulse didn't quicken and her breath catch in her throat, she might have been successful at the ruse.

Praying her heart wasn't beating so loud that he could hear it, she swallowed her alarm as well as her pride and leaned even nearer. "If I could but try and catch the aroma of the tea . . ."

She couldn't abide the thought of looking into Gowan's eyes, so she kept her gaze on his mouth. It didn't help her composure in the least when she saw him flick his tongue over his lips lazily, as if he were tasting something delectable.

Nick swallowed hard. "Don't be alarmed," she told him. "Think of this as nothing more than a scientific experiment." The advice delivered, both to him and to herself, she brought her nose on a level with Gowan's lips and sniffed.

The first whisper of his breath was enough to make Nick forget both her apprehensions and her caution. She leaned even nearer. "I can smell damiana," she said to herself. "And cloves." Frustrated at not being able to make a more thorough analysis, Nick sat back. "If only I knew for certain."

The smile that brightened Gowan's expression didn't simply tickle his lips. Like the morning sun coming up over the mountain, it transformed his entire face. It crinkled the corners of his mouth. It sparkled in his eyes like day glow off water.

This time, he was the one who moved nearer.

Before Nick even realized what was going to happen or had time to react to it, he had one arm around her waist. He flattened it against her side, his thumb playing up and down her ribcage. "I think there might be a solution to that little problem," he said, bringing his mouth a hair's breadth from hers. "You need to know for certain what kind of tea they served me, am I right? Perhaps a taste of my lips might help."

Four

All her life, Nick had kept herself apart from other people. All her life she had spoken her charms and cast her spells, watching humbly and in awe as they took hold. All her life, she'd seen others yield to the power of her magic.

But she'd never felt herself fall prey to such a thing.

Until now.

Now, she sat as if spellbound, unable to move, though that's what she knew she should do, unwilling to break the unlikely link forged of the moment, no matter how preposterous her head told her heart it might be.

At the first tentative brush of Gowan's lips against hers, she found herself falling under his spell. When the kiss lasted for more than a second or two, her resolve melted. When his mouth moved over hers and he parted her lips with his tongue, her determination dissolved completely.

Her heart beating wildly against Gowan's, her head back, Nick cursed herself twice. Once because she hadn't anticipated what was on his mind and moved to prevent it, and a second time because in spite of herself, the moment his lips met hers, she didn't give a second thought to how he tasted. She was too busy enjoying the kiss. Though she knew he would never admit it in a thousand lifetimes, she knew Gowan was, too.

His pulse racing beneath Nick's fingertips, he tugged her nearer, crushing her breasts against his chest.

That small portion of her brain that was still functioning

logically told Nick to move away as quickly as she could, to put some space between herself and the man at the same time she distanced herself from the frightening emotions he was stirring in her. It told her that Gowan's behavior was far too presumptuous to be proper. It informed her that his touch was too brazen to be prudent. It warned her that he tasted like damiana and cloves and that his arrival here was hardly coincidental. It reminded her that he was the Earl of Welshpool and as such, a threat to all she held most dear.

That was enough to bring her to her senses.

Her hands at his shoulders, Nick pushed herself away from Gowan. She leapt from the bed. "It is worse than I thought!"

Gowan laughed, the kind of languid, secret laugh shared by lovers. "Oh, no. You're wrong, my girl," he said, making a grab for her hand. "It's much better than I thought."

Nick snatched her hand away and moved out of his reach. "You are a vile man. That is not what I meant and you know it. I simply meant . . . I meant . . ." She could not say what she meant, not with the taste of him still warm upon her lips.

Nick scoured the back of her hand across her mouth and even though she was certain she would see his eyes filled with a merriment bought and paid for at her expense, she dared a look at Gowan. It did her spirits little good to see that she was wrong.

He didn't look the least bit amused. He looked satisfied and a little out of breath, as if their encounter had unsettled him as much as it had her. There was one decided difference. While she wanted nothing else than to be done with him, it was obvious he wanted more.

One look at the undisguised desire that still glimmered in his eyes and Nick's thoughts coalesced with dreadful certainty. "Good God," she moaned. "They have really done it this time. It's working."

She knew she didn't have a moment to spare. Nick

dashed to the cupboard. Her fingers nervously sorting through the bottles on the shelf, she found what she was searching for—a tonic made from skullcap. She hurried back to the bed and held the bottle out to Gowan. "Here," she said. "Drink this. Quickly."

"Don't be ridiculous." Gowan pushed her hand and the bottle aside. He looked over at her cupboard and his top lip curled. "Do you think I've forgotten that you tried your damnedest to maim me for life with the contents of a bottle very like that? It was one thing having the wretched liquid poured on me. I am certainly not going to drink anything that came out of that cabinet of horrors."

Frustrated, Nick sighed. She propped her hands on her hips. "And where do you think theirs came from?" she asked with a knowing look at the door. "The aunts did not get the tea they brought you from the kitchen, I can tell you that much. They have a cabinet of their own. In the small room at the back of the house. Do you trust anything that came out of it? I am not certain I would. If you did not notice, they can be a bit vague at times. And distracted. I would venture to say you are safer by far drinking something from one of my bottles than you are from one of theirs."

For a second, she thought she'd convinced him. Gowan glanced at the door and though he tried not to show it, she noticed a slight wavering in his maddening self-possession. His lips pinched the way a man's sometimes do when he is thinking over a problem. His eyes narrowed. But instead of admitting he was wrong and she was right, as he surely would have done had he been the least bit sensible, he let out a harsh laugh.

"What are you saying, that your aunts are trying to poison me?" Massaging the back of his neck with one hand, Gowan looked at her in wonder. "It hardly seems likely. They have no reason. Besides, what harm could the three of them ever do anyone? They're such sweet old ladies."

Enough was enough, and Nick had had more than enough. "Sweet old ladies . . ." She sighed and raised her gaze to the ceiling. "And every one of them a rheibes." The Welsh word was second nature and it slipped out before she had a chance to consider that he would not know what it meant. When he gave her a blank stare, she sighed again. "Those sweet old ladies," she told him, "are witches."

She got exactly the kind of reaction she expected. It did little to soothe her temper and even less to enhance her opinion of the young earl. It was the same reaction she always got from those who thought they were terribly modern and absurdly civilized, though coming from a man as insufferable as Gowan, it was more gratifying than usual. His mouth fell open and for one blessed moment, he was actually at a loss for words.

His brown eyes wide, he stared at Nick, then at the door through which her aunts had disappeared such a short time ago. He looked over at her cupboard and at the little bottle in her hand. He raised his eyes to hers and started to say something, but though his lips moved, no words came out. He cleared his throat and tried again. This time, the only thing that escaped him was an enormous laugh.

This was not the usual reaction, and Nick barely held her temper.

Gowan hardly cared. He laughed so hard, his cheeks turned red and his eyes brimmed with tears and even then, he only laughed more. Finally, holding his sides, he collapsed against the featherbed.

"Witches!" Gowan slapped the bed and struggled to sit up, his voice still bubbling with amusement. "That is most excellent. Really." He wiped the tears from his eyes. "I never would have expected a show of humor. Not from you."

"Then you'll not be disappointed. I am not trying to be humorous, m'lord," she said, biting through his title. "I am simply telling you the truth. As a kindness. And a warning."

"And what is it exactly that you're trying to warn me about?" Gowan tried his best to look sober and concerned, but his eyes flashed with enjoyment. "Are they trying to turn me into a toad, do you think? Or perhaps they're the type of witches who eat travelers lost in the woods. Is that why you were so worried about my being here?" He raised his eyebrows and leaning forward, he snatched Nick's free hand. Like a fisherman hauling in his catch, he reeled her to the bed. "Hoping to save all the best parts for yourself?"

"Really!" Nick stopped herself just short of screaming with frustration. She fought to bat Gowan's hand away, but that was little use. He wound his fingers through hers and held fast. The more she struggled, the tighter his grip and the tighter his grip, the more she struggled. Finally, she surrendered and this time, she couldn't keep herself from screeching.

"You said it yourself," she told him through clenched teeth. "Not one hour ago. You said there was a snowstorm. You said how unusual it was at this time of year and how the whole thing came on so fast and so furiously as to seem like—"

"Magic." Gowan finished the sentence for her. He sat up, suddenly looking a little less cheerful.

The look did not last long. His gaze slipped from her breasts to her waist and back up again and Gowan's eyes glazed over. He slid his left hand from Nick's fingers to her wrist and from her wrist to her elbow. He tugged her nearer and lowered his voice, and though he kept at least the thread of their conversation, it was obvious his thoughts were far from what he was saying, and dangerously close to what he was looking at.

"Magic!" He chuckled, settling his right hand at the smooth curve where Nick's waist met her hip. "It was a figure of speech. Nothing more." He slid his hand from her waist up and over her ribs. "You can't possibly be serious."

Nick didn't wait for any more. She tugged free and darted

across the room. Her back to her cabinet, she turned and though her voice trembled nearly as much as her knees, she faced him and told him as much of the truth as she dared.

"I would love to tell you you are right," she said. "Honestly, I would. I would like nothing more than to tell you the whole thing is a lark. I would like you to go away believing it, for you deserve to find out for yourself how wrong you are. But I cannot do that. Not this time. You have to believe me because you have no choice. And if you do not believe me . . . if you do not cooperate and do as I tell you, we will both suffer the consequences."

Gowan got up from the bed. It was obvious she'd spoiled his pleasantly amorous mood and just as obvious that he was not at all happy about it. But at least he knew enough to keep his distance.

He did a turn around the room, examining the colored candles set on the tables, and her collection of eagle and hawk feathers laid out in the corner. He was so intent, she might have thought he'd forgotten about her altogether if he hadn't scowled over at her every now and again.

"You're not making any sense at all," he said, fingering the pots of herbs that sat on a wooden bench near the window. "If we're both to suffer the consequences then the least you can do is explain what terrible doom awaits me. What did they give me to drink? And why? What am I to your aunts?"

"You are the earl." Like a bather dipping one toe in water that might be far too cold, Nick inched her way into the explanation. "They gave you damiana and cloves and Lord knows what else mixed in with your tea. It is . . ." Certain her cheeks were flaming just as her voice was cracking, she looked away. "It is . . ." With a mumble of defeat, Nick gave up the fight. She blurted out the whole of it before she could convince herself to stop. "It is a love potion."

"A love potion?" She had Gowan's full attention now. His eyebrows raised, his expression an absolute study of amazement, he swung around to face her. "Why would your aunts care if I fall in love and who on earth do they wish me to fall in love with?"

Nick didn't answer. How could she? She crossed her arms over her chest and stood back, waiting for him to reason his way through to the one and only possible solution.

It came barely a second later. Gowan's eyes flew open wide. His expression soured. He retreated a step and would have backed up even more if he hadn't found himself up against the window. He held out both his hands as if to ward off something unpleasant. "You're not serious. They don't really want . . . You mean, they're trying to make me . . . They want me to . . . to you?"

Nick wasn't sure if she should laugh or feel insulted. She set aside both emotions as unproductive and decided to take full advantage of the situation while Gowan was still stunned. She lowered her voice and advanced on him, laying the possibilities out before him like the gates of hell yawning at his feet. "That's right. They want you to fall in love." She poked one finger into his midsection. "With me." She pointed at herself at the same time she caught his gaze and held it. "Think about it, m'lord," she suggested, her voice like warm honey. "The two of us. Together. Forever and ever. Sunup to sundown. Day and night. What do you say to that?"

Gowan darted a look to both sides, searching for an escape route and when he did not find one, he swallowed so hard Nick could see his Adam's apple bob. "It's insane. That's what I say. It's mad. You're all mad. It is some cruel prank, surely. I am certain your aunts will come to their senses after they take the time to consider it. Are they that desperate to find you a husband that they must resort to trickery?"

The affront was nearly enough to make Nick forget herself. She backed away and balled her hands into fists at her sides.

He'd touched a nerve and Gowan knew it. The momentary wavering of Nick's self-control was enough to make him recover his senses and his sense of humor. A slow, impudent smile chasing the confusion from his face, he joined in the game.

He advanced on her in just the way she'd done to him, one step forward for each one Nick took back, eyeing her up and down the whole while. When he had her pinned against the far wall, he brought himself up short. He stopped and cocked his head.

"You're a frightfully vexatious little thing," he said. "But certainly even you can't be all bad. You're passably pretty," he added, gliding a look like fire as far down as her waist and back again to her face. "That ought to be enough to attract a suitor or two. At least until they got to know you better. Of course, once they found out that you're all raving lunatics . . . Still, there's no end to what men will put up with to get a woman in bed. You must have at least one beau somewhere in these godforsaken mountains. Why would your aunts have need of me?"

It was not something Nick was willing to explain to him—not now, not ever—and she scrambled for some explanation that would satisfy his curiosity.

Gowan saved her the trouble. "That's it! Of course!" A triumphant smile transformed his expression. A gleam of admiration in his eyes, he stepped back, as if the answer was startling, but not altogether unexpected. "They're after the title, aren't they? The way so many women were in London. Who would have thought it?" He shook his head in wonder.

"You don't seem a tufthunter, but I suppose even a girl like you isn't immune to the temptations of a fortune and a peerage. Or was it the aunts' idea? I must admit, it is a damned sight more inventive than some of the schemes I came across back home. Invitations to balls, yes." He smiled, as if remembering all the splendor and excitement that must certainly attend such events.

"Intimate dinners afterward, certainly." Gowan quirked his brows. "Discreet suggestions from desperate Mamas and Papas, absolutely." He rolled his eyes. "But never did any one of them try a magic potion. At least as far as I am aware. It is most extraordinary. Those sweet old ladies . . . They're trying to secure your place as the next Lady Welshpool."

Gowan was closer to the mark than Nick dared to admit, to him or to herself. The thought did little to calm her and even less to soothe her temper. She tossed her head and raised herself up on the balls of her feet so she could more easily glare directly into his face.

"And do you think I'd want anything to do with your title or with yourself?" She dangled the bottle of skullcap in front of his nose. "Why do you think I am trying to give you this? In spite of what the aunts might wish, I want nothing to do with you, Gowan Payne. You're insufferable. And arrogant. You're pretentious and entirely too pleased with yourself, and the sooner you drink this and be gone, the sooner I will be at peace. That would be an end to the aunts' schemes. And to my worries."

Gowan gave her an indulgent smile at the same time he laid one hand on her arm. "You needn't worry," he told her, looking at her as one might at a child. "I certainly have no intention of falling in love with you. There's nothing on heaven or earth that could make that happen. Or in hell. I'm sorry. I suppose I am not accustomed to these odd country rituals. You really believe in all this magic trumpery, don't you?"

Nick might have wished for his logic, but she certainly did not want his pity. She told him as much with one withering look. "You needn't speak to me as if I am some poor addlepated creature," she told him. She pulled her arm from his grasp and held it tight to her side. "What I believe is none of your concern, just as what you believe is none of mine. But if you do not believe in the power of the aunts' potion, how do you explain the way you've been acting? You thought me diabolical a short while ago. And now . . ."

Though she tried to keep her gaze on Gowan, Nick could not. She found herself looking across the room. There was an impression in the featherbed from the place he'd sat and she imagined it must be warm still from his body. The thought crawled through her like melted candlewax, spreading heat.

It was a place she dared not go, physically or mentally, and Nick forced her thoughts from it and back to the problem at hand. "You tried to kiss me," she reminded him though she was sure he needed no reminder. His gaze followed hers to the bed and his eyes twinkled. It only served to make her angrier. "You did kiss me. And would have done more given half the chance. If I am so diabolical, if I am so despicable, explain yourself. What made me suddenly so alluring that you could not help yourself?"

"Well . . ." It was clearly not something he'd stopped to consider. Gowan ran a hand through his hair. "A man does these things," he said, but even as the words left his mouth, she could tell that even he did not think them sufficient. He looked at her sheepishly from beneath the lock of hair that fell over his brow. "Doesn't he?"

"Not any man who is a gentleman." Nick glared at him. "And although I have seen little proof of it, I will take your word for it that you are a gentleman."

"But a potion . . . ?" Wrestling with the thought, Gowan stroked his chin through his growth of stubble. "A potion could make me do that? A cup of tea? It's not possible. No." He rejected the notion with a quick slash of one hand through the air. Though his words had the ring of certainty, he could not keep his gaze from being drawn back over his shoulder toward the bed. His face flushed and he drew in a deep breath and let it out again slowly. "If it was possible . . . not that it is, of course, but if it was . . . You think my wanting to kiss you . . . You think my wanting to . . . You think that had something to do with . . . ?" Gowan's face paled. "Good Gad! Perhaps you'd better give me some of that potion of yours."

Relief flooded through Nick and she moved forward quickly, before he had a chance to change his mind. There was a small fire burning in the hearth across from the bed and a kettle of water set on the fender before it. Snatching a cup from the mantelpiece, she poured some of the hot water into it. She opened the skullcap and splashed it into the water. As always, she did not measure the dose. She judged its potency by its color, and when it was the exact shade of yellow-green that told her it was neither too weak nor too strong, she set the skullcap aside. On her way back across the room, she retrieved a purple candle from the cabinet.

She handed Gowan the cup. "Don't drink. Not yet," she instructed him. She passed her hand over the candle and a flame sprang to life. Holding the candle in both hands, she stood in front of him with it. That done, she signalled him to drink while she concentrated, mind and spirit, on the flame that danced between them.

The fire swayed to the rhythm of their breathing, the flame bending first toward Gowan, then to Nick. She let it bounce one way, then the other, waiting for it to quiet as their breaths fell in tempo one with the other. When they breathed as one, the flame stood straight and Nick kept her gaze upon it, watching as it blurred before her eyes. The flame lost its shape, and its color, and even its heat as she lost herself to the power of the magic. She drew in a deep breath and felt the power flow through her, filling her body and her mind, calming her, linking her to the magic that tingled like lightning through her veins.

Nick knew it was time to begin. Her voice was low, and

even to her own ears, it sounded as if it came from very far away. She chanted the words of power. "Smoke and fire, change the spell. Keep this gentleman strong and well. Open his eyes and let him see. Change his heart from thoughts of me."

She did not need to think if the spell would work. She felt its potency around her in the very air itself. Like a mother, it embraced her. Like a lover, it caressed her. It sizzled over her flesh. It pounded through her bloodstream. It lifted her spirit.

It made her mind soar and her heart glad. It spiraled through her and left her dizzy and weak, and when it was over, she came around to find herself right where she'd always been, staring at the little yellow candle flame.

Nick sucked in a sharp breath. As was usual when she came out of a trance, she felt a bit as if she'd been struck in the stomach. Holding the candle in one hand, she pressed the other to her heart. Only when she was sure she could look at Gowan evenly, did she bring her eyes up to his.

She expected him to be finished with the drink, but one look at him and at the cup told her he hadn't touched a drop. The cup was full. Gowan's mouth was hanging open.

"You?" Like an animal caught in a glaring light, he blinked rapidly. He cleared his throat uneasily the way people are wont to do when they are astonished. "You're one of them? That is, you think you're a . . . a . . . ?" Because he could not bring himself to finish his question, Nick decided he did not deserve an answer.

She leaned closer and watched with perverse pleasure as Gowan recoiled, doing everything in his power to avoid contact with her. "It's part and parcel of the spell," she told him, motioning to the cup with one finger. "It will not work if you do not drink."

"Drink. Er . . . Well . . . Yes." It was clear Gowan didn't know if he should be amused by Nick or afraid of her. He backed away another step, then another. He eyed her. He looked at the cup in his hands. Apparently deciding the potion was the lesser of two evils, he lifted the cup to his lips.

Just as he did, a sound filled the air all around them. It was like the noise of a hundred humming insects, and startled, Gowan lowered the cup.

Nick recognized the sound instantly, and every fiber of her being went on the alert. She knew there wasn't a moment to lose. Darting forward, she nudged Gowan's hands, urging him to finish the potion. "You'd best drink and be done," she told him, her misgivings growing even as the volume of the sound increased. "It's the aunts. They're trying to—"

It was too late.

Just as Nick touched the cup, the potion inside it seethed and spit like a pot at the boil. The mixture turned from yellow-green to dark brown.

"Jesus Christ!" Gowan's eyes went wide. He would have dropped the cup if Nick hadn't wrapped her hands around his to steady them. "What the hell—?"

The potion secure—at least for the moment—Nick didn't wait to answer Gowan's questions. She spun toward the door. She stomped her foot and raised her voice above the relentless humming. "Belle, I know this is your work," she called. "You can stop right now." She got no answer though she knew her aunt was not far away. Like some people could feel rain in the air when it is yet hours off, she could feel Belle's presence on the other side of the door. She would recognize the hum of Belle's rough magic anywhere.

"You'll not overtake my spells." Nick tried again. "You know it yourself. Hold off, Belle, and let me be."

Again she got no answer. The humming continued.

Nick drew in a breath that was far more unsteady than she liked. Her arms close to her sides, she fought to maintain her self-control. "Listen to reason, Belle, for you know

I will not allow what you're about. I will do all I can to put a stop to it."

Nick had to admit, she was annoyed at her aunts' schemes. She was irritated at their audacity. Had she been entirely honest with herself, she also would have admitted to being afraid. Afraid that everything happening around him would cause Gowan to take flight. Afraid that if he did, he would not have a chance to drink Nick's potion. Afraid that once he was gone and the aunts' spell had its time to work, he really might fall in love with her.

The thought was enough to frighten anyone.

Nick did not usually make a show of her powers. They were a sacred gift and as such, were not meant to be paraded about for entertainment or to best her rivals. But this was an exception, she decided with the kind of clarity of mind and will that comes in a crisis. This was serious.

Calling up her energies, gathering her power, Nick whirled back toward the cabinet. She grabbed a handful of dried woodruff and sprinkled it over the cup.

The humming stopped. The tea was yellow-green once more.

"Drink," she told Gowan. "Before they try again."

Changing the aunts' spells was apparently easier than changing Gowan's mind. If he had been unsure of Nick earlier, now he was all too sure. He held the cup in both hands on a level to his chest, as if it were a shield that could ward her off. "No. Thank you." He backed away from her, one careful step at a time. "It was one thing being asked to drink something green. But then to have it turn brown . . ." He glanced at the cup as if checking to see if it had changed again since last he looked. "And then green again. No. I think not. I think it might be best if I—"

He made a move for the door at the same time Nick did. There was something, at least, she'd inherited from her Aunt Tildy. She could move like the wind when she had to. She beat him to the door and flattened her back against it, her arms out at her sides, her hands against the wall on either side of her.

"I will not let you by," she said, holding her chin steady and her head high. "Not until you drink."

For a moment, she thought Gowan would challenge her. His eyes glinted. His jaw tightened. A vein at the side of his neck pounded out his exasperation. "Mother of Mercy." He grumbled the words through clenched teeth. "If that is the only thing that will release me from this madhouse . . ." Clutching the cup so tightly Nick feared it might splinter, he lifted it to his lips and drank.

To his credit, he hardly pulled a face at all. When the cup was drained, the skullcap finally gone, Nick let go a sigh of relief. "There. That's better." She relaxed against the door. "Now you can go back where you belong. Why don't I—"

The words were barely out of her mouth when the window across the room burst open. A wind as cold as a winter gale blasted through the casement. The force was enough to topple the potted plants on the bench near the window. It scattered the papers lying on a nearby table. It exploded against Gowan and knocked him off his feet.

He landed right up against the door. Right up against Nick.

"Tildy, how dare you?" Nick squirmed beneath his weight. She brandished a fist at the open window. "I know it's you," she screamed, "and you can stop. He's had the skullcap."

As quickly as the wind came, it died.

Nick fought to catch her breath. She waited for Gowan to move away.

He didn't.

Almost too afraid to look, she slowly raised her gaze to his. She found him smiling, his eyes lighting the way they had when he sat on the bed, naked except for the blanket that barely covered anything at all that he'd meant for it to cover.

A terrible misgiving assailed Nick. She whispered a prayer that he'd drunk the skullcap in time and swallowed hard. She forced herself to speak.

"How do I look to you?" she asked.

"You look . . ." Gowan had a bemused sort of smile on his face. She'd seen the look before. It was the same look she'd seen on the faces of the shepherds from further up the hills when they had been with their flocks the whole of the summer and came down to the village in the autumn feeling randy as rams. Gowan stretched lazily, his body full against hers, every hard plane of his body fitted against every one of her curves. He lowered his mouth so that his lips were a fraction on an inch from hers, his voice as seductive as a lover's. "You," he murmured, "look awful."

Nick mumbled a curse at the same time she shoved Gowan away. It might not have been such an easy task if he wasn't laughing so hard.

"Awful," he said again when he was far enough from her to look her up and down. "I look at you now and all I see is you, and one look is enough to convince me that you are peculiar, and wilful, and a damned sight too odd even for a man with my sometimes singular tastes. It seems your potion worked, my little witch."

Nick was so relieved, she paid no mind to the sarcasm in his voice. "Thank goodness." She breathed a sigh. She glanced over her shoulder toward the door. "Now perhaps you should leave before they try something else. Come. Come on." She snapped the door open and went into the outer passageway. "Let us get you back to the train station in Beddgelert before they do any more damage."

"But I'm not going to Beddgelert."

Her hand still on the door, Nick froze. She turned back to Gowan. "Of course you are." Even to her, her words sounded forced. She knew they were as much a hope as a statement. "There's a train this evening, I'm sure. You can be on your way back to London and—"

"I'm not going back to London."

If Nick didn't know better, she might have thought she'd touched a nerve. Gowan's face went as hard and gray as the slate that was quarried from the nearby mountains. "I'm headed toward Rhyd Ddu," he said, sounding none too pleased with the prospect. "And to the Lodge beyond. I'll be staying for at least the summer."

All summer.

The aunts would have all summer to try to work their wills.

It was too awful to even consider.

Her heart sinking, her mind working furiously to unearth a solution to the hideous problem, Nick led the way down the stairs. Before she got to the bottom, she had her answer. At the door, she turned to Gowan, a smile on her face.

"And do they know in the village that you are coming?" she asked, as innocently as she could.

"Yes." Gowan stood aside while she grabbed a blue cloth sack that sat on the table near the door. He let her lead the way out over the doorstop with its chalked design. "I wired ahead before I left London. I let the staff at the Lodge know that I was on my way and I'm sure by now, the entire village has got wind of it." He puffed out his chest, looking suddenly less like the patient she'd doctored these past days, and more like a man who saw at least some light at the end of a very dark tunnel. His eyes gleamed and he smacked one flattened hand against his stomach.

"I can't wait," he said. "A nice, hot dinner. A cup of tea. A fine bottle of brandy from the cellars. Ah!" He grinned over at her, making it clear it all sounded infinitely preferable to what he'd endured here. "I've never visited before, you know. I imagine the folks of the village are preparing quite a warm reception for their new earl."

Nick stepped out into the sunshine and her spirits soared like the hawk that was circling high overhead. "Preparing a welcoming? Oh, yes, m'lord," she purred. "I am certain they are."

Five

"I do believe they have at least some affection for each other." Bustling back and forth between the table and the hearth, Clea nodded eagerly, as if the gesture might give some substance to her statement.

Belle looked at her as if she'd lost her mind.

Tildy liked to think herself infinitely more patient than Belle, but this time, even she could not contain herself. She looked at Clea, too, and though it was not a gesture that was either characteristic or becoming, she clicked her tongue.

"Really, Clea." Tildy tried her best to retain her composure, but after the chaos of the last few minutes, it was nearly impossible. She was not as young as she used to be, she reminded herself, and the wind-working spell she'd cast in an attempt to keep Gowan from drinking Nick's potion had drained the last of her energy. Quite obviously, the charm Belle cast had done the same to her.

Belle sat across the table and although she kept her head high and her shoulders back, there were dark smudges of fatigue beneath her eyes. Tildy could well understand why. She was feeling much the same, and she supposed she must look just as exhausted.

She knew her hair was a fright. It floated in wild disarray around her head and hung into her eyes, and she pursed her lips and blew it aside. She sat with her shoulders bowed and watched Clea at the hearth. Blessedly, when she came back to the table, it was with the teapot in hand.

Carefully, Clea filled Belle's cup, then came around the table to pour for Tildy. "I do not mean to say that they are in love," she said, her eyes taking on that wistful look that sometimes crept into them when she thought her sisters weren't watching. "Though it would be easy enough to fall in love with a man who looks as he does."

Clea's sigh was echoed by Tildy, who remembered all too well the glimpse she'd had of Gowan behind the blanket, and even by Belle who, in spite of her efforts to remain as dispassionate as ever, was as appreciative of a man's physical attributes as any woman Tildy had ever met.

Sensing that her sisters were reading her thoughts as well as her emotions, Clea pulled herself back to the chore at hand. She poured herself a cup of tea and handed around a plate of buttery biscuits. "That's ridiculous, of course. It's too much to expect that they could have fallen in love, don't you think? At least so soon. But they did leave here together . . ." She left the statement dangling, as if to keep open all its possibilities. "And strike me silly if I'm wrong, but when they walked out, I would swear that Nick was smiling."

Being reminded of the problem was enough to make the longing on Belle's face disappear in an instant. Her lips pinched tight with displeasure, she dipped her biscuit into her cup. It left a crust of crumbs floating at the surface, and watching her sip her tea through it, Tildy made a face. "She was smiling right enough," Belle said. "That is what worries me so."

"Oh." This was clearly too complicated a matter for Clea to reason her way through. While she made the attempt, she broke a biscuit in two and nibbled on the smaller half. She squeezed her eyes nearly shut, her effort at concentration so intense as to be almost palpable. "But we want them to like each other." She looked from Belle to Tildy. "Don't we?"

The brief rest was enough to restore at least some of Belle's energies and all of her acerbity. She poured herself another cup of tea and dunked another biscuit, and when she spoke, her voice was as brisk as ever. "You forget, Clea, that Nick has vowed to do all she can to avoid the earl. She warned us she would when we first heard the news that he was on his way. Foolish girl! She simply will not listen to reason."

"Perhaps we are the ones who are being unreasonable." Tildy finished one biscuit and started in on another. She knew it was a mistake to speak her mind, but she was too weary to care. It was an opinion she'd expressed more than once since news of the earl's arrival spread over the mountain. This time, like all the times before, it threatened to escalate their discussion into an argument.

Belle tapped her spoon against the rim of her cup. "Do you think it's something I want to do to the girl? It is not, Tildy Rhys, and you know it. It was not to be cruel to Nick that we made the decision. But she has a responsibility. As her mother did before her, rest her soul." Even Belle was not insensitive to a mention of the dead. She bowed her head as did the others.

The moment gone, the tribute briefly paid, Belle went on. "Nick knows her duty. It would be easier on us all if she would simply accept it. Once each generation, we must have someone marry. And Nick is the only one left. Only this time . . ." In spite of her every attempt to keep herself reserved, Belle could not suppress the shrewd gleam that lit her eyes. "This time, we'll beat the Welshpools at their own wicked game. They thought they were safe. They thought one of theirs would never marry one of ours. We'll prove them wrong, Tildy. And the curse will be broken."

Tildy knew Belle was right. It was the only chance in this generation for setting things aright. Yet something about the whole plan niggled at her insides, though she could not say what it was. She knew one thing for certain, and again she cast aside her discretion and spoke her mind. "Nick will not go quietly."

"She will not." Belle shook her head solemnly. "That is what worries me so."

"Oh, dear!" The color drained from Clea's face. Her eyes grew wide. She pressed one hand to her mouth. "That is why it wasn't good for Nick to leave here with a smile on her face. Do you think she's planning something?"

It was a question not deserving of an answer.

Tildy reached for another biscuit and chewed it thoughtfully. "I hope it's nothing like she did to Tabor Blount."

This time, it was Belle who clicked her tongue.

Though three years had passed since the incident Tildy referred to, none of them would ever forget it. Tabor was a young man from a distant village who knew nothing of the craft practiced by the Rhys family or of Nick's skill at it. He learned his lesson right enough, the day he tried to steal a kiss from her. He left Rhyd Ddu with a rough lesson in magic that as near as Tildy could remember had something to do with his trousers catching fire.

Tildy reached for the last biscuit on the serving plate. "That poor man," she said, but even she wasn't sure if she meant Tabor or Gowan.

Belle drained her cup. She drummed her fingers against the tabletop. "If only there was some way of knowing what Nick has planned."

There was, of course, and they thought of it as one.

Tildy was the first to leap from her chair. She hurried to the cupboard where they kept their herbs and potions.

"Yes. Yes. Of course!" Behind her, she heard Belle's voice, high and tight with excitement. "We can at least see what she's doing and perhaps do something to counter it."

"We can indeed," Tildy agreed, and reaching into the cupboard, she drew out their seeing crystal.

* * *

"Damned odd, that's what you are. Odd and troublesome. And did I mention infuriating?"

Gowan wasn't sure why he was bothering to tell Nick exactly what he thought of her. The last he'd seen of her, she was at least a hundred feet ahead of him. Like one of the sure-footed goats he'd once seen on a mountainside in Switzerland, she scampered up a path that had gotten steeper and more torturous since they left the cottage.

She was out of sight completely now, but that didn't keep Gowan from continuing his tirade. "And intolerable." He called out the words.

His fit of pique should have made him feel better. It generally did. Today, it did little for his mood and nothing at all for his composure. He listened to the last of his words echo back at him from the face of the nearby mountains and was reminded only of how isolated he was.

That didn't make him feel one whit better, and it certainly did not make him feel any more favorable toward a guide who, ever since they'd started on the path to Rhyd Ddu nearly a quarter of an hour ago, had taken every opportunity to dash on ahead and leave him struggling to catch her up.

Gowan shoved aside a branch of whatever kind of shrubbery it was that was blocking his path. He'd never been keen on shrubbery, never been interested in gardens or glasshouses or the things that grew in them. He wasn't interested now, except that he wondered why such devilish things as this need exist at all. Whatever this greenery was, it had branches that curled over the footpath like the tendrils of some Welsh Medusa. And thorns an inch long.

One of the barbs tore into his thumb and he winced and swore and sucked at the wound.

No sooner did he release it than the branch sprang back and caught him from behind. One of the spines grazed his neck and he felt a trickle of hot blood behind his ear.

"Damn!" Gowan untangled himself from the hellish plant. Using a large boulder for a prop, he dragged himself to the next place where the track levelled off. He glared into the distance.

There was no sign of Nick, no sign of any living creature. The mountains rose to both sides of him, slate-colored walls barricading him from the rest of the world. There were few trees about and those that were must have been buffeted by the winds that screamed over these mountains during a storm. Their trunks were bent. Their limbs were twisted. They were nearly bare, their buds just beginning to swell in the spring sunshine. Here and there, a single red berry hung from a branch like a drop of congealed blood.

It was a bleak world, and desolate, not at all like the green and fertile holding where Nick and the aunts had their cottage. The clouds above Gowan scuttled by at the whim of a breeze he could not feel, and although he heard rustlings in the undergrowth that grew along the side of the track, he saw no animal, large or small.

Nick must have come this way, Gowan thought, stopping long enough to dab at the scratch on his neck with his handkerchief. There was no other path that led from this one. No way to go but up. Yet if she had, there was no evidence of her. It was as if her passing was no more substantial than the mist that settled on the mountaintops. Something he could neither touch nor feel. As fleeting as a smile.

"Are you ready now to go back to Beddgelert?"

Gowan looked up. Where she came from he couldn't imagine, but Nick was perched atop a boulder that sat full in the sunshine not twenty feet away. She dangled one leg over the side of the huge rock. The other she had propped on a convenient foothold. She had one elbow on her knee. Her chin was in her hand.

It was not meant to be an enticing pose, but Gowan could not fail to notice that it exposed a good deal more of her than she might have realized. He had an excellent view of one leg, or at least as much of it as could be seen beneath stockings that were sturdy and black and far more functional than they were fashionable. As unbecoming as they were, he couldn't help but admire the way they fit. They displayed her shapely calf to best advantage. Even her stout black boots could not hide the fact that her ankles were slim and well-proportioned, or that her feet were as tiny as the rest of her.

"It's far easier to go down the mountain. Especially for a man not used to the rigors of country life."

Nick's comment drew Gowan out of his reverie. He brought his gaze up from her leg to her face just in time to see her smile. It was a look that didn't strike him as being friendly. It was far more challenging, as if she was daring him to dispute anything she said. "If we start soon, you'll be in Beddgelert before tea and on a train home by suppertime."

"Except that I am not going to Beddgelert." Gowan hauled himself up the last few feet to where Nick sat. Reluctant to let her see how short of breath he was, he sat down with his back to her and propped himself against the boulder. "How many times do I need to tell you, or am I not making myself clear? I'm headed to the Lodge. I will be living at the Lodge. At least through the summer."

Nick leaned over, her face directly above his, her hair draped to both sides of it like an inky curtain. "Are you certain?"

"Yes, I'm certain." Gowan glared up at her. He hoped his words did not sound as bitter to her as they did to him. Heaven forbid she should ask him to justify his reticence. He had no need to explain that the Lodge was his last refuge, the last retreat of a desperate man. Not to this woman.

To her credit—and there was little else he was willing to give her credit for—she didn't ask. Humming softly to herself, Nick rummaged through the blue cloth sack she'd brought with her. Gowan heard something crunch and when he looked up, he saw her eating an apple.

She took a huge bite and ignoring Gowan completely, chewed away quite happily. Juice dribbled down her chin and she wiped it away with one finger. When she'd finished the first mouthful, she took another bite and sighed contentedly, as if the fruit were the most delicious and satisfying of its kind since Eve plucked one of its ancient kin from the tree in Eden.

A warm breeze wafted the scent of the apple in Gowan's direction. Even though he told himself he was almost to the Lodge where a sumptuous hot meal would, no doubt, be readied for him, he could not help but remember that he'd had little more to eat in the past three days than a few bites of the aunts' bread and butter and a mouthful of Nick's odious tea. His stomach rumbled.

Perhaps Nick didn't hear. It seemed more likely that she did and that she simply didn't care. She went right on eating and when she was finished, she tossed the apple core onto the ground where the animals could finish it off. She reached into her sack and pulled out a second apple.

Gowan watched as she polished the apple against her sleeve. He stared as she raised it to her mouth. His own mouth watered. He licked his lips.

Ready to take a bite, Nick paused and looked a him. As if she'd forgotten he was there, her expression went from blissfully content to slightly sour, the mere sight of him enough to spoil the taste of the apple. Her mouth turned down at the corners. Her lower lip pinched.

It was an expression Gowan had seen dozens of times on the faces of dozens of women who were trying their damnedest to look pouting and provocative.

Nick looked neither. Nick looked positively nettled. "You wouldn't like one, would you?" she asked.

It was not the most gracious invitation he'd ever gotten, nor was it offered with even the slightest trace of civility.

Perhaps that was why Gowan so enjoyed accepting it.

Nick tossed the apple down and he might have taken a bite quickly before she could change her mind and withdraw the offer, if it were not for the fact that he didn't quite trust her. Before he dared a taste, he looked over the apple carefully. He even sniffed it to be sure it was an apple and only an apple and not something steeped in or soaked by one of Nick's strange potions.

He thought he'd been discreet enough, but his examination did not escape Nick's notice. Her look went from sour to insulted. " 'Tis only an apple," she said. "And if you do not believe it, give it back. It is untouched by magic. You have my word for it."

That did little to console him.

The first bite Gowan took was a small one. It tasted like nothing more or less than an apple, and relieved, he took another mouthful.

The apple was crisp and delicious. The fact that he'd bested Nick by accepting it when she clearly expected him not to, was even more appetizing. With the taste of the apple in his mouth and the sun warm upon his face, Gowan settled himself against the boulder. Feeling very pleased with himself, he relaxed for the first time since he'd woken in the strange little cottage with the even stranger aunts all around him. He closed his eyes.

The next thing he knew, he felt something wet against his cheek, and the puff of a hot breath in his face. Startled, Gowan sat up. He opened his eyes to find himself nose to nose with a brutish looking horse.

The animal was as white as snow, but its color was the only thing about it that was the least bit innocent. It had a broad body and legs the size of tree trunks. Its mane was shaggy and thick. It hung over eyes that looked like bits of black glass and gleamed at Gowan as if the creature were sizing him up for a meal.

As near as Gowan could tell, that is exactly what the

beastly thing was doing. It snorted directly into his face, showing a set of teeth that, in spite of their yellowish color and the fact that a number of them were missing, looked to be very serviceable indeed.

"What the devil!" Gowan jumped to his feet. He wasn't nearly quick enough. Before he could move far enough away from the animal, it took his entire hand into its mouth.

Behind him, Gowan heard laughter. "It's your apple he's after, not your life and limb." Nick came bounding down the path, her skirts flying around her ankles. "You needn't look as if you are about to die."

"Who are you to say how I should look? You weren't attacked by the savage." Gowan tugged his hand free and dried it against the leg of his trousers. The horse, apparently, did not much care. He contently chewed all that was left of Gowan's apple. "It nearly took off my fingers."

Nick obviously didn't think there was much danger in that. She laughed again and reaching into her sack, she drew out another apple. She held it in front of her. The horse caught the scent immediately and lost all interest in Gowan.

Safely out of its reach, Gowan leaned against the boulder and pulled his handkerchief from his pocket. He wiped his face and his hands.

Nick smiled over at him slyly while she fed the horse out of her hand. "You do not get on well with animals, do you? First Cat and now this." The smile never left her face, but she shook her head sadly. "That will teach you to fall asleep with food in your hands, especially out in the open."

"Sleep? Did I?" Gowan looked around. If the slanting shadows didn't tell him he'd been asleep, the soreness in his neck and shoulders should have. He stretched and bent his head, working out the pain.

"It is my fault. I'm sorry." Nick didn't look at him, but Gowan didn't have to see her face to know that this time, she actually meant what she said. He could hear it in her voice. The sharp tinge of regret combined with a trace of chagrin and made her accent thicker and even harder to understand than usual. If he didn't know better—and if he didn't think her a creature completely incapable of such a response—he might even have said that her face flushed with embarrassment. Disguising her discomfort, she reached up and scratched the horse's ears.

"You have been abed these past days and it was not right of me to expect you to walk all this way, or to hurry on so fast you had to run to keep up. I did not realize it until you nodded off. I suppose even earls do not have a limitless supply of energy." Sliding her hands to either side of the horse's head, she laid her cheek against its broad muzzle. "That is why I've brought Horse." She twined one hand through the animal's mane and motioned for Gowan with the other. "Come on then. Climb up. You can ride the rest of the way into Rhyd Ddu."

"I think not." Gowan feared he answered all too quickly. As soon as he saw the twinkle in Nick's eyes, he knew he was right.

Her head tipped to one side, she studied him carefully. "You mean you do not want to ride?" she asked, though it was clear she knew full well that was exactly what he meant. "Horse's owner will not mind, if that is what worries you. He has no master. He roams the mountain freely and comes when he's needed. Everyone about here sees to his needs."

"Charming." Gowan managed a smile that must surely have looked as stiff as it felt. "It isn't that. It's—"

"He is a good horse. And gentle." Nick walked toward him, the horse following right behind her. "He will not move at more than a trot if you tell him."

"Yes. I'm sure." Gowan backed up a step. "He's a fine horse."

"But still, you do not want to ride." Nick ambled forward. She stopped directly in front of Gowan and the horse hung its huge head over her shoulder. It nuzzled Gowan's chin with its nose.

Nick couldn't possibly have missed the way every muscle in Gowan's body tensed. Not surprisingly she wasn't about to let him get by without at least some mention of it. In a performance as accomplished as any West End ingenue Gowan had ever seen, she opened her eyes wide. "You're not afraid of Horse, are you, m'lord?" she asked. "For if you were, you might certainly be better off back in London where you could hide yourself from dangerous wild creatures such as this."

"Afraid?" His pride wounded, Gowan pulled back his shoulders. "Why should I be? We have horses in London, if you are not aware. Thousands of them. Horses that pull cabs and wagons and coaches and such. I see horses every day."

"But do you ever get close to any of them?"

If Gowan didn't know better, he'd wonder if Nick didn't have some way to communicate with the animal and make it do her bidding. As if in response to her every word, the horse nodded its immense head. It puffed a wet snort directly into Gowan's face.

A man could only tolerate so much.

Gowan sidestepped both Nick and the horse. He dashed up the path. "I'll walk the rest of the way, thank you, if it's all the same to you."

She didn't reply—thankfully—and Gowan didn't wait for either her or for her answer. He went right on, and he might not have known she was following him at all if he didn't hear her mumble now and again in Welsh. He didn't think she was talking to him. He supposed she must have been talking to the wretched horse.

After a few minutes, she fell silent and Gowan was just as glad. Perhaps they could get to Rhyd Ddu without further incident.

He might have known things would not be that easy.

* * *

"Off with you! Go! Shoo!" Tildy clapped her hands and waved her arms, scattering the doves in the birdbath. "Be gone with you!" She flapped her skirts and watched the birds retreat to the top of the garden wall, and when they were gone, she waved to Belle and Clea. "This will do, don't you think?"

Clea was skeptical. She walked up the garden path with her head to one side, studying the birdbath as if she'd never seen it before. "The crystal would surely work better."

"If Tildy hadn't broken the crystal." Belle threaded her way between Clea and a bed of blue-flowered speedwell. "I suppose it may work," she said, though she did not look thoroughly convinced. She plucked a dove-gray feather from the birdbath and cast it aside, and Tildy watched the water ripple from her fingertips.

The colors of sky and cloud swirled before her eyes, dapples of sunshine lighting it until it sparkled like jewels. The movement settled slowly, until the reflection became more distinct, like the images in a mirror. Tildy saw the billowy white clouds scuttle by on a bed of purest blue. She watched as a kestrel circled high overhead, sailing on the breeze. It wasn't long before she saw something else beside: the reflection of three faces bent over the birdbath.

Tildy whisked away the stray strand of hair that hung in front of her eyes. "I think it will work quite nicely," she said. She did not need to glance up to see either of her sisters. She could view them perfectly in the water.

Clea would try anything, that much was certain, and having no better suggestion to make herself, she was willing to at least have a go at Tildy's. Belle was still not satisfied, but it was clear she knew she had little choice. Her lips were pinched. Her eyes were narrowed. She was trying her best to think of an alternative, and much to Tildy's delight, she was having little luck.

They'd already considered and abandoned every one of Belle's suggestions: the window glass (because it was in diamond-shaped panes that made a clear reflection impossible), the well water (because drawing it up in a bucket left too little surface for the three of them to scry), the candle flame (because it was a bright afternoon and the images would be too vague).

This was the only choice left, and because it was Tildy's idea, it was hardly to Belle's liking.

"We can but try," Belle said with a sigh. She held out her hands.

Tildy took Belle's right hand. Clea took her left. Tildy and Clea joined hands. The circle complete, the power already beginning to flow between them, Tildy lowered her voice to a whisper.

"It seems to me," she said, "that the water may work just as the crystal did. If we calm ourselves . . . If we focus . . ." She drew in a deep breath and let it out again slowly and in the smooth surface of the water, she watched her sisters do the same.

"Just like the crystal," she reminded them, and she did not give Belle the opportunity to point out—yet again—that it was her fault they did not have that instrument to consult. "As when we use the crystal, we've joined hands. Now we must think. Think about what we wish. And speak the words of power. As in the crystal, we'll see what we wish to see."

"Will we?" Clea was not certain. She had that look about her eyes, the one that always reminded Tildy of a lamb separated from its mother and frantic for reassurance. In the water, Tildy saw her dart a glance to both sides. "And if it doesn't work?"

"Of course it will work." Belle may not have been truly certain, but as always, she sounded confident. It was one of the things Tildy admired most about her. "We need only quiet our minds and still our fears. We need only concentrate. Concentrate."

Tildy felt her eyes flutter and close. She felt her chest rise and fall to a rhythm that joined them all. She felt the worries drain from her mind and the cares flow from her spirit. She felt herself fill with the power.

"We speak our wish." She heard her own voice, hushed in reverence.

"We speak our wish." Clea echoed her words.

"We speak our wish." Belle said the words, too, and Tildy felt her tense, ready to speak the old spell they always used when they looked into the crystal.

Tildy felt a small stab of regret. She wasn't sorry she ate so many biscuits, and she was certainly not sorry that they were so delicious and buttery. She was sorry that she hadn't thought to wipe the butter from her hands before she picked up the crystal.

As if Tildy's regrets were clouding their powers, Belle cleared her throat, instructing Tildy to empty her mind. That done, Belle went on with the spell.

"Crystal of seeing, crystal of life, a mirror to our Nick ye be. Let us see what she's about. Let us see. Let us see."

When the last of Belle's words glided away on the breeze, Tildy opened her eyes. The image she saw in the birdbath was as distinct as ever, a circle of clear water, its surface reflecting the sky and the clouds and the sisters. There was nothing else.

At her side, Tildy heard Clea sigh.

"Hush. Don't despair. Not yet." Tildy couldn't say why, she only knew it was too soon to give up. It was as if she could feel the magic. Its vibrations were in the air around her, getting closer by the second. She saw the surface of the water shift, as if the very elements themselves could feel the passing of the power. The image of sky and cloud darkened. The colors melded.

Tildy held her breath, waiting for the reflection to shift, expecting at any second that the waters would swirl and when they stilled again, she would see a vision of Nick and the young earl.

Instead, all she saw was feathers. There was a splash and a spray of water flew at them. A fat gray dove landed in the center of the birdbath.

"Shoo! Shoo!" Tildy waved her hands at the offending creature. Its eyes black and shiny, it stared right back at her and she was certain, had it been able to lift its beak into a mocking sneer, that is precisely what it would have done. Instead, it flapped its wings, flinging water all about. Its opinion thus expressed, it fluttered away.

Tildy whisked a drop of water from the tip of her nose, gathering her dignity along with her pride. "Well," she said, "that was not as successful as I hoped."

Belle and Clea had no comment. Belle was too busy drying her spectacles against the skirt of her gown. Clea glanced overhead, watching for another assault.

"Perhaps we might try again?" Tildy ventured into the suggestion carefully, bracing herself for the disapproval she knew was sure to come.

To her surprise, it didn't.

Setting her spectacles back on the bridge of her nose, Belle sniffed, but she did not object. As always, Clea was eager to cooperate. They joined hands again and kept their eyes open, watching for intruders, and once they felt the magic tingle in the air like lightning off the mountain, they said the spell again.

This time, it worked.

No sooner had the last words faded from their lips, than the water shivered. The colors trembled. The shapes shifted. The images in the water danced.

And when they settled again, the sisters were looking at Nick. She was standing in front of Gowan and she had Horse with her. Its huge head was draped over her shoulder.

"Look! They're on a hillside." Clea's voice quivered with excitement.

"Yes, but where?" Belle bent closer, studying the landmarks. "Surely they haven't gone the long way about. To Rhyd Ddu?"

Tildy couldn't help herself. She had to laugh. "That's our Nick," she said, her voice warm with affection. "I thought she'd try something of the sort. She's taken him through Hell's Gate."

"Well, she shouldn't have." Belle's voice was as icy as the look she shot into the birdbath. "We agreed—"

"Yes, *we* agreed," Tildy pointed out. "Nick did not. She never will. You know that, Belle. She's a stubborn girl and you know it yourself, for it's a trait she inherited from you."

"As she inherited her recklessness from you." Belle did not say the words as a condemnation, but simply as a statement of fact. Realizing that bickering would get them nowhere, she brushed off the entire argument with a shake of her head. "It changes nothing," she said. "Nick knows that. She must do what she must do. As must we."

"Yes." Tildy let go the word along with a sigh. It did her heart no good to know Belle was right. "Let's do what we must then and be finished with it."

"Hmm. Yes." There was a note of pensiveness in Belle's voice. "They do not look at all happy with each other and it seems to me, that is not a good way to begin a romance." Her eyebrows raised, she looked to each of her sisters in turn. "Something must be done."

Six

Gowan followed the path to where it finally began its descent. A broad valley spread at his feet, a palette of slate-gray shadow and fields in every imaginable shade of green. Directly below was one of the small lakes that, even after such a short time in Wales, he had come to realize were as much a part of the landscape as the mountains and the mist. Not far beyond, he caught the wink of sunshine against glass, and the stubby spire of a small church. They were nearly to Rhyd Ddu.

He quickened his pace.

From what he'd heard of the Lodge, Gowan knew it was not in the village. But it was no more than a mile beyond, and merely the thought of finally being so near a warm bath, a hot meal, and some well-deserved peace and quiet was enough to give him a second wind.

Before he'd gone a hundred paces, he saw a woman coming the other way on the path.

"Dydd da!" The woman called to Gowan as soon as he was in sight. It didn't take her long to realize he was a stranger. She still smiled as she passed him, but he couldn't help but notice that she eyed him uncertainly. Her apprehension disappeared the moment she spied Nick coming up behind him. The horse, Gowan noted with a sigh of relief, was nowhere to be seen.

Chattering in brisk and completely incomprehensible Welsh, the woman reached into the pocket of the white apron she wore over her gown, pulled out a wedge of cheese, and pressed it into Nick's hands. She kissed both of Nick's cheeks.

Gowan could remember being welcomed so warmly only a time or two in all his life, and that only at a certain house of delight over near the Strand where the girls knew a well-paying gentleman when they saw one. He watched Nick and the woman and wondered at the whole thing. Nick didn't seem to think it at all unusual.

"This is Mrs. Hopkins," she explained in English, looking over at him. When the woman saw that Nick was acquainted with the stranger, her opinion of him changed instantly. She beamed him a smile and made a quick curtsy, holding the skirt of her dark dress out to both sides of her stout body.

"And does Mrs. Hopkins hand cheese to everyone she meets on the path?" Gowan asked, giving the woman a small bow of acknowledgment.

"Ach, no!" Apparently, Mrs. Hopkins understood enough English to answer for herself. She laughed heartily and grabbing one of Nick's hands, she gave it a squeeze. "Not for everyone, sir. But for our Little Nick, well . . ." Mrs. Hopkins's florid cheeks flushed two shades deeper. She beamed her way around a watery smile. "She's a wonder worker, if you don't know it, sir. That's what our Little Nick is. And this small bit of cheese . . . Ach! It isn't nothing, sir. Not compared with what she done."

"Really." In spite of himself, Gowan was interested. He stood back and let his gaze slide from Mrs. Hopkins to Nick. "She is certainly a wonder, I'll attest to that much," he said, and while Mrs. Hopkins may have missed his meaning, it was clear Nick did not. She narrowed her eyes and wrinkled her nose at him. "And I certainly know all she's done for me. And *to* me," he added. "But tell me, Mrs. Hopkins, what has Nick done for you?"

"You are a stranger in these parts and no mistake." Mrs.

Hopkins dispensed with her emotion with a series of discreet sniffs. She wiped her eyes and giggling like a girl, she waved one hand in Gowan's direction as much as if to say she knew he was having her on. "There's not a soul in Rhyd Ddu or anywhere else in all of Gwynedd who doesn't know. She saved my Owain's life. That's what she did. She healed him when he was sick."

"Did she now?" Gowan could not have been more surprised if Mrs. Hopkins informed him that Nick had sprouted wings and taken flight. "I'm afraid I am more familiar with her immense capacity to damage people rather than to repair them."

The barb may have missed its mark with Mrs. Hopkins, but it was certainly not lost on Nick. She gave Gowan a withering look. He tossed one of his own back at her.

The only solution to the stalemate seemed to be filling the uncomfortable silence that followed it. Mrs. Hopkins looked back and forth between Nick and Gowan. "And where are you two headed this afternoon?" she asked.

"We're on our way to Rhyd Ddu," Gowan answered. He stretched and rubbed the back of his calves. He was unaccustomed to any exercise more strenuous than twirling a young lady across the dance floor, and he felt his muscles already tightening. He had no doubt a hot bath would be in order before the hot meal he was anticipating at the Lodge. "And a damn long time it is getting there."

"And no wonder!" Mrs. Hopkins shook her head in amazement. "If you're coming from the cottage, you're going the long way about, aren't you? And right through the heart of Hell's Gate! You could have been to Rhyd Ddu long ago had you taken the other track—the soft, smooth one through the fields."

"Other track?" Gowan rounded on Nick. "Smoother track? That is a despicable thing to do to a man, Nick, and furthermore—"

"And furthermore . . ." Nick interrupted him without a

qualm. She turned to Mrs. Hopkins. "You have not had a chance to meet our guest. Have you heard news that the new earl is on his way?"

"Who hasn't?" Mrs. Hopkins's expression curdled like old cream. She mumbled something in Welsh and spit on the ground. Gowan did not have to understand the language to catch her meaning. Surprised, he stepped back and signaled Nick that perhaps an introduction was not in his best interest at the moment.

He might have known she'd pay him no mind.

Nick flashed him the kind of smile he imagined a cat might give a mouse right before it pounced. "Well, here he is," she said with a sweeping gesture toward Gowan. "Live and in the flesh. And fine flesh it is, too, I can tell you that much, for I've seen a good bit of it with my own eyes."

Mrs. Hopkins tossed a look at Gowan that could only be described as baleful. She patted Nick's hand. "I'll let them know in the village," she said, and with that and a final warning to Nick to be watchful and take care, she hurried on.

Gowan watched her go. "I have the distinct impression that woman didn't like me."

Not the least bit concerned, Nick fell into step beside him. "Did you now?"

"I did, indeed, and if I was a betting man, I would wager you know why. I've never set foot in this part of the world before. What am I to Mrs. Hopkins that she should think of me so?"

"You are the earl." Over her shoulder, Nick gave him a meaningful look. At least he supposed it was a meaningful look. He'd be damned if he could decipher what it meant.

Gowan knew he'd get no further explanation from Nick, not when she was so obviously disinclined to give it. Unwilling to engage in what was sure to become another battle of words and wits, he changed the subject. "What did she mean? When she said you saved someone's life. She wasn't serious, was she?"

Nick darted him a look. It wasn't much, but it was enough to tell Gowan that while he was trying to avoid one conflict, he'd obviously walked right into another.

"We are not a people likely to carry stories when it comes to something as meaningful as life or death," Nick told him, her words as solemn as her expression. Her eyes darkened, reflecting the somber beauty of the hills. "Owain is her husband. He was ill most of the autumn and got worse when the winter cold set in. Mrs. Hopkins called me. Torri 'r clefyd." It was one of those Welsh phrases that seemed to have no simple English translation. Nick's dark brows dropped low and she searched for one.

"To break the disease," she finally said. "With magic."

That was too much.

Gowan pulled to a stop. He turned to face her, laying one hand on her arm to keep her in place. He controlled his disapproval but he could not quite control the note of wonder that rose in his voice. Or his skeptical chuckle. "They actually let you near their sick with your potions and your poisons?"

"I've never poisoned a soul." Nick yanked her arm free. "Leastways not yet." Without another word, she spun away and forged on ahead.

"Damn!" Gowan grumbled to himself. It seemed even when he tried to be careful and temper the disbelief that must surely greet her peculiar assertions, he could not say the right thing to Nick. He watched her bolt down the rough track, her movements so quick as to be nearly frantic. She stopped only once, and then only to dart a look over her shoulder, as if making certain she'd left him well and far behind.

Something about the look put Gowan in mind of another time he'd been in the wilds. He'd done it only to oblige some friends who'd referred a particularly wealthy and not especially unhealthy old woman to him for consultation. It was a coup of sorts, in London medical circles, and it required at least a token repayment.

Unfortunately in this case, repayment meant a weekend of sporting in Scotland. And more unfortunately still in this instance, sport meant hunting.

It was an odious sort of pastime. Gowan decided that much after less than an hour at it. It was bad enough a man had to rise before the sun, worse still when he did it in the cold. It was even more dreadful when he was obliged to do it simply to trail some poor, unsuspecting animal about over wetland and moor with the sole intention of killing the thing.

Gowan shuddered.

Just once that weekend had he gotten close enough to even see a deer. Once was enough. He would always remember how frightened the animal looked when it caught the scent of its pursuers. He'd never forget the way its head went back and its eyes gleamed with terror.

It was exactly the way Nick looked right now.

The thought brought Gowan up short. It wasn't anger that had sent Nick scrambling away. Not this time. Gowan was certain of it. This wasn't a declaration of war, it was a retreat, and he marveled at it at the same time he puzzled over its cause.

It might have been what he said. That was the first explanation that came to mind, and the simplest, but Gowan knew instinctively it wasn't correct.

Nick was not a woman who ran from words. Though he'd known her no more than a matter of hours, he was certain of that. Nick's will was too strong. Her mind too fixed. She was not the type who gave ground. Not an inch of it. She would never give way in an argument or recoil from a challenge. She would never back down from a fight. He could tell as much from her manner as he could from the set of her chin and the silver fire that sometimes flashed in her eyes like lightning. He could tell simply because he could always tell these things about women.

In spite of his bothersome thoughts about Nick, Gowan found himself smiling.

It was one of his talents, he admitted to himself, it was a boon that clearly put him at an advantage in all his dealings with women. He always knew which were obstinate, and over the years, he'd learned to maneuver his way around them. He knew which ones were intractable, and much time and experience had taught him they needed to be controlled with a firm hand. He could judge at a glance which were more trouble than they were worth, and he'd learned to steer far clear of those who were.

Nick was an unfortunate combination of all three. She was surely obstinate. She was obviously intractable. She was certainly more trouble than she was worth.

Then why did he find himself wondering what was going on inside her head?

The question made Gowan uncomfortable, and to hide his uneasiness, he quickened his pace. He watched Nick bound over the rocky path, and he couldn't help but notice the appealing way her hips swayed with every movement. Nor could he ignore her hair. It swung out behind her, the color like onyx in the late afternoon light.

The thoughts that crept up on him were not in the least comfortable, but damn him, they were pleasant. He remembered how Nick tasted when he kissed her and how her body felt pressed to his.

And he knew why she'd run from him.

It wasn't his words that caused Nick to take flight, it was the fact that he'd touched her.

He'd taken her arm. He'd held her in place. He'd stood no more than a foot from her and it made her uneasy. Hell, it made her more than uneasy, it made her as nervous as a cat. Just as it had back at the cottage.

It was a puzzling thought and Gowan turned it over in

his head while he hurried to keep pace with Nick. As much as he tried, he found that as difficult as trying to ascertain what might be going on behind that pretty face of hers. She knew every twist and turn and she took advantage of it to press on. She was nearly out of sight when Gowan saw her skid to a stop. Her hands on her hips, her mouth open, she stood as still as if she'd come up against a wall.

Tildy pursed her lips and blew a strand of hair out of her eyes. "That's done it," she said, her voice barely audible above the clamoring of her own heart.

"That's done us in, you mean." Clea dropped to the ground beside where Tildy was already slumped against the birdbath. "I feel as if I've run a hundred miles."

"We've never tried the likes of it before." Belle's voice sounded just as tired but she was not about to show herself as weak as her sisters by giving in to the fatigue as they did. She stood at the birdbath, her arms straight and propped to both sides of it. "It makes one quite lightheaded, does it not?"

Tildy didn't answer. She couldn't. If this whirling in her brain was what Belle called lightheaded, then she supposed Belle must be right. Again. She forced herself to focus her eyes on the door of the cottage and she didn't dare to look away for fear her stomach would rebel.

"I've never felt this dreadful in all my life." Clea was a decided and quite unbecoming shade of green. She pressed her hands to her heart. "Perhaps we've tried to do too much."

"It will be worth it," Belle broke in.

"Yes," Tildy agreed. "If it works."

"What's done is done, and if we haven't been successful, well . . ." Belle pulled herself upright and headed toward the cottage. "All we can do is watch and wait."

* * *

Gowan couldn't imagine why Nick looked so mystified. There was nothing here that looked any different from the rest of what he'd seen on their beastly trek over the mountain.

Except for the river.

He followed Nick's gaze down to the water. It was a swift-running little river that was not nearly as wide as it was treacherous looking. The water appeared to be as deep as it was fast. It cut the track neatly in half, tumbling over boulders and pooling here and there in small, clear basins where the reflection of cloud and sky showed as clear as the images in a mirror.

There was nothing surprising about the river, as far as Gowan could tell, except that it was damned inconvenient. He bent at the waist and peered both upstream and down. "Where's the bridge?"

Her lips pursed, Nick took a step closer to the water, so absorbed in her own thoughts that if she hadn't answered his question, Gowan might have thought she'd forgotten his presence completely. "There is no bridge," she said, her voice as distracted as her look.

Gowan snorted his disbelief. "What do you mean there's no bridge? There has to be a bridge. How else did Mrs. Hopkins come this way?"

Nick didn't answer him. She picked up a pebble lying nearby and pitched it into the river. It did what all pebbles do when they smack into water. There was a faint plunking sound and a splash. It was exactly what Gowan knew would happen, but Nick didn't look very happy about it.

Gowan was a practical man. He understood, no doubt better than anyone, that he was far from perfect. But he was also enough of a realist to know that he had his assets as well as his liabilities. He was loyal to a fault once he found a person deserving of his loyalty. He was reasonable until pushed beyond the brink, honest unless the person he was dealing with did not deserve his honesty. He was reasonably easygoing when unforeseen catastrophes such as inheriting the earl's title and troubles did not crop up to confound him. He was an intelligent companion, a clear-headed professional, a good conversationalist. He could be thoroughly charming when it served his purpose. He was an adequate physician, a damned good card player, and quite a skilled lover, if he did say so himself.

What he was not, was patient.

He sighed and with a restless kick, sent another pebble tumbling into the water. "Mrs. Hopkins couldn't have crossed on her own," he reminded Nick. "The water's moving too swiftly. And it looks to be far too deep. You had as good a look at her as I did. She wasn't wet—not even around the edges. And if I recall correctly, Mrs. Hopkins had sufficient edges to soak. If there's no bridge, how did she cross?"

Nick chewed on her lower lip. Her eyes gleamed as if she was formulating a theory, one she didn't like in the least. "She wasn't wet because there wasn't anything here for her to get wet with," she said.

It was as inelegant an explanation as it was confusing. Gowan tried reasoning his way back through it again. "You're saying there's no bridge. I understand that much. But are you telling me that when Mrs. Hopkins came this way, there was also no water?"

Nick didn't answer him and it was her silence more than anything that made Gowan ill at ease. He considered putting one hand to her brow to see if she was burning with fever. He might have done it, too, if he didn't fear getting so dangerously close to her when she was spouting such nonsense. He stepped back instead and eyed her carefully.

"What do you mean, no water? The river's certainly here now. And it looks to be as old as the mountains. It didn't just materialize out of nowhere, did it? Things like rivers don't simply appear as if by—" A thought too incredible to even consider occurred to him and Gowan's words trailed off.

It was impossible. That's what it was.

Of course it was impossible.

And anyone who thought otherwise must surely be as mad as May-butter.

It was high time to set the poor girl right.

Gowan straightened. He tugged down his waistcoat. He cleared his throat. He fixed Nick with the kind of authoritative look he was used to giving to doddering old dears who carried on and on about their sciatica and their rheumatism and the ague that kept them from sleeping but never seemed quite bad enough to keep them from taking tea with just the right people in all the right places. The look had always worked for Gowan in his surgery, there was no reason to think it would not work now.

"No." He slashed one hand through the air, the motion effectively cutting through whatever outrageous explanation Nick might be prepared to offer. "Don't tell me. Don't even try to tell me. It's a wonderful lark, Nick, but it's gone on long enough. Please. You have made it quite clear what you think of me, but allow me the respect of not treating me as you might a simple-minded fool. Don't tell me your aunts had anything to do with—"

"Of course they did." Nick mumbled a Welsh word that didn't sound a bit too pleasant. Frustrated and angry, she spun away, then spun again to face him. "How else do you explain it?" she asked, jabbing one finger toward the water. Her eyes flashed the kind of silver fire Gowan had remembered as so warm and appealing. It looked anything but, now. It looked piercing and ominous, like the silent lightning that forewarns of a storm.

Still, Gowan would not yield. Doddering old ladies were prone to bluff and bluster, too, he reminded himself, and he never surrendered to them. He stood his ground, his eyes blazing back into Nick's, his manner cool and just aloof enough to goad her into a burst of anger.

"How else could there be water where there was none before?" Nick's question ricocheted like a shot off the surrounding hills, rolling back on itself and them. "It had to be the aunts doing, though where they found the stamina is quite beyond me. They've been busy today, that is for certain. They have tested their powers again and again. I shouldn't wonder if their magic—"

"Nick, Nick, Nick." Gowan scratched a finger idly behind one ear. "I really must insist. No more talk of magic. I simply do not believe it. Any of it. No matter how you try to convince me, you're blathering—"

"Blathering, am I?" Nick's jaw went rigid, her hands curled into fists. "You say you do not believe in our magic, but tell me, mun, was it twattle, what you saw back at the cottage? What of the wind that nearly blew you down before the aunts knew you had a chance to drink the tea I gave you? And the tea itself? It changed color. Explain that to me, for you saw it with your own eyes."

"I've seen conjurors pull rabbits out of hats, as well." Gowan crossed his arms over his chest. "Really, Nick. I am a physician, a man of science. I can no more believe in magic rivers than I can believe in the kind of hocus-pocus healing you and Mrs. Hopkins seem to think possible. And I am not a hermit. At least I never was before I consigned myself to this wretched place. I've spent a good deal of my adult life being entertained. Music halls, fairgrounds, theaters . . ." Out of deference to the fact that while Nick was not a lady by any means, she was certainly a young woman and as such, should not be scandalized, he kept himself from mentioning the other types of places a man of wealth and breeding went in search of entertainment.

"I've seen hundreds of magic tricks," he said and he nearly laughed aloud when he thought he'd seen them in both the places he'd mentioned and the ones he didn't.

"Some were done quite well, as was yours," he added almost as an afterthought. Nick did not look at all pleased by the compliment, and Gowan hurried on.

"Others . . ." He shook his head. "They are as transparent as rock crystal. It doesn't take much genius to fit the pieces together. Back at the cottage, you sprinkled something in the tea to make it change. That much is clear. I may not have seen it just as I did not see how you caught the candle on fire but then, that's why they call it sleight of hand. And as for the wind through the window . . ." He shrugged and glanced around. "A trick of nature, surely, not of man. Or woman."

"Is that what you think?" Nick returned the look with one of her own, but though his was tolerant, hers was anything but. It crackled through the air like the electricity he'd seen manufactured by generators. "You've a good deal to learn, Mr. Gowan Payne, Earl of Welshpool," she said. "And you'll have a great deal to apologize for once you speak to the folk of Rhyd Ddu and find that I am right. There's not a soul in the village who's seen or heard of this river. I can tell you that as surely as I can tell you my own name. You'll see, once we reach the village." She cast a glance at the river and her expression clouded. "If we reach the village."

Gowan had not considered the likelihood of that. He eyed the position of the sun, low against the mountaintops, and the long shadows where evening mist was already gathering against hillside and in hollow. "And if we don't?" he asked.

"It is my guess that's exactly what they want, though it seems a poor use of their powers to me." Nick had that distracted look about her again. She studied the river from all angles. "I do believe," she finally said, "that the aunts would like to see us spend the night on the mountain."

"Together?" The word was no sooner out of Gowan's mouth when the sense of the whole thing came rumbling at him with all the subtlety of an ox cart. "Another of their schemes to snare both me and my title, is that what you'd like me to believe?" He chuckled.

A morning of bizarre surprises and an afternoon of straining every nerve and sinew left Gowan with little more than his sense of humor. The whole thing was beginning to have the peculiar appeal of an absurd stage play. He held onto that thought—and his temper—as long as he could, and pieced together his hypothesis.

"Let me venture a guess. We spend the night here together and in the morning, we're the talk of the village. That's it, isn't it? What happens then? Am I automatically expected to ask for your hand in order to preserve your honor? Or do you make a great show of it, bewailing the loss of your virtue while you drag me kicking and screaming to the altar?"

"You're as arrogant as you are small-minded," Nick snapped. "I've told you before, I want nothing to do with you or your wretched title. I'd like nothing better than to see the last of you."

Gowan knew he should have let the matter drop, right then and there. He should have walked away and let it die. He might have done it, too, if he wasn't so bloody annoyed at Nick for all she'd done to him. He deserved some restitution, that was for certain.

He deserved it because she led him through this wasteland the locals called Hell's Gate. He deserved it because she summoned that brute of a horse and he swore she did it only to confound him. He deserved it because she was trying her damnedest to get rid of him and damn it, but he'd be damned if he'd let her.

The course of Gowan's revenge was obvious.

When Nick stepped back, Gowan stepped forward. She might have tried to move even farther away but the terrain sloped down to the river. He had her for certain this time and to prove it, he slid one arm around her waist. "I'll play your game," he said, settling one hand at the small of her back, the other at the gentle curve where her waist met her hip. "You say the aunts want to see us trapped in this infernal place for the night. Very well. I believe you. But perhaps that wouldn't be so very bad."

He couldn't tell if Nick's outrage was caused by his nearness or by the fact that she was so staggered. Whatever the cause, it was well worth the effort. She could think of nothing to say. She stood there as stiff as a pound of candles with her mouth hanging open, and Gowan congratulated himself. He had won this one small skirmish. The rest of the battle, he reminded himself, lay ahead of him, and the strategy was all too clear.

When Nick struggled to break his grasp, he held her tighter, barely controlling the laughter that threatened to break his all-too-solemn expression. "Perhaps after a night together, you won't find me so odious." He slid his fingers through hers and brought her hand up. He grazed a kiss over it, from her knuckles to her fingertips. She shuddered at the touch, but he paid it no mind. He deserved that bit of satisfaction, too, for all she'd done to him. "Perhaps it is time for you to face your fears."

"Is it, now?" Nick's voice was tight and it cost her a good deal, but she stood her ground. Standing this close, she needed to raise her chin to see him fully and he looked down at her and watched the anger suddenly dissolve from her expression. That in itself should have been enough to warn him. "Very well, m'lord," she said. "I do believe you are right."

"I am?" Gowan couldn't help himself. Shocked at her easy acquiescence, he dropped her hand and stepped back.

It was the only chance Nick needed.

She raised her hand and putting her fingers to her lips, she sounded a sharp whistle. In a matter of moments, the horse appeared.

He lumbered forward and nudged Gowan from behind.

Nick laughed and patted the horse's broad back. "Here

you go, m'lord. You needn't worry about being trapped here for the night. Horse will get you across the river."

Gowan turned to face the beast. It immediately snuffled a wet welcome directly into his face. The fiendish thing didn't look any friendlier now than it had when it tried to devour his hand. "But I—"

Nick didn't wait to hear any more of his excuses. Her hand beneath the horse's massive head, she guided the animal over to where a broad, flat boulder poked from the ground. "You can step on the rock," she said, holding the horse steady, "and mount him easy enough from there. Come on, m'lord. What are you waiting for?" Her eyes sparkled. Her voice was as spirited as the water that flowed at their feet. "It is time for you to face your fears."

She had him there.

The thought settled somewhere between Gowan's heart and his stomach, feeling for all the world like the remains of a bad dinner. He had no choice and he knew it. It did not make the walk over to the boulder any easier.

Gowan climbed the rock with no trouble. Gathering the courage to mount the monster of a horse was another matter altogether.

Carefully, he leaned forward. Gingerly, he stroked the horse's back. "Nice horse." He said the words not as if they were the truth, but more like a prayer. "Good horse."

He might have kept right on spouting senseless endearments if he hadn't caught Nick's eye. She was enjoying every minute of his discomfort and that in itself was enough to goad Gowan into action.

Without another thought for what he was doing or what the consequences might be, he climbed onto the horse. Once he was atop the brute, Gowan sat as still as stone, surveying the mountainside from a vantage point that was far too high for his liking.

His spirits as low as he himself was high in the air, Gowan chanced a look at Nick.

It was enough to cheer him immediately.

Nick stood at the horse's head, a look so much like astonishment on her face that Gowan couldn't help but laugh. He realized there was nothing he could have done in all the world that would have surprised her more. She had expected him to bolt and run, not to take up her challenge, and now that he had, her smugness wilted around the edges.

But there was more than simple disappointment in her expression, more than just wounded pride, and Gowan took a closer look. Was it his imagination, or was there the slightest trace of new-found respect gleaming in her eyes?

Unaccountably, the thought made Gowan feel remarkably satisfied.

The animal was as gentle as Nick promised. It stood perfectly still, waiting for him to settle himself comfortably. That wasn't difficult, either. Though Gowan was tall, his legs long, the horse was more than big enough to accommodate him with room to spare.

The thought made Gowan feel even better. He sat back, and waited to make his move.

"Well, there you have it." Nick refused to look at Gowan and he hoped it was because she was so angry at having been bested. She gave the animal a friendly pat. "Horse will get you across and keep you dry, I'll venture. The village is no more than a few minutes straight on after that. They'll tell you the way from there to the Lodge." She glanced up. Whatever spark of admiration he may have seen in her eyes was gone. "With any luck, we won't be seeing each other again."

"Oh, no!" Before Nick could move away, Gowan grabbed her hand. He held on tight, pulling her toward the horse. "You'll not get away so easily. Damn it, Nick, you called this beastly horse here purposely to annoy me. You can't expect that I won't have my revenge. If I'm to ride . . ."

Raising his eyebrows, he patted the horse's broad back, directly in front of where he sat. "So are you."

Gowan didn't think he could have looked nearly as terrified at seeing the horse as Nick looked right now. At least he hoped not. Shaking her head, she backed off.

"Oh, no. If you're worried about me, send Horse back when you're done and I'll—"

"Worried? About you?" Now that Gowan was up on the horse and relatively comfortable, he found he almost liked it. There were certain advantages to looking down on the world, not the least of which was that Nick found it devilishly hard to fight him off. "It's my own self I'm worried about," he said. "Come on. Right here." Again, he patted the horse. "You can keep me warm as we cross."

Except for two spots of bright color in her cheeks, Nick's face went pale. She tensed as if she was making ready to run, but before she could, Gowan bent and lifted her into his arms. He swung her onto the horse and set her in front of him.

"There you have it, Nick," he said, wrapping both his arms around her and pulling her close against him. "It seems I'm not the only one who must learn to face my fears."

Seven

Nick wasn't sure what was worse, the certainty that Gowan would prevail or the realization that once he did, she would be at his mercy.

Neither scenario was to her liking. She hated nothing more than being bested, especially by a man. At least she always had. She had the unpleasant suspicion that she would find other things she hated even more now that Gowan Payne had come to Rhyd Ddu.

For his part, Gowan did nothing to allay her fears. Before she could think to move, he seized her wrist and dragged her toward Horse. Before she could react, he leaned down and wound one arm about her waist. He was quicker than she imagined and far stronger than he looked. Before Nick could pull away, he lifted her into his arms.

"Gowan Payne, you insufferable man!" Nick beat her fists against his chest. She kicked and screeched and cursed Horse that he was so gentle and so obedient that he did little more than stamp and whinny at all the commotion instead of rearing and knocking the honorable Lord Welshpool on his dishonorable ass.

"You're a monstrous Saxon and that's for certain." Her arms pinned to her sides, Nick's words came out in a series of staccato gasps.

"There you have it, Nick." Gowan laughed. "It seems I'm not the only one who must learn to face my fears."

"Afraid? Of you?" She managed a laugh to match his.

It might have sounded genuine if it were not for the fact that her voice caught over the words. It was easier to glare at Gowan than to argue with him, especially with his arms so tight around her. Nick snapped her head up. She might have proceeded to give him the kind of glower that had been known to wilt men at twenty yards if it were not for the fact that she found his face only inches from hers.

She expected it. Of course she expected it. She simply wasn't prepared for it. Or for the feeling that shot through her when her eyes met his.

This close and with the evening light slipping over the rim of the mountains and shining full on his face, Gowan's eyes were as brown as walnuts. There was a sparkle of laughter in them, a glint of mischief, a trace of good humor that should have made her feel more inclined to amity and less to mayhem.

It didn't.

The more Nick looked into Gowan's eyes, the more certain she was that this was not the place for her to be. If she needed the proof, she need only listen to the erratic beating of her heart and the way the blood rushed inside her ears until she was deaf to all but its sound. She need only realize that she was numb to every sensation but the press of Gowan's body against hers. It was a feeling unlike any she'd ever had and it did more than simply astound her.

It confounded her. It made her angry. It drove her to distraction nearly as thoroughly as the feel of Gowan's arms around her, and the whisper of his breath against her cheek, and the fact that this close, she could see a touch of red in his beard, and the hint of a smile around his lips. There was the slightest suggestion of some emotion other than amusement in his eyes, and though she'd never seen anything like it in all her days, Nick knew immediately what it meant. It meant that while he might be seeking his harmless revenge for all she'd done to him, the game could end just as quickly and unexpectedly as it had begun. It meant that it could change to something far more serious, something she had neither the right nor the wish to even consider.

"Here you go, my girl." The sound of Gowan's voice brought her out of her thoughts and made her realize that, sometime while she was lost in her errant notions, she'd stopped struggling completely. Gowan loosened his hold long enough to pat the seat in front of him. He smiled and winked at her. "Take a seat. Right here."

Her teeth clenched so tight her jaw ached, Nick spun around. "I do not wish to ride." It was the truth and she dared to speak it though she did not venture to add that she would sooner submit to the ride—or to nearly anything else—than she would dare even another second of gazing into Gowan's eyes.

Behind her, Gowan chuckled. He waited while she tucked her skirt discreetly beneath her and swung one leg over to the other side of the horse. "I know. I do not wish to ride, either," he said, echoing her accent. He set it aside just as easily as he'd slipped into it and with a snicker, fell back into his own nearly incomprehensible way of speaking. "But here we are, and here we'll stay. The two of us. Together. You don't expect me to handle this beast of a horse on my own, do you?"

It was Nick's turn to chuckle. "You're afraid of Horse."

Gowan linked his arms around her waist. He leaned over her shoulder, tipping his face, no doubt to better be able to see hers and to gauge her reaction. "You're afraid of me."

Nick kept her eyes forward. "Told you before, I am not."

Gowan leaned over even more. "And I know for a fact that you, my dear girl, are a liar."

There was no answer to that, not one that was both true and that she was willing to offer either to him or to herself, so Nick said nothing. She twined her fingers through Horse's mane and gently kicked his sides, and when he clumped forward, she jerked back and into Gowan's arms.

This time, he was the one who chuckled. The sound was

rich and far too satisfied for Nick's liking, and the fact that he took the opportunity to tighten his hold on her did little to alleviate the uneasiness it caused. He was sure to mock her for it, but this once, Nick didn't care. She sat up as fast and straight as she could and inched forward and before Gowan could say a thing, she nudged Horse to a trot.

"Damn animal!" Behind her, Gowan's voice sounded as rough as the terrain. He grabbed hold of Nick and held on for dear life. "Must he go at such a pace?"

Nick glanced over her shoulder. It brightened her mood considerably to watch Gowan flop about like wash on a line on a windy day. "Oh, no, m' lord," she said quite innocently. "He has no need to go at this pace at all." Still looking at Gowan and enjoying his discomfort very much indeed, she gripped Horse tighter with her knees, took a firmer hold on his mane, and prodded him into a canter.

It was a wonderfully devilish plan and it might have worked like a charm if Gowan did not decide to retaliate with one of his own. The faster Horse went, the tighter Gowan held on to Nick, until his arms were full around her in a smothering embrace and he was close enough for her to feel every inch of his body against hers.

His chin was on her shoulder. His cheek grazed hers. His beard prickled her skin. He linked his legs around hers and pressed his chest to her back until she could feel the contour of every muscle and the quick, distinct pulse of his every heartbeat.

Other parts of him were even nearer.

Nick's cheeks flushed and a feeling very like panic fluttered through her. It was not an emotion she was accustomed to, nor was it one she liked. Still, there was little she could do to control it.

Their bodies moved together in perfect rhythm to Horse's smooth movements, causing a singular friction that made Gowan purr like a contented cat. He was quite enjoying himself. There was no doubt of it. The hard evidence was pressed right against Nick's nether cheeks.

It was a blessing when Horse finally splashed into the river and kicked up a stream of cold water. It splattered Nick's dress and flew over her shoulder, catching Gowan full in the face.

"Damn!" Gowan was startled enough to sit back.

Perhaps it was the sweet feeling of relief that made Nick laugh. Perhaps it was, rather, that Gowan had gotten his deservings for all the things he'd no doubt been thinking and for all he'd made her feel that she had no business and no wish to feel.

Nick glanced over her shoulder in time to see him shake his head. Droplets of water flew every which way, sparkling like diamonds in the light. With a sniff, Gowan gathered his dignity. "Damn me if it doesn't feel like real water," he said. "As wet as real water. And as cold. There's no magic here, I'd wager, at least not the kind you'd have me believe in."

It wasn't the first time that day that Nick wished she had the time and opportunity to cast a spell. He deserved to be shown the error of his ways, that was for certain, and she tucked the thought aside and swore she'd bring it out again when the time was right.

It took no more than a little while for Horse to ford the river and as soon as all four of his feet were on dry land again, Nick wiggled out of Gowan's grasp and dropped to the ground. "Is there no magic?" she asked, looking up at him. "I'm thinking it must be magic that got you atop a horse."

Gowan dismissed the observation with a decorous little snort. He straightened his shoulders and looked down his nose at her. "Devil take it," he said, "but I think I'm actually beginning to enjoy riding."

"Good." Nick turned her back to him and headed down the path. "Then you'll know how to dismount without my help," she called over her shoulder.

Gowan sputtered something. It may have been a curse. It may have been a plea for help.

Nick liked to believe it was the latter.

She pulled herself to a stop and turned to him. "What was that, m'lord?" she asked. "Are you saying you'll be needing some assistance?"

Some of Gowan's maddening arrogance melted in the bright light of reality. Cautiously, he peered over both sides of the horse, as if measuring the distance to the ground. But though he might have been cautious, he was not about to show himself cowardly. He narrowed his eyes and shot her a look.

"If you can get down, so can I," he announced.

It was a solemn moment, or perhaps it might have been if he didn't look for all the world like one of those poor persons who squeeze their eyes shut and hold their noses before they dare go into the water. Nick bit her lower lip to stifle a laugh. She watched as Gowan strained forward, caught Horse's mane, and swung his leg over the side. He balanced himself for a moment, took a deep breath, and plumped to the ground.

He landed safely enough, as Nick suspected he would. When he did, his legs gave out. Nick suspected that would happen as well. Like a man who has never set foot on a boat and cannot find the way to stand once he does, it took Gowan a bit to adjust again to the feel of the land beneath his feet. After no more than a curse or two, he righted himself. He was hobbling just a bit and that was to be expected, too, from a man who had apparently never sat a horse before.

Gowan brushed his jacket and tugged his waistcoat into place. "Infernal animal!" He looked back over his shoulder, but Horse was already gone and the simple fact of that only seemed to confound him more. "Carriages make far more sense. They are more comfortable and they are safer."

"But we have no carriages here." Nick started down the track and Gowan fell into step beside her. "It is far too rugged, as you can see. Here, it is easier to walk from place to place. Besides, none of us here in Rhyd Ddu is rich enough to own a carriage. Not like you."

"Rich." Gowan added a bit of a hurumph to the word that made it sound more like a curse than a blessing.

Nick had never stopped to consider how other people felt about their surfeit or lack of money. She was rich enough for her own liking, rich in all the things that really mattered in this world. She chanced a remark simply to see how he would respond. "You are rich, aren't you? You are the earl."

"I am the earl. Yes." Gowan stopped long enough to bend and pluck a thistle from the leg of his trousers. He flicked it onto the path and went on walking, leaving her question unanswered.

In spite of herself, Nick was intrigued. She didn't want to be. Yet there was something about the way Gowan avoided her question that piqued her curiosity. Gowan was a puzzle and as with all puzzles Nick had ever come up against, she found it difficult to rest without finding the answers.

She told herself it was unwise. She told herself she would regret it. She told herself to stop before the words tumbled out of her mouth and she could never take them back. She asked the question at any rate, even though she was not at all sure he would answer it. "You do not want to be here, do you?"

Gowan's laugh rang through the hills. "Haven't I made that clear enough? London. Rome. Hell, I'd settle for a place as vulgar as Brighton right about now. But here? In Wales?" He kicked a pebble that lay in the path. "I can think of a thousand places I would rather be."

"And a thousand people you would rather be with?" Nick offered the remark more as a hope than a comment.

Gowan did not disappoint her. "A hundred thousand," he said with a wicked smile. "Two hundred thousand. Though I must admit . . ." He snatched her hand and even before she had pulled to a stop, he spun her around to face him.

When he spoke, his voice was hushed, his eyes, gleaming. "You make a man immensely comfortable seated on a horse with him."

By now, the panic was familiar—like an acquaintance the likes of whom she was not pleased to see. Nick recognized its face and rued its arrival. She knew the taste of it at the back of her mouth and the feel of it, like a hand around her throat.

Unfortunately, the right way to deal with it was as foreign as ever.

She hid her uneasiness behind idle chatter. "You do not want to be here, but here you are. It seems a curious thing to me. What would make you leave the elegance of London for our little village?" The answer hit her as surely and as abruptly as the water that had done her the favor of slapping Gowan's face back at the river. "Are you running from someone?"

"Someone. Something. There's little difference, is there?" Gowan shrugged. It was a careless gesture, one like so many Nick had seen before, and she knew precisely what it meant. It meant he cared a great deal. "It hardly matters at any rate," he added, so nonchalantly that it made her wonder what else a man such as this could hide and how well he could do it.

He wound his fingers through hers and if he was doing it to distract her and keep her mind from the subject, he had found a remarkably effective method. It was difficult enough to keep her thoughts in order when he was standing this close. It was nearly impossible when he was touching her.

"But there are places you'd rather be?" Nick's question was far too breathy for her own liking, her words trembling so that Gowan could not fail to notice.

He chuckled and took a small step closer. "You'll not catch me that easily," he said. "And you will certainly not convince me to head back to Beddgelert. Not after that beastly trek over the mountains. Here I am and here I'll stay." When he saw the sullen expression on Nick's face, he laughed all the harder. "Oh come now, Nick. It's not as bad as all that. Look at what we've accomplished in one afternoon. We know we cannot abide each other, and that's as a good a beginning to any relationship as any I've ever found. It puts us on a nice, even keel right from the start. You know, if we could endure five minutes together without arguing, there might be something between us." He quirked his eyebrows and smiled down at her, as if waiting for her to admit that he was right.

She didn't, she didn't dare, and Gowan's smile turned into a broad grin. "We've both learned to face our fears, too, haven't we? I certainly did. I rode that damned horse, though I pray to God to never have to do it again. And you . . ." With his fingers still wound through hers, he rubbed his thumb across her palm. "You've learned that I won't bite. At least not until I get to know you better. Tell the truth, Nick. It wasn't so very awful, was it?"

It wasn't.

The truth of it stuck in Nick's throat along with the certainty that if she spoke the words, she'd live to regret every one of them. She had no choice. She pulled away and hurried down the path.

It was not awful riding with Gowan. The thought beat through her brain in perfect tempo to the pounding of her heart. It was not awful being that close to him and feeling the curiously comforting sting of his beard against her skin and the warmth of his legs wrapped around hers.

None of it was awful.

Perhaps that was why the whole thing frightened her so.

"This is it?"

Gowan couldn't help himself. His question was, no doubt, as rude as it sounded, but he could hardly be held accountable for it.

The village of Rhyd Ddu lay before him in the gathering twilight, and if he thought Beddgelert remarkably quaint and old-fashioned, it was Paris compared to this.

There wasn't much to Rhyd Ddu, at least not as far as Gowan could see, and the more he could see, the more certain he was of the terrible truth.

A small village green stood directly in front of him at a place where four crossroads came together. In the very center of it was one of those singularly Celtic crosses that are sometimes seen in the countryside. It was a tall, unwieldy looking ornament of gray stone carved all over with whirls in a pattern much like he'd seen chalked onto the aunts' front doorstep.

Not an impressive monument by any means. That was Gowan's first thought. He reconsidered when another look around confirmed his worst fears: the tiny green and the massive cross were the highlights of the place.

A certain colorful and quite descriptive figure of speech came to Gowan's head and almost made its way past his lips. He controlled the outburst, not because he didn't think it relevant but because Nick was walking at his side and, damn it, if she didn't look at the village like the queen herself would beam at a map of the Empire.

One look at her confirmed Gowan's worst fears. "This is it." It wasn't a question this time. It was a simple statement of fact. His spirits plummeted.

To his left, there was a row of cottages and the stone church whose stubby spire he'd seen from the summit at Hell's Gate. To his right was another line of plain, sturdy houses. There was a larger building that might have been a pub or an inn toward the far end of the street and beyond that, something that with the help of a large dose of imagination might have passed for a shop.

There was nothing else.

Though he hadn't noticed her watching him, Nick must have been, at least enough to measure his mood. At his side, she grinned. "What were you expecting?" she asked. "A place as grand as Beddgelert?"

"It would have been a start at least." Looking about, Gowan grumbled. "Tell me, what is it you people do for amusement?"

"We have the occasional Saxon in," Nick answered, glancing at him and smiling that impish smile of hers, the one that lit her eyes with sparks like the reflection off the tinsel on a Christmas tree. "That is an amusement of a sort, I suppose. They come to climb our mountain." She looked over to where the face of Snowdon loomed over the village. "Mostly they lodge in Beddgelert, but there are times they are forced by wind or weather to tarry here for a night or two. Iain puts them up at the Dragon and we always find a good bit of gossip to keep us busy after they are gone again. You are a strange race, you English."

"Are we so different?" Gowan wasn't certain he'd like her answer, but he asked the question nonetheless and prepared himself to defend the honor of England. "We are the same people, more or less, and subjects of the same queen."

"Perhaps." Nick's gentle laugh tickled the evening air. "Do you see anything here around you that says the mountains care who's king or queen or why it matters? We are the people of the mountains and the red dragon of Wales fires our blood." As if trying to make some sense of the notion, she shook her head. Her hair caught the last of the light, glistening like a fresh stroke of India ink. "It is difficult to see a kinship with others, especially you English. You are an odd race, with your haughty manners and your peculiar accents."

"Peculiar, indeed."

Nick ignored the aside. "Most of the folk in these parts raise sheep or cattle up in the hills," she said. "There are a few here in the village who do not live off the land—people such as the vicar and Iain at the Dragon. But they are like everyone else, up with the sun and to bed with it.

There's little time for amusement. And less still for wasting." She darted him one of those glances that he'd already come to recognize—the kind of look that told him she was about to say something she knew he wouldn't like. "Are you sorry now you came?"

"Sorry has nothing to do with it. I—"

Gowan's words were interrupted by a high-pitched bellow. "It's Little Nick! She's here!" He heard the voice long before he caught sight of its owner. Out of the gathering twilight, a child materialized from behind the stone cross. He darted into the road and pulled to a stop a hundred paces or so in front of them and propping his fists on his hips, he looked Gowan up and down.

From this far away, Gowan guessed the boy was no more than ten or twelve. He was short for his age, and solid as a stone wall, with the kind of broad-barreled chest so often seen in children who lived in rural areas. He had a powerful, clear voice that perfectly matched him in appearance. It had all the subtlety of a train whistle and Gowan imagined it carried just as far. "Little Nick's here!" the boy yelled.

Like magic, the door of every cottage on the road snapped open. Warily, as if they were measuring the prudence of the thing, folks stuck their heads outside.

"It's Little Nick right enough!" A lady in the cottage nearest to them smoothed down her apron and came out on the stoop. She dropped a quick curtsy in Nick's direction. "And she's got his very self with her," she added.

Nick did not seem to think the incident at all astonishing. She went right on walking, and when other folks came outside and waved and smiled, she smiled back, acknowledging their greetings.

By the time they got as far as the stone cross, the entire village seemed to have appeared as if out of nowhere. There were people out on doorsteps, people gathered in gardens. There was a tall, reed-thin man of the cloth with his back against the front door of the church. And another man, short and pudgy, was stationed outside the Dragon, his arms crossed over his broad chest, his bald head glistening in the last rays of the sun.

"I say! A welcoming committee!" Gowan rubbed his hands together and smiled, his mood brightening at the thought that there were at least some people in these god-forsaken mountains who knew their manners.

Though the prospect of being scrutinized by every man, woman, and child in the village did not thrill him, he supposed it was to be expected. There were certain responsibilities, after all, that came with his position: a certain *noblesse oblige.* Being received in a town where he was the chief landowner and the only member of the peerage was certainly one of them, and Gowan was only surprised that he had not thought of it sooner and expected that it would happen.

Remembering his disheveled appearance, he brushed at his jacket and glanced over his clothing to check for wayward thistles. "I'm afraid I hardly look the part of their earl right about now. I do hate to disappoint them. What do you think? Am I at all what they were expecting?"

Nick nodded solemnly. "Oh, aye, m'lord. I do believe you are that and more."

Her approval buoyed his spirits, though Gowan was at a loss to say why. It may have been that for all her faults—and they were legion—Nick at least knew the respect owed his rank. It appeared the rest of the village did as well.

Gowan pulled his shoulders back and marched on ahead. Perhaps Rhyd Ddu wasn't such an awful place, he told himself. They knew how to welcome an earl, that was for certain. Smiling, he waved to the villagers. "Good evening." He tipped his head, acknowledging a group of women in a nearby garden. "Hello."

The women didn't respond. One of them, a crone who looked as if the slightest breath of wind would blow her out over the mountains and into the ocean, spat on the ground. Another woman shot a black look in Gowan's direction.

"Yes. Well." Hiding his confusion, Gowan coughed politely behind his hand. He refused to let his smile sag.

There was a crowd of old men standing near the stone cross, and he headed that way. "How do you do?"

The men turned their backs on him.

Gowan was not a man prone to imaginings, at least he never had been before. Neither was he the type who saw offenses where none existed. Still, he had a bad feeling about this.

A very bad feeling.

The reaction was the same everywhere, from the young lad who had originally announced their presence to the hulking brute of a young farmer who stood outside the pub. The man was as sturdy-looking as the very mountains themselves. He looked so much like the lad that he might have been his father, but Gowan suspected he was an older brother, instead. He was dressed in rough working clothes and his eyes were dark and as piercing as bits of broken glass. He chose the precise moment Gowan and Nick walked past to spit a stream of brown tobacco juice. It missed Gowan's boots by no more than an inch.

"Nick . . ." Hoping to make the move as circumspect as possible, Gowan inched closer to Nick's side. He kept on walking and prayed that she would not stop. He did not think this was a place he wished to linger. "Is this the way they always treat strangers here?"

Nick turned to him, her expression as innocent as can be. "Never seen it before," she said.

He remembered her peculiar rambles about witches and her powers, and another thought struck him. "Is it you?"

A lady of the village chose that moment to dart across their path. She pulled herself to a stop in front of Nick and dropped her a curtsy. The woman was so nervous, she could barely keep still. She clutched a bottle of some dark liquid to her chest and darted a look in Gowan's direction, and when she saw that he was looking back at her, her hands shook so badly, she very nearly dropped the bottle. Her face went pale. Her eyes went right back to Nick.

"Been meaning to bring this to ye, Little Nick." She shoved the bottle at Nick and Nick accepted it with a smile. "To thank you."

The lady was gone as fast as she'd come.

Nick turned the bottle over in her hands. "Ah!" She sniffed the cork. "Dandelion wine," she said, and why she sounded so inordinately pleased by something that sounded so excessively awful was far beyond Gowan's reasoning. She tucked the bottle into her sack and went on walking. "Now what was that you said?" she asked. "Are they acting this way because of me?" Her smile was as saucy as her question. "What do you think, m'lord?"

Gowan didn't know what to think. Nor was he prepared to figure his way through it with the entire village staring at him as if he were the main and the most outrageous curiosity in a halfpenny sideshow.

It was the first time Gowan was thankful that the village was so small. In a very few more minutes, they were past the row of cottages and the pub and the shop that might not have been a shop at all. Gowan chanced a look over his shoulder.

The entire village was standing around the stone cross, and they were all looking in his direction.

Gowan let go a rough breath. "What was that all about?"

It was as if Nick could contain herself no longer. She threw back her head and laughed. "Welcome to Rhyd Ddu," she said, and it was all she would say.

Gowan hardly had time to think about it.

Before he knew it, he saw a chimney rise up over the trees ahead.

"The Lodge!" He breathed the words like an answer to some long-said prayer. It had been a lengthy journey, and a strange one, and relief at finally being at an end to it swept over him.

His steps suddenly lighter, he hurried in the direction of the house. It wasn't long before he came upon the evidence of what must have been, at one time, a fine and impressive drive. The stone was cracked now and overgrown with moss and vines, and vegetation encroached from every side.

Even that was not enough to deter Gowan, not with the prospect of a hot bath, a warm meal, and a bottle of brandy so close at hand. He thrust aside the branches of the nearest shrubbery and continued on. From up ahead he saw the warm glow of a single light winking at him like the promise of sun after a long day of storms. He quickened his pace.

Feeling suddenly more at ease with life in general and even with Nick now that he was on his own property, he turned to thank her. "I appreciate your bringing me all this way," he said, "I—"

Gowan's words fell flat. Nick was gone.

"Damned odd." He mumbled the words and chanced a glance around. There was no sign of Nick. It was as if she'd been swallowed by the shadows.

"Damned odd." Gowan added the invective one last time, just in case she might be lurking somewhere where she could hear it. There was no use trying to make sense of the girl, he decided, and without another thought of her, he continued up to the house.

"The brandy first," he promised himself, sidestepping a massive tree sprouting from the center of the overgrown drive. "And then the meal. Roast mutton, or some of that fine beef I hear they raise in these parts. Or perhaps I'll have the . . . the . . ."

Gowan's words faltered along with his steps.

The closer he got to the Lodge, the better he could see it. And the better he could see it, the more certain he was that he didn't like at all what he was seeing.

What at one time must have been as fine a country home

as any ever built had some time ago fallen into a state of abominable disrepair. Gowan remembered the family legend that attributed the Lodge to the second earl, a blustering old rogue who was awarded the lands and the exclusive rights to hunt and fish them for his service to Henry VIII.

"That was probably the last time the place saw paint and plaster." Gowan's words sounded as dispirited as he felt.

The chimney he'd seen over the trees was intact, but it was nearly the only thing about the place that was.

There were three other chimneys that Gowan could see. Two of them had collapsed completely. The third teetered on the brink. The windows on the far side of the house were boarded. The roof at the back of the building was gone completely. The shrubbery reminded him of one of those photographs he'd seen of the South American jungles: dense to the point of nearly impassible.

"There must be some mistake." Gowan grumbled the words, more to give himself the courage to go to the front door than because they made him feel any better.

"There has to be some mistake."

But he knew there wasn't.

There was a sign carved into the stone to one side of the front door. It proclaimed the place, "The Lodge."

If Gowan needed any more proof, it came the next instant.

The front door snapped open.

"Thank the Lord!" The lady who came to the door reminded Gowan of a crane. She was tall and as thin as could be. She was well on in years, at least sixty if her graying hair was any indication, and she had the kind of pinched expression lean people have when they get older. She wasn't smiling now and judging by the fact that her face was perfectly free of laugh lines or wrinkles, he imagined she never did. If she ever had the occasion, he imagined the expression would be so unfamiliar as to make her look as if she'd bitten into a rancid pudding.

The woman pressed one hand to her heart and heaved a sigh of relief. "And if I wasn't the most worried of creatures!" She didn't sound worried. She sounded ruffled, like a governess who has misplaced her charges and instead of considering the peril of the children, considers only her own inconvenience. "It's a blessing to see you, m'lord, and that is for certain," she added solemnly. "Finally, one of the Welshpools here to stay again. We've kept the place in order for you, m'lord, as much as it has been possible. You simply must come in and—"

The lady's word dissolved in a mutter of embarrassment.

"You must forgive me, m'lord." She dropped him a low and showy curtsy. "I do carry on so. I am Mrs. Pritchard. Your housekeeper."

In spite of himself, Gowan couldn't help but remember what Nick had said about the haughty manners of the English. This woman was as Welsh as the very mountains themselves. Gowan could tell from her accent. Yet her manners were fit for a reception at St. James's. As was her bearing.

She may not have been as cordial as he'd like, but it was a far better welcome than he'd received in the village, there was no doubt of that. In an effort to appear a little less rumpled and a little more deserving of his housekeeper's approbation, Gowan pulled back his shoulders and lifted his chin.

"It is good to be here." He lied. "And not a moment too soon. I am devilishly hungry, Mrs. Pritchard, and as thirsty as any three sailors."

Gowan sensed that Mrs. Pritchard would like nothing better than to wring her hands. She didn't. It would have been a show of emotion far below her dignity. "You'll have to forgive me, m'lord," she said, and damn him if she didn't make it sound as if he was the one who really needed the forgiving. "I've nothing ready. Not now. Your trunks were delivered three days ago, but there's been no sign of you. Well, you can imagine my concern."

"I was detained." Gowan couldn't even begin to explain. Not now. He was saved the trouble when he saw Mrs. Pritchard's expression go hard.

"Not by that, I pray."

Gowan turned to follow Mrs. Pritchard's gaze.

Nick stood near what he supposed used to be a large and sweeping lawn. It was overrun with greenery now, the shadows so deep he might not have seen her at all if she didn't smile.

"May the good Lord help us." Mrs. Pritchard backed a step farther into the house.

It was an interesting reaction, and so unlike anything he'd seen in Rhyd Ddu that Gowan couldn't help but be intrigued. He looked from Nick to Mrs. Pritchard. "What do you know?" he asked. "About Nick."

Mrs. Pritchard sniffed. "I know there are those in the village who are foolish enough to believe in her powers. I know there are those who consult her and her aunts for things best left to others—physician and clergyman. You were not injured by the minx, I pray, m'lord."

"Injured?" It seemed an absurd question, at least now that he was away from Nick, and Gowan laughed. When he looked back toward the lawn and found Nick gone, he was not the least bit surprised. "I am quite undamaged, Mrs. Pritchard," he admitted, but he couldn't in good conscience leave it at that. "Though she did try her best to do me in a time or two."

"I'd not treat it so lightly, m'lord. Not if I were you." As if sharing a confidence, Mrs. Pritchard leaned nearer. "You do know why they call her Little Nick, don't you, m'lord?" she asked. "There are those in these parts who say she's the daughter of the devil."

Eight

"Mrs. Pritchard! There is a cat in my breakfast!"

At the sound of Gowan's voice raised in surprise and consternation, the cat sitting on the sideboard lifted its head and turned to where he stood rooted at the door of the morning room. The cat's eyes glittered like jewels in the morning light. Its black coat glistened like the finest India ink. It took one look at Gowan and, obviously convinced he was hardly worth its interest, went right back to doing what it had been doing when he walked in.

The fact that the cat was feasting on the kippers that had been laid out for Gowan's breakfast was one thing. The realization that the damned animal looked all too familiar was another all together.

"Mrs. Pritchard!" Gowan called again.

"A cat, m'lord? Surely you must be mistaken." A tray of morning coffee clutched in both hands, Mrs. Pritchard bustled in from the kitchen, her steps as confident as her words. "I'd no sooner have a cat in the house than I would a—"

Gowan stepped back to allow her into the room, and at first sight of the cat, her words dissolved and her face went as hard as a brick.

"It is not my responsibility and I'll tell you that right here and now, m'lord." Mrs. Pritchard didn't seem to mind the cat nearly as much as she minded the prospect of being blamed for its presence. She gave the animal one frosty look before she proceeded to the table to arrange the coffee service.

"It is the house. That's what it is," she said, taking the sugar bowl and the creamer from the tray and setting them to both sides of the coffeepot. "The roof's gone completely in the great hall. There's hardly a window left in the old west wing. That is how they get in. Cats, birds, bats. There is an owl that roosts in what used to be the library and though I have yet to see it—thank the Lord—I am quite certain there is something living in the butler's pantry. I am very much afraid it is something unpleasant." Mrs. Pritchard closed her eyes for a second and shivered.

"It is a disgrace to the name of the family," she added. Taking the single china cup and saucer from the tray, she set them one atop the other with a decided clink, as if to emphasize her point. "Surely you see it as such, m'lord. A disgrace to your family and to mine, which has served yours faithfully for so many years."

The dishes laid, Mrs. Pritchard pulled herself up and stood stiff and erect. She massaged her left arm with her right hand. "I had thought that now you were here, things might change. I do believe you will agree with me or I would not dare broach the subject. It is time to use the family fortune to restore the Lodge to its former glory, or at least to keep the vermin outside where they belong."

Cat replied before Gowan ever could, though he suspected it was not the same reply he might have given. The animal lifted its elegant little head, and damn him if it didn't give them both a haughty sneer.

Gowan sneered back. "Yes, well . . ." He watched the cat take another gulp of his breakfast. He rubbed his chin and considered his options, which seemed at the moment to range from letting the creature devour everything in sight to risking his hide again as he had done once before, by making the mistake of getting too close.

"Well, that is easier said than done." Carefully, Gowan

advanced on the cat, keeping up his conversation with Mrs. Pritchard in an attempt to lull the creature into complacency. "You see, Mrs. Pritchard . . ." His words dissolved and Gowan pulled to a stop, considering the problem.

Mrs. Pritchard would not see. That much was certain. There was no way she'd understand that the glory of the earls of Welshpool was long faded, their fortune long spent. There was no chance she would listen if he told her the twelfth earl had left the thirteenth nothing more than debts. There was no way she'd comprehend the fact that the Lodge could never be restored to its former glory, not with Gowan's purse empty and his debts as high as the crumbling ceiling.

Cat finished off the kippers and started in on a plate of bacon and, grateful for the distraction, Gowan pointed at it. "The state of the house seems hardly to matter at this moment. That thing is eating my breakfast!"

"Aye." Mrs. Pritchard set the flatware in its proper place. She glanced over her shoulder at the cat. "So it is. Pardon me for mentioning it, and for being so forward, for that is what I suppose I am being when I tell you the truth, but it is your house, m'lord. It is your roof that is collapsed and your windows that are missing. If there are animals inside where they do not belong, I simply cannot be expected to—"

"No. No. Of course not." Gowan supposed that Mrs. Pritchard was right. Owing to the fact that there was no other staff here at the Lodge—no outside men, no butler, no maids of all work, not even a cook—there was no one else who could be expected to dispense with the cursed creature. If someone was going to toss it out, it would have to be him.

"Here Cat. Nice Cat." In those infrequent moments when he was feeling introspective, Gowan admitted he may have done a foolish thing or two in his life. But he knew he was certainly no fool himself. The scratches he'd acquired at his last meeting with Cat may have faded, but they were not forgotten. Keeping his voice down, he held out one hand, offering Cat a truce and hoping the animal couldn't read minds so that it didn't know what he really wanted to do with it. "Good Cat. Why don't you just—"

Before he was within a foot of it, the cat attacked. The hair along the ridge of its spine rose as if it had been charged with a bolt of electricity. Its mouth opened in a vicious snarl. It raised one paw.

But this time, Gowan knew enough to keep well clear of it.

Cat swiped at him and missed completely. The animal was as surprised as it was annoyed, but just as Gowan expected, it wasn't about to show it. With the kind of gesture he'd seen countless overindulged young ladies use to great effect, it tossed its head. With that, it leapt from the sideboard and disappeared.

Gowan didn't even bother to look for the cat. He knew he wouldn't find it. Grumbling to himself, he poured a cup of coffee and sat at the table with it. "Of all the infernal beasts . . ." Under the disapproving eye of Mrs. Pritchard, who had warned him more than once since his arrival four days ago that sugar was costly and as such was to be used prudently, he loaded his cup with sugar and stirred it fitfully.

In the past four days, he had done his best to keep himself from thinking about Nick. He'd been fairly successful at it, too, if he didn't count the scores of times he thought about her when he woke in the morning, and the untold number of times she crossed his mind before he fell to sleep at night. He hardly gave her more than a thought or two when he was shaving. He barely thought about her at all while he was eating the tasteless meals Mrs. Pritchard prepared, or washing up in icy cold water, or exploring this beastly mess that he had the unfortunate luck to call home.

But the cat, damn it, had brought more than chaos with it into the morning room. It had brought a reminder of Nick and this time, try as he might, Gowan could scarcely keep her from his head.

The thoughts came unbidden, as sudden as the sun cresting from behind a bank of thunderheads, as sharp and as clear as the reflections in a mirror: Nick sitting in her rocking chair back at the cottage, looking as sleek and as self-satisfied as her cat. Nick out on the hillside, the sun shining on her face, burnishing her cheeks until they shone red like the apple she had sought to keep him from eating. Nick astride the horse, her hair smelling of lavender, her body pressed against his, triggering the rise of more than just his imagination.

Gowan shifted uncomfortably in his seat. The fact that Nick was the most annoying, the most wilful, and the most demented of women he had ever met made his preoccupation with her all the more mystifying. It made him all the more resolved to put her from his head.

And now it seemed that even Cat was determined not to let that happen.

Banishing the thoughts, Gowan tapped his spoon against the side of his cup. He peered under the table and over in the corners. As he suspected, there was no sign of Cat. "How did the blasted thing find its way here?" he asked, though if he was asking himself or Mrs. Pritchard, even he wasn't sure. "That's what I should like to know. All the way over the mountain . . ." He shook his head in disbelief. "It's a hellish trek from Nick's as I well know."

"Nick's?" On the best of days, there was little rosiness in Mrs. Pritchard's sallow complexion, but what was there completely drained away. Her face was left the color of fireplace ashes. "Little Nick? Are you certain?"

"Of course I'm certain." Gowan reached for a piece of toast. It was dry and hopelessly hard and he cast it aside without even attempting to take a bite. "I'd recognize those claws anywhere. I've seen them before and at much closer range. I do believe I have the scars to prove it."

"Just as I expected." Mrs. Pritchard stood at the table with her shoulders pulled back, like a soldier awaiting inspection. She looked none too happy about the turn of events. Her chin trembled the way Gowan had come to learn it always trembled when she was incensed, which was often, and often for dubious reasons. She rubbed her left arm.

"Begging your pardon, m'lord, but someone needs to speak the truth out in the open and speak it soon," she said. "That woman has designs on you and no mistake. I thought as much when I saw the way she was watching you from the wood t'other night. Hussy! It is shameful. That's what it is. And I am not sorry I've done what I've done to put an end to it."

"Wait. Wait." Gowan swallowed a mouthful of Mrs. Pritchard's watery, tepid coffee and held out both hands to stop her flow of words. "What are you talking about? First of all, be certain, Mrs. Pritchard, that Nick has no more designs on me than I do on her. And I find her exceedingly . . ." He struggled for the word.

Loathsome was not quite right, for Nick was far too handsome a woman to be considered loathsome by any stretch of the imagination.

Neither was ghastly an accurate description.

Nick was far too clever to be spoken of as dull. She was far too winsome to be taken for insincere.

But she was defiant. That was for certain. And vexatious. And too cagey for her own good. In spite of her slight size and delicate appearance, Nick was not the type of woman who could be easily managed. Her chin was slightly squared. Gowan remembered that well enough, and he'd seen the same feature on enough women to know what it meant.

It meant Nick was stubborn. Headstrong. Opinionated. It meant if she wanted a thing enough, she would never take no for an answer, and that she would never say yes when she didn't mean it.

It meant she was the type of woman he would do best to steer well clear of and that, Gowan promised himself, was exactly what he was going to do.

"She's . . ." Aware of the fact that Mrs. Pritchard was still watching him and that the silence was all too telling, Gowan searched for the right word. "Disturbing," he finally said, and he slapped the table, positive that there was no more fitting description. "Nick is disturbing. That is exactly what she is."

Mrs. Pritchard could not have looked more sullen had she bitten into a lemon. Her lips puckered. Her brows formed an ominous vee over her small, dark eyes. "Disturbing." She nodded as if the single word held within it the fate of the entire Empire. "That is exactly what I was afraid of."

Before Gowan could ask what she meant, Mrs. Pritchard thrust her hand into the pocket of her starched white apron. She pulled out a small, folded piece of paper and shoved it toward Gowan. "Here. Take it, m'lord. It seems to me you'll have need of it right enough, and heaven help you."

Gowan accepted the paper and turned it over in his hands. Waiting for some explanation as to what it might be and what it might be for, he looked at Mrs. Pritchard and found her trying her best to maintain her dignity while fighting a wave of embarrassment that was so unlike her, it made Gowan all the more curious.

Mrs. Pritchard's hands trembled where she had them clutched at her waist and her face was suddenly as pink as a girl's. She could not meet Gowan's eyes, but kept her gaze firmly on the floor directly in front of her. Like the good soldier she was, she drew in a breath and started into her explanation.

"It is Papur y Dewin, m'lord," she said very quietly, as if the walls themselves had ears and she was afraid not only that they might hear, but what their reaction might be.

"Papur y Dewin." Gowan rolled the unfamiliar syllables

over his tongue. He waited for more and when Mrs. Pritchard was not forthcoming, he prodded her. "Do I eat it? Read it? Burn it? You have to help me out, Mrs. Pritchard, for as everyone in this cursed place never ceases to remind me, I am no more than a mere Englishman. I have no understanding of things Welsh."

"Papur y Dewin. It means the wizard's paper, m'lord." This much confessed, Mrs. Pritchard shuffled her feet and chanced to raise her eyes to Gowan's. "There is a man. In Beddgelert. My mother was acquainted with his mother, you see, m'lord, or there is no chance that I might know such a person myself. There are those of the locals who do think they need his services now and again, and he is only too eager to oblige, provided the right amount of money changes hands."

"And . . . ?" Gowan waited for more.

"And I do not believe any of it. I wish to make that perfectly clear." All her starch back in spades, Mrs. Pritchard raised her chin. "I am not prone to imaginings as are those of the village. My family has always lived here in the Lodge and as such, we are above such ignorance. But there are those who do believe in it, m'lord. There are those we believe in Little Nick."

"Believe in Nick? You mean in her powers? I am certainly not one of them." Gowan laughed and tossed the square of folded paper onto the table. "If this wizard's paper of yours has something to do with Nick's wild claims . . ." He twitched his shoulders, as if discarding the very thought. "The girl's dotty and so are those aunts of hers. If this has anything to do with what they call their magic—"

"Oh, it isn't magic, m'lord. Not precisely." Mrs. Pritchard looked more uneasy than ever, but she was true to her nature and what Gowan had learned was her iron-hard determination to prove herself right and most of the rest of the world wrong. Holding her left arm close to her body, she retrieved the paper with her right hand and handed it back to him. "I dare say it is why our families are so perfectly matched, m'lord, and why they have been these hundreds of years. I no more believe in these silly folkways than you do, and you can imagine my chagrin at having to purchase it from the man in Beddgelert. But there are times that a man must take action. And a woman, as well. The paper is not for magic, m'lord. Not in and of itself. It is for protection from the magic."

Gowan might have pointed out that the two things sounded one and the same to him. He would have if Mrs. Pritchard didn't looked so remarkably serious about the whole thing.

While he grappled with a way to explain his position in a manner she might understand and accept, he unfolded the paper. What he saw made him shake his head in amazement.

"Abracadabra." He read the top line of the paper out loud. The rest of it seemed completely unintelligible until he looked at it more closely. "Abracadabra," he said again below his breath. "It says the same thing all the way down." The word was written in full at the top line of the paper. The next line down, it was written out except for the last letter. The next line lacked one more letter still, and the next after that even one more, until the whole message tapered down into an inverted pyramid and ended with the single letter, "A."

"Abracadabra." Gowan nearly laughed out loud. "I've heard the word used a hundred times on stage by a hundred different conjurers. It is a nonsense word, to be sure."

Mrs. Pritchard frowned. "Nonsense in London, perhaps. But it is an old word, m'lord, and there are still those in these parts who do believe in its powers. You must keep the charm." Mrs. Pritchard reached for the paper. She refolded it in precisely the manner in which it had been given to her and handed it to Gowan. "Even though the two of us are not foolish enough to believe in such things, there are those who do. This may be of some use against them."

Mrs. Pritchard made a small, encouraging gesture with her right hand. "You must keep it in your pocket at all times," she told him. "It is the only way you will have protection."

Because he did not know what else to do, at least while his housekeeper was standing over him like a solicitous hen over a wayward chick, Gowan tucked the paper into the pocket of his trousers. That done, the subject, he hoped, as safely behind him as the paper was, he rose from the table. "There it is and there it will stay," he assured her, patting his pocket. "Only tell me, Mrs. Pritchard, what exactly am I being protected from?"

Finding him hopelessly dull, Mrs. Pritchard shook her head sadly. "Why, Little Nick, of course. Little Nick and all witches."

It was fitting that Gowan didn't have the chance to reply, for he had no idea what he might have said. Before he could answer, Cat appeared as if out of nowhere, leaping onto the breakfast table with a caterwaul that sounded like a banshee's cry.

"Jesus Christ!" Gowan didn't stop to think of how outraged Mrs. Pritchard might be at his blasphemy. Startled, he grabbed for the cat, hoping to scoop it into his arms. He missed the cat and hit the coffeepot instead. The pot overturned and like lava from Vesuvius, coffee shot everywhere.

Cat, seeing the disaster as an obvious invitation to join Gowan in a cup of morning coffee, dipped its whiskers into the liquid. One taste was enough. With a scornful snarl and a noise that sounded for all the world like a grunt of disgust, it bounded from the table and disappeared out the door.

Gowan grabbed for the nearest serviette to blot the coffee stains on the front of his shirt.

Mrs. Pritchard surveyed the damage. "It is the house, m'lord," she said. "Something must be done about the house."

Even while Gowan was trying to think of the best way to reply, he saw Mrs. Pritchard rub her left arm again. It was not a nervous habit. Women like Mrs. Pritchard did not allow themselves nervous habits. This was something more, and it provided Gowan the perfect opportunity to change the subject.

"What's wrong with your arm?"

The question was so unexpected, it caught Mrs. Pritchard off guard. She looked at Gowan in wonder. "M'lord?"

"Your arm. Something's wrong."

Mrs. Pritchard looked down at her left arm as if she'd forgotten it was ever a part of her. "It is nothing, m'lord." She flexed her arm as if to prove it and even though she tried her best to maintain her reserve, Gowan made note of the spasm of discomfort that crossed her face. "I cut myself a day or two ago. The wound has not healed. That is all. It is nothing to worry about."

"But I am worried." Gowan realized he was speaking the truth even before the words were out. It was obvious that Mrs. Pritchard was in pain and just as obvious that she was too stubborn to do anything more than grit her teeth and suffer through it. He crossed the room and stood in front of her, his hand out. "Come on. Roll up your sleeve. I want to see it."

Mrs. Pritchard could not have looked more surprised had he asked her to strip down to her frillies. Her face shot through with color, she blinked very rapidly and stammered over an accounting of why his request was completely out of the question. "My lord! A woman simply does not show a man her arm upon his asking. Think of the impropriety!"

Gowan did think of it, and he might have smiled at the thought had not Mrs. Pritchard been so upset. A certain kind of woman showed a man her arm. He knew that well enough. And she'd show him a great deal more if the price was right and both their moods suitable.

Gowan cast the thought aside and concentrated on Mrs.

Pritchard. It was not the first time he had run across such misplaced modesty in a lady of breeding, and as easily as some people slip into their overcoats, he slipped into a cajoling voice to combat it. "Mrs. Pritchard." He smiled and inched closer. "It is something that needs to be looked into and since I am the only other person here, I believe I should look into it. Go ahead, then. Roll up your sleeve. Let me take a look."

Mrs. Pritchard chewed her lower lip. Her chin trembled. Begrudgingly, she undid the button at the cuff of her left sleeve and rolled it up above her elbow. She had a small square of linen tied over her forearm and she undid it gingerly and held her arm up for Gowan to see it better.

"It's not large," Gowan said, almost to himself, examining the inflamed skin around the wound and the cut itself, which was obviously infected. "But it is serious. You really need to see a physician."

No sooner were the words out of his mouth than the irony of the statement caught him. He dropped his head into his hands and chuckled in amazement. "I do believe I have become quite addled since I have been here in Wales," he said. "It must be the mountain air. Or perhaps you are right, Mrs. Pritchard. Perhaps I am bewitched."

For once, Mrs. Pritchard was at a loss for words. She stared at him, her mouth open.

Gowan didn't take the time to explain. A singular sensation tingled through him, one that reminded him of his days in school when treating small wounds and illnesses successfully had always left him feeling so inordinately proud of himself.

"Stay right here." He gave Mrs. Pritchard the kind of look that told her it was not a request, but an order from the master. Without another word to her, he headed for the door.

"Now where the devil did I leave my medical bag?" Being careful to skirt the place in the main entryway where the floor was worn and the boards cracking, Gowan bounded up the steps two at a time.

"My medical bag, clean cloths, iodine." He ticked off the list as he headed for his room, feeling suddenly more energetic than he had in as long as he could remember. "There should be just what I need to—"

In the middle of the stairway, Gowan stopped dead. He shot up straight as an arrow and punched one fist into the palm of his other hand. "That's it!" He hurried to the top of the stairs.

There was a long gallery on the first floor with a decrepit bannister that looked down over the main entryway. Being careful not to put too much weight on it, Gowan placed both his hands on the bannister and looked around the shabby old house.

He had never been the kind of man who believed in divine intervention. The Divine certainly had better things to do than meddle in the affairs of mortal men. Nor was he the type who believed in coincidence.

The dilapidated old house, Mrs. Pritchard's injury, and his need for money seemed on the surface to have little in common, yet thinking of those three things had started an unassailable chain reaction inside his head.

"By the Lord Harry, that's it!" he said, his own voice tight with excitement, echoing through the empty house. "There is a way to make at least some money in this hellish place. And I know exactly what it is!"

Nine

"He's gone and done what?"

Nick could scarcely believe her ears. She stood near the hearth, her hands on her hips, and stared at the aunts. The feeling that had started inside her as amazement quickly turned to outrage. "Are you sure you heard properly? Are you certain?"

"As certain as certain can be." Tildy set her market basket on the table. "We heard it from Rena, and you know Rena. She may be the vicar's wife, but she has her ear to everyone's door and her nose in everyone's business. She knows what's happening in the village seemingly before it's ever happened."

"And she assured us it is true." It was a leaden day, and cool for the first week of May, and Clea removed her cloak, folded it, and set it over the back of the nearest chair. "It must be true," she said quite simply. "For after we heard it from Rena we heard it from every other soul in the village. It is the talk of the town."

"He is the most conceited, the most arrogant, the most meddlesome man on the face of the earth!" Too irritated to keep still, Nick did a turn around the room. "It's a personal insult. That's what it is, and why you two aren't seething about it is beyond my comprehending. He's a sly one, he is, that mankie beggar. He—"

"I have the distinct feeling we are discussing the Earl of Welshpool." Belle came in from the garden. She wiped her boots on the carpet set before the door and brushed her hands together. Her expression as free of emotion as her voice, she watched Nick pace from the window to the hearth and back again. "What has he done that you are in such a state?"

Nick pulled to a stop. Her voice rose an octave. "Done? What he's done is gone and opened a . . . a—"

"A surgery. He's opened a surgery." Tildy was infinitely calmer than was Nick and while Nick was still spluttering over her words, she took over the telling of the story. "According to Rena and the others, he's taken a room at the Lodge and outfitted it with his medical instruments. He has opened a doctor's surgery."

"Has he now?" As if she was thinking through the thing, Belle's eyes narrowed and her lips pursed. But though she may have looked thoughtful, she hardly looked upset. For that matter, neither did Tildy or Clea.

Puzzled, Nick eyed them cautiously. There were times when she would eagerly exchange the powers she did possess for the talent of reading other people's thoughts. This was one of those times. Try as she might, Nick could make as little sense of the aunts' logic as she could of their attitudes.

"And is that all you have to say about it?" She looked from Belle to Clea to Tildy and knowing it was with her middle aunt she'd find the most sympathy, she kept her gaze there. "The man walks into Rhyd Ddu as right as can be and sets himself up in a surgery, and the three of you have nothing more to offer than an accounting of the facts? It seems a queer thing, to be sure, and just as queer on his part. He did not come all this way with the health of the people of Rhyd Ddu on his mind, and you can be certain of that. He never dreamed of opening a surgery. Not until he met us. Don't you see? He's done it deliberately. As an insult. And a challenge. He's set himself up in competition to prove that he's better than us. And that we are no more than foolish women with our foolish, old-fashioned ways."

"Oh, dear." Mumbling to herself, Clea dropped into the nearest chair. "She's right, you know. I never thought—"

"No, I'd venture none of you did." Nick didn't give Clea a chance to finish for she was sure if she did, they'd be off in another direction with not a care for the original subject or a worry that it had been left far behind. "Perhaps now you see why I was so anxious for him to leave. You three wanted him to stay. You encouraged that. And more."

They had not spoken of the love potion, or the magical river, or the aunts' plans for Gowan, not since Nick returned from Rhyd Ddu that first night and told them in no uncertain terms that she had had enough of their schemes and their sorcery. They had no need to speak of it further, as far as Nick was concerned, and she gave them each a pointed look. "You should be ashamed. All of you. It was your doing and now look what's happened."

Clea looked anxious. Tildy looked reluctant to take sides either way. Belle, however, looked as solid as Gibraltar. And just as impenetrable.

A direct assault was in order.

"You of all people should see what this could mean." Nick spoke directly to Belle. It was the kind of sensible, straightforward argument that was so like her eldest aunt's thinking, she knew it could not fail. "The people of Rhyd Ddu hardly have use for another doctor. Why do they need him? They have us."

This was a bit of logic none of them could disagree with. Apparently seeing it as such and as an end, at least temporarily, to the tension that vibrated in the room like thunder, Tildy used the opportunity to bustle over to the hearth. She set the teapot on the fire. "Apparently the folk of the village agree with you. We heard . . ." She looked over her shoulder at Clea as if waiting for her to corroborate the story, and when Clea nodded, Tildy went on. "Though Gowan's surgery has been opened nearly a week, we heard there isn't a soul who's gone near."

"That's a blessing." Nick didn't sound as if she meant it. Even to her own ears, her voice sounded as tight as the knot of emotion in her stomach and as bitter as the taste of anger in her throat. "You've seen the man. You've spoken to him. He's a pompous ass with not a care in the world for anything other than himself. He can't possibly know what he's about."

"Yet he is a physician." Clea nodded, pleased with her own deduction.

"A physician!" Nick shuddered. "A Harley Street physician as he was so quick to point out. I've been talking to Iain over at the Dragon. He knows a thing or two about the Saxons. He's heard of this Harley Street and he knows what goes on there. Overpriced doctors dispensing advice to overindulged ladies. That's what Iain says and I have no doubt of it. We have no need here of a physician such as that. Him with his schoolbook medicine and his fancy ways."

And his eyes as warm as a summer's evening.

The thought crept up on Nick and nearly upended her, and she was grateful that she had at least the presence of mind not to speak the words.

She could not so easily keep them from her head.

In spite of the anger that bubbled through her like Tildy's tea water in its metal pot, she could not easily forget the time she'd spent with Gowan or the havoc those few hours had since caused in her mind and in her heart.

When she closed her eyes, he was right before her, as clear as he had been that day at Hell's Gate. His eyes lit when he looked her way. She could not forget that. Or the way the corners of his mouth lifted just the slightest bit when he smiled, as if it was something he did not do nearly often enough and he wasn't sure how to deal with it.

He was an exasperating man. There was no doubt of that.

And if she needed more proof than he'd given her on the walk over Hell's Gate and the ride through the river, she need only think of him sitting haughty as a haul-devil, in his surgery at the Lodge.

But exasperating or not, she could not forget him. She knew herself well enough to admit that and more. Gowan Payne, thirteenth Earl of Welshpool and the man she would have wished to avoid more than any other in the entire world, tugged at her heart like no man ever had. And that meant she was in danger of losing all she held most precious.

Perhaps that, most of all, was what angered Nick so.

"We have no need of him. None of us." She spoke too quickly. She knew she was trying to convince herself as well as her aunts, and she prayed they would not realize it.

She need not have worried. Clea was too engaged in looking excessively woeful, her delicate nature upset, as always, by even the slightest hint of a squabble among them. And if Tildy was not really too busy readying the tea to pay much mind, at least she pretended to be.

Only Belle held her ground, and even before she opened her mouth to argue the point, Nick knew what she was going to say. She braced herself for it, for Belle's words and for the truth of them.

Even being ready to hear them did little to lessen their potency, and nothing to ease the pain.

"He's all they'll have." Belle's pronouncement was as solemn as the peel of a death knell. "He and his kind. He's all the people of Rhyd Ddu will have when we are gone."

Nick met the argument head on. "And when we are gone," she said, "it will not matter to us."

Belle paid her no mind. She went right on as if lecturing before a crowd, her voice even and as calm as if she were reading from the market list Tildy had taken with her to town. "Someday all the folk of these parts will have to depend on outsiders, on men whose learning comes from

Saxon medical books and Saxon medical schools. They'll have no experience of this place or of the people. They'll have no knowledge of the woodland or the plants. And what learning they do have will never make up for their lack of magic."

Nick refused to give in to the power of Belle's words. She swung around and faced her aunts. "It is not my doing, and it is not my problem." She looked from one of them to the other, daring them to deny the truth. "There's nothing I can do."

"You could give them daughters." It was Belle who spoke, of course. Belle was the one who always pointed out everything that was painfully obvious.

Nick raised her chin and squared her shoulders. She could never quarrel with Clea, for Clea was too gentle a soul. She could never fight with Tildy, for Tildy was too big-hearted to press an issue, especially one she knew distressed Nick. There was nothing keeping her from arguing with Belle, for Belle would never give an inch. And neither would Nick.

"I could give them daughters." Though she knew she wasn't deceiving anyone, not even herself, Nick's voice was deceptively calm. "Or I could give them sons. You forget to mention that much, Belle. Conveniently. You overlook the fact that I could bear boys as easily as girls. And do you also conveniently forget that the power is something for the females of our line only? Males cannot possess the magic."

This, at least, was a point none of them could argue. They could only stare at her, their silence as eloquent as any words.

"I would do anything. You know that sure enough." Nick could face up to their silence and their arguments. She could not withstand the pleading looks in three pairs of eyes. "Anything in the world but this."

"Daughters would carry on our magic." Tildy was not

as heartless nor as singleminded as Belle. Nick knew why she took over the argument. She wanted to try to explain in her own way, without Clea's sentimentality or Belle's cold, hard logic. Tildy's voice was hushed and smooth, the way it used to be when Nick was young and needed to be calmed of some childish fear. "If there were daughters of the Rhys line, the people wouldn't need Saxon physicians. Your daughters would take care of the people of Rhyd Ddu just as we have done. They would continue the magic. We would see to it."

Nick didn't wait to hear any more. She had no use for Tildy's patient explanations, or Belle's arguments, or Clea's worrying. This was not some childish fear, some bwbach that prowled the night and haunted her dreams. This was real. Too real.

Retrieving her blue cloth sack from the corner of the mantelpiece, Nick headed to the door with it, determined to put some distance between herself and the aunts and their troubling reasoning. She stopped at the doorstep, and turned to her aunts.

"No," she said, and even as she spoke, she found her anger gone. Her words rang with confidence and calm assurance. "It will never happen. The price is far too high. I've more power than the three of you. You've said it yourselves often enough. More than the three of you combined. I will use it against Gowan Payne. Wait and see."

And holding on to the thought and to the tears that threatened to betray her, Nick headed up the mountain.

When she was gone, Tildy let go a long, trembling breath. Ignoring Clea's sniffles, she turned on Belle. "You did not have to be so hard on the girl," she said. "She's heard it all before. More times than enough. She knows her duty and—"

"And sometimes she needs to be reminded." Belle poured a cup of tea and sat at the table with it. "All things considered," she said, "I think it went remarkably well."

"Well?" Even Clea could not let such a statement go unchallenged. "You heard her, Belle. Nick is angry with us. That weighs heavy on my heart, indeed."

"And on yours, I suppose?" Belle looked at Tildy. She clicked her tongue. Cradling her teacup in her hands, she beamed a smile at her sisters. "The two of you may fret away your hours. I am not worried. Whatever plans Nick has, I think she has finally met the man who is her match. He is not a man who will be easily dissuaded. And I for one am very pleased to hear that he has set up a surgery. Don't you see what it means?" She looked from Clea to Tildy and when neither of them offered an answer, she provided one herself. Her smile widened. "Ladies, ladies!" She shook her head and actually laughed aloud. "It means he is planning to stay!"

"Blast!" Not caring where it landed or what it might damage on the way there, Gowan flung his hammer to the other side of the surgery. He shook the pain from his hand.

He knew better than to curse in Mrs. Pritchard's presence, and he congratulated himself for keeping his language so remarkably bland. With his finger smarting like the devil and his patience long past the breaking point, all he really wanted to do was let go with a mighty oath. A stream of graphic invective, that's what was in order. One designed to describe exactly what he thought of hammers, nails, timber, and, most especially, those men foolish enough to think they could handle them when they clearly—and quite painfully—could not.

He bit back the words while he shook out his hand. He could not take the chance of cursing in Mrs. Pritchard's presence. He knew that. If he did not, he need only take a look at the pinched expression on his housekeeper's face.

Mrs. Pritchard stood at the other end of the wooden plank, doing her best to dutifully hold it still while he attempted to hammer it. Though he had been acquainted with his housekeeper for barely more than a month, he knew exactly what she wanted to say. She was about to remind him as she had so many times in the last weeks, that she could not possibly tolerate the use of vulgar language under what she so euphemistically called "her roof."

He did not need to alienate his housekeeper. Not when she seemed his only ally in a village replete with people whose behavior ranged from cool to unfriendly to openly hostile. And especially not now, when he needed her help.

Gowan swallowed his anger. He leaned back against the desk. "I am no joiner, Mrs. Pritchard. That is for certain." To prove his point, he held up his hands for her to see.

Three of his fingers were bruised and if he was any judge of injuries, that number was about to escalate to four. His left hand had a scrape along the back of it, from the knuckles clear down to his wrist. His right hand had fared better, he supposed, with only an assortment of small puncture wounds, a cut that was not as deep as it was wide, and two split fingernails.

"It seems a poor trade indeed for what we've accomplished." Looking around the room, Mrs. Pritchard shook her head sadly.

Gowan followed her gaze. "A bally mess. That's what it is."

Mrs. Pritchard was hardly an optimist, yet even she was not heartless enough to speak the whole truth. "There are no more gaping holes in the floor," she said, though her skeptical expression hardly matched her encouraging words. She took a step forward and carefully poked the toe of her boot against one of the boards Gowan had found in the cellar. He'd cut and fit it to fill a hole and if he did say so himself, he'd done a bloody poor job of it.

Gowan mopped his brow with his handkerchief. "It's ugly, right enough," he admitted. "But at least my patients won't turn an ankle when they come to call."

"If you ever have any patients."

Mrs. Pritchard's words stung, but then, Gowan supposed that is exactly what she intended. When he winced, she pulled back her shoulders and clutched her hands at her waist.

"I've never made a secret of my feelings, m'lord, and I'm not about to do it now. I feel as terrible as I can about the way the people of the village have turned their backs on you, but I remind you, as lord of these lands and master of this place, you have your responsibilities. Engaging in trade . . ." Mrs. Pritchard's shoulders trembled.

Gowan couldn't help himself. He smiled. "Being a physician is not exactly trade, though I will admit, the money from paying patients would be useful. We need more timber, Mrs. Pritchard, and a skilled craftsman or two wouldn't hurt. Besides, I am a physician by training. It seems a likely enough way to pass the time here in Rhyd Ddu, where the only doctoring the people know is what comes out of the bottom of Nick's blue sack."

He hadn't meant to mention Nick. He'd vowed to himself he wouldn't. All these past weeks, he'd struggled to put her from his mind.

And lost every battle.

Uneasy at the thought and all the memories it brought into his head, Gowan rose from the desk and went over to the windows. The room he'd chosen for his surgery looked over the front of the house. It must have been a grand view at one time. Now, one of the windows was boarded completely. The other was cracked. Beyond the window, he could see the overgrown drive and the vegetation that encroached on the house like an invading green army.

Gowan sighed. It was a dismal existence here at the Lodge. Was it any wonder his imagination kept wandering?

"Believe it or not, Mrs. Pritchard, back in London, doctors are accepted into polite society." The comment was a bit off the subject, and that was just what Gowan needed—something to keep his thought's of Nick at bay.

Mrs. Pritchard obviously didn't believe a word of it, but she was just as obviously too well aware of her station and her duties to argue. She sniffed instead, an imperious sort of sound that Gowan suspected was far more intimidating than any argument she might have brought forward. "Be that as it may, it does no good for your reputation. Accepting money for services rendered . . ." This time the tremble was more violent than ever. "It smacks of trade, and no mistake, and I'd not be surprised if the people held it against you."

It was enough to make Gowan laugh, though he feared the sound of it was not as merry as it was cynical. "Would it matter? I should have known I was in trouble the day I went into the village to announce the opening of my—" He made a sweeping motion, taking in the room, and his spirits fell along with his voice. "My surgery." He hauled in a deep breath. "No one would come near me. No one would speak to me. I don't suppose I should be surprised that in the three weeks I've had surgery hours, I haven't had one patient. Not one. Tell me, Mrs. Pritchard, what is it? I am not so disagreeable a fellow, am I?"

"Oh, no, m'lord." Mrs. Pritchard's face paled at the very thought.

"And I have attempted to be pleasant, haven't I?"

"Oh, yes, m'lord!"

"And yet they treat me as if I carry the plague. Yesterday that little fellow . . . the one with the broad chest and the booming voice who greeted me so strangely the first night I came to the village . . ."

"Dafydd, m'lord." Mrs. Pritchard supplied the name and from the tone of her voice, he knew she did not approve of the child. "Dafydd Phillips."

"Dafydd. He's the one. He took one look at me as I headed toward the Dragon and cried out as if the devil himself had made an appearance in the village. It was no surprise to me that by the time I got there, the pub was as empty as a church on Monday. Not a soul about. No one to pour me an ale." Gowan was just as puzzled as he was angry about the whole thing. "Do the people here about always treat strangers so?"

It gave Mrs. Pritchard no joy to admit the truth. "Oh, no. Not usually, m'lord. They may be ignorant and they have some old-fashioned ways, but they are known to welcome travelers who come to climb the mountain."

"Perhaps I should take up climbing." Gowan mumbled the suggestion to himself.

The sarcasm was beyond Mrs. Pritchard. She shook her head. "It would make no difference, m'lord," she said. "Begging your pardon, but the fact that you are English is bad enough. That's what they think. It's made even worse by the fact that you are the earl."

It was as surprising a suggestion as it was incredible. Gowan gave her a skeptical look. "Correct me if I'm wrong," he didn't need to say it, he knew Mrs. Pritchard would, "but I have always supposed that members of the aristocracy are held in some high regard by the common folk. It worked like a charm in London."

"London is London, m'lord. And I dare say that in London, folks are more learned and less likely to dwell on the things of the past. Here . . ." She puffed out a sigh of exasperation. "Old Rolph, the Second Earl of Welshpool, he was a cruel man, m'lord. And as hard as he was heartless. He visited no end of miseries upon the people of the village. They've never forgiven him."

"The Second Earl?" This was too much. Gowan threw his hands in the air. "That must have been hundreds of years ago!"

"Yes, m'lord. But that hardly matters here. A year is as good as a hundred to these people. And a hundred years as good as a day."

"But I—"

"Yes, m'lord. I know." Mrs. Pritchard nodded solemnly. "It makes little sense to you or me. But our Christian duty tells us we must remember that they are simple folk down in the village. It is the only explanation for their folly. According to family records, the second earl was in residence here for well on twenty years. Even at that time, m'lord, my family served yours." Mrs. Pritchard was excessively pleased with the thought. Her cheeks darkened and it took all of her formidable self-command to keep herself from smiling.

"When he died, his son inherited the title. But he never visited. He kept to his estates in England, as did most of the earls of Welshpool after him. We've hardly ever been visited by one of your ancestors, m'lord, which explains the state of the house."

"And when one of them dared journey to the Lodge?"

"You can well imagine the kind of reception they received. Much the same as you, m'lord. And some even worse. I am sure your family history records it, though I've no doubt the hostility of the deeds has been lost through the years. If I am not mistaken, it was the fourth earl who came down with a mysterious malady while on a visit to Rhyd Ddu." She gave Gowan a knowing look. "He recovered soon after he returned to England. And it is said that the seventh earl met a band of ruffians on the road not far from here, though it is known full well there never were such as those in these parts. He suffered two broken legs, as the story goes, and injuries to—"

Mrs. Pritchard's face flushed with color. "To other portions of his anatomy," she concluded in a small voice. "As I recall the story, m'lord, it is the reason his brother's sons inherited."

Gowan was hardly able to help himself. He winced and shuddered and tried his best not to think about it. "Well at least that explains why the people in the village act the way they do," he said. "Do you suppose I might be able to win them over, Mrs. Pritchard?"

"It seems hardly worth the effort, if you catch my meaning, m'lord. Still . . ." Mrs. Pritchard glanced around the room. "There are those men of the village who would make short work of the house. There are many who are skilled craftsmen and it would certainly serve our purpose to have their help. If only we could—"

Mrs. Pritchard's words were cut short by the sound of the front door bell.

For a moment, Gowan didn't move. Neither did Mrs. Pritchard. The sound was so unexpected, and so amazing in light of everything Mrs. Pritchard had told him, all he could think was that there must be some sort of mistake.

But there couldn't be.

The words drummed their message of hope inside Gowan's head.

There wasn't a soul who could chance upon the Lodge without being aware of where he was and who the master of the property might be. And that could mean only one thing.

"It's a patient!"

Gowan and Mrs. Pritchard spoke the words in unison.

The realization of all they meant followed close behind.

Smoothing her hair and straightening her starched white apron, Mrs. Pritchard headed for the door. Gowan glanced around.

There were timbers leaning against the room's only two chairs and the only way to conceal them was to hide them behind the threadbare draperies. He accomplished that in little time and turned to the desk. It was covered with scraps of woods and coated with a sprinkling of sawdust, and he swept his arm across it, brushing it all onto the floor behind the desk where no one could see it.

By the time Mrs. Pritchard tapped on the door to announce his very first patient as physician to the people of

Rhyd Ddu, Gowan was seated behind his desk, a medical journal open in front of him.

"M'lord?" Mrs. Pritchard poked her head into the room.

"Yes, Mrs. Pritchard?" Gowan snapped his medical book shut and leaned back, looking for all the world the picture of the perfect society physician: terribly learned, slightly world-weary, and just bored enough that he would welcome the arrival of the next person who might wish to consult him.

Even his well-studied manner could barely mask his excitement. Without trying to be too conspicuous, he craned his neck to look beyond his housekeeper. "Is there someone here?"

"No, m'lord." Mrs. Pritchard looked nearly as disappointed as Gowan felt. "No person, but someone did leave this." Mrs. Pritchard held out a small parcel wrapped in a clean white cloth and tied with string. "It appears to be a gift of some sort, if I am not mistaken."

"Is it now?" Setting aside his disappointment, Gowan rose and went to take the parcel from Mrs. Pritchard. "Well, I suppose that's nearly as good a sign as a patient, isn't it? Perhaps it's a sort of peace offering from the village. What do you think?"

Whatever Mrs. Pritchard thought, she had the sense not to say it. She handed Gowan the parcel and stepped back to watch him open it.

Inside the cloth wrapping was a small cake.

"I say!" Gowan's smile went ear to ear. "Seedcake! I haven't had seedcake in a dog's age. I think we are making friends, don't you, Mrs. Pritchard? Why else would someone send a seedcake?"

He didn't wait for Mrs. Pritchard to answer. Gowan took the cake over to the desk and broke off a piece. It was still warm and it smelled as delicious as anything he'd ever imagined. Even one small taste was enough to remind him that while Mrs. Pritchard was a competent cook, she was hardly imaginative. For the last weeks, his meals had consisted of little more than boiled meat, potatoes, and leeks.

"Mrs. Pritchard!" He waved her closer. "Would you care for some?"

Mrs. Pritchard turned up her nose. "No thank you, m'lord. There is no card to say who sent it, m'lord, but it is clear the cake is from someone in Rhyd Ddu. I am not fond of eating the cooking of the people in the village. It is plain and simple tasting."

"Plain, yes. And simple. I will give you that. But this is delicious. We must find out who sent it and send our thanks." Gowan took another bite. The cake was certainly as good as he told Mrs. Pritchard it was, but he suspected his enjoyment of it came from more than its taste.

The gift of the small seedcake meant someone in the village of Rhyd Ddu was willing to forget four hundred years of hostility with the earls of Welshpool and give him a chance.

Gowan finished the piece of cake and brushed the crumbs from his hands. "When we find the cook, we must also ask for the recipe," he suggested. "It has quite an unusual flavor. Like cloves."

Ten

"This is chwys mair. You remember that, don't you? And this, mintys mair."

Nick looked sidelong at Dafydd Phillips. The boy was on his hands and knees beside her, elbow-deep in buttercups and fragrant spearmint.

"I remember the mintys mair right enough," Dafydd replied with an earnest shake of his shaggy head. He breathed deep and a smile cracked the solemnity of his expression. "The smell's a wonder and no doubt!"

Pleased by both the quickness of his mind and his accuracy, Nick smiled back at him. "Ah yes, the scent is fine! But do you remember what the plant is used for?"

This was not as easy a question. Dafydd sat back on his heels. He was as exuberant a child as any Nick had met, but she also knew he was too bright to speak without thinking and shrewd enough to know if he held off, he might yet wheedle the answer out of Nick and be saved from the trouble himself.

She did not let him have that satisfaction.

As if she had all the time in the world and she was more than willing to spend it waiting, Nick busied herself separating the leaves she'd already picked from the purple-blue flowers of the mintys mair. Once she had them sorted, she deposited them into her blue sack. "Well . . . ?" She looked at Dafydd expectantly.

He plucked yellow petals from the buttercups and rubbed

them through his fingers. "Well, I believe mintys mair might taste as fine as it smells."

"That is certain." Nick fought to control a smile. "But it has other uses."

Thinking very hard, Dafydd squeezed his eyes shut. "Toothache," he ventured, opening one eye to watch Nick's reaction.

"No." She shook her head. "Not toothache, Dafydd, and not baldness, for that is certain to be the next thing you'll guess."

Dafydd conceded defeat with all the good grace any eleven-year-old boy could. "It's too much for me to remember." He stopped himself short of sticking out his lower lip, but only, Nick suspected, because he did not want to appear childish.

"There's too much to learn."

There was much to learn. Nick knew it. She also knew that Dafydd was too valuable a pupil to discourage. "You'll learn it, right enough." She ruffled his dark hair. "It takes time. That's all. And you're well on your way. We only learned yesterday where to find the mintys mair and what it looks like. You're right, it does smell wonderful." She bruised a leaf of the spearmint plant and drew in a breath of the aromatic oil.

"And it tastes as good as it smells. You remembered that, too. I know you also remember that its smell and taste are the reason we mix it with other herbs that don't taste as good. Besides its aroma and flavor, mintys mair works to excite the vital energies and . . . ?" She dangled a bit more of yesterday's lesson in front of him, waiting for him to supply the rest.

"And it relieves muscle spasms!" Proud as old Cole's dog, Dafydd sat up straight and beamed her a smile.

"Yes!" Nick applauded. "And—"

"And it's wonderful for flavoring jellies."

Startled both by the suggestion and the voice, Nick turned around.

Gowan Payne stood not ten feet away, and how he'd gotten so close without her knowing it was a mystery to Nick. Her heart suddenly pounded hard against her ribs, and she told herself it was from the shock of seeing him and the fact that he'd appeared out of nowhere.

She was surprised. That was all.

That was all she would allow it to be.

Holding tight to the thought, Nick scooped the rest of the plants she'd picked into her sack and tied it shut. She ignored the smile on Gowan's face, but it was not as easy to ignore the way her hands were suddenly trembling, or the fact that her breathing was as quick and as erratic as the gurgle of the small stream that flowed not ten feet away.

She had a sharp knife with her, and paper and ink so that Dafydd might try to sketch the plants they found, and she collected them and arranged them in a neat pile.

It was make-work, nothing more, a poor attempt to keep the disturbing fact of Gowan's presence out of her head.

And it didn't work.

When last she'd seen him, Gowan's face was rough with the stubble of a three days' growth of beard. He was clean-shaven this morning and even after only one look, Nick was certain it was an improvement. Though the beard had been a perfect match for his prickly personality, it did little for his appearance. It hid the firm line of his jaw and the tiny scar on his chin that somehow softened his every expression.

Just as she'd expected that day at the cottage, now that his hair was clean and combed, it shone like finely polished mahogany. His clothes were trim and brushed, his shoes were polished to a shine that reflected the morning sun.

He was as agreeable a sight as any Nick had ever seen, and that in itself was enough to warn her to keep her hands busy and her mind on other things.

She rearranged the stack of drawing paper, and though the blade of the knife was as clean as it could possibly be, she wiped it against her skirt.

If Dafydd was just as surprised to see Gowan, he at least, had the sense to keep his head. When Gowan took a couple of steps nearer, Dafydd hopped to his feet. He curled his hands into fists, pulled back his shoulders and stood over Nick as if he was ready to defend her to the death if need be.

Gowan was hardly intimidated. In fact, he looked as if he might be tempted to laugh. "Excuse me. I didn't mean to startle you." He smiled at them both, but his gaze stopped and rested on Nick. "Either of you."

A rush of some unfamiliar emotion surged through Nick. Uncomfortable with it, she started to her feet. When Gowan offered a hand to help her up, she had no choice but to take it.

"It hardly matters that you are here. We need to be on our way. Dafydd and I are going to see Old Wallace." Once she was standing, Nick pulled her hand from Gowan's as quickly as she could. She tucked it into the pocket of her skirt, somehow comforted by the fact that at least there, he could not take hold of it again and she would not be forced to endure the warmth of his touch any longer. Looking over her shoulder to where a rocky path climbed along the side of the mountain, she turned, eager to be gone and to set aside all thoughts of Gowan and the peculiar feelings he brought forth from her. She lifted her sack. "We were just about to leave."

"I'll walk along with you."

It was not what Nick expected and it did not make Dafydd the least bit happy.

This time, the boy did not hesitate to stick out his lower lip. He balanced on the balls of his feet and though Gowan towered over him, he glared up at him before he turned his attention to Nick. "If the likes of him is to be with us, I'll be gone." And with that, Dafydd stalked away.

"Dafydd!" Nick took a few steps to follow him, but it was clear from the start that the boy was too quick for her. He was out of sight before she ever had a chance to catch him up. A feeling of panic bubbled up inside her, and try as she might, she could not convince herself that the feeling had anything to do with the fact that Dafydd had left her to deal with Old Wallace on her own.

"Dafydd!" Trying not to sound nearly as frantic as she felt, Nick called to him again, hoping to elicit his sympathy. "I need your help with Old Wallace, you know that well enough. I cannot handle him alone. Dafydd!"

There was no answer and after only another few moments, the sound of Dafydd's boots crunching upon the rocky path faded and disappeared.

"That boy's head over heels in love with you. You know that, don't you?"

"That is the most ridiculous thing I have heard in an owl's age." Her mouth open in protest, Nick spun around. One look at Gowan told her she might not have bothered. He was smiling that maddening half-smile of his, his eyes glimmering a color like acorns in the morning light. Convinced he would say anything to aggravate her and determined not to give him the pleasure, she set her annoyance aside, holding it as tight inside her as she was holding her blue sack in front of her "I've been teaching Dafydd the old ways. That's the whole of it."

"Really?" Gowan looked from Nick's sack to the stack of paper still sitting on the ground at her feet. "And who taught you?"

It was a simple enough question, and no secret at all, yet Nick found herself reluctant to answer. There was something about sharing this bit of herself with Gowan that made her uneasy. It was too personal a thing, far more familiar than his caress as they rode Horse across the water, more intimate even than his kiss.

Too uncomfortable to keep still, Nick picked up the paper and the knife. She headed up the path that led to Old Wallace's. "The aunts, of course." She answered Gowan's question as if it were nothing more than a inquiry as to the weather. She would have been more than happy had he left it at that.

Of course, he didn't.

Gowan fell into easy step beside her. "And who taught them?"

Nick fixed her gaze straight ahead. "Their aunts. And it was their aunts before them who gave them the knowledge."

"Yet you are teaching a boy."

Damn him for being so quick to pick up on the essence of the thing.

Nick shot a look at Gowan out of the corner of her eye. "Dafydd is a fine lad. And as quick as can be. He's interested in healing and that much of our art I can, at least, pass on to him. The people in these parts will need someone to take care of them when the aunts are gone and I am too old to do it without help. Dafydd cannot learn the whole of it, of course, even if I wished to teach it to him. The magic cannot be taught. It is a gift handed down to the women of our family."

"And you're saving it for your daughters?"

He was too close to the mark for Nick's comfort, too close by far. A change of subject was in order. She gave him a casual glance. "You've put on weight since last I saw you. That is certain. Mrs. Pritchard's cooking must surely agree with you."

If Gowan was surprised by her reticence, he didn't show it. He smiled and patted his stomach. "I do believe it is this country air that agrees with me. It must be. It can't be Mrs. Pritchard. Mrs. Pritchard cooks like the devil. Her meals are dull, tasteless, and invariably bland. And those are the good ones!"

Nick couldn't help herself. The admission was the most genuine thing she'd heard pass Gowan Payne's lips, and the most humorous. She laughed.

It was the wrong thing to do. She suspected as much the second the sound was out of her mouth. She knew it for certain when Gowan took her laughter as a good sign. He wound his fingers through hers and tugged her to a stop.

Nick could see that she'd been right about his eyes. They were the color of acorns, but this close, they were also as warm as a winter's fire. Just like a fire, they sparkled when he looked down at her, their brown depths lighting with coppery sparks. An expression that was not quite a smile played its way over his lips.

He brought his free hand up, tracing the lines of laughter on Nick's face with one finger. "There's a side to you I don't know, Nick. You can be merry enough when you forget yourself."

Though Nick's smile felt frozen, the rest of her was suddenly hot. Her cheeks flushed. Her breath caught in her throat.

And Gowan did not fail to miss a bit of it.

A slow smile stole over his lips and crinkled the corners of his eyes. "You forget, the life of a gentleman is one of endless boredom. We make an art of reading between the lines of other people's conversations. It's the only way we can amuse ourselves through long hours of dreary social calls. You cannot change the subject so quickly and think I won't notice, Nick. You haven't told me why you're sharing your knowledge with Dafydd. It seems all too clear to me, you should be saving it to pass onto your daughters. I can picture it now!" He tilted back his head and as if the scene of all he was imagining was laid out there before him in the fat, white clouds that scuttled overhead, he laughed.

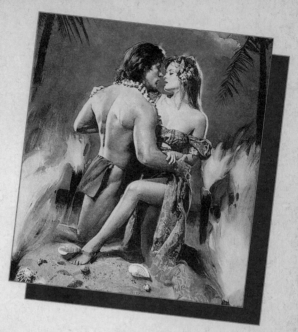

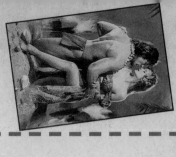

"Belle, Tildy, and Clea in charge of training the little darlings. It would be a sight indeed!"

"Indeed it would, but it will never happen." Nick's smile melted under the heat of Gowan's touch. Her words felt tight against the ball of emotion that suddenly clogged her throat. "I will not be having any daughters."

"Is that so?" Gowan seemed to think the statement nothing more than an interesting, if inconsequential, prediction. His smile spread even more as he flattened his hand against her cheek. "What makes you so certain of that?"

If his smile was disturbing, his touch was unendurable. Nick turned her face away. "I won't marry. That's all there is to it. There won't be daughters because I won't marry."

To Nick, it seemed as serious a thing as they had ever discussed, yet Gowan chuckled. "I wouldn't give up so easily. I haven't told a soul how you treat a man. Honestly! There must be more than one young swain here about who would have you. If not Dafydd, what about that strapping brother of his?"

"Hugh?" Nick's voice closed over the name. There was a time years ago when she was as taken with Hugh as was every other girl on the mountain. He was tall and sturdy, and as handsome a lad as ever there was, with a singing voice as sweet and musical as an angel's.

It was never really love she was feeling. The distance of time had taught her that much. The feeling that had crept through her like melting candle wax each time she met Hugh in the village or came across him on the path that led up to his small landholding had more to do with her awakening awareness of men than it ever had to do with Hugh himself.

Still, the memories of that summer when Nick was sixteen were as distinct as they were poignant.

At the time, she thought Hugh shared her feelings. She learned her lesson right enough the day she discovered there was only one thing Hugh ever wanted from her—the same thing he wanted from every other girl on the mountain.

The one thing Nick would never give him.

She coughed, clearing the emotion from her throat. "Hugh is no more than a friend. As is Dafydd. Besides, Hugh's too busy to notice me. He's spent the last months wooing Iain's daughter to his bed, and if he doesn't know it, he'd best be careful. Iain's not a man who will allow that for long. It takes no magic to know they'll be betrothed by the time summer's out." A show of bravura was certainly in order, if for no other reason than to vex Gowan and make him think none of it mattered a bit. Nick tossed her head. "I wouldn't have Hugh in any case," she said. "No more than I would have you."

It apparently wasn't much of a threat. Gowan threw his head back and laughed. "Is that so? Then tell me why your cheeks are as red as apples, Nick." He skimmed his hand over her cheek, then slid it down her neck so that his fingers were wound through her hair at the back of her head and his thumb was flat against the hollow at the base of her throat. "And why your heart is racing."

His heart was racing, too. Nick could feel each pulse through his skin.

She braced herself against the sensation and the quick, unmistakable wave of longing it brought with it. She knew her voice would be no more steady than the erratic beating of her heart, but she spoke nevertheless. She had to, or be overwhelmed completely by the painfully sweet emotions sweeping through her. She raised her chin. "You tell me. You are the doctor."

She had not meant it as a challenge, yet that was exactly how Gowan perceived it. He pulled away and the sound he made was halfway between a laugh and a roar of outrage. "That's what this is all about! You're afraid of me, aren't you, Nick? You and your aunts. Now that the people of Rhyd Ddu have a real doctor—"

"A real doctor? Is that what you call yourself?" The spell of his touch broken, the warmth and the scent and the nearness of him safely and thankfully removed, Nick's self-consciousness disappeared. She stood toe-to-toe with him, her blue sack between them like an unbreachable wall. "You with your city ways and your city airs. A real doctor? Is that why there isn't a person alive who'll come near that surgery of yours?"

"That's where you're wrong." Gowan pointed one finger at her. "I'll have you know I'm winning over someone at least. Why, in the past week . . ."

Whatever else he said was lost on Nick.

She stared at his hands in morbid fascination, her gaze wandering over the assortment of cuts and bruises that marked his skin.

". . . cakes and biscuits and . . ." Gowan's words dissolved. "And what in bloody hell are you staring at?"

Nick could hardly help herself. Her good sense warred with her curiosity. There was never really any doubt which would win. She deposited her sack on the ground and bent nearer, taking Gowan's hands in hers. She turned them over for a closer look, her trained eye automatically assessing the cuts and bruises that marred his skin. "You must have been in a right fair dust-up. And from the looks of things, I'd say you lost."

"Lost indeed." Gowan puffed out a sigh of exasperation. "I've been working at the Lodge, if you must know, and it is no work for a gentleman, I can tell you. See that." He nodded, indicating his left hand. With one finger, Nick followed along the scrape that went from his knuckles to his wrist. Though it was well on its way to healing, she could tell it must have been painful enough when it was fresh.

"That's what comes from cutting the damn timbers to fit into the damn holes in the floor. And that . . ." Gowan indicated his other hand and automatically, Nick's gaze traveled that way. His hand was covered with an assortment of small injuries and when she touched the most recent looking of them, he winced. "That's what comes from hammering and nailing and fighting the mice in the cellar when I hazard a trip down there to search for the damn timbers to fit into the damn holes."

Nick's astonishment could not have been more complete. She stepped back and might have stepped away if Gowan didn't close his fingers over hers. Her curiosity had caused her to make a disastrous mistake, she knew that as soon as he tightened his hold. Because she could not escape either her blunder or Gowan, she carefully looked him up and down, cursing him inside her head as she did.

He was not the man she thought him to be—not completely—and the realization of it did little to soothe her and nothing to relieve her amazement. There was even less she could do to quiet the voice inside her head that told her there was more to Gowan Payne than she ever imagined. Perhaps he was not as pampered and indolent as she thought him. Perhaps he was not as idle or as willing to accept matters as they were presented to him. Perhaps he was as stubborn as she was herself, and inclined to take things into his own hands and mold them to his liking.

This time when Nick cursed, it was herself she aimed the words against. How many times in the last weeks had she promised herself she would not let Gowan break down the barriers between them? How he'd found his way past this one was as much a puzzle as why she wasn't making a move to dislodge her hands from his.

Eager to fill the strained silence between them, Nick scrambled for something to say and prayed he would not notice that her voice sounded as shallow as if she'd run up the mountain. "You have not told me what you are doing here. You are far from the village, to be sure, and even farther from the Lodge."

It was, apparently, a question Gowan was not expecting. It hardly mattered. As if it was somehow answer enough, he hauled Nick closer and he smiled down into her eyes. "I was on my way to the cottage."

"You were? Why?"

Gowan allowed another smile to creep across his expression. He bent his head and the warmth of his words ruffled the strands of hair that floated around Nick's face. "To see you, of course."

Nick reminded herself that in the time Gowan had been in Rhyd Ddu, she had heard some amazing things, but this was the most amazing of them all. "Me? Why?"

Gowan caught himself on the brink of an answer. Before the words could cross his lips, he blinked, but whether it was because he was surprised by her question or by the answer he'd nearly given, Nick couldn't say.

His face screwed into an expression of absolute bewilderment, and as if the words hurt, he stepped back and let go of Nick's hands. "Damned if I know." He squeezed his eyes shut. "I was drinking my coffee this morning and finishing a piece of seedcake. The idea struck me. It's as simple as that." He opened his eyes. "I decided I wanted to come see you."

Nick looked at him in wonder. "And what is it you were planning on doing once you saw me?"

Gowan shrugged. He laughed. "I haven't the slightest idea." He shook his head, as if trying to clear his thoughts. "It must be this damned mountain air. Too little oxygen, that's what it is. It's got my head in a muddle." He wrinkled his nose, talking to himself. "What was I going to do when I saw you?"

There was no answer, and even if there was, Nick was not at all sure she wanted to hear it. Scooping her sack into her arms, she headed up the path. "Well, whatever the reason, you've seen me now. You can go back to your Lodge and your empty surgery."

"Or I could come along. You did say you needed help with Old Wallace . . . ?"

Nick's shoulders sagged along with her spirits. She'd told Dafydd as much. There was no denying that, just as there was no avoiding the fact that there was nothing she could do to change Gowan's mind. He'd decided he would come with her, and come with her he would.

There would be hell to pay if Old Wallace discovered who Gowan really was. The thought struck Nick out of nowhere. It was the only thing that made the journey worthwhile.

Her mood brighter, her steps brisk, Nick led the way to the small holding that lay in a narrow green valley just to the other side of the mountain. Gowan walked at her side at an easy pace, and the quiet closed around them, the aromas of the morning and the spring kicking up from the path, scenting the air.

"Your cat came to visit."

After so long a silence, Gowan's comment startled Nick. She wasn't about to let him know it. Shifting her sack from one arm to the other, she gave him a quick, disinterested glance. "Cat's a curious creature," she said. "And did you get the coffee stains out of your shirt?"

The expression that dashed across Gowan's face made the aggravation he'd caused her this morning seem nearly worthwhile. He jerked to a stop and stared at her in wide-eyed wonder. "How did you know about the coffee? Don't tell me . . ."

Nick laughed. She went right on walking. "Very well," she said. "I won't."

Old Wallace's farm did not look any different today than it had the last time Nick had been there. Or the time before. Like the mountains themselves, the small landholdings that dotted them were unchanged from generation to generation. She was used to seeing Old Wallace's small garden choked with its weeds, and the low crumbling wall that edged the path that led to his door. She'd seen Old Wallace's scraggly goats a hundred times, and the tumbledown outbuildings that lay upon the land as randomly as if they'd been tossed there by some uncaring hand.

But one look at Gowan told her the place was as odd to him as it was familiar to her.

"He's blind." The front gate was hanging askew. Nick carefully pushed it open and stepped aside so that Gowan might pass. "Old Wallace. He's blind. And very old. He cannot tend to things as once he could."

"That explains it." Gowan's gaze traveled over the tiny, whitewashed cottage with its faded blue door.

Nick went up the walkway. "Iain and Hugh and the other men of the village will let their own work wait, one day soon when the weather is fine. They'll mind the garden and patch up the house." She stopped at the door and knocked.

"It'll do you well," she explained, keeping her voice low. "The fact that Old Wallace is blind, I mean. In case you have not thought of it. He's as balky as his goats. It is bad enough you're a Saxon. He'd not be pleased to see the Earl of Welshpool walk into his home as fine as how-do-you-do. If you're wise . . ." She gave him an unmistakable look, one that said she believed he was not. "You'll keep your mouth closed and your odd, foreign accent to yourself."

Gowan looked as if he wanted to protest. He didn't. But only because Nick didn't provide him the chance. She knocked again and the door swung open.

"Little Nick?"

They heard Old Wallace's voice before they ever saw the man. It had always seemed to Nick that when God was handing out bodies and voices to go with them, Old Wallace must have somehow missed his place in line. He was as frail a man as ever there was. His spindly arms and long, scrawny legs never failed to remind her of the goats out back. What was left of his hair was thin and the color of December snow. Like the whites of his eyes, Old Wallace's skin was as yellow as new churned butter, a symptom of the disease that racked his body.

His voice, though . . .

Nick found herself smiling.

Old Wallace's voice was the voice of an orator, the voice of a preacher. It boomed through the tiny cottage like thunder in a summer storm, rumbling his welcome.

"Bore da, Nick." Old Wallace stepped into the square of sunshine let inside by the open door. With one hand, he leaned on his cane while with the other, he waved her into the house. "Sut mae?"

"I'm find, Old Wallace. And you?"

"As well as the Good Lord allows. I've not much of an appetite these days and I sleep a good deal more than I like, but . . ." He gave her a toothless grin. "I'm still as much a heartbreaker as ever."

"I have no doubt of that." Nick kissed Old Wallace's cheek. Laughing, she set down her sack on the table near the hearth.

Old Wallace never moved. Aware of another presence, he turned blind eyes toward the door where Gowan stood. "And who's this? He's too broad and tall to be Dafydd, I can tell as much even without my eyes. And my ears tell me he's far too quiet to be Hugh."

"A friend." Nick cast a glance at Gowan, reminding him to hold his tongue. She bent her head toward Old Wallace, but kept her eyes on Gowan, daring him to defy her warning. "He doesn't say much," she confided. "He has a heart of gold, but a mind that is no more clever than one of your goats. He asked if he could walk along with me and I did not have the heart to say no to so simple a creature."

"God bless you, Little Nick." Old Wallace patted her arm. "And you," he turned toward Gowan. Raising his voice, he spoke very slowly, as one might to a foreigner or a dull-witted child. "Welcome and come in. Nick will get you a drink, what do you say? Ale? Would you like a cup of ale?" Smiling and nodding, Old Wallace went over to a chair set at the other side of the room. He settled himself and leaned forward, both hands upon his cane. "You've been knowing Nick awhile, have you?"

Gowan opened his mouth to answer, but Nick broke in before he ever could. "That's right, Old Wallace. He's the poor, witless son of an old friend." She gave Gowan a sweet smile and gestured him closer to the fire. "He's come to help out of the charity of his poor, simple heart."

Gowan stomped over to the hearth. "No more clever than a goat, am I?" He looked no happier than he sounded, but at least he remembered to keep his voice low enough so that Old Wallace could not hear him. "I'll have you know—"

"Here. Take this." Nick denied him the opportunity to rant and rave, not so much because she was afraid Old Wallace might hear, but because she knew it would only aggravate him more. She reached into her sack and handed him a fine, heavy piece of iron.

The metal was shaped like a hen's egg and nearly that size, too. She watched Gowan weigh it in his hand.

"Heat that over the fire, will you?" Her head already filled with the list of other things she needed to get done, she waved toward the hearth absently. "The tongs are there on the mantelpiece."

Gowan looked at the metal. He looked at the fire. He looked over his shoulder at Old Wallace. "What the hell are you planning to do with that?" His words whispered at her like the hiss of the flames.

As if Old Wallace could see her, Nick kept a smile on her face. She was not used to being questioned, and she kept her voice low, too, and her temper barely in check. "I am planning on using it in Old Wallace's treatment, if you must know. Just as I've been using it to treat him and others with a like affliction since I toddled along next to the aunts to learn their ways. There. You've had your answer. Now keep the rest of your questions to yourself, or you'll have him after you with that cane of his."

Old Wallace leaned forward, listening very closely. "My cane? What about my cane?"

"Not cane, Old Wallace." Nick shot Gowan a look, reminding him his tongue would yet cause trouble. "Flame. I said flame. Our friend here is going to heat the iron in the flame until it is good and hot. I'll pour the ale."

Without another word, Nick headed to the larder where Old Wallace kept his ale. She poured a half cupful and brought it back to the fire. In spite of Gowan's questions and his obvious skepticism, he'd done exactly what she'd told him. He had the iron down in the center of the fire.

"There you have it." Nick watched the gray metal heat until it was the exact right color, red like a glowing ember. When it was, she instructed Gowan to lift it and drop it into the cup of ale.

"But—" Gowan caught himself in time. Shaking his head, he did as he was told.

The ale hissed and steamed, the aroma of grain and yeast rose in the air, scenting the cottage.

"Ah, I can tell you're about your work, Nick." Old Wallace took a deep breath and nodded enthusiastically. "The sound reminds me of the fairy falls of the Cynfael."

"Indeed it does." Nick took another cup from the cupboard and handed it to Gowan. "Fill this with boiling water," she directed him.

He did as he was told, though he didn't look any less skeptical than before. Gingerly lifting the kettle that sat to one side of the hearth, Gowan filled the cup. He handed it to Nick.

"A pinch of saffron. That's what's needed." Nick dug in her sack for the herb. She sprinkled it over the water and that done, she combined the mixture with the ale. Her voice hushed, her head bent, she held her hands above the cup.

Nick took a deep breath, centering herself and her thoughts. Quiet descended over her like a blanket, its completeness broken only by the small sounds of the cottage:

Old Wallace's labored breathing, Gowan moving uneasily at her side. Nick refused to let the sounds destroy her concentration. She allowed them to blend with her thoughts, merging into a kind of hum inside her head that calmed her and caressed her. The sound pulsed through her bloodstream. It beat to the rhythm of her heart.

The power surged through her, and Nick caught her breath. Her eyes flew open. Even after so many years, the first whispers of the magic always came as something of a wonderful surprise.

Nick's skin tingled. Her heart raced. She smiled, listening to her own voice reverberate through the tiny cottage, marveling at the way the words grew out of the magic and flowed from her lips, as if she was not speaking them herself, but only providing a voice for some other, higher power. "From the crown of thy head to the sole of thy foot, may the Lord heal thee."

The spellwork spoken, the magic done, she exhaled, emptying herself of the power.

She did not move, not even when she heard Gowan let out a sharp snort of disgust.

"There you have it, Old Wallace," she said, pointedly ignoring Gowan. "A tablespoonful every day for five days. You remember that right enough, don't you? After that a tablespoon and a half each day."

"I remember, Little Nick." Old Wallace hoisted himself out of the chair and came over to the table. "Did you leave a spoon where I could find it?"

"Right here." She took his hand and laid it over the spoon she'd set next to the cup upon the table. "I'll be back to check on you at week's end."

Old Wallace squeezed Nick's hand. "Bless you, Little Nick," he said. "And you," he added louder and slower for Gowan's benefit.

Outside the cottage, Nick pulled in a breath of sweet mountain air. The sun was barely higher in the sky than it had been when they went into the house, yet it seemed hours since she'd been out in the air. Using her magic always left her drained and sleepy and she set her sack down at her feet and stretched.

"It's a beautiful day." She did not offer the comment for Gowan's benefit, but said it more to herself.

At her side, he grunted.

Nick refused to acknowledge him. Lifting her sack into her arms, she headed toward the path. Before she got there, Gowan grabbed her arm to stop her. It took every ounce of his concentration for him to control his temper as well as his voice. His face was red from the effort.

"Hot iron and ale? Water and cooking saffron? Are you mad, Nick? Or just completely foolhardy?"

Nick's fatigue vaporized under the blistering heat of Gowan's remarks. Yanking her arm from his grasp, she drew herself up to her full height and glared at him. "And what is it you're objecting to? Are your Harley Street sensibilities offended by the fact that I took no money for my services? Or are you the one who is jealous this time? Did you not know how to treat the disease?"

"Treat it!" Gowan ran one hand through his hair. Too frustrated to keep still, he turned from her, then just as quickly spun around to face her again. He jabbed one finger in Nick's direction, emphasizing his point. "Didn't you notice the color of the old man's skin? And his eyes? Didn't you notice the smell?" Fighting for control, he dragged in a rough breath. He clenched his jaw. He closed his eyes, and when he opened them again, they were as hard as the shale of the mountains and as unyielding as the ground beneath their feet. Gowan controlled his temper and his voice, speaking to her as she imagined he might to a green medical student with little experience of life and even less of the healing arts.

"There is an odd, sour smell to the old man, Nick, in case you never noticed. It is faint, I realize that. You probably never remarked upon it, or if you did, you may have thought it came from some stale bit of food or soiled clothing in the cottage. I realize you have no training and no way of understanding the symptoms, but they are as clear as they can possibly be to me. The signs are unmistakable. A first year medical student would know as much. The old man has liver disease."

Gowan may have found the strength to control his anger; Nick never even tried. Her temper flared and exploded out of her along with the words she simply could not contain. "The old man's name is Old Wallace and I know full well his liver is diseased."

"Then you should also know that liver disease is incurable. There isn't a reputable doctor in the civilized world who doesn't know that. It is irresponsible to give the old man false hope. That ale and hot iron treatment of yours can be no more effective than your ridiculous hocus-pocus act."

"It has kept him alive this long."

"Luck, pure and simple. There isn't a thing you can do for the old man, Nick, and you might as well admit it. He'll be dead before the spring is out."

"Will he?" Like ice, the anger inside Nick solidified. She raised her chin. "I wouldn't be so sure of that, doctor." She made certain she put enough emphasis on the last word so that it sounded more an insult than an appellation. "I wouldn't be sure of anything, except that you are not welcome here." With that, Nick spun away.

Gowan's words slapped into her back as she hurried toward home. "Welcomed or not, here I am and here I'll stay. I swear it, Nick. If for no other reason than to bring at least some little bit of sanity to this place. Modern medicine. That's what's needed here. A little modern medicine and a great deal of common sense."

"Oh no. There's where you're wrong." At a place in the path where it rose before it curved to head around to the other side of the mountain, Nick turned. Gowan was still where she'd left him, standing some hundred yards away. She raised her voice and pointed a finger at him, and her words rang through the air like the clear toll of a bell. "I'll swear my own oath here and now, by all that is sacred to me and all the magic I have at my command. I swear, Gowan Payne, before this summer's out, you will be gone from this place."

Eleven

Her skin would be as smooth as silk and as white as alabaster. Her lips would be moist, the words that whispered past them inviting him closer. Her eyes would shimmer in the moonlight with a look that would make him shiver. A look that would make him want her more than he'd wanted anyone or anything in his life. A look so tempting as to make him forget himself and make him reckless enough to take her.

Gowan's drawn out sigh rippled the air of the empty surgery like a fretful breeze. He shifted in his leather chair, crossed his legs, uncrossed them again. He folded his hands on the desk in front of him, pressing them together until his knuckles were white.

The pressure and the slight pain it caused his bruised joints and cut fingers should have been enough to take his mind off the thoughts that were running rampant through his head.

It didn't.

No matter how hard he tried, he could do nothing to rid himself of the images of Nick that rose up in his mind like ghosts in a graveyard.

Images of her face radiant with a desire as poorly concealed as his own. Images of her eyes flashing her impatience and her longing. Images of Nick, always images of Nick, her hair down around her shoulders, her naked skin incandescent in the moonlight.

Gowan dashed the thought from his head. It was certainly not the first time in the past weeks that such ideas had made their way into his mind. And something told him it would probably not be the last. He didn't understand it. Not at all.

If he wasn't so rational a man, he might actually believe the nonsense Nick had told him about magic love potions and secret spells. Why else did thoughts of her keep rattling around inside his head?

With another sigh, he reached for a second piece of the delicious seedcake that had been delivered to his door that morning. He nibbled the cake thoughtfully, working his way through the problem in the systematic, analytical way he'd been taught to diagnose disease while he was up at University.

"What are the symptoms?" He asked the question as well as provided the answer.

"I can't stop thinking about her." He shrugged as if the gesture might somehow explain away his baffling behavior. "Morning, noon, and night. I think about how she looks and what she wears and how she'd looked if she wasn't wearing anything at all."

Gowan's heart skipped a beat and a feeling like fire shot through his belly.

He shook his head sadly, the way he'd done so many times back on Harley Street when he was forced to deliver bad news. In those days, his diagnoses were fairly standard: ague, the gout, dropsy, all things that most people would have considered nothing more than inconveniences and inconvenient reminders that they were getting older. His wealthy and pampered patients, though, considered them not only serious but serious insults to their constitutions, their characters, and their family names.

Ague, the gout, and dropsy were nothing compared to this. "This," Gowan told himself, "is serious."

He rose from his chair and paced to the windows, his

hands clenched behind his back. "And your diagnosis, doctor?" His question trembled on the late spring air.

"That's as easy as can be," he answered. His voice was as dispirited as the feeling that, at the admission, sunk like a lead weight inside him. "It's obsession. Pure and simple. There's no other word for it. I'm obsessed with the girl. Though for the life of me, I cannot say why. It certainly isn't her personality!"

He snorted at the very idea. "She was surely no more pleasant at the old man's home yesterday than she has been any other time I've come across her. And that temper of hers!" He felt a shiver crawl over his shoulders.

"Still . . ." The single word trailed into the silence.

"Still, I cannot stop thinking about her."

There is was, as plain as day. Out in the open. The incredible truth.

And it made no more sense now than it did when he refused to speak it.

Completely puzzled, Gowan returned to his desk and finished the piece of seedcake. There was a swallow of Mrs. Pritchard's weak and tasteless coffee left in his cup and he downed it and grimaced. Even the cold coffee was not enough to cool the heat that pounded through his body or dampen the thoughts that continued to clamor through his mind.

He knew there was only one treatment for this disease.

"No, that isn't quite right." Again he found himself talking to himself. "There are two possible treatments. I could locate and join the nearest monastery." Sarcasm laced his voice, and he laughed at his own ridiculous suggestion. "Or . . ." Gowan's laugh faded. His cynical smile disappeared. He could no more understand the how and why of what was happening than he could touch the moon, but he did know one thing for certain: it was time to face the truth. There might not be a cure for what ailed him, but there was surely a treatment.

He dropped into his chair and when he spoke, he thought his voice must certainly echo the astonishment that swept through him like leaves before a brisk autumn gale. "The solution is simple," he told himself, shaking his head and wondering that he had not thought of it before. "I will simply have to make love to the girl."

Gowan's plan was certainly much easier and much more pleasant to invent than it was to implement.

He thought about the ways it might be done all through luncheon, and if Mrs. Pritchard wondered why his lordship sometimes sighed over his flavorless boiled mutton or why he looked distracted and slightly on edge over the dry bread and thin butter she served him as afters instead of a sweet, she did not comment on it. She did, though, inquire once as to the Abracadabra charm she had given him, and when Gowan assured her it was still in his back pocket, Mrs. Pritchard looked as relieved as it was likely for a woman of her disposition to look, and as grimly satisfied as ever that things were going her way.

In his surgery again after lunch, Gowan continued to think his way through the problem. No nearer a solution now than he had been earlier, he glanced around the room, hoping to discover some distraction that might free his mind of his maddening preoccupation with Nick.

But like yesterday and the day before and the day before that, the place was as quiet as a tomb. There was no sign of patients on the long wooden bench that served as a waiting area in the passage outside his surgery, no sign of visitors at the front door or coming up the long, overgrown drive that led from the village.

"Damn! Not even a sign of more seedcake." Gowan let the draperies on the front window fall back into place. In the last weeks, gifts of seedcake and biscuits had arrived almost daily.

Eager to discover the identity of his anonymous benefactor and anxious to occupy the endless, all together too quiet days, he had spent countless hours watching at both the front entrance and back. He had threaded his way through the wild greenery around the house to spy on the road. He had even ventured to climb the somewhat tenuous stairs that led up to the top floor of the old west wing, thinking he might from there have a better view of the grounds and the road beyond.

It was all to no avail. There was never any sign of anyone, and the next thing he knew, there were the scrumptious gifts, left in a place he would have sworn he was watching so carefully, and nary a sign of who had brought them.

This day would seem to be no different from the others and silently, Gowan cursed both himself and his own bad luck. Just when he needed something to keep his mind off Nick, he could think of nothing that might supply the distraction.

Nothing at all.

Even as the thoughts were rattling through his brain with all the subtlety of a West End harlot dressed in a full blaze of crimson satin and tawdry lace, he heard the front bell ring.

Gowan had always considered himself something of a realist, but he simply could not control his reaction. The thought that it might be a patient bubbled inside him like the effervescence in a champagne glass. He hurried to his desk and artfully posed himself behind it, a medical book in hand.

When the door snapped open he expected to see Mrs. Pritchard. Instead, Hugh Phillips came galloping into the room. His eyes wild, he took a look around and seeing Gowan at the desk, he sped that way and slid to a stop right in front of it.

Moving at a somewhat less considerable, if no less determined pace, Mrs. Pritchard arrived in the room right behind him.

"No manners. None at all, m'lord." Mrs. Pritchard's face puckered into a formidable scowl. As if he were a particularly unsavory exhibition at a zoological park, she glanced sidelong at Hugh. "I tried to stop him at the door. I did my best to find out what he wanted. He insisted that you are the only one who can help."

Hugh didn't allow her the chance to say more. He was wearing a rough cloth cap, and he pulled it from his head and held it directly in front of him in both hands like a shield over his broad chest. "Beggin' your pardon, m'lord." Hugh's handsome face reddened from the tip of his dimpled chin to the roots of his coal-black hair. "I mean, doctor. I mean, your lordship, sir." Clearly ill at ease, he kept his gaze fixed somewhere above Gowan's head. "What I mean to say your lordship, sir, doctor, sir is that we've no time to waste. And no time to spend explaining things to those who cannot help." He lost his self-consciousness long enough to shoot a sideways look of his own at Mrs. Pritchard, one that clearly said he thought as little of her as she did of him.

Remembering himself, Hugh cleared his throat and looked back again at the empty air four feet above Gowan's head. "What I'm meaning to say, sir, is this. We're needing your help, your lordship, sir. Up at the farm. Your doctoring help."

"Dafydd?" Gowan popped out of his chair. He wasn't sure why, but a picture of Hugh's young brother rose in his head. Perhaps it was Hugh's sense of urgency that made him think the worst, perhaps it was the look of alarm that darkened Hugh's expression or the worry that shuddered through every word he spoke.

"No. No." Hugh dismissed Gowan's fears with a shake of his head. "Not Dafydd. It's Peder. And he's bad, sir. Mighty bad."

"Peder?" Gowan looked toward Mrs. Pritchard, hoping she'd make sense of it all for him. She shrugged her bony shoulders. "No matter." Gowan darted from behind the desk. "Get my medical bag, Mrs. Pritchard. It's packed and near the front door." He turned to Hugh Phillips. "Lead the way, man," he said, and stepped aside so Hugh could do just that. "Lead the way."

A lifetime of traipsing over the steep hills and mountains of Gwynedd had equipped Hugh Phillips with a stamina that was quite as formidable as was his physique. He sped on ahead as if the devil himself was after him, leading Gowan past the village and onto a track that was obviously little used because it was so treacherous.

His heavy medical bag weighing him down, his boots slipping on the rocky path, Gowan scrambled to keep up. "This Peder . . ." Gowan shifted his bag from his left hand into his right. "What exactly is wrong with him?"

Hugh raised eyes as blue as a summer sky to the small steading that lay not far beyond, the gray mountains like a theater back cloth for its green fields. The whitewashed cottage gleamed in the afternoon light and Hugh narrowed his eyes. "You'll see for yourself soon enough," he said.

Gowan puffed along at Hugh's side. "Yes, I realize that. But there are other considerations. If I'm to treat the patient, it would help for me to know at least something about him."

"His name's Peder."

"Damn the Welsh for their recalcitrance." Gowan grumbled to himself. "I know his name is Peder," he said aloud. "You told me as much at the Lodge. But you haven't told me anything else. You haven't even told me why you need my help."

Hugh snorted. It was not a friendly sound. He kept on walking. "That is as simple as simple can be. Wouldn't have come for the likes of you if there was anyone else."

Damn the Welsh for their honesty.

Gowan paused under Hugh's stinging rebuke and cursed whatever distant and long-dead ancestor it was who had turned the entire population of Rhyd Ddu against him before they'd ever met him. "I've been led to believe that no one comes to me for their medical care because there is, indeed, someone else." He caught up with Hugh and held on as tightly to his temper as he did to his medical bag. "What about Nick? If this Peder needs help so badly, why not ask Nick for her advice?"

Hugh grunted. "Not a job for Nick," he said quite simply and as if that was all he needed to say, he trudged on ahead.

Gowan had definitely had enough and more. He stopped and set down his bag down. "You're like an old woman, Hugh." He hurled the challenge at Hugh's broad back. "You talk a good story but there's no substance to it. That cock won't fight! I'll not move another inch until you tell me what I'm up against. If you won't tell me what's wrong with Peder, tell me at least something. It will help me form a picture of him inside my head. How old is he? You can tell me that, at least."

Without missing a step, Hugh rounded on Gowan. He looked at him as if he was the simplest man who had ever walked the earth. "It's happy I hope you are that you've stopped and wasted valuable time. Peder is all of four years old, if you must know it, doctor." He spit out Gowan's title in much the same manner Nick always did. As if the word tasted bad. "Is that enough to get your Saxon feet moving again?"

It was enough. It was more than enough.

Gowan realized as much when he found himself a full hundred yards ahead of Hugh. He arrived at the gate that led into the cottage garden long before Hugh had a chance to round the last bend and set foot on the path that led to the gate. Glancing at the house and wondering what waited for him behind its closed door, Gowan pushed the gate open.

He was sorry as soon as he did.

Like thunder rumbling over the mountains, Gowan heard an ominous sound.

It started as a low snarl and grew into furious barking. Before he had a chance to swing the gate shut and put himself safely on the other side of it, five howling dogs charged around from the back of the house.

It was too late to retreat and too early to panic. Gowan froze in place and positioned his medical bag between himself and the dogs. They were a breed he'd never seen before, with short, stubby legs and long bodies covered with coarse, tan-colored fur. Their ears were pointed.

So were their teeth.

"Damn." Gowan glanced over his shoulder to see if Hugh was at hand. The burly young farmer was suddenly as relaxed as he had been frantic only a short time before. He loped along, his arms swinging, and if he noticed the commotion, he paid it no mind.

Gowan grumbled another, coarser word as one of the dogs, heavier and more vicious looking than the others, attacked the bag and sunk its teeth into the leather.

"Of all the places in all the world!" Gowan rapped the bag sharply toward the dog and watched with no small sense of satisfaction as the animal fell backward. It was on its feet again in an instant, growling its displeasure and helping one of its fellows get to work on chewing Gowan's bootlace. "I have to find myself exiled in a country with more animals per square mile than people." Gowan shook his foot. The dogs kept right on chewing.

He decided on a different tack.

"Good dogs. Nice dogs." Gowan offered the dogs a smile. They didn't much care. While two of them worked on his left bootlace, the others kept circling. And barking.

When Hugh was finally close enough so that he could

no longer pretend nothing was happening, Gowan raised his voice. "Fine dogs," he said. He kept a stiff smile on his face while he shook loose the dog that had decided to nibble on the leg of his trousers. "You raise them, do you?"

Hugh beamed at the wretched animals as a mother might at her brood of children. "Aye. They're a wonder and no doubt. That's Artur there." He inclined his head toward the biggest one of the pack, the one who had already taken a taste of Gowan's bag and looked to be considering taking a taste of Gowan himself.

"And this one's Tristan." Hugh indicated the dog chewing on Gowan's trousers. "The bitch over there is—"

"Yes, I'm sure." Gowan kicked Tristan away. "No time for that now. What of Peder?"

"Peder! Yes, of course." As if he'd forgotten all about the urgent mission that had brought him to fetch Gowan, Hugh's face paled. He slapped his thigh. "Enough! Go on!" He pointed toward the back of the house and the dogs disappeared in that direction.

Gowan looked down at his shredded pant leg. "Charming," he mumbled.

"Thank you." Smiling, Hugh pushed his way through the gate. "There's a bitch in heat if you're interested in a pup."

Gowan did not answer. He followed Hugh down the garden path and when Hugh turned toward the outbuildings instead of the cottage, he pulled to a stop.

"In there?" Gowan eyed both Hugh and the byre where he was headed with out-and-out suspicion. Puzzled, he looked back toward the cottage. "Why isn't a sick child inside? What's he doing in there with the animals?"

"And who said he was?" Hugh had that disgusted look on his face again. "You go through." He pointed toward the byre. "And out the door at the back. You'll see for yourself soon enough." Before Gowan could ask him to explain further, Hugh disappeared around the other side of the barn.

Gowan pushed open the door and peered inside. It was

still daylight and it was unlikely that any of the byre's residents would be in from the fields, but he stepped inside cautiously nevertheless. The stalls he saw were clean. They were filled with fresh straw. They were empty.

Feeling a little more confident, if no more sure of what he was supposed to be doing, Gowan did as he was instructed. There was a door at the far end of the byre and he opened it and walked out into a fenced farmyard.

After the darkness inside the cowshed, it took a moment for his eyes to adjust to the bright sunshine. He squinted and looked around. The farmyard was no more than twenty feet across and probably another twenty deep. It was closed in on three sides with a stone wall. The fourth wall was formed by the back of the byre. Hugh was outside the enclosure, leaning over the wall to Gowan's left.

"There you have it, doctor." Hugh grinned and tipped his head toward the far side of the enclosure. "There's Peder for you."

Gowan turned in the direction he indicated. He even took a step that way, eager to get to work.

What he saw made him stop dead in his tracks.

"It's a . . ." His mouth suddenly dry, Gowan found it hard to get the words out. He stared in utter amazement at the huge animal on the other side of the pen. An animal that was staring right back at him, its small, dark eyes shining like shards of broken glass. The animal was as big as Gowan's desk back at the surgery. It was as black as hell. "It's a . . . It's a bull."

"Not just a bull." Hugh sounded offended. "That there's a genuine Welsh Black, your lordship. And in case you're no judge of cattle flesh, let me tell you one thing. Peder there, he's destined for greatness, he is. He's a handsome animal, don't you think? He'll make a fine stud when his time comes."

"Indeed."

Peder pawed the ground. He took a step forward. Gowan took a step back.

"You'll have to excuse Peder if he's acting a bit peculiar." Hugh went right on, his words as casual as if they'd been passing the time over a pint at the Dragon. "He's usually as gentle as a lamb, you see, and as mild as a day in May. But he has this problem, doctor. That's why I fetched you."

Peder raised one massive hoof and stomped the ground. He tossed his head and his horns glinted in the sunlight.

"Problem?" Gowan took his eyes off the bull long enough to glance at Hugh. He knew better than to move. Though he was a city man born and raised, he'd heard enough stories about bulls and how they were attracted to quick movements. "What sort of problem?"

"Nothing serious. Not for a Harley Street doctor." Hugh pointed one hand at the bull. "See. See there. The ring's come loose from his nose. It's dangling there like a leaf in a wind storm. He's in pain, poor darlin', and he's sure to do some damage to himself it it's not taken care of soon."

"What?" Whatever trepidation Gowan felt melted beneath the heat of his anger. "I'm a doctor, Mr. Phillips. I do not treat animals. It seems you're the one who's wasted time. Yours and mine."

Hoping for the best, fearing for the worst, Gowan turned his back on Peder. He was about to step back into the byre when someone stepped out of the shadows inside and blocked his way.

It was Nick.

Somewhere in the back of his mind, Gowan knew the sight of her should have warmed him much the way his fantasies of her had been warming him of late. He knew it should have cheered him. He was certain it should have reminded him of the vow he'd made to himself just that morning.

It didn't.

In his imagination, Nick's lips were moist and swollen

from his kisses. In reality, they were curved into a self-satisfied smile. In his dreams, Nick was willing and docile, vulnerable to his every touch. In reality she was as stiff as a poker, as petulant as any Society debutante Gowan had ever met, and as damned pleased with herself as he had ever seen her.

His fantasies went up in flames and his temper along with them. "What the hell are you doing here?"

Nick didn't answer. She looked beyond Gowan to where Peder still pawed the ground. "It seems what there is of your reputation will be in shreds after this, doctor." A smile played its way around her lips. Her hair was down around her shoulders and she shook her head and laughed. "Are you ready now to go back to where you came from?"

"Is that what this is all about?" Gowan glanced from Nick over to where Hugh was leaning against the wall, laughing. "Do you really think you can get rid of me that easily?"

"I think Peder could." Nick's smile grew wider by the second. When Gowan could think of nothing to say to her, she turned her attention to Hugh. "I told you he would not do it, Hugh. A Harley Street physician is too good for the likes of us. He would never humble himself to tend to a bull."

"Even a prize bull?" Hugh seemed to find the idea impossible to comprehend.

"Or perhaps he's not too good for us." Nick cocked her head. Her hair tumbled over her right shoulder, grazing her arm, brushing her breast. "Perhaps I was right all along, Hugh. Perhaps our esteemed earl simply does not have the courage."

"Courage be damned!" Gowan moved so quickly, Nick barely had time to grasp what he was up to. He slammed his medical bag down on the ground and in one fluid movement had his jacket off and was rolling up his shirtsleeves. "You won't be rid of me that easily, Nick. That's for damned sure. I've told you before, I'm not leaving. I think I'm beginning to understand why Hugh came to me and not to you on this matter. Perhaps you are the one who doesn't have the courage to deal with Peder."

"Perhaps I am too smart to want to be trampled to death." Nick tossed a scathing look at Gowan. It should have made her feel better. It should have made him aware of exactly what she thought of him.

Unfortunately, he didn't see it. He'd already picked up his bag and turned his back on her. He was headed straight across the paddock.

"Sorry, Nick." Hugh vaulted over the stone wall. Pulling his cloth cap from his head, he ran one beefy hand through his hair. He watched Gowan make his way toward the bull one careful step at a time. "I'm going to have to help him. We can't let the poor, stupid man be killed."

"Why not?" Nick tossed a look at Hugh as cutting as the one she'd given Gowan. This time, at least, it did not go unappreciated. The way it always did when he realized he'd done something to displease her, Hugh's face reddened.

"You know we can't let anything happen to the man." Hugh's broad face broke into a smile. He clapped his cap back on his head. "Besides," he said, heading across the enclosure, "I'd hate to see Peder dirty himself with Saxon blood."

Twelve

"Of all the stubborn, obstinate, foolish men!" Nick leaned against the door of the byre, grumbling to herself. She watched Gowan near Peder much in the same way she'd seen people who had heard of her witchcraft approach her . . . Slowly . . . Carefully. As if they were certain she'd do something unexpected and astounding the moment they let down their guard. Something that might involve an assault, and a great deal of pain, and a good deal of blood.

Except that she knew in her case, it wasn't likely.

And in Peder's, it certainly was.

Nick chewed on her lower lip. She was not one who ordinarily spent a good deal of time rethinking her decisions, or regretting them, yet she wondered now if this plan of hers was as brilliant and as faithworthy as it sounded when she and Hugh had first invented it.

Nick was not usually prone to cursing herself, either, and she didn't need to be reminded that it was something she'd done with a good deal of regularity ever since Gowan had come to Rhyd Ddu.

"Damn!" She mumbled under her breath. The oath may have been meant for herself as so many others had. Or it may have been aimed at Gowan. "Why must you be so mulish?" she asked, keeping her gaze on Gowan and speaking to him though there was no way he could hear her. "Why must you be so set in your ways? Why must you be so damned brave?"

The last word trembled on Nick's lips. It shivered through her mind along with the realization that it was not a quality she'd thought to find in Gowan Payne.

"One look at Peder was supposed to send you running for home." Her words shook in much the same way as her insides did. To her dismay she realized that the closer Gowan got to the bull, the more she felt as if she was being stirred in one of Tildy's potions. She was anxious and alarmed. Her hands were shaking.

There was no use cursing herself this time, Nick knew, and wrapping her hands around her arms, she held on as tight to herself as she did to her emotions, and watched Gowan get as near to the bull as he dared.

Sensing a threat both to his territory and to himself, Peder pawed the ground. He snorted. His tossed his head and the metal ring that hung loose from one side of his nose glimmered in the afternoon sun. The movement was obviously enough to cause the animal pain. He bellowed. His eyes flashed.

Gowan took another step forward, and Nick heard his voice drifting on the breeze. "The damned thing does speak English, doesn't he?" Gowan asked Hugh. Hugh didn't answer. As canny as he was experienced, Hugh kept his eyes on the bull and his concentration to the task at hand.

Gowan either didn't recognize the danger or didn't care about it. He murmured to the animal, his words low, vibrating on the air like the whisper of a lover. "Well, whether you speak English or Welsh, I'll tell you one thing, old Peder. We're going to take care of that nose of yours. That's for certain. And do you know why?"

As if he understood every word Gowan said and didn't agree with even one of them, Peder gave voice to his displeasure. His harsh bellow echoed through the steading.

"There's a fine fellow!" As remarkably calm as any man could be looking into Peder's black eyes, Gowan took another step closer. "If you cannot figure it for yourself, I'll tell you why I'm bound and determined to help you, my friend. See that woman over there?" Gowan tipped his head in Nick's direction, but even he knew better than to take his eyes off the bull. "She thinks I can't do it. She thinks I haven't the skill. Or the nerve. We'll prove her wrong, won't we, boy?" Another step brought Gowan within ten feet of the bull.

"We'll show her what we're made of. And we'll show her that it will take more than an animal to send me packing. She's tried before, you see. First a cat, then a damned horse. That didn't work, either."

Gowan took his eyes off Peder long enough to look over his shoulder and flash an icy smile in Nick's direction. It only took a second.

It was one second too long.

Peder saw his advantage and took it. He lowered his head and charged.

Nick caught her breath and held it, and she did not let it out again until Gowan jumped back safely out of the way.

The bull ran past him. With Peder at a safe distance, at least for the moment, Hugh grabbed a loop of rope from where it lay atop the stone wall. When the bull charged again, he flung the rope over Peder's massive head. The bull stomped and roared, but Hugh was nothing if not obstinate, and nearly as strong as Peder was himself. He yanked on the rope as hard as he could and tied the end of it to a nearby post.

Peder thus secured, Hugh stepped back to let Gowan get to work.

Gowan grabbed his medical bag and snapped it open. Nick saw his chest rise and fall, as if he'd taken a slow, steadying breath. He bent over the bag and came up holding something that caught the afternoon sunlight. The moment he reached toward the bull with it, Peder reared his head and brandished his horns.

Gowan took one, startled step back and let go with a

word as appropriate as it was colorful. Recovering in less than a heartbeat, he tried again.

"You'll do it yet, Gowan Payne. Just to spite me, you'll doctor that animal." Nick's anger grew in direct proportion to her amazement. She would not be defeated so easily, she vowed that much to herself.

Where the idea came from, she was not at all sure. It flitted through her mind, its passing as soft as the brush of a fairy's fingers, and when it was gone, it left her feeling more cheered than she had felt since Gowan took his first step toward Peder.

"Magic." The word skipped over Nick's lips and tugged her mouth into a smile. "I have tried to defeat you honestly, Gowan Payne," she said. "But it seems you will not see reason. There is only one solution. You leave me no choice. I simply must use my magic."

Closing her eyes, Nick forced herself to focus her thoughts. She scarcely ever used her magic for her own purposes. She called on it to cure disease, and to cast the love spells the girls in the village demanded. She summoned it when farmers needed help with their calving or when the crops wilted and the mountains needed rain.

This was just as important a cause as any of those, she told herself, opening her eyes again. This time, her own heart was at stake.

Folding her arms across her chest, Nick raised her chin. She stared at Peder and at Gowan's back as he reached toward the animal again. Gathering herself and her power, she whispered one word.

Peder reared and bucked. Startled, Gowan flinched. He stepped back and knocked into his medical bag. His feet went out from under him.

Nick giggled. Gowan made a pretty picture, seat down in a pile of muck.

Pulling himself to his feet, Gowan wiped his hands against his trouser legs. She heard him mumble a word she could not quite understand. Something told her it was for the best. He picked his medical instrument out of the mud and brushed it against his shirt sleeve. He went to work again.

So did Nick.

She concentrated and whispered the word.

This time, Peder threw back his head and bellowed.

Nick laughed.

Gowan could not help but hear her. He tossed a withering look over his shoulder. His chin set, his lips pulled into a thin line of determination, he turned again to Peder.

"That's the last time you'll do that to me, dammit." Gowan's roar was nearly as hostile as Peder's. "You'll stand still and let me clean the blood off your bloody ugly face. And then you'll let me pinch that damned ring shut. You hear me, you damned, ugly animal?"

Hugh looked offended. Peder looked ready to fight.

Nick waited for Gowan to make the next move.

Still grumbling, Gowan pulled a cloth and a brown glass bottle out of his medical bag. He opened the bottle and spilled some liquid into the cloth. He got as close to the bull as he could and, extending his arm, he reached to wipe the blood off Peder's face.

Nick whispered the word of power.

Nothing happened.

"What?" Surprised and dismayed, Nick jerked upright and looked around. That's when she saw the source of the trouble.

There they were. On the other side of the farmyard. They'd hoped to hide there without her knowing, she could tell as much from the fact that they kept themselves to the shadows.

But Nick's eyes were better than they imagined. And her instincts were as true as ever. She felt the tremor in the strength of her magic. She sensed a power working against hers. She knew it could only come from one place.

The aunts.

Belle, Tildy, and Clea stood on the other side of the wall, their eyes closed in concentration. Nick could not imagine what had brought them to Hugh's steading, or how long they'd stood watching silently without her knowing it. But she did not even have to think upon it to know why they were there.

They were there to counter each of her spells and to cast spells of their own, ones that would render Peder docile, and make it possible for Gowan to finish his work. They were there to ease Gowan's way, and lessen his risk, and to raise the opinion of him in Hugh's eyes. For they knew as certainly as Nick that whatever happened there in the paddock, Hugh would recount the story not once but one hundred times before the week was out, and if Gowan was successful in his endeavor, each telling of it would further elevate the young doctor's courage, his skills, and thus, his reputation.

After they had given Nick their solemn promise that they would not interfere, and they would not meddle, and they would certainly not use their powers to try and bring to pass the union they so desired and she so feared, the aunts were there to thwart Nick and to do everything in their power to help Gowan.

It was a devious plan, and so in keeping with their characters, Nick wondered that they had not tried something very like it sooner.

She did not have time to think upon it.

In the seconds she'd taken to speculate as to the aunts' intentions, Gowan had already cleaned the blood from Peder's muzzle. There was no time to lose.

Nick drew in a deep breath. She waited until Gowan had his hand on the ring that hung unfastened to one side of Peder's nose. This time, she knew better than to try a simple spell or to even attempt to be subtle about it. She waved her hands and wove her words carefully. This time, she said the word of power aloud.

Peder stomped and tossed his head. Gowan grabbed his hand and sucked it, as if he'd been bitten. Even Hugh flinched.

On the other side of the low stone wall, Nick heard a rather satisfying sound, three sharp intakes of breath. She looked that way and found her aunts staring back at her in astonishment.

Belle was decidedly annoyed. She never did like it when Nick displayed a power more potent than hers. Tildy was flustered. Her hair hung in her eyes. Clea was distressed. She cast a wide-eyed glance at Peder and another pleading look in Nick's direction.

"Oh, no." Nick shook her head. She did not need to speak too loudly. She knew her aunts heard every one of her words. "You will not convince me with your pitiful looks or your pleas for mercy. I will have him gone!" Nick thrust one hand out toward Gowan and the animal.

Peder kicked and reared.

The aunts may have been impractical to a fault. They may have been unreasonable. They may have thought only the best of Nick who, in spite of their insistence on meddling with her life, they loved as dearly as if she were their own.

But they knew a declaration of war when they saw one.

Belle's face went hard as a butter crock. Tildy pursed her lips and blew a curl of hair from her eyes. Clea blinked rapidly, like an animal surprised by bright light.

They linked hands. From where she stood, Nick could not hear the words they said, but she saw their lips move in unison, and she saw what the power of their charm did to Peder. The animal stood as still as a stone.

It did not take long for Hugh to catch wind of what was happening. He was no more comfortable in the presence of magic than most, and more than once in the years she'd known him, Nick had seen him react to the terrifying wonder of it all. He swallowed hard and ran one finger around the inside of his shirt collar. He darted a look between Nick and the aunts and his handsome face paled.

As far as Nick could tell, Gowan was too busy concentrating on Peder to realize what was going on around him. Even if he did realize there was something afoot, she was certain he would believe it had more to do with the laws of nature and the erratic state of Peder's temper than it did with magic.

At Peder's last uproar, Gowan had put a safe distance between himself and the animal. Now he closed in on it again, and this time when he neared, Peder never moved.

"Not for long." Again, Nick waved her hands. Again, Peder tossed his head. Again, Gowan swore and started anew.

Nick knew what would happen next. As sure as she knew the names of the flowers in the fields and the ways to employ each and every one of them in the healing of the sick, she knew the aunts would try again.

As one, they closed their eyes. They began their spell.

The moment they did, Peder stopped writhing. His eyes glazed over. His tongue lolled out of his mouth. He stood transfixed, a creature bespelled, and when Gowan grabbed onto the metal ring that dangled from his nose, Peder never moved a muscle.

Nick heard the click as Gowan pushed the ends of the ring together.

And then she heard something else.

A sneeze.

Nick turned in time to see Tildy drop her hands from those of her sisters. She saw her middle aunt scratch her nose and push a curl of silvery hair out of her eyes.

Whatever magic the aunts had woven dissolved as quickly as it had been created. Peder snapped out of the spell that held him. He roared. He reared. With a furious tug, he broke free of his rope.

His eyes gleaming vengeance, his horns shining like steel in the last rays of afternoon light, Peder put his head down and charged. Straight for Gowan.

"No!" Nick felt her heart jolt at the same time a scream of warning erupted from her. She knew it was no use to look to the aunts for help. They clucked like chickens, and already Clea was wringing her hands, making it impossible for them to join their powers together by linking their fingers.

There was only one thing to do.

Spreading her arms and raising her voice, Nick called on all her power. The air crackled and what had been but a gentle breeze all day grew into a howling wind that advanced like an invisible hand through the farmyard.

It touched Peder and the animal froze in his tracks. He crumpled to the ground no more than a foot in front of Gowan.

For what seemed an eternity, Gowan didn't move. Neither did Hugh. Part and parcel of the spell that still crackled in the air, Nick fell back against the doorway. She pressed one hand to her heart as if that might slow its frantic pounding. She passed her other hand over her eyes, fighting against the fatigue that overwhelmed her as surely as her magic had overpowered poor Peder.

Her head hammering in time to the frenzied rhythm of her heart, she closed her eyes and allowed herself to be swept into the nothingness that always enveloped her when she finished a spell. She floated there much the same as her magic had floated on the wind, suspended somewhere between the physical and the ethereal worlds. As the magic subsided, her heartbeat slowed, bit by bit, and the blackness ebbed and finally withdrew.

When Nick opened her eyes again, Hugh was on his knees beside Peder, his ear pressed to the animal's heaving side.

"He's fine, Hugh." Nick's voice trembled nearly as much

as her knees. She braced herself against the door of the byre. "He'll be as right as ninepence in a bit. Give him an extra measure of hay tonight and he'll forgive all we've done to him, I think."

As surely as if he had been as bespelled as Peder, Gowan's head snapped up at the sound of Nick's voice. He spun to face her, his expression as startled as any she'd ever seen.

Before he could begin a barrage of questions that was sure to end in skepticism, objections, and, undoubtedly, a row, she turned and headed out of the byre.

"Here!" Behind her, she heard Gowan's voice and the scramble as he rummaged through his medical bag. Apparently not finding whatever it was he was looking for, she heard him shove the bag at Hugh. "You take care of the damned beast!"

The urgency that vibrated in Gowan's voice did not bode well for Nick's retreat. By the time she made her way out of the byre, across the yard and as far as Hugh's garden, she could hear Gowan's boots crunching against the path behind her.

Before she got as far as the gate, his hand was on her elbow. He closed his fingers over her arm and pulled her to a stop and in a movement that made her head spin, he turned her to face him.

Gowan looked remarkably happy for a man who had so nearly met an untimely and quite grisly end. There was a smile on his face that crinkled the corners of his eyes.

Now that he'd taken hold of Nick, he did not seem to know what to say. He opened his mouth and snapped it shut. He opened it again. The smile on his face got wider. The sparkle in his eyes brightened.

Nick attempted to yank her arm from his grasp. "If you're expecting an apology, you'll get none from me."

Gowan did not rise to the challenge in her voice. He didn't let go of her, either. His eyes flickering, he smiled down at her. "I don't know how you did it, Nick. I'm not sure I want to know how you did it. But you did! By the Lord Harry, you did. You saved my life!"

Nick let go a sigh of frustration. As much as she hated to admit it, she knew it was true. "Yes. I did." She sounded no more pleased by the confession than she felt. "I did not do it willingly," she said, her look as frosty as she could make it beneath the heat of Gowan's touch. "You should know that here and now. Hugh loves that animal like a brother. I did not want to see anything happen to it."

She expected Gowan to object. He didn't. He laughed, a warm sound that rippled the air between them. "That's not why you did it and you know it. Admit the truth, Nick, for I think you know it as surely as I do."

Nick could have sworn there were still some vestiges of her magic in the air. She could feel it all around them, tingling against her skin like the first brush of a spring breeze, trembling, like the whisper of a lover's kiss. It made her head buzz and her heart pound. It made it impossible for her to lie to Gowan, and more impossible still to keep her voice from quavering when she told him the truth.

"I wanted to frighten you. That was all. I thought you'd leave. I certainly never meant to see you hurt. When Peder charged . . ." Nick cast a glance around the steading. She would have liked to explain to him the aunts' part in the whole thing. Of course, they were nowhere to be seen. "I had to do something," she admitted with no great relish. "You might have been killed."

It did not seem a humorous thing to Nick, yet Gowan laughed again. "Would you have minded so very much?"

"It's what you wanted, isn't it?" she glared at him. "Why else would any man get so near a beast as large and dangerous as that? You've a death wish and no doubt."

Gowan seemed disinclined to argue the point. His smile widening, he slid his hand down her arm and wound his fingers through hers. "Perhaps . . ." He raised her hand to his lips, his words shivering over her skin. "Perhaps like the gallant knights of old, I am willing to give my life at the behest of my lady love."

"What!" Nick yanked her hand out of Gowan's grasp and hid it behind her back. She put the other hand with it, just for safekeeping. "You're daft, that's what you are."

"No." Gowan shook his head and if she thought her hands secure where they were, she had surely been wrong. Gowan grabbed for them. Before Nick knew what was happening, or could do anything to prevent it, his arms were around her. He kept them there, his fingers trailing slow circles over her back.

"If there's one thing I'm not, it's daft, Nick." Gowan drew her closer. "I'm the most logical of men. Always have been. But you should know that I am also a man who knows what he wants and who will do whatever he must to get it."

As spellbound as Peder ever was, and surely as stunned as the poor animal might have been had he had any understanding of what was happening to him, Nick stared into Gowan's eyes. They were bright with longing and dark with desire. They flashed and sparked with a barely contained yearning that rumbled in his voice and caused a smile of unbridled eagerness to play its way around his lips.

There was only one explanation for a look such as that. Only one reason for his actions.

"They've charmed you." The words tumbled out of Nick with icy certainty. Automatically, she searched the yard again for any trace of her aunts. "They've taken hold of your head and of your heart. They've—"

"No, no, no!" Gowan brushed the word against her lips, the single syllable pulsing like a heartbeat between them. "I haven't seen a trace of your aunts in weeks."

"Yet it is the only thing that can account for your behavior." Nick's words might have sounded far more convincing had they not caught in her throat, right at the spot where Gowan pressed a soft, moist kiss against her neck.

He reached one hand up to nudge aside the collar of her gown and his tongue skimmed the hollow at the base of her throat.

Against every instinct that screamed the warning of it through her head, Nick closed her eyes, permitting herself the pleasure of the feeling that tingled over her skin, allowing herself to be swallowed by a sensation so like the sweet oblivion that resulted from her magic that it took her breath away.

It was certainly folly. Nick knew it. It was folly to let Gowan show such reckless intimacy. It was folly to so savor the sensations that were sweeping through her, and to tell herself that after the madness was over, all could be just as it had been before.

Folly. All of it.

And Nick was powerless to stop it.

"I've been meaning to call on you. To tell you how I feel." Gowan's words brushed her ear. "There isn't an hour that goes by when I don't think about you, Nick. You're like a drug, eating away at the life of me."

Folly.

The word echoed inside Nick's head.

It was folly to let Gowan believe in a love that was certainly no more than an illusion cast and created by her aunts. It was folly to pretend that it could ever be anything more.

Folly.

An indiscretion he could walk away from. One he was sure to forget.

One she never would.

The thought roused Nick from the peculiar enchantment caused by the brush of Gowan's lips. It settled in her soul, chilling the secret places warmed by his touch. Her heart squeezing with the ache of longing she knew would always fill her, Nick pushed away.

Ignoring the flicker of desire that glimmered in Gowan's

eyes, she forced her gaze to his. Nick was not quite sure how she did it, but she gave him a smile. "You smell like a barnyard."

"Do I?" Gowan wrinkled his nose. He sniffed the air and his expression went sour even as a warm and thoroughly delightful smile lit his face. "Mrs. Pritchard will be appalled!"

He backed away a step. "You'll have to excuse me. This is hardly the way to make an impression on a woman. I'll call on you when I'm more . . ." He searched for the word and finding it, he chuckled. "More aromatic!"

Delighted to be rid of Gowan and all the unsettling emotions he brought to life, Nick sighed with relief. She was about to turn away in as dignified a retreat as she could manage, when he took her hand.

"Before I go, I think there is something you should know, Nick." Gowan's voice was low and as tempting as the look that shimmered in his eyes. "I've made a promise to myself. Before this summer's out . . ." Grinning, he leaned nearer and whispered the last of it in her ear. "Before this summer's out, I will have you in my bed."

His smile brighter than ever, he turned and walked away.

Nick could not say how long she stood there dumbstruck, staring at the spot where Gowan had been. She only knew she was snapped out of her stupor when Hugh came to stand beside her. He stood as near to her as he dared, following her gaze to where Gowan disappeared onto the path that led back to the village.

"You're in a fine mess."

"You're not telling me anything I don't already know." Nick shook her head, puzzled by the whole thing. "We've got to do something and we've go to do it quickly. He wants to—" She could not bring herself to say the rest aloud. Her cheeks grew hot and before he could notice her embarrassment, she sidestepped away from Hugh and went as far as the gate.

When she got there, she drew in a deep, calming breath and turned. "I think we need to have a talk with the boys in Beddgelert. To invite them here to Rhyd Ddu."

Hugh didn't understand. Not at first. Finally, the significance of her suggestion dawned on him. His eyes went wide and his mouth dropped open. "You mean—?"

"I don't see that we have any choice."

"But you saved the man's life!"

"I don't want to see him dead!" Nick's voice trembled with the feelings that rocketed through her. She folded her fingers into her palms and held them there, clutching tight to her emotions. "I only want to see him gone from here. If we can arrange something between the boys there and the boys here . . . ?"

Hugh didn't answer, but it was clear, the more he thought about the idea, the more it appealed to him. "It is not Gwylmabsant yet." He tried one last argument to dissuade her, the look in his eyes telling her if he succeeded, he would be disappointed.

"No. It is not the Saint's Day. Not our's or Beddgelert's. But even so, we could try."

A slow smile spread over Hugh's face and he rubbed his beefy hands together, savoring the thought. "Yes. Yes." He nodded. "It just might work. He is the earl, after all, he cannot refuse."

"No. He cannot." Nick turned to scan the path toward the village. There was no sign of Gowan and she breathed a sigh of relief at the same time she wondered why she felt so bereft at losing sight of him. "We've got to do something," she said, more to herself than to Hugh. "And we've got to do it soon. Before it is too late."

Thirteen

Staring at the raindrops that streaked the glass, Gowan congratulated himself. For all the other annoyances and inconveniences visited upon him these last weeks, at least he'd had enough proficiency and presence of mind to do something right. He'd gotten the window in his surgery repaired well enough to keep the wet out and the heat—what little of it there was—in.

Turning from the window, he went over to the fireplace. Mrs. Pritchard had managed to kindle a small fire in the grate from the even smaller store of coal in the cellar. Gowan chafed his hands over the flames, marveling at the fact that three days of wet and cold in Wales could feel far wetter and far colder than weeks of rain in London.

Still rubbing his hands together, he did a turn around the room. He knew his restless mood had less to do with the weather than it did with the sense of isolation that sat over the Lodge, as real and as oppressive as the fog that blanketed the mountains. In London, there would have been endless amusements to fill the cold, endless hours: the theater, the opera, music halls, gaming dens, houses of pleasure. With a little imagination and a pocket full of banknotes, a man could occupy himself for an eternity.

Here . . .

Gowan grumbled a word suitable to both his humor and to the occasion.

"Here I meet bulls." Automatically, he rubbed his backside and the huge purple bruise that had shown up within hours of his run-in with Peder "And I watch the rain."

The gloomy thought still foremost in his mind, Gowan went to his desk and sat down. It was bad enough that the weather could so influence his mood, worse still because he knew exactly why the incessant rain annoyed him so.

It confined him to the house.

It restricted him to the Lodge.

It kept him away from Nick.

Gowan drummed his fingers against the desktop. He flipped through the pages of a weeks-old *Times* that had finally found its way to him through the post. He sat that way for some time, and when the front bell rang, he was certainly surprised, but he knew better than to be hopeful.

Sitting back in his chair, Gowan waited for the moment Mrs. Pritchard would come marching in, her face as dour as the weather.

She did not disappoint him.

The door snapped open and Mrs. Pritchard stepped into the room.

Gowan fully expected her to be carrying some small gift, another of the delicious little seedcakes or one of the equally delectable cordials that had been arriving of late with some regularity.

She was not.

Mrs. Pritchard's hands were empty. She clutched them at her waist. She cleared her throat. "There are some . . . er . . . some gentlemen . . ." She gave the word a curious inflection and darted a glance over her shoulder into the passageway and the front door beyond. ". . . some gentlemen here to see you, m'lord."

Gowan hardly needed to be told.

From out in the passageway, he heard the crump of heavy boots and the low rumble of voices.

Not just gentlemen by the sound of things, but a good many gentlemen.

Gowan rose and stood behind the desk. "Did they say what they wanted?"

"They did not." Mrs. Pritchard spoke quite precisely, as if she did not find the telling of it any more satisfactory than the incident itself. "Though certainly I asked. It is my duty, after all. As housekeeper here, it is my responsibility to speak to everyone who might come to call, to determine what they want, and if it is important enough for me to interrupt your work."

Mrs. Pritchard's lips pinched. Her mouth puckered. Though she fought like the devil to keep her eyes on Gowan, he couldn't help but notice that she glanced around the room. Her look said all there was to say about what she thought of that work, and of the lack of it.

She brought herself back to the matter at hand with a shake of her angular shoulders and another glance toward the passageway. "Why they cannot understand that I must fulfill my obligations, is beyond me. They said it was for your ears and yours alone. Expressly, what they said is that it is a matter of which they must speak directly to the earl."

"Did they?" The situation was becoming more and more curious. Gowan rounded the desk and went to the fireplace. Posing himself before it, he clutched his hands behind his back. He raised his chin. He pulled his shoulders back. When he thought he looked as much like an earl as it was possible to look in a room pieced together from cheeseparings and candle ends, he nodded, instructing Mrs. Pritchard to show his callers in.

They were not what he expected, though what he expected, even Gowan wasn't sure.

The group that filed into the surgery was led by Hugh Phillips. He had Iain, the pubkeeper from the Dragon, with him, as well as another dozen lads Gowan recognized by face but did not know by name. They were men from the village and the surrounding steadings, each one of them brawnier than the last, and they tramped in and arranged themselves in single file along the far wall, leaving Hugh and Iain up front to approach Gowan.

"Hope we're not disturbing your lordship, m'lord." That Hugh suddenly found a set of manners and the demeanor to go with them was nearly as surprising as the fact that he had the audacity to be here at all after the Peder debacle. He twisted his cloth cap through his hands. "There's something me and the boys here need to talk to you about."

"Well, not precisely." Iain stepped forward. He wasn't wearing a cap, and his bald head glistened with rain water. "It ain't exactly talkin' we're needin' to do, your lordship. It's not time for talk. Not no more." Iain punched his left fist into his open right hand. "It's time for action."

Gowan was no farther along the road of enlightenment than when they entered the room. He looked from one man to the other, waiting for more of an explanation.

It came from Hugh.

"It's those damned bastards from Beddgelert." As soon as the words were out of his mouth, Hugh reddened from the tip of his well-shaped chin to the top of his well-proportioned forehead. He looked around to be sure Mrs. Pritchard had left the room, and when he was sure she had, relief swept across his face. "They've communicated with us, sir. They've made their position right clear. There's no way out of it now."

It was not the first time since he'd come to Rhyd Ddu that Gowan felt like a man adrift in a very small boat on a very large ocean. Hoping he didn't sound nearly as uncertain as he felt, he looked from Hugh to Iain and back again to Hugh. "No way out of what?"

It's a challenge, that's what it is!" Iain's voice rattled the windows and shook the walls. "A direct challenge. And there's no way we can back down. They've insulted our honor. They've offended our dignity. They've as much as said they know there's no way we can stand the test. That's why we've come to you, you being the earl and all. You've got to stand shoulder to shoulder with us, m'lord. You've got to lead us to victory."

Gowan was not known, to himself or to others, as the kind of man who indulged in flights of fancy. Before he could stop them, images of feudal warfare rose in his mind. Hand-to-hand combat. Pitchforks and staves. Fighting to the death in the streets of Rhyd Ddu.

It was appalling. And uncivilized. It was insane. But before Gowan could tell them as much, there was a general clamor from the men along the wall.

"We'll show them blokes from Beddgelert!" a tall, wiry lad called out. His statement met with a roar of approval.

"Wait a minute!" Gowan put out his hands, signalling the men to quiet down. "This is a little drastic, don't you think. I can't imagine what these chaps from Beddgelert said, but—"

"They said we couldn't win!" Another of the men near the wall stepped forward. He had a square jaw and a dimpled chin. His eyes shone with the fire of battle. "We'll show 'em, won't we lads?"

This time, the entire room shook with their thunderous shouts.

Gowan tried again. "Surely there are better ways to settle quarrels." He directed his comments to Hugh and Iain on the off chance that they might be the two most level-headed of the group. "We simply cannot resort to violence. If we sit down and talk it out—"

"Talk!" Someone echoed Gowan's word. The rest of the men laughed. Even when they stopped, Hugh kept right on laughing. He stepped forward and wiped tears from his eyes. "Seems your thinking is all wrong, your lordship, sir. We ain't talking about fighting them boys from Beddgelert. Not exactly."

"Oh." There was little else Gowan could say. He felt some of the tension that had been building inside him dissolve. "Good. Fine." He managed a weak smile. "Then what are you talking about?"

Hugh's eyes gleamed. His face split with a wide smile that revealed his perfect, pearly teeth. His tongue wrapped around a single word and when he spoke, it was with all the passion of a man for his mistress.

"Rugby."

Before he even realized what he was doing, Gowan found himself smiling back. "Rugger? They've challenged us to a match?"

"That they have!" Iain ran his tongue over his lips. "This Saturday. Noon precisely. We'll show them beggars. Excuse the phraseology, your lordship, but they've been spoilin' for a game. We'll show 'em for certain."

Gowan wasn't sure what Hugh and the rest of them expected from him. As one, they stared at him, gauging his reaction. He couldn't say why, but something told him they weren't expecting enthusiasm.

He was not at all sorry to disappoint them.

For the first time since he'd set foot in Wales, Gowan felt completely at ease. This time when he stood straight and tall and threw back his shoulders, it was with good cause. "I was a fair inside center back at school, you know," he said, and he applauded himself for being enough of a brick not to tell them the whole truth. He was more than a fair inside center. Far more. He was a stellar inside center. His play was legendary, his reputation without equal.

Hugh poked his head toward the tall, wiry lad with the square chin. "Ewell there, he's our inside center. Has been since we played together as boys."

"Very well." Gowan refused to let them know how disappointed he was. "Outside center, then. Surely you'll be needing one of those."

"No." With one hand, Iain rubbed his chin, while with the other, he motioned toward a boy with broad shoulders and a ruddy complexion. "Selwyn here is our outside center."

Gowan had never been a man to believe in the supernatural. He needed only think of Nick's wild claims and her aunts' even wilder behavior to remind himself of that much. Yet he swore at that very place and time, he could see into the future. He knew what was coming and suddenly the pieces of the puzzle fell neatly into place.

They were not here to invite him into the game. They were not here to welcome him—finally and quite belatedly—to the community. They were here to challenge him. They were here to defy him. They were here to make him a proposition they fully expected him to refuse.

Damn them, they would not win so easily. Gowan lifted his chin while he surveyed the group. He kept it high as he met Hugh's gaze eye-to-eye. "You want me to play fullback."

For all his attempts at passing himself off as an unassuming man, Iain was not stupid. Though it was certain Hugh was not bright enough to realize what was going on, Iain saw clear enough that Gowan had worked his way through to the truth of the thing. He had the good sense to look at least a bit shamefaced at his part in it.

"Want ain't the precise word," he said, sucking at his teeth and scratching his ear. "You see, it's like this, your lordship, sir. Once every year, we get together with the lads from Beddgelert for a match. It's somethin' of a tradition, you see. We . . ." He looked over his shoulder at the men against the wall. "Me and the other lads, we always save the spot of fullback for the earl. As an honor of sorts." Iain shuffled his feet against the threadbare carpet.

"Beggin' your pardon, sir, and not to pass judgment on your ancestors even though it don't make no difference if I don't say what I think of them because you already know anyway how we all do feel, but the last earl, he was here for a match one summer well on twenty years ago. Refused to come out of the Lodge to join us, he did. So did the earl before him. It don't look good." Iain shook his head woefully. "Them folks in Beddgelert don't have their own earl like we do. To have your own earl and never have your opponent see hide nor hair of him, it's damned embarrassin', that's what it is."

Better to be embarrassed then to be dead.

The thought rumbled through Gowan's head along with a lengthy list of logical, sensible, and quite rational reasons why he should refuse their ridiculous challenge and show them the door immediately.

In a game played without protective equipment and with no rest but one five-minute period between halves, fullback was by far the most dangerous position on the field. It was a position where Gowan had no experience, and no training. The fullback was the last line of defense for his team, the man who tried to stop the attacking team and the one who was himself generally attacked *en masse* by the opponent.

The position generally went to the tallest, most strapping, and strongest player. By all rights, it should have gone to Hugh.

Except that Hugh's teammates didn't want to see his blood smeared over the field.

And it was clear that's exactly where they wanted to see Gowan's.

It was an ugly thought. Uglier even than standing toe-to-toe with Peder. So was the idea that if the team from Beddgelert was anything at all like the burly lads there in the surgery, Gowan knew beyond a doubt that he was no match for them.

It was foolish to say yes. It was asking for trouble, or worse. It was suicide.

Those were the facts. Plain and simple. Studying them left Gowan no choice.

Raising his chin and squaring his shoulders, he glanced from man to man. He kept his gaze on Iain far longer than he had on the others, and on Hugh even longer than that.

Gowan smiled and accepted.

* * *

"An entire half played and no score." Hugh wiped a trickle of blood and a smudge of mud from his brow with the cloth Nick offered him and shook his head sadly, disappointed by the turn of events. "It's a devil of a situation, is it not?"

"It is, indeed." Nick pursed her lips and thought through the problem.

"Their wingers are fine, tough lads. That's certain enough. And their forwards . . ." Hugh let out a long, low whistle. "It's like hitting a brick wall. Did you see the stand-off and the center trying to get the ball down the field when the match began? They didn't play with the Beddgelert boys last year, that's right enough. I would remember lads as stout as those. And the centers! Did you see the way they came at me when—"

"Hugh." The last thing Nick wanted to hear was a recounting of every play of the first half. She interrupted without a qualm, hoping to remind Hugh of why they were really there. "Hugh, you're thinking about rugby."

Surprise was etched in every muddy line of Hugh's face. "Of course I'm thinking about rugby. And whatever else would you want me to be thinking about at a time like this, woman? The second half starts in five minutes, there must be some strategy we can use to—"

"Hugh!" Nick tapped the toe of her boot against the rain-soaked ground. The skies had cleared only that morning and the sun was shining bright, but the field was saturated. Here along the sidelines where the folks of both Beddgelert and Rhyd Ddu had laid their blankets and set up their picnic lunches, the grass was merely damp. At the center of the wide, open area where the match was being played, it was gone completely. The field was a sea of mud, a good deal of which coated Hugh from head to toe.

"Hugh, I thought we arranged this match for a very particular reason. You're not supposed to be thinking about the game. You're supposed to be thinking about the earl."

"Him?" Hugh poked his chin toward the other side of the field. Nick followed his gaze to where Gowan stood apart from his teammates. Just as they glanced that way, the boys from Rhyd Ddu opened a bottle of liquor and passed it around. Iain was the last of them but Gowan to take a swig. He started to pass the bottle back to the first man, thought better of it, and handed it around to Gowan.

It wasn't much. Just a small gesture. Yet there was no mistaking the fact that Gowan was pleased by it. He accepted the bottle and took as big a draft as anyone else and when he was done, he wiped his mouth in the sleeve of his muddy shirt.

Hugh shook his head in amazement. "It's a wonder, make no mistake about that, Nick. We've done all we could to bring him down. He's been hit, jabbed, and cuffed about the head. His nose is bloodied, his left eye is nearly swollen shut, and I know it as God's honest truth that his right arm was nearly pulled from its socket because I am the man who yanked on it when he was down in a ruck. He has yet to give up. As a matter of fact, he's as happy as a sand-boy. I've never seen a man who loves rugby more."

It wasn't what Hugh said, it was the way he said it, as if it was the grandest praise he could ever give a man, dead or alive. Nick swallowed the sour taste of defeat that rose in her throat. "But Hugh—"

Hugh wasn't listening. One of his mates waved the bottle at him and he trotted over to join them.

"A fine match, don't you think, dear?" Tildy came up behind Nick, chittering like a small, excited animal. She looked to where Gowan was taking another drink and smiled, her cheeks rising like plump, round apples. "We've brought refreshments, you know." Tildy looked over to where Belle and Clea had laid out a plain but satisfying looking meal on the blanket set a slight distance from all the others. "That is, if you are thirsty, dear."

Nick spun away from the disheartening scene of male camaraderie taking place across the field. "I am not thirsty."

"You're still angry at us then?" Tildy's shoulders sagged. She bent her head and looked up at Nick from behind the wisps of hair that floated in front of her eyes. "You haven't forgiven us for trying to save the poor boy's life at Hugh's, have you?"

Nick hauled in a breath designed to calm her frazzled nerves. It did little to help. She managed to keep her voice even, but only because it was Tildy she was talking to, and she couldn't bear to offend her kind-hearted middle aunt. "Don't you understand? You may have thought to save his life, but it didn't work. And I am the one who had to finish what you'd begun. He took it as a good sign, Tildy. He thought I saved him because I . . . because I . . ." The rest was far too awful to put into words. Nick's face reddened. Her voice smothered behind the lump that blocked her throat.

Tildy patted her arm. "I know, dear. It's clear how he feels about you. I suppose, in a way, it is a blessing. Far easier than if he did not love you at all." She sighed and fluttered a hand over her face, waving aside a wisp of hair that dangled in front of her like the gossamer tissue of a spider's web. "I know how frightening the whole thing can be. Before your mother met your father, I thought I might have to be the one." Even after so many years, Nick could see how the memory disturbed Tildy. Her eyes filled with tears. Her lower lip quivered.

"Our magic is the most precious gift we have. And yours more rare than most. The three of us . . ." She looked toward her sisters and a bittersweet smile crossed her face. "We are not as skilled as you, Nick. We never will be. You have a special gift. I know it's hard to believe, but I do understand what you're feeling."

Nick's voice sank beneath the weight of her worries. "Yet you support Belle's cause. You think I should—"

"Good afternoon, Tildy. Nick."

Nick did not have to turn around to know Gowan had come up behind them while they talked. Even if she had not recognized his voice, she would have known he was there. She could feel his nearness. It vibrated in the air like a physical thing. It tingled through her as did his touch, and like cyw haul, the small orbs of light that sometimes surrounded the sun, it surely bespoke misfortune.

"You sound fairly merry for a man who has yet to score a try." Nick's own demeanor was as cold as Tildy's smile was warm and welcoming. She erased any trace of emotion from her face before she turned to him. From Hugh's account and what she'd seen herself of the match, she expected to find evidence of the sound thrashing Gowan had taken on the field, but she hardly expected anything like this.

Gowan's nose wasn't merely bloodied. It showed every sign of being broken. It sat slightly askance in the middle of his handsome face, and Nick was sure there would be a small but permanent bulge at the bridge of it.

Gowan's eye was not simply swollen. It was black and blue. He grinned at her, his teeth dazzling white against his mud-spattered face. "We'll get them in the second half, that's for certain."

Nick hardly knew what to say. The man did not belong on the playing field. He belonged in bed with a poultice of comfrey on his eye and another of boneset on his nose.

And it was all her fault.

Guilt coursed through Nick like water in one of the fast-running streams in the hills. She bit back the exclamation of mortification that nearly escaped her lips and forced herself to sound as cold and unfeeling as she wished she felt. "You're as daft as Hugh."

"Am I?" Gowan seemed to take her appraisal as something of a compliment. "He's a better player than I thought he might be. Did you see the way the centers came at him when—"

"Really!" It was too much for any woman to take. Nick twitched her shoulders and turned away. When she did, it was to the sight of Tildy watching her carefully, a look as artless as morning sunlight upon her face. Beyond Tildy, Belle and Clea mirrored her expression.

Too flustered to face the aunts' pretended innocence, too ashamed to speak to Gowan. Nick mounted as hasty a retreat as she could. "I wouldn't worry about the second half if I were you." She tossed the remark over her shoulder as she hurried away. "There's never been anyone killed in the second half. Not for years and years."

She might have known Gowan would not take the warning to heart. His laughter echoed over the field.

Gowan was still laughing as the second half of play began. He took his place behind Ivar Brown, the village baker and threequarter back who was, that day, playing winger, and waited to make his move. It did not take long.

Gowan took off toward the opposite goal. His arm stiff, his palm open and flat, he handed off a player from the Beddgelert team. He dodged around the man and came up alongside Ivar who saw him coming and tossed him the ball.

"Come on, ye ruddy Saxon!"

Nick would recognize the booming voice anywhere. She turned to find Old Wallace up on his feet, cheering like a madman.

So was every other man, woman, and child from Rhyd Ddu, including the aunts.

Nick stood numb with wonder and amazement. For one second, the thought of using her magic crossed her mind. With the help of her powers, she could stop Gowan easily enough, just as she'd stopped Peder. She could bespell Gowan and make it impossible for him to become the champion of the game and the idol of the crowd. She could put an end, once and for all, to what was quickly turning into a full-fledged disaster.

Fortunately, she did not have long to think upon it. The next thing Nick knew, one of the Beddgelert lads stepped out of nowhere and planted himself directly in front of Gowan. It was too late for Gowan to sidestep him. Too late for Gowan to stop.

He slammed into his opponent at full speed. The man had shoulders a mile wide and a chest that looked to be carved out of solid stone. Gowan hit him and bounced backward. He slammed to the ground. The ball popped out of his hands.

"Damn! You blinking, bloody . . ."

Old Wallace, who was being supplied a narrative of the action by the man who stood beside him, seemingly did not care that there were women and children present. He let loose with a string of invective voiced loudly and with great feeling.

His sentiments were echoed by everyone in the crowd.

While Nick glanced at the crowd, play on the field continued. She turned back to the match to find the Beddgelert team had the ball and all but one of the Rhyd Ddu boys were after it.

The one who was not was Gowan.

Still laying where he'd been downed, Gowan raised himself on his elbows. He shook his head. From where she stood, Nick could not clearly see his face, but it was obvious he was wonky. He staggered to his feet. He shook his head again. His arms out at his sides as if that might help steady the world that was whirling around him, he balanced himself and watched the action going on down field. Hauling in a deep breath, he joined again in the fray.

Much of the second half went the same way.

Each time the lads from Rhyd Ddu took the ball toward the Beddgelert goal line, they were driven back. Each time the Beddgelert boys fought their way to the other side of the field, they were repulsed. Most times, Gowan ended up in the very center of the action.

By the time there were only two minutes left to play in the match, there was so much blood mixed with the mud on Gowan's shirt and trousers, it was difficult to tell where it might be coming from, or even if it was all his.

"Oh, dear." Watching a man from the Beddgelert team hand off Gowan much more roughly than he should have, Clea winced. Tildy closed her eyes. Belle continued to watch, but even her cheeks were pale.

"Men really are the most incredible creatures, are they not?" Clea's voice was breathless. Her eyes were wide. "They actually seem to be enjoying themselves. It's hard to believe. It is so very rough-and-tumble."

They all should have known Tildy would not miss the opportunity to offer her opinion. She opened her eyes and they gleamed with mischief when she glanced around. "Yes," she said. "And from what the village women tell me, it is not the only thing that will take a tumble tonight. This rough play surely stimulates more than just the lads' good sportsmanship."

"Tildy! Really!" Belle's expression went as hard as a bone. "It is the liquor, surely, that excites their bold natures as well as their desires. If you have not noticed, they miss no opportunity to pass their bottle, even while the ball is in play."

"Drink or no drink, mark my words." Sure of her prediction, Tildy nodded solemnly. "We will be whelping a babe or two come winter."

They might have gone on like that forever, Nick knew, Tildy and Belle taking two sides of an issue as they always did and arguing it to death. This time they did not, but only because Clea happened to notice that something remarkable was happening on the field.

"Look!" Clea pointed.

As one, Nick and the aunts turned to stare at the action. They were just in time to see Gowan snatch the ball from one of his opponents and race downfield with it.

"He's done what?" Old Wallace's face went from sour to ecstatic as the fellow next to him delivered the news. "He's done what?" Clutching his friend's arm, the old man leaped about, cheering. "You get 'em, you mangy Saxon bastard!" Old Wallace's shout was half encouragement, half warning. It was taken up by the rest of the crowd.

"Get 'em!" Even Clea and Tildy took up the call. Belle was clearly above joining in such nonsense, but Nick could not fail to notice that she was holding herself so tense and stiff, even her knuckles were white.

The ball still in his hands, Gowan crossed the halfway line and headed straight into a solid line of Beddgelert forwards. He darted and dodged his way around every one of them, so covered with mud, he was nearly impossible to tackle and hold on to.

"He's going to do it! He's going to do it!" Tildy and Clea hugged each other and shrieked.

All around the field, the faces of the Rhyd Ddu people radiated their excitement. The folks who had traveled there from Beddgelert were equally excited, but for just the opposite reason. Their combined shouts of hope and screams of dismay echoed through the surrounding hills and reverberated through Nick's head.

"He is going to do it." Even Nick could not keep herself from repeating the cry, though hers was not nearly as enthusiastic as either Tildy's or Clea's. Her heart sinking as her well-laid plan was obliterated right before her eyes, she watched Gowan eat up the muddy ground between himself and the Beddgelert goal line.

Just as it looked as if he might cross the line and score the winning—and the day's only—try, the powerful Beddgelert man who had downed him earlier stepped into Gowan's path. There was no way around the man and no time to make a decision. In one smooth movement, Gowan let the ball drop and kicked it.

Less than a second later, the Beddgelert man slammed into him. They both went down in the mud.

There was hardly anyone in the crowd who noticed. The people of Rhyd Ddu and the people of Beddgelert held their breaths and watched as the ball sailed over the goal post.

The Rhyd Ddu team won by a score of three to nil.

"He's done it! He's done it!" Tildy and Clea danced with joy. Even Belle smiled. Not one to miss a moment of the excitement, Old Wallace raced onto the field, congratulating both Rhyd Ddu and Beddgelert players as he went, though how he knew who was who was a mystery to Nick.

An open bottle already in his hand, a smile like a sunbeam lighting his face, Hugh ran over to retrieve his cap which he'd left with Iain's daughter. He clapped it on his muddy head and stopped just long enough to talk to Nick. "Ain't it the grandest thing? The best match ever, that's for certain. We're all on our way to the Dragon now to talk about it. Come along, Nick. Bring your aunts. Everyone's going. Even the folks from Beddgelert."

And everyone did go.

Her hopes dashed along with her scheme, Nick watched the crowd thin. Now that the match was over, Rhyd Ddu lads and Beddgelert boys trudged back to the village and the evening of drink and conversation that awaited them, their arms linked, their voices raised in song. They were followed by the spectators, the men already arguing every play of the game, the women exchanging gossip.

Eager to be left alone to give free rein to her disappointment and her misery, Nick waved her aunts on ahead. Thinking that she might collect herbs on her way back to the cottage, she'd brought her blue cloth bag with her. She went to retrieve it at the base of the oak tree where she'd left it, and when she turned back to the playing field, it was deserted and as quiet as a tomb.

Except for one grimy body still sprawled in the mud.

For a moment, Nick thought about turning around right then and there and pretending she hadn't noticed him. She thought about leaving him right where he belonged, and letting him find his own way home.

The next moment, she cursed herself twice: once for having a conscience, and a second time for listening to it.

With a sigh that streamed through the quiet air like the murmur of wind through the trees, Nick picked her way over the field. Gowan lay where he'd been dropped, his arms out at his sides. His eyes were closed, an expression so vacant and so like sleep on his face, Nick wondered if he was dead.

He wasn't.

When her shadow slid over him, Gowan opened his one good eye. He tried to smile and winced instead. His lip was split, his chin caked with a streak of dried blood. So was the cut on his brow. His nose was still bleeding. His eye was blacker and more angry-looking than ever. When he spoke, his voice came out thick through his swollen lips. "Nick!" he said. "We won!"

Fourteen

Struggling to raise himself on his elbows, Gowan glanced around the empty field. What there was of his smile dissolved. "It seems I am still only a ruddy Saxon, even if I did win the match for them."

"It seems you are." It was an easy enough thing to acknowledge, Nick told herself. At least it might have been before that day. Now, she found herself wondering why the truth was so very difficult to admit. Perhaps it was the sad fact that even after all he'd done for them, the lads of Rhyd Ddu had deserted Gowan. Perhaps it was the fleeting wistful look that crossed his poor, battered face when he realized it.

"They've gone to the Dragon," Nick told him and she took no joy in the telling. "And I suppose you know, you have no welcome there." Uneasy with the truth, and all too aware of the guilt that spread through her when she thought about her part in the plot that had left him there in the mud, beaten and bleeding, Nick concentrated on Gowan. She took a long look at him and shook her head, her practiced eye noting the cuts and bruises that showed and imagining the multitude of them that did not.

"You're in need of some tending, that is for certain." She glanced around the field. "Come on." She offered Gowan a hand up. "Let's get you over near those trees where I can take a better look at you."

It wasn't easy getting Gowan up on his feet. It was harder still shepherding him to the sidelines where it was less muddy and where they would both be more comfortable. Nick tried holding onto his hand, but he slid from her grasp. He would have gone right back down in the muck if she hadn't shot out a hand to hold him up and wrapped the other around his shoulders to keep him there. Even that did not make the task much easier. He was far taller than she, and in his coating of mud, he was as slippery as a salmon.

"It's no wonder they couldn't bring you down during the match. They couldn't hold onto you." Nick adjusted her grip at the same time she took Gowan's right arm and linked it around her waist.

How he did it, she was not sure, but Gowan smiled without wincing. "They couldn't bring me down because I was bloody marvelous!"

"Bloody is the word right enough. There's no doubt of that." In the shade of the oak, Nick untangled herself from him and helped him sit, his back to the tree. She knelt beside him and rummaged through her bag. "I did not think to be treating battle injuries. There is not much here that will help what ails you. I only brought those things I thought the ladies of the village might be wanting."

"Really?" Gowan groaned and stretched his legs out in front of him. He leaned his head against the tree. "And what is it the ladies of the village are wanting?"

"The usual." Nick took a bundle of lavender from her bag and set it on the grass beside her. She did the same with a small bunch of dried violets and a sprig of dill. "Some of them ask for mixtures with the power to make a man love them. Others want to lessen their man's ardor. I know which herbs to bring when I am coming to the village." Shaking her head, Nick closed her sack and sat back on her heels. "I do believe you are in need of more than I have here."

"I don't know about that." Gowan took her hand and wound his fingers through hers. "When everyone else deserted me for ale and song, you stayed. That makes me feel better already."

Nick's gaze slid down to where their hands were linked. Gowan's were coated with mud. They slid over her's smoothly, the cool mud a peculiar counterpoint to the heat of his skin.

Suddenly, Nick felt as if she'd played in the rugby match, too. Her breathing was just as irregular as Gowan's, and she was sure her heart was pounding just as hard. She fought for something to say, some bit of conversation that would take her mind off the slippery trace of his fingers over hers and the response it was eliciting from deep inside her.

"I cannot resist the beaten and the battered." Her words were as uncertain as they sounded. "It is a character flaw, I know. If there are those who are ailing, I find myself ministering to them."

"Nick, you may minister to my needs until your heart's content." With a grunt of pain, Gowan managed to sit up. He caught Nick's other hand and pulled her nearer.

Even through the coating of mud that was quickly hardening like the bottom of a dry riverbed, Nick could not fail to see the expression of longing on his face. It sparkled in the bit of a smile he found the strength to offer her.

"You can't possibly kiss me." Somehow, Nick had thought to make her protest much more forceful. It came out sounding breathless instead.

Even though it caused a spasm of pain to cross his face, Gowan chuckled. "Is it the mud you're objecting to?" A smile still on his face and a glint of mischief in his good eye, he brought one very grimy hand up. He cupped Nick's chin and stroked her cheek, leaving a muddy trail in his wake. "There are more kinds of comfort than those that can be obtained from your crumbling plants and noxious potions, Nick. That's all I've ever asked of you, you know. Let me show you some of them."

The feel of his hand against her skin was like sunshine after a storm. It dulled Nick's mind at the same time it heightened every one of her senses. The heavy, earthy fragrance of mud blended with the smells of blood and sweat and tingled through her. The sounds of his rough breathing mingled with hers like the sweet harmony of a choral piece.

As if he were the lodestone and she the element called to its bidding, Nick leaned toward him. She nuzzled her cheek against his hand. "It isn't the mud." Her voice was a whisper. "It's the . . . the . . ."

"And it can't possibly be the fact that I'm injured." Gowan traced a pattern of swirls over Nick's back and she heard his velvety laugh close to her ear. "If I didn't know better, I'd venture to guess that you had something to do with the whole, mad scheme. You are just cheeky enough, I think. And far too clever for your own good. Did you think fifteen stout lads from Beddgelert could accomplish what Peder could not?"

The last thing Nick needed was a reminder of her perfidy. She swallowed her shame and opened her eyes, but she did not dare meet his. "I—"

He did not give her the chance to confess her sins. Gowan grazed a kiss over Nick's eyes, forcing her words to vanish and her eyes to close again.

"I don't want to hear about it." Like the delicate touch of a feather, his statement brushed her skin. "I don't want to hear your reasons . . ." He kissed the very tip of her nose. ". . . Or your complaints . . ." He skimmed his mouth to her ear and traced its shape with the tip of his tongue. ". . . Or your arguments."

His hand at the back of her head, he spread his fingers through her hair. He pressed his forehead to hers and though Nick could not see him clearly so close, she knew he was smiling.

"I don't want you to say anything, Nick. I only want you to let me kiss you."

"Tildy was right, then." It was a ridiculous thing to bring up at a time like this, and Nick knew it. It wasn't her fault. It was as if her mind and her body were suddenly working quite independently of each other, and at quite disparate purposes.

Her body wanted nothing more than to surrender to the tantalizing promise of Gowan's touch. Her mind was not so easily tempted. She scrambled for some bit of conversation that would fill the expectant silence that trembled on the air between them.

"Right? Was she?" Gowan moved back far enough to look into Nick's eyes. "There's a strange occurrence if I ever heard of one. Tildy? Right?" He did not say it with malice, but with a twinkle of devilment in his good eye and as much of a smile as he could manage with his poor, misshapen lips. "What is it Tildy was right about?"

Now that the time had come to explain, Nick found herself uncommonly embarrassed. She averted her eyes and tore at the grass with anxious fingers. "About men," she explained, her voice no more assured than the sudden skip of her heart. "She says that after vigorous physical exercise . . ." That served no purpose but to lead her further into trouble. Nick cleared her throat. "That is, she says that after playing in a match such as you did . . ." That was not much better.

Nick bit back her shame and forced herself to look Gowan in the eye. His good eye. "She says that after athletic competitions, men are more likely to feel amorous."

"Did she?" Gowan's dark brows might have shot up in surprise had they not been hardened in place by his coating of mud. "I didn't realize Tildy was so very sophisticated. How does she know such things?"

"Just because we are none of us married women does not mean we are not worldly wise." Nick held onto the simple explanation like a drowning man grabbing for the last handful of dry land he might ever touch. She wrapped her fingers around it and held on tight, using it to steady the frantic beating of her heart and the flood of unfamiliar and disturbing emotions that threatened to engulf her. "I've seen as much myself. Each time the Beddgelert club plays the lads from Rhyd Ddu. There will be much merrymaking in the village tonight. And not all of it will be drink and song at the Dragon."

"Tildy's a wise woman." Gowan inched closer. His breath brushed her lips. "It would be a shame for the man of the match to miss out on such an important part of the celebration, don't you think?"

Before Nick could answer, he took a curl of her hair in his hands and gently stroked it against his own cheek. "There's only so much a man can take." His words trembled on the rough breath that escaped along with them. "I do believe I have reached that limit, Nick. I've even stopped trying to make sense of the whole thing. Why I feel the way I feel doesn't seem to matter very much any longer. I know only one thing. I've spent days thinking about you, and nights dreaming about you, and the time in between thinking about you and dreaming about you, wanting you."

He twisted the curl around his finger, his gaze so intent upon it, it seemed the most important thing in all the world to him. He unwound the ink-black ringlet and brushed it against Nick's cheek. He glided it over her eyelids and across her nose. He slipped it down her neck and up again before he grazed it against the hollow at the base of her throat.

The smooth, repeated motion was as strangely hypnotic as Gowan's dark gaze. It mesmerized Nick. It held her spellbound. When he slid his mouth to hers, Nick offered no protest.

Bewitched by the flavor of him, and his nearness, and the frenzied beating of his heart so close to hers, Nick invited him to deepen the kiss. When he parted her lips with his tongue, she could no more have resisted than the moon could have withdrawn from the sun's inescapable hold.

He was salty and hot, and the taste of him coursed through her along with the feel of his thumb drawing long, slow strokes across her neck.

Years of loneliness and longing rose up in Nick, so sharply painful as to make her heart ache and her eyes fill with tears. Still, she did not back away. There was as much danger as there was warmth inside the circle of Gowan's arms. There was as much anguish waiting at the end of his kiss as there was promise in it, and more of the isolation that was her lot in life—a separateness made all the more excruciating by this small taste of intimacy.

It did not matter. Not here. Not now.

All that mattered was the warmth of his mouth against hers, and the slow, seductive swirl of his tongue. All that was important was the unbridled sting of passion that heated Nick's blood and the realization that overwhelmed her brain as surely and completely as desire engulfed her body. It was not any man she longed for. It was not any man who could fill the empty places inside her, not any man who could make her forget all that was at stake.

It was this man.

Right now, nothing else mattered in all the world.

Gowan broke away long enough to slide one arm around Nick's waist and the other over her shoulders. In one smooth movement, he turned her around, and with an effort that made him wince from the pain at the same time he smiled from the successful completion of it, he laid her on the ground and stretched himself out beside her.

"I would not have waited so long to kiss you if I knew you would respond so enthusiastically." A tiny smile tickled the corners of Gowan's mouth, cracking the trickle of blood that was dried on his chin. He propped his elbow against the damp grass and cradled his head in his hand, touching a look that burned like fire all down the length of her.

His dark gaze brushed her face. It skimmed her neck. It skipped from one to the next down the row of bone buttons at the front of her gown, lingering there until she was sure he could count each fierce pulse of her heart where it slammed inside her ribs.

Bringing his hand up, Gowan followed the path his eyes had laid. His forefinger slid down the row of buttons and back up again while he trailed his thumb over her breast.

Nick caught her breath but she was too far under his spell to bridle her desires. She looked up into his face and saw her own reflection there in his eyes, her pupils as wide and dark as his. Her mouth was open slightly in surprise. Her lips were parted, her tongue flicking between them, a silent invitation.

Not sure if the purr of contentment she heard was coming from him or from herself, Nick snuggled closer.

"Your poor face!" She knew she was not as moved by pity as she was anxious for any excuse to maintain the physical contact between them. She reached up one hand and stroked his cheek. "It's getting worse by the moment and I have nothing to give you for it."

"Nothing but yourself." Gowan pressed a kiss into the palm of her hand and another to the inside of her wrist. He glided his tongue to where her long, tight sleeve hugged her arm and slipped it beneath the fabric, sampling the flavor of her and smiling his approval against her skin.

"I've been here nearly two months." Gowan's voice was like the rumble of summer thunder. "And all those two months, this is all I've ever wanted."

It was all she wanted, too. It was what she wanted more than anything in the entire world.

Nick bit back the sob that threatened to expose her deepest fears and her most troubling thoughts. How could she explain that it was the exact reason she had to do all she could to be rid of him?

She was saved the trouble when Gowan pulled away.

Even beneath his layer of dirt, she could see the blood drain from his face. "Damn! Look what I've done to you!" Gowan's gaze followed the trail of mud that coated the front of her gown. Grimacing from the effort, he sat up and dug a handkerchief out of his back pocket. It was no cleaner than the rest of his clothing, but he dabbed at Nick's face with it, and when he realized he was not removing the mud as much as he was simply spreading it around, his face screwed into a painful expression made all the more pathetic by his injuries.

Disgusted with himself and with his efforts, Gowan shook his head. "I can't believe it! Here I am trying my damnedest to impress you and—"

"It's not nearly as bad as all that." Disarmed by his sincerity as well as his futile attempts at restoring her to some kind of tidiness, Nick smiled. She brushed off her gown and rubbed the mud from her cheek.

"Isn't it?" How he did it, Nick was not quite sure, but Gowan managed to pull himself to his feet with no more than a smattering of groans. He offered her a hand and helped her up, and when they were standing face-to-face, he didn't let go. He wound his fingers through hers and held her in place, his hold on her as firm as his gaze was intense.

It was just as well he held her, Nick knew. Her knees were weak from his touch. Her head was still spinning from the effect of his kisses. In the swirl that was all that was left of her reasoning and her judgment, she knew she should take this opportunity to leave as quickly as she could. In her heart, she yearned again for the brush of lips and the exhilarating touch of his hands.

She stood her ground, her gaze locked with his, and when he brushed a kiss across her mouth, she knew without a doubt she would cast aside both her reasoning and her judgment in exchange for even one more taste of the ecstasy he offered.

"This is no way for a man to make love to a woman. That's as sure as sure can be. And not the way I have imagined it should be done." He was careful to keep his distance. He wiped one hand against the leg of his trousers, examined it, and wiped it again. It was hardly cleaner than when he began, but it was, at least, drier. Satisfied of that much, he cupped Nick's chin and raised her face to his. "Promise me one thing."

Nick could not have refused if she wanted to, and right then, she was not sure she wanted to. She could not make herself speak, so she nodded instead.

"Promise me you'll come to the Lodge tonight."

The invitation rippled on the air between them, as tempting as any she'd ever received.

"I . . ." Even Nick wasn't certain what she was going to say. She tried again, waiting for the words to tumble out of her mouth. Hoping when they did, they would be the right ones. "I . . ."

"You could bring your herbs and your poultices." A mischievous gleam lit Gowan's face. "At least that is the excuse we could use for your visit."

"Mrs. Pritchard would not like that at all." It was a ridiculous objection, but all Nick could think to say.

"Mrs. Pritchard!" Gowan's expression was a mix of exasperation and amusement. "Mrs. Pritchard is my housekeeper. Not my mother. It's none of her concern if I decide to have a young lady in to visit." Gowan inched closer. He traced the outline of Nick's lips with his tongue.

"It isn't that as much as it is me." Nick tried her best to explain. It wasn't easy when Gowan was standing this close, and harder still when he chose that particular moment to rub his thumb back and forth over her chin. "She doesn't believe, you see. In our magic. She doesn't—"

"It's not your magical powers I'm the least bit concerned about. It's the rest of you. The very physical rest of you." Gowan tapped the tip of her chin with one finger and gave her a look that made her feel as if she were made of wax, and he was the hot sun, slowly but surely melting her. "And you haven't promised yet. Do it, Nick. Tell me you'll come see me. Pretend it is to nurse the injured if you must. Or to drop off one of those bally potions of yours. I don't care what reason you use. Just promise."

"I . . . I can't."

"Can't promise or can't be there?"

"Can't promise. Can't be there." The longer Nick stood so close to Gowan, the more confused she felt. She stepped back and drew in a deep breath. The air did not seem so heated this far from him and her head cleared enough for her to gather her wits. "I cannot promise. I will not be there. I—"

He stopped Nick's protest with a kiss.

"Promise me, Nick." Gowan raised his mouth from hers long enough to let his words vibrate against her lips.

"No." Nick shook her head. It was a feeble gesture at best and she was sure it was no more convincing than the words that strangled against the ball of emotion in her throat. "No. I can't. I—"

He kissed her again.

"Promise me, Nick."

In the heat of his kiss, Nick's resolve evaporated along with her resolution. The only thing left in its wake was a desire so powerful, it filled every inch of her, usurping command of her mind and her heart.

As if her body was no longer under her control, she felt herself nod her agreement, and she could not have done a thing to stop it had she tried.

"You'll be there?"

She nodded again.

"Eight o'clock? That should give me time to get myself cleaned up." He looked at her as one might at an especially naughty child who had a tendency to tell falsehoods. "You're telling me the truth, aren't you? You'll be there?"

Nick swallowed hard. "Yes." It was impossible to even think about the assignation and breathe normally. She took a step back and clutched her hands together at her waist, fighting for control. "I'll be there. I—"

Something lying on the ground caught Nick's eye. She bent to retrieve it. "This must have fallen out of your pocket," she said, picking up the small square of paper. "When you pulled out your handkerchief."

Nick wasn't sure when she realized what it was she had in her hands. She might have believed it was nothing more than it looked to be if Gowan's mouth hadn't fallen open at the same time his cheeks went as red as summer strawberries beneath his veneer of mud.

Nick turned the paper over in her hands and her heart leaped into her throat. She should have recognized it at once and she might have if her head wasn't so addled and her mind so filled with thoughts of Gowan and all his seductive promises.

"Papur y Dewin." Nick's voice sounded as hollow as she suddenly felt. She looked from the paper to Gowan. "It's Papur y Dewin, isn't it? You had it in your pocket. You're carrying the wizard's paper."

"Nick." Gowan rolled his eyes and clicked his tongue. It was a gesture so like the kind Nick imagined he might give an overly hysterical patient that it served little purpose other than to send her anger soaring. "Nick." He reached out, whether for her or for the paper, she wasn't sure.

She didn't wait to find out. Refusing to relinquish the charm, Nick clutched it tighter and backed away. Too optimistic to want to believe the truth of the thing, too pragmatic not to, she unfolded the paper and held it open in her hands.

Through the haze of tears in her eyes, she looked down at the paper and saw the all-too-familiar charm, Abracadabra written over and over, each line of it losing one letter of the word until the whole thing was shaped into an upside-down pyramid, its pointed bottom the single letter "A."

Nick was not sure if it was rage or disappointment that filled her. She thought it was, rather, something in between. Some emotion that snatched away all the warmth of Gowan's skillful kisses and left her feeling cold. Some terrible sensation that made her realize she had been dangerously close to surrendering all that was important to her for something that was no more than a sham offered by a man as false as his promises.

When she spoke, her voice wavered on the fine line between disbelief and anger. "A charm against witches. That's what it is." Nick raised her eyes to his, daring him to lie. "But I suppose you know that, don't you?"

Where he thought to find himself in the middle of planning an especially delicious rendezvous, Gowan found himself in the middle of an argument instead. Frustrated, he raked one hand through his mud-caked hair. "You don't think I believe it, do you?" he asked, attempting a laugh that was meant to be charming and was instead both awkward and painful. "All that nonsense about charms and protection against witches. . . . It's a lot of tripe and onions, that's what it is."

"Then why carry it?" Nick held the paper up between her thumb and forefinger, eyeing it as if it were a snake that might at any moment take it into its head to bite. "You say you don't believe and yet you keep it with you. Are you that afraid of me?" There was a glint of challenge in her eyes, a fire that, the next second, flared at another thought.

"Or do you think it will give you a power of your own?" Nick's voice rose with wonder and simmered with hostility. "The power to have your way with me. Is that why you thought you could treat me so?" For a moment, her gaze fluttered to the ground where only minutes before they had laid side by side, their hearts entwined as nearly as their desires.

"No. Nick, I—"

She didn't give him time to explain. Her eyes glowing with anger, her shoulders rounded with something he hoped was disappointment but knew was disgust instead, Nick flung down the charm. She ground it under her heel into the mud.

"There's for your wizard's paper!" Her lips twisted with distaste, she shot the words at him. "And our arrangement. Man of the match or not, you can be sure of one thing, my lord earl. You'll be spending this night alone."

With that, Nick turned from him and walked away. She was already across the field and on the path that led to the village when Gowan found his voice.

"But, Nick . . ." She went around a bend and disappeared from his sight and Gowan's words dissolved along with the last of his expectations.

"Damn!" He punched one fist into his other hand. He was sorry the moment he did. A pain shot through his fingers and up his arm. He shook it out and weighed his situation.

It did not take him long to make up his mind.

In spite of a cramp in his right leg that made it feel as if it was being wrenched from his body, regardless of the fact that he could scarcely see where he was headed and the realization that he must look as bedraggled and just as filthy as what the cat pulled in from the gutter, he went after her.

He limped across the playing field. He hobbled to the road. Moving as quickly as he could with muscles that felt suddenly as if he'd run straight into the side of a moving lorry, he rounded the corner, and ran squarely into Hugh Phillips.

"There you be!" Hugh put out one hand, but whether it

was to keep Gowan from falling or to keep himself upright, it was difficult to tell.

It was obvious that in the short time since the end of the match, Hugh had done far more than was necessary to quench his thirst. He grabbed onto Gowan's shoulder and looked at him a bit uncertainly, as if trying to focus his eyes.

"Been lookin' all about for you, your lordship, sir." Hugh gave Gowan a muzzy smile. "Ain't we lads?" He looked over his shoulder at the group of men, both from Rhyd Ddu and Beddgelert, who were coming up the road behind him. Even one look at them told Gowan they were in no better shape than Hugh. They passed a bottle between them and one of them took a drink, wiped the lip of the bottle with his sleeve, and offered the liquor to Gowan.

Busy craning his neck to look for any sign of Nick, Gowan accepted the bottle, but he didn't take a drink. When he realized she was already out of sight, his spirits plummeted along with the last of what was left of his hopes.

"Eight o'clock." He mumbled to himself. "Just a few short hours!"

His fantasies of a delightful evening of passion dissolved in the cold light of reality and he turned to Hugh and the others.

"I can't imagine why you'd be looking for me." Gowan hardly cared if they noticed his disappointment and his aggravation. His voice was laced with sarcasm. "Why would you want to find me? Last I heard, I was a ruddy Saxon."

"That was afore you won the match!" Ivar, the baker, gave Gowan a congenial slap on the back. With a motion of his hand, he urged him to take a drink.

Gowan ignored him. He glanced toward the undergrowth that grew along both sides of the road, hoping Nick was still somewhere about.

She wasn't.

A single thought pounded through Gowan's brain: his

plans for the evening were in ruins. So was whatever tenuous relationship he might have been able to forge with Nick in those quiet moments after the match.

With a sigh of resignation, he raised the bottle to the men around him and took a good, long taste, drinking both to them and to himself, and to his bloody bad luck.

Hugh beamed him a smile. "You see, the way we have it figured . . ." He leaned closer and wagged one muddy finger in Gowan's face. "The way we have it figured, any man who can play rugby as well as you . . . well, you can't be all bad. Even if you are a Saxon!"

The other lads let out a cheer and before Gowan could protest, they hoisted him up on their shoulders and carried him in triumph to the Dragon.

By the time the celebration was over, the people of Rhyd Ddu had decided that the Thirteenth Earl of Welshpool was not nearly as odious a person as they'd once thought him to be. After all, the man could play rugby, and he played it with a passion that could not be denied. It was a significant and quite admirable quality, and it said a good deal more about his character than did simply the unfortunate place of his birth or the fact that he happened to be related to the wrong sort of family.

Neither was the earl a poor sport. He fully understood when they explained they'd left him behind at the field by mistake, forgotten where he lay in the mud.

He hardly blushed at all when late in the evening as the ale flowed as freely as the conversation, Hugh regaled the crowd with the story of Peder. As a matter of fact, Gowan laughed the loudest of them all when Hugh came to describe his first encounter with the prize bull, and took over the telling of the story when it came to the part about Hugh roping and holding the beast while he tended to it.

If the folk of the village had any question about Gowan's capacity to hold his liquor, that concern was alleviated, too. He proved himself quite as capable as Hugh or any of the other lads whose thirst was renowned and whose ability to quench it, legendary.

Though his voice was not nearly as agreeable or as melodic as Hugh's, he was a fair singer, as well. He did not hesitate to join in the songs that rattled Iain's rafters, even though he did not know the Welsh words and had to, most times, simply hum along.

If the people of Rhyd Ddu had any cause at all to worry about their new earl, it was only once during the revelry.

It was the only time in an evening replete with merriment, song, and a good deal of drink, when his attention wandered and his singing trailed away. It was the only time his smile vanished and as wistful a look as any of them had ever seen crossed his handsome face.

And that, only when the tall clock that stood in one shadowy corner of the Dragon struck eight.

Fifteen

The music of harp and fiddle swirled through the evening air, merry tunes played in perfect rhythm to the merry footsteps of the men and women who twirled across the makeshift dance floor.

Standing to one side, a cup of ale in his hands and a smile on his face, Gowan tapped his toe in time to the music. He could hardly help himself. The mood was infectious, the air alive with laughter, singing, and the conversation of people who had only so short a time ago been hostile strangers.

Now they were friends.

Gowan was as amazed at the abrupt and startling turn of events as he was at the fact that each time he thought about it, his insides filled with a warm and comfortable feeling he had never had before.

"What do you think, Mrs. P?" Mrs. Pritchard was standing at his side and he turned to her. "Is our celebration a success?"

Mrs. Pritchard snorted. "Our celebration?" She put just enough emphasis on the first word to let him know she thought it a poor choice. "I had nothing to do with it, may I remind you, m'lord. I was not the one who decided to let the village folk have their heathen festival here at the Lodge."

"Heathen? Is it?" Gowan laughed. He lifted his glass in

greeting to Hugh when he whirled by on the dance floor with Melvina, Iain's handsome, large-boned daughter in his arms. "I thought it a long tradition. In both England and Wales. People have been celebrating Midsummer Night for thousands of years."

It was obviously the first thing he'd said in as long as she could remember that Mrs. Pritchard deemed accurate. She raised her spare and ruler-straight eyebrows and her upper lip puckered. "You've said it yourself, m'lord, though it seems you had no idea you were supporting my argument when you did. People have been celebrating the eve of summer for thousands of years. No doubt, the holiday is of pagan origins." Her shoulders shook with the spasm of distaste that coursed through her. "There's nothing but trouble can come from that. I have never participated in such nonsense myself. I would not have this year had you not invited the entire village here."

Gowan was having too fine a time to pay any mind to Mrs. Pritchard's dour predictions. He chuckled and nodded a greeting to Mrs. Hopkins and her husband, Owain. "Yes. And a splendid plan it was, wasn't it? It took a good deal of work to get the place ready, but even you must admit, it was worth every minute." He glanced around and his smile got wider.

Ladies in their finery and men in their Sunday best filled what was at one time the extensive and quite impressive gardens of the Lodge. The area was neither extensive nor impressive these days, but it was a fine sight more presentable than it had been only a week earlier when he'd decided that this year's Midsummer fest should be hosted by the new earl.

Hours of backbreaking work, by Gowan and the other men of the village, had cleared away most of the weeds, revealing paths that had long been choked with bramble and smothered in gorse and heather. The footpaths crisscrossed through the surrounding stands of trees, and lovers, the young and the not so young, walked arm in arm there. Their shadows intertwined in the light of the flaming torches that marked the boundaries of the paths.

The torches mirrored the light of the bonfire that burned in the center of the garden, its embers piled high, its flames leaping to the heavens, rivaling the light of the stars just beginning to glitter in the twilight sky. The flames twisted and danced, washing the revelers in their orange light.

Those who were game enough ran around the bonfire, getting closer and closer to its flames with each passing. As a host and a physician, the display struck Gowan as slightly foolhardy and more than a bit dangerous. But as Hugh had explained when it all began, it was as much a part of the festivities as was the drinking and the song. The closer a person got to the flames, the better, and those who were bold enough to run through the ashes on its edge and cause sparks to fly, were certain to have good luck all year.

Gowan shifted his gaze from the fire that burned bright at the center of his own garden to the bonfires that glittered like fallen stars over the surrounding hills. Each had been kindled to welcome the warm, bright days of summer and chase away the spirits that those who believed in the old ways said prowled this night.

The tune ended and finding it impossible to applaud with his ale cup in his hands, Gowan offered the musicians a smile of appreciation.

"It was a stroke of genius. You have to admit that, Mrs. P." He tried again to brighten his housekeeper's mood, leaning toward her and lowering his voice so that she might think he was sharing a confidence. "They'll talk of this night for a long time to come. Not only of my hospitality, but of your efficiency."

"And expect more of the same." Mrs. Pritchard's lips pinched. "There's only so much mingling those of your station should do with those of theirs." She was so intent on looking down her nose at the people around her, she missed the inelegance of her own statement. "Before you ever know it, they'll think they have the right to come traipsing through the Lodge any time they please. That's all we need." Mrs. Pritchard's sigh fluttered through the evening air. "All of them," she said, underscoring the last word with a roll of her eyes. "Here!"

"Not all of them." Gowan fought to keep his voice as dispassionate as was possible. It was not an easy thing to do. Try as he might, he could not stop himself from scanning the crowd, searching for the flash of midnight-black hair and eyes as gray and unwavering as the ageless mountains that surrounded them.

Like the last time he'd looked for Nick, and the time before, he saw no sign of her, and he shook his head, not sure if the feeling that settled in his gut was one of disappointment or relief.

Gowan knew that one portion of his mind and his heart—and certainly other parts of his anatomy—wanted nothing more than to see Nick and hold her again in his arms. If he had any doubt of that, he need only think of the endless succession of restless nights he'd spent since the day of the rugby match. He could hardly close his eyes but he could see her there in front of him, her lips moist and inviting, her cheeks red with the sudden, startling awareness of her own desire and a passion that rivaled his own.

Another more sensible part of him couldn't help but remember the very different look on Nick's face as she ground the abracadabra charm into the mud.

Her eyes had flashed. Her skin had gone pale. Her expression chilled until it was as cold as stone.

Nick was angry, that was certain. But try as he might to blame his reluctance to face her again on her wrath, Gowan could not. He'd certainly seen Nick angry before, and he had no doubt he'd see her angry again. He could deal with Nick's anger; he had been dealing with it since the very first day they met.

No, it wasn't Nick's anger that made him nervous about seeing her.

It was her pain.

Even so many days after their clash over the Papur y Dewin, the thought made Gowan uneasy. He shifted uncomfortably and tried to make himself concentrate on the dancers as they went by. It was a fruitless endeavor at best and it left him feeling more self-conscious and less untroubled than ever.

No matter what else Nick had been feeling—anger, disgust, even hate—what she felt most was the sting of betrayal. His betrayal. Gowan knew that, and the realization left him chilled in spite of the heat of the bonfire.

"I do not see the Rhys sisters. Or Nick." Not certain if it was to quench his thirst or to drown the emotion that trembled in his voice and threatened to betray him, Gowan took a drink of his ale. He tried his best to sound no more concerned than would any proper host. "Are they like you, Mrs. P.? Averse to spending this night with the folk of the village?"

Before Mrs. Pritchard could answer, a buzz of whispering voices curled through the revelers. As if all Gowan did not dare say was enough to conjure both his fondest wishes and his most dire apprehensions, the crowd parted. Belle, Tildy, and Clea came side by side into the garden. Nick was right behind them.

The drone of voices tapered and drifted away. The music stopped. Silence fell over the garden, a stillness broken only by the crackling of the flames and the swish of ladies skirts as the crowd parted to allow Nick and the aunts closer to the fire.

Passing like wraiths through the crowd, silent and solemn, they went to stand before the dancing blaze. They linked hands and spoke, their voices so low, Gowan had to strain to hear them.

"What's happening? What are they doing?" Gowan's own

voice was hushed to a whisper. He looked to his housekeeper for an explanation.

Mrs. Pritchard's eyes narrowed, but whether from disapproval or because the flames were so bright, Gowan really couldn't say. "They are blessing the fire," she said. "There are those who believe it as necessary to the festivities as lighting the blaze."

Gowan watched as Nick reached into her blue cloth sack. She pulled out a small parcel and set it before the fire. "And now?"

"Solod." The single word from Mrs. Pritchard meant nothing to Gowan and he looked at her in wonder. "The food of the messengers of the dead," she explained, and though he had the distinct feeling she would have liked to roll her eyes and click her tongue at his naivete and the superstitious beliefs of the villagers, she did not. She kept her gaze on Nick and the aunts, her eyes wide, her voice low, and Gowan couldn't help but notice that with one hand, she made the sign against the Evil Eye.

"Little Nick is leaving cheese and a small loaf of bread. For the ghosts, the spirits of the dead who walk this night."

"Hungry spirits, are they?" As quaint as the custom was, it was difficult to pay much attention to the supernatural when the physical occupied Gowan so. At the first sight of Nick, his gut had tightened and his heart had begun a sort of erratic rhythm that, had he been one of his own patients, would have made him confine the poor fellow to bed.

Bed.

There was a thought.

And not one likely to calm him one whit.

His gaze fixed on Nick, Gowan watched her finish the ceremony. She moved back from the fire and once the aunts had joined her at the edges of the crowd, a cheer went up and the music began again.

Gowan sucked in a breath, one designed to bring him from the realms of the magical back into the land of the living. But even once the spell was broken, he could no more shift his gaze from Nick than he could expel her from his thoughts. He watched an endless stream of well-wishers line up to greet her and the aunts, and if Nick was even a trace as uneasy being in Gowan's garden as he was having her there, she showed no sign of it.

Her hair shimmering in the firelight, her skin as radiant as pearls, Nick greeted each person in turn. She accepted the small tokens of their admiration they brought with them, dropping bottles of wine, wheels of cheese, and loaves of bread into her ever-present sack until the sides of it bulged and it looked much too heavy to lift.

The music played on, and once or twice when Gowan wasn't looking, someone refilled his glass. The sky above the garden darkened to indigo. It deepened to black. And still, he watched Nick, until the line of well-wishers dwindled and she and the aunts were left alone.

While the aunts talked among themselves, their heads bent and their voices low, Nick watched the dancers out on the floor. Though she had a smile on her face, Gowan knew better than to be deceived by it. He'd seen her smile before. She didn't do it nearly often enough, but when she did, it was a bright smile, as unabashed as Nick was herself and as genuine as any smile he had ever seen.

Nick's smile as she watched the dancers was bittersweet, and something about it made Gowan examine her more carefully. It didn't take him long to realize that her smile did nothing to disguise her look of wistful longing. It took less time still for him to see that even the deep shadows where she stood with her aunts could not hide the fact that beneath the hem of her dark gown, she was tapping her toe in time to the music.

Gowan had no intention of speaking his heart, especially to Mrs. Pritchard, yet the words came out of him as if of their own accord. "No one's asked her to dance."

"M'lord?" Startled from whatever sullen silence kept her

thoughts as grim as her expression, Mrs. Pritchard turned to him.

Now that he'd begun, there was no turning back, and Gowan knew it. He tipped his head toward where Nick and the aunts stood watching the festivities. "I wouldn't expect the aunts to dance," he said. "Belle would certainly want to lead. Tildy would leave her partner exhausted and confused. And Clea . . . she seems far too timid to get out on the dance floor with people watching all around. But Nick? She's the most fetching woman here. I'm surprised no one's asked Nick to dance."

"It is a ghost night, m'lord. I've told you as much."

"And other nights?" Gowan couldn't help himself; Mrs. Pritchard's answer was hardly helpful. It left his own questions still tapping at the back of his brain. He could no more not ask her to explain than he could keep himself from drawing in his next breath.

Mrs. Pritchard, who prided herself in anticipating the every need and whim of the master of the house, was this time, clearly confused. Even the light of the fire could not soften the look of absolute bewilderment on her face. "Other nights? There's not a soul who would dare. This night or any other night."

"You mean Nick's never danced?"

Mrs. Pritchard did not need to tell him his question was ridiculous; she said as much with a lift of her shoulders and a shake of her head. "I really couldn't say. I told you, m'lord, I am not often present on such occasions. But it does not take much to figure one's way through the thing. There's not a man on the mountain or in all of Wales who is brave enough to get so close to a witch."

Mrs. Pritchard's explanation was so straightforward and so honest, there was no earthly reason it should have made Gowan feel the way it did. But it did.

It made his blood boil. It stirred some demon inside him

he had not even realized existed. Some devil that urged him to take action and damn the consequences.

At that moment, Iain happened to walk by. Gowan grabbed Mrs. Pritchard's hand and thrust it into the hand of the publican. "Here. Why don't you and Mrs. Pritchard have a dance?"

He didn't wait to hear what either Iain or Mrs. Pritchard might say. The last thing he saw as he wound his way through the crowd and over to the far side of the garden, was the couple as they spun by on the dance floor. His feet moving furiously, his arms tight around his partner, Iain had a grin on his face as impish as any Gowan had ever seen. Mrs. Pritchard looked nothing if not surprised. Somehow, her hair had come loose. It floated behind her like the tail of a galloping horse. Her eyes were wide, her cheeks were as red as apples, and damn him for a fool if he was wrong, but Gowan could swear she actually had a smile on her face.

Brushing his hands together, he dismissed all thoughts of Iain and his housekeeper and concentrated on the problem at hand. He pulled his shoulders back, and prayed he had the strength—or was it the folly?—to stand up to whatever Nick had in store for him.

The entire time they'd been at the festivities, the aunts had done no more than talk among themselves and exchange pleasantries with the people around them. It was no wonder Nick noticed so sudden a change in their demeanor. Out of the corner of her eye, she saw Tildy poke Belle in the ribs with one elbow. She turned to see Clea twittering as only Clea could.

By the time Nick realized Gowan was headed straight for her, it was too late to do anything but stand her ground and wait for him.

Like one of the ghosts said to haunt this night, he materialized from the far side of the bonfire. The shifting flames threw patterns across him so that one moment he was caressed with fire, the next, with shadow. The strange, stirring light made him look unreal, so much like the images of him that had of late been frequenting her dreams, that Nick caught her breath and held it, expecting him to disappear at any moment.

He didn't, and she watched as a burst of sparks erupted out of the fire, reminding her that she was very much awake and still very angry at Gowan for his treachery. They had a great deal to settle between them, not the least of which was the Papur y Dewin.

Clutching her hands at her waist, Nick prepared a broadside, rehearsing inside her head all the things she'd wished she'd said to him that day she discovered that he carried the wizard's paper.

It would have been decidedly easier to concentrate on her anger if Gowan did not look quite as splendid as he did. In the days that had passed since the rugby match, his wounds were nearly mended. His lip was healed. The gash on his brow had closed. His eye was no longer swollen. If it wasn't for her training and the gift she had for treating illness, she might never have noticed the slight discoloration along his cheekbone and jaw. If nothing else, the color made his cheekbones more distinct and made his face look as if it had been carved from stone.

A stranger coming on the festivities unaware would have had no trouble recognizing Gowan as lord of the manor. His dark trousers and jacket fit him as only finely tailor-made clothes could. His white shirt with its stiff collar and white tie were radiant in the light of the fire.

He looked marvelous, right enough. Nick admitted that much to herself.

And she'd be damned if she'd let him know it.

She braced herself, ready to lash out at Gowan the moment he came near.

He didn't give her the chance.

With no more than a nod and a smile in the aunts' direction, Gowan pulled to a stop in front of Nick. "Dance with me?"

As suddenly as every clever and indignant salvo entered Nick's head, it was gone completely, blown away by Gowan's perfectly preposterous invitation.

"They're starting." Gowan glanced over his shoulder. The fiddler was tuning his instrument. The dancers were lining up, men opposite their women partners.

Nick ran her tongue over her lips, and refused, on matter of principle, to look over at her aunts. She had no need. She knew they were watching the little drama as if their very lives depended on it: all ears, all eyes, and with all their hopes as far aloft as they could possibly get. "I . . . I can't."

"Can't?" Gowan looked down at her with something like amusement sparkling in his eyes. "Or won't?"

"Can't." Nick shuffled her feet. It was bad enough that her aunts were watching so carefully. It was worse still when she realized the rest of Rhyd Ddu had stopped what they were doing to watch, as well. Nick had no doubt they knew exactly why Gowan had crossed the garden, just as she had no doubt they were, each and every one of them, amazed by his courage as well as his foolishness. If they thought him a brave man before that night, they had certainly been mistaken. The collective intake of breaths Nick heard could only mean one thing: they never thought any man brave enough to hazard a dance with a witch.

Nick tossed her head and threw a look over Gowan's shoulder to where the folk of the village waited expectantly, their curiosity piqued and their expressions anxious. "Can't. Won't. There's little difference as far as I can see."

"Then you don't want to dance?" Like an apple on a tree, Gowan dangled the question in front of her. When she hesitated long enough to make it look like she might not answer it at all, he took a step back and turned away.

"I . . ." Nick could hardly help herself. The temptation

was too great. She darted forward and laid one hand on his sleeve. "I do," she admitted. "More than anything." She swallowed her pride and lowered her voice. "But I can't. I've never danced, you see. I don't know how."

She expected Gowan to be surprised and she would not have been at all astonished if he was appalled at her lack of social grace as well. Instead, he threw his head back and laughed, and before she could either object or withdraw, he grabbed her hand and dragged her out onto the floor.

"It's easy," he said, leading her to a place at the end of the line of waiting women. "They're doing the kinds of country dances I learned when I was a boy. You must have watched enough times to know them by now. We'll move through a series of figures. Just watch the top couple." He glanced toward the head of the line where Hugh waited across from Melvina. "We'll do as they do when it's our turn."

Nick suspected it sounded far easier than it looked, and she was sure it would have been far less stressful had not every person there been watching so closely. It was little consolation when she realized they were no longer watching her. They were carefully watching Gowan, waiting, no doubt, to see what terrible fate might befall him as a result of his indiscretion.

Ignoring them all, especially Gowan who was standing across from her beaming like a man who had just won a particularly savory prize at an especially difficult game, Nick concentrated on the music.

Because she could not watch Melvina easily without bending at the waist and peering down the long column of ladies waiting their turn to complete their figures, Nick watched Hugh. When the music began Hugh approached Melvina. He bowed, and moved back into place. Melvina moved forward and curtsied to him before they linked arms, spun around and each went back to their respective starting places.

The figure was repeated by the next couple, and the next and the next down the line. Watching each of them in turn, the tension wound tight in Nick, like a clock spring. The boisterous rhythm of the music made it nearly impossible to keep still. When the couple next to them finished the figure, Nick caught her breath and waited.

Like a person dreaming, she watched Gowan move forward until he was at the center of the line between the men and women. He stopped there. "I owe you an apology." He bowed and moved back into place.

Following the pattern set by the other dancers, Nick moved forward to the center of the line. She curtsied. "There's the first bit of truth you've spoken in as long as I can remember."

Again, Gowan moved forward. He linked his arm through hers and for one giddy moment, he twirled her around, his voice coming out of the swirl of excitement and music that surrounded her. "Then you forgive me?"

She didn't answer. She couldn't catch her breath, and even if she could, she was not certain what she might have said.

The next thing she knew, Nick was back in the place where she'd started, slightly out of breath, but whether from the dance or the heady feeling of being so close to Gowan, she really couldn't say.

She chanced a glance at him. "Do you?" He mouthed the words.

Nick used the excuse of the music and the whirl of activity to pretend she didn't understand.

For what seemed far too long a time, they stood there staring at each other, waiting for the interminable figures to be completed by the couples ahead of them. When it was their turn again, Gowan clasped one arm around Nick's waist and led her down the center of two lines formed by the other dancers. He hardly watched where he was headed, his gaze was so intent on Nick.

"I asked if you forgive me."

"The wizard's paper is a very powerful charm."

"Yet it didn't work."

They parted at the top of the line, turned, and met again at the middle, prepared to come back down.

No sooner was Gowan's arm around her again, his hand steady and warm against the curve where her waist met her hips, then he turned to her, a question in his eyes as well as on his lips. "Well, did it?"

It didn't, and Nick knew it. If the charm had any power, they wouldn't be dancing together. But simply because she recognized a thing as true didn't mean she had to admit it, especially in this instance. She met Gowan's probing look with one of her own, daring him to contradict her. "It is a charm against witches."

"Yes." Gowan admitted as much with a long-suffering sigh. "It is. But I wasn't the one who—"

For good or ill, it was all he had time to say. They returned to their place at the bottom of the line and parted company again.

As if dancing alone to the rhythm of his frustration, Gowan folded his arms across his chest and for the next few beats, stomped his feet restlessly. Even that, apparently, was not enough to help.

"Damn!" His voice rang out, louder than the music. It was so thunderous and so unexpected, Nick sucked in a sharp breath.

She was not the only one who was startled. The musicians stopped playing. The other dancers froze in place. More than one person standing alongside the dance floor stood as if spellbound, their ale cups raised to their lips along with their hopes of a little excitement and a bit of gossip to add some spice to the flavor of the evening. Their mouths open in surprise, their eyes sparkling with the conviction that they must surely have been right all along and the poor man must certainly have been affected by his nearness to Nick, the entire crowd stared at Gowan.

There wasn't a soul who dared dispute him or ask what it was that distressed him so. He was the earl, after all, and even in a village where they put little stock in a man's title and less still in his lineage if he happened to have the unfortunate luck of being born on the wrong side of the border, they knew enough to know rank had certain privileges.

This was one of them.

If the earl decided that the music should end or that the festivities themselves were over, it was his right.

Gowan's footsteps pounded against the wooden dance floor in perfect rhythm to the throbbing of Nick's heart.

"There's only so much a man can take! Don't you think?" Gowan cast a glance all around. "A man makes mistakes, doesn't he? Damn, but I've taken all I'm going to take. There's no reasoning with the woman." He poked one finger in Nick's direction. "She's as stubborn as a blacksmith's bootlace and as headstrong as any woman I've ever met. There's only one thing to do."

Nick might have protested had she had the opportunity. Or the presence of mind.

She had neither. She stood as transfixed as was the rest of the crowd, waiting to see what Gowan might do next.

He did not make her wait long.

Without another word, or another look at her, Gowan strode over to the musicians, bent his head, and whispered something to them.

The fiddler looked at the harpist uncertainly. Both men shrugged but it was clear from the start, they did not dare to disagree, not with a man who was bewitched and acting like Tom o' Bedlam because of it. They nodded and consulted each other. By the time Gowan walked away from them, they had already begun the strains of a slow and rhythmic tune.

As little as Nick knew of music and dancing, she knew

it was not qûite a waltz, for she was sure the musicians, being local men, never heard the kind of waltzes that she knew were so popular in cities. This was more of a two-step, the strains of it achingly sweet, the melody, mesmerizing.

The folk of Rhyd Ddu were more than aware of the proper etiquette that accompanied such a momentous occasion as the playing of something that did, at least, approximate a waltz. They stepped back and allowed the earl to lead the dance.

His expression devoid of emotion, but his eyes sparkling, Gowan crossed the dance floor and this time when he bowed to Nick, it was the low, stately sort of gesture she imagined he had practiced countless nights in countless drawing rooms with countless young ladies. When he held out his hand, though, his smile was only for her.

"May I have this dance?"

At the same time mortification caused a rush of blood to surge into her cheeks, Nick's voice caught in her throat. "I . . . I could scarcely follow the figures when I had other dancers to watch. How can I possibly—"

He didn't listen to her objections.

Wrapping one arm around Nick's waist, Gowan took her hand in his and swung her into the dance.

Sixteen

It was terrifying.

Trying desperately to keep her composure at the same time she worried about her balance, Nick chewed on her lower lip and looked down at her feet.

"None of that." Gowan loosened his hold on her long enough to crook one finger beneath her chin. He raised her face to his and when her feet hesitated and she lost count completely, he hardly seemed to care. With the ease of long practice, he guided her back into the rhythm, each movement so effortless and so unobtrusive as to make it seem as much her doing as his.

Now that he had her attention, Gowan slipped his hand from her chin to her throat. He stroked his thumb across her skin. "I didn't ask them to play a waltz so you could stare at your boot tops," he said.

The heat of his touch tingled through Nick. It produced a dizzy feeling in her head quite apart from the lightheaded sensation brought on by the swirling, hypnotic steps of the dance. Perhaps Gowan was both conscious of her confusion and sympathetic to it. He caressed her neck for no more than a moment before he moved his hand away. He circled her waist again and with the slightest bit of pressure, he drew her closer.

"I'm sorry if I had to be so dramatic about it, but you have to agree, I've been pushed far beyond my limit." He raised his brows. "And there are certain things a man can say to a woman only when she's in his arms. I wasn't getting a chance to talk. And you weren't listening at any rate. We've some things we need to discuss, Nick."

Nick ignored the reflection of the bonfire that turned his eyes from brown to copper. She ignored the firm hold he had on her hand and the way the pulse in his wrist drummed against hers. Even though she was certain, to her dismay, that she had lost what little control she had of her will, she fought to govern her voice. "Such as?"

"Such as the fact that it doesn't matter where I got that blasted wizard's paper any more than it matters that I don't believe in such nonsense. It's a silly sort of thing. That's what I think. But you put a great deal of stock in it. I realize that, too. That's all that's important. I want you to know, I never meant it to offend you. And I certainly never meant to hurt you. I'm sorry, Nick."

His words rippled the air between them, as tender as his look, as warm as a caress. They warmed Nick through.

It was a delicious feeling, and as dangerous as it was delectable.

Struggling to rid herself of it, she grappled for the words to fill the uncomfortable silence. "It was kind of you to ask me to dance."

"Kind?" A half-smile of puzzlement and disbelief lit Gowan's expression. "I am hardly a charitable institution. You know that. Kindness had nothing to do with it. And neither did proving anything to the people of the village, in case you're about to accuse me of that."

They twirled closer to the bonfire and Nick saw the aunts there watching along with everyone else who was not out on the floor.

"I asked you to dance because I wanted to dance with you."

"And you're not afraid?"

Gowan smiled. "I could no more be afraid of you than I could be of the sun that rises in the morning sky, or the moon that lights the night." He bent closer, his mouth against hers. "I've told you before, Nick, I love you."

Nick's heart thudded to a stop, as did her feet, so quickly that Gowan nearly tripped and brought them both down in a heap. While he was still recovering from the surprise, she yanked her hand out of his grasp.

"I have to go." Nick didn't care that when they stopped dancing, so did every other couple on the floor. She didn't care that every pair of eyes was on them and that, already, tongues were wagging. Panic snatched her breath and blocked her throat and nothing could erase it, not even the look of absolute bafflement on Gowan's face.

"I can't stay." She backed away a step and looked from side to side, hoping to determine the best route of escape. "That is, I don't want to . . . I can't . . . Good night!"

Without another thought to the scene she had caused or the mortification she could already feel heating her face, Nick ran off the dance floor.

Deserted so unceremoniously and so publicly, there was only one thing for Gowan to do. He stood in the center of the floor and stared like a simpleton, his gaze fixed to the place where only a second ago, Nick had been.

"Damn!" As stunned as he had ever been, he mumbled the word below his breath and watched Nick retreat hell-for-leather. He hardly had time to think the predicament through.

The next thing he knew, Nick spun around. Her dark skirts flying, she bounded back up on the dance floor and darted over to him.

Her face was red from her brow to her chin. Her hands were shaking. She refused to meet his eyes. Before Gowan could say a word or recover from the surprise of seeing her again so soon, she raised herself on her toes and kissed his cheek. "Thank you," she said. "For the evening. For the dance."

And before he could recover enough to reply, she was gone.

Gowan knew without a doubt that the folk of the village would talk about that night for years to come. He could hear their voices inside his head: the ones who told of the earl who'd been enchanted. The ones who spoke of the beautiful young witch who had cast her spell over him. The ones who remembered how they stood, their mouths open and their brows raised, when against all that was sensible and all that was sane and all that was both wise and proper, he went chasing off into the night like a madman, looking for her.

It did him little good.

Gowan was already to the place where he'd last seen Nick when he realized he'd never find her. Not if she didn't want to be found.

"Damn!" Slapping one hand against his thigh, he pulled to a stop and tossed a scathing look over his shoulder at the people who were watching him as if he were some especially peculiar attraction in a circus sideshow. "Damn!"

The echo of his curse had barely died when the aunts appeared. It was a complete mystery to Gowan how they found their way to his side so quickly. They simply were there. They stood shoulder to shoulder and as one, gazed into the deep shadows where Nick had disappeared before they turned their collective attention in his direction.

"Poor dear." Clea shook her head sadly, her expression so vacant, it was impossible for Gowan to gauge which of them she meant, Nick or himself.

"She hardly knows how to handle you, I'm afraid," Tildy added.

"She hardly knows how to handle me?" Though he feared it was far too late to save face, Gowan was eager to disguise his frustration. He crossed his arms over his chest and settled his weight back on one foot. "If I could look inside her head, I swear it would be as chaotic as a church jumble. I'm convinced the woman doesn't know what she wants. One second she's warmhearted and affectionate. The next—"

"She's frightened half to death."

The statement was extraordinary enough in itself. Coming from Belle, it was doubly remarkable.

"What's that you say? Nick? Frightened?" Gowan could hardly help it. He laughed. "As frightened as the pope is of the devil! I've never known a woman who was braver. Or more steadfast. Frightened you say? Impossible!"

"It is a fine night for a walk, I think." With a shake of her head that sent her silvery hair flying, Tildy changed the subject completely. She gave Gowan a scramblebrained look, as if she hadn't been following the conversation at all. "The moon will be up soon and the sky is clear. They say a night such as this is wondrous. More so on the mountains. On the mountains, it is magic."

Magic was the last thing Gowan wished to think about. He let go a sigh of frustration.

Beneath the full power of the glare he shot at her, Tildy's face paled. "Or perhaps not," she mumbled. Hugh walked by with a cup of ale in his hands and Tildy took it from him. Clutching it tightly, she held it out to Gowan, a peace offering of sorts. "Perhaps you know best, m'lord. Perhaps you should stay here with your guests. After all, it is a celebration . . ."

Presenting the cup to Gowan, Tildy let the rest of her apology go unspoken. When Belle and Clea turned to leave, she followed in their wake, but not before she glanced over her shoulder at him one last time. Tildy's face broke into a smile. Her eyes glittered like fallen stars.

It was no wonder Nick was so impossible.

The thought settled in Gowan's gut, tugging at it like the remnants of a bad meal.

What effect must a lifetime with the aunts have, when even a few moments with them left a man feeling as if he'd been sucked in by some Celtic Scylla and spit out again by a Welsh Charybdis?

Gowan shook his head to clear it, but by then the rankling question would not be so easily dislodged. There was nothing for it but to wash it away.

Holding up the cup in mock salute to the three weird sisters, he drained it and went in search of something—anything—that would take his mind off Nick.

He never found it.

The buzz of conversation around Gowan did nothing at all to soothe his restlessness. The laughter of his guests did even less. It was damnably hot near the fire and he went to stand farther from it, loosening his tie as he did. When the music began again, he found it intolerably loud, and he moved farther still from the commotion.

Taking up a stand at the edge of the garden where he would be neither noticed nor bothered, Gowan passed one hand over his brow. The dancers out on the floor faded and blurred. He shook his head. The firelight dimmed. As if there were an invisible hand around it, cutting off his air, his throat tightened.

"Damn!" More annoyed than alarmed, Gowan grumbled to himself. Though he didn't remember how much he'd had to drink, it was painfully clear it had been too much.

The realization made him feel even worse.

He had never had the problem in London. That was for certain. Back in London, he was known as a man who could hold his liquor with the best of them.

Hell, he had been the best of them.

Now here he stood like a green and callow boy whose first taste of liquor had gone right to his head. His insides were twisted. His heart was pounding like an army band. He had yet to go to sleep, and already, he was feeling like the morning after the night before.

Irritated, Gowan decided there was only one thing to do. It was the same thing he always did back in London in the wee hours of the morning when the cards were long since set aside and the pretty faces on the painted trollops were long since faded, when the liquor bottles were long since empty and the obligatory camaraderie that had sustained him through an evening with tiresome colleagues and toadying acquaintances had long since paled.

He would walk it off.

By the time Gowan realized he felt better, he had walked all the way from the Lodge to the track that led over the mountain and to the aunts' cottage beyond. He stopped and eyed the path as if there were some monster lying in wait on the other side of the mist that was just beginning to collect in the hollows.

He may have been foolish enough to torment himself with a dance with Nick. He may have been indiscreet enough to allow thoughts of her to nudge aside everything else in his head and take up permanent residence in his heart.

But he knew better than to risk either his pride or his reason in another confrontation with her. At least that night.

With an express and quite explicit admonition to himself to put all thoughts of what lay at the other end of the path out of his mind, he turned and headed toward home.

Instantly, the weight on his chest felt as if it had been lifted. "That's better." Gowan drew in a deep breath. He knuckled his eyes and noticed, with more than a little relief, that his vision had cleared. The stars above his head shone bright and distinct. The outlines of the mountains that loomed over him were unclouded.

Stretching, he savored the feeling that shot through his head and refreshed him like a slap of cold water. It wasn't the way he usually felt after a night of consuming too much liquor in too little time.

It was the way he felt a day or two later.

Fresh. Alert. With the world open to him like an oyster and the fire of ambition and excitement in his gut. It was as if, suddenly and for no reason he could fathom, his head was open to not only the probabilities of life, but the possibilities, as well.

Humming a tune, Gowan skirted the village and came around the Lodge from the back side. When he got there, he pulled to a stop and looked around in astonishment.

The garden was deserted.

The dance floor was empty. There was little left of the bonfire other than a smoldering mound of twigs and an occasional spark that caught in the night air and disappeared on the breeze. The torches that lit the paths were out. The musicians were gone.

So was everyone else.

Automatically, Gowan felt in his fob pocket for his watch. It was nearly midnight and he found himself endeavoring to tally the distance he'd covered on his walk with the amount of time that had passed.

It was no use.

It made no sense. No sense at all.

Shaking his head and promising himself he'd work his way through the problem in the morning, Gowan headed across the garden and toward the house.

He was almost there when he saw something out of the corner of his eye.

A flash. Nothing more. A flash that came from the stand of trees at the far side of the garden. An instant's light that glimmered like moonlight against water.

It was hardly a curious thing, or it might not have been except that he was certain there was no water there, and the moon was, at that moment, hiding behind a fat, fleecy cloud.

The light winked at him again and curious, Gowan approached the place where he'd seen it spark. He told himself it was probably nothing more than an animal, or some hapless and quite squiffy lad who had lost his way in the dark. He held the thought, completely ignoring the small voice inside his head that reminded him both of Mrs. Pritchard's warnings and Tildy's predictions.

It was a ghost night. So Mrs. Pritchard had said. It was a night when the messengers of the dead roamed through the misty mountains, searching for the gifts of bread and cheese left beside countless fires.

Tildy, of course, had not taken nearly so dreary a view. She had told him that such a night on the mountain was magic.

Given a choice, Gowan thought he would much prefer the magic.

Chiding himself for giving either theory even so much consideration, Gowan headed down the path that led into the trees. The torches had sputtered out long ago. The darkness was complete except for the flash of light that teased him again from up ahead.

In spite of the stern lecture he gave himself about the impossibility of ghosts and the improbability of magic, Gowan paused when he came to the clearing at the center of the trees. He looked all around.

There wasn't anyone there.

Not sure if he should feel relieved or perhaps alarmed, he stepped into the clearing and took another look. Even in the dark, he knew it would be difficult for someone to hide there. Though tall trees surrounded the area like a living wall, there was little more in the center of them than a carpet of bracken broken only by an outcropping of stone and a tussock or two of heather.

And an aroma.

Staggered by the realization, Gowan took a deep breath. The scent was not like bracken and heather at all, but something else. Something he had never smelled before. Something that tingled through his blood and sparkled through his head like the bubbles in a champagne glass.

His brain spinning, his blood sizzling, Gowan took a step into the center of the clearing and looked up. Above him, a million stars danced in the sky. Here and there, a cloud drifted by, a fat sheep in a field of onyx. Moonlight trembled from behind one of the clouds, lighting its edges with silver.

Gowan could have sworn he was alone, the only living being in a universe as vast as it was exquisite, and surely the only person in the garden. Yet in the brief flicker of moonlight, he could have sworn he saw something move near the far trees.

"Is someone there?" His heart suddenly in his throat, he narrowed his eyes and focused his gaze across the clearing. "I said, is someone there? Are you—?"

The moon floated out from behind a cloud and silver light flooded the tiny clearing. For the first time, Gowan knew he wasn't alone.

Nick was there with him. Standing not ten feet away.

Gowan pulled in a breath so sharp it stung his lungs. His heart banged against his ribs, right before it rose into his throat. Like the moonlight that flowed from the heavens, his gaze moved down from Nick's face, and a sensation as sweet as it was piercing squeezed his heart and tightened through his gut.

Nick's hair was loose over her shoulders. It covered her breasts and trailed to her waist, but there was no mistaking that except for her veil of hair, there was not a thing between her skin and the soft night air.

She was completely naked.

Seventeen

Nick's skin was as smooth as silk and as white as alabaster. Her lips were moist. The words that whispered past them invited Gowan closer.

He may have been startled. He may even have been stunned. But Gowan knew one thing for certain. He was not stupid. He did not hesitate and he did not wait for her to ask again. In two strides, he closed the space between them and scooped Nick into his arms.

She felt like a dream. She looked like a vision, her eyes shimmering in the moonlight, her pupils so wide as to look black and deep, bottomless enough for a man to get lost in.

Gowan breathed in the incredible scent that blanketed Nick like a cloud. The aroma brought to mind the heather and bracken that surrounded them, but there was more to it than that. It was the perfume of the woods and the mountains, the fragrance of the night and the stars. It was the incredible and quite distinct aroma of desire, and it sizzled through his bloodstream like a drug.

Surely as aware of the hunger that pounded through his body as she was of her own, Nick pulled away from Gowan just enough for him to see all of her she wanted him to see: the veil of inky black hair that brushed her shoulders and hid her breasts, the silky plane of her belly, the secret shadows that lay below, so near the place where his hands caressed the smooth curve of her hips.

When she was certain he had seen all and appreciated

it, she stepped back. As wanton as any Cyprian who worked the houses of pleasure in London's fashionable districts and as bold as one of the street whores who walked the alleyways in the city's shabbier quarters, she tossed back her hair.

Moonlight flowed over her shoulders. It touched her breasts. It turned her skin from alabaster to silver.

Nick followed the path the moonlight traced. She smoothed her hands over her shoulders. She trailed them down even further. Her eyes never leaving Gowan's, she slowly traced the shape of her breasts with one finger, and in spite of the heat that shot fire through his body, Gowan shivered.

When she reached for his hand and brought it to her heart, he was like a man spellbound. He stood transfixed, feeling neither the stroke of the breeze that tossed the leaves above their heads nor the touch of Nick's hand. He felt nothing. Nothing but her heart pounding out the message of her desire against his palm.

The realization was enough to cause Gowan to pull himself back to reality. He came around to find Nick watching him carefully, a sly smile on her face. Looking as satisfied as a cat with its whiskers in a bowl of cream, she laid both her hands over his and bit by excruciating bit, she guided him over every inch of her silky flesh. She smoothed his hand along one breast, then the other. She glided it over her ribs and down to her abdomen. She tucked it between her legs.

With a moan of delight, Nick caught her lower lip between her teeth. She arched her back and tilted her hips. She rocked against him, the movement smooth and slow, the rhythm hypnotic, tempting him to deepen the touch.

Gowan caught his breath. Nick might not have been able to read the thoughts that ran rampant through his head, but she could surely see the evidence of his desire. Still smiling, she slipped one hand across the front of Gowan's trousers and when he groaned, she laughed and tore at his clothing.

Her fingers impatient and eager, she drew his tie away from his collar and tossed it over her shoulder. She worked free the mother of pearl studs at the front of his shirt and dropped them to the ground. Tugging his shirt open, she pushed it down over his shoulders.

A tiny smile tugging her lips, Nick took hold of his hand and led him to a place where the bracken was soft and deep. She knelt and patted the place beside her, inviting him to lay with her.

In spite of the taste of desire that filled his mouth and blocked his throat, Gowan managed a tight laugh. Damn him for a fool but beneath the uncharacteristic and quite candid look Nick aimed directly at the front of his trousers, he could swear he was blushing.

An inexplicable and quite queasy sensation filled Gowan. The long days of wanting Nick and the still longer nights of dreaming about her solidified inside him, robbing him of his speech, rooting him to the spot.

What other reason could there be? What else would account for the small niggle of uncertainty that suddenly gnawed at the edges of his desire and left him doubting himself, and her, and each and every one of the delicious temptations she so openly offered?

"Too much. Too soon." Gowan could swear he had not spoken the words or even thought them through, yet he knew full well the sound of his own voice. And he knew what he said was true.

Even after all these months of wanting Nick, even after all these months of waiting for her, there was no denying the fact.

This was too much. It was too soon. It was too fast. Everything he'd ever wanted was right there before him, and he was completely incapable of moving, and damnably and inexplicably reluctant to take Nick as he had dreamed of taking her a hundred times before.

As eager to disguise his uneasiness as he was to change

the angle from which Nick was scrutinizing him, Gowan dropped to his knees beside her. "There's no hurry, darling," he said, running a hand through her hair. "We have all night!"

With a click of her tongue, Nick tossed her head and moved away, just enough that he found himself with his hand poised in midair. Her lower lip crinkled into a pout. "It is what you want, is it not?"

Without waiting for his answer, she lay back. She dug her shoulders into the bracken and ran her hands the length of her body. "I am what you want." She took Gowan's hand and brushed it through the triangle of dark hair between her legs. "I am all you've ever wanted."

There was no denying it was true. *This* was what he wanted. *She* was what he wanted. But if that much was true—and Gowan would wager his soul it was—why did his insides feel suddenly as if they'd been twisted into knots?

Gently, Gowan pulled his hand from her grasp. "Yes. It's what I want. More than anything. You're what I want, Nick." He trailed a finger down her cheek. "More than anyone. Ever. But—"

"Then love me." Nick's eyes sparked. An all-too-familiar razor's-edge of anger sliced through her words at the same time an equally familiar and equally disturbing look of betrayal settled in her eyes.

It was too much for him to face. Gowan squeezed his eyes shut. When he dared to open them again, the sight of Nick lying naked and eager before him dimmed and blurred. The moonlight faded until it was nothing more than a milky smear. The emotion that had started as desire soured and the heat in Gowan's blood cooled. He passed a hand over his eyes.

Through the haze that clouded his vision, Gowan saw Nick's jaw tighten. With a visible effort she controlled the hurt and anger that simmered in her eyes and trembled over her lips. She raised herself on her elbows and giving him a smile that was as seductive as any he'd ever seen, she traced the shape of his ear with her tongue.

"I am all you want, Gowan Payne. And you can have me. But only now. Only tonight."

"But, I—"

"Take me. Now. Tonight!" Her grasp urgent and insistent, Nick plucked at the buttons at the front of his trousers. "You must love me. You must. You must obey the magic."

"Damn the magic!" Gowan gripped her shoulders and holding her at arm's length, gave her a shake. "I don't care about the magic. I care about you."

Her eyes wild, her face as pale as death, Nick stiffened in his arms. "But it is your wish."

"My wish. Yes. It's what I've been wishing for ever since I set foot in this damned country." Gowan's head spun. His vision faded. "But it's not my wish . . . not like this."

"It is the magic." Nick wasn't listening. Or perhaps she simply didn't care. She clung to Gowan and laying back, she pulled him down on top of her.

"Your wish. Your wish."

Her voice whispered in his ear. It filled his head. It was the last thing Gowan heard.

"My wish."

The sound of his own voice startled Gowan awake. He opened his eyes to find himself flat on his back in the center of the small clearing. The sky above his head was bright blue and sunlight streamed down on him, warming his face and setting off a furious pounding in his head.

"Damn." The oath scratched its way out from between his parched lips, and he squeezed his eyes shut against the light. In spite of the fact that his head felt as if it were stuffed with cotton batting, he fought to gather the tangled strands of his memory and weave some picture, however incomplete, of all that had happened the night before.

"My wish." He repeated the words. Though he was sure they had something to do with the uneasy feeling that twisted through his gut, he was not at all certain what that might be. "My wish," he said again, turning the thought over in his head and hoping that by speaking it out loud, it would help make some sense. "My wish. And Nick!"

His eyes flying open, Gowan sat up like a shot. Automatically, he thrust his hands out to his sides in search of the soft touch of Nick's skin.

He came away with only a handful of bracken.

"Damn!" Gowan cast the greenery aside and glanced around.

He was alone. There was no sign of Nick anywhere, and except for his tie, which he saw tangled in a heather bush, and his mother of pearl shirt studs, which littered the ground around him like fallen stars, there was no sign that Nick had ever been there.

Anger coursing through his blood like liquid fire, Gowan jumped to his feet as quickly as his pounding head would allow.

"No sign of her now, no. But she was here," he muttered, heading toward the path that led to the garden. "She was here. I'm certain of it. And by the Lord Harry, it seems to me, we have a good many things to discuss."

When he got to the place where the bright sunshine met the dark shadows under the trees, Gowan saw that he had been wrong. He was not alone. He pulled to a stop and watched as one of the black shadows uncoiled. It stretched. Settling back on its haunches, Cat glanced up at him with the most disinterested of looks and, satisfied that he was hardly worth the trouble, the animal turned its full attention to bathing itself.

"She was here, wasn't she?" Gowan didn't stop to consider that before he ever came to Wales, he would have thought any man who talked to cats to be quite mad. Though he hardly expected Cat to answer, he asked the question. "Where has she gone? Home?"

The animal paid him not the least mind, but went right on washing its right foreleg.

"Yes. Of course she has. She's gone home." As if he could see through the mountains and to the cottage that lay beyond them, Gowan shot a look in that direction. He had already run down the path that led him to the village when he pulled himself to a stop. With his shirt open and a night's stubble of beard on his face, he was hardly fit to be seen in public. Even a man burning with anger knew that much.

He turned and headed to the house to bathe and change his linen, and when he looked back as if to signal Cat that he was neither foolish or ill-bred enough to make a call in such a state, he saw that the animal was gone.

Gowan dismissed Cat without another thought. He had more pressing matters to consider. He knew without a doubt that there was no way he would ever school his temper, but he must, at least, rehearse his words. He must think what he would do and what he would say and how he might feel when he demanded an accounting of all that had happened in the little clearing under the light of the ghost night moon.

And that, he vowed, was exactly what he was going to do. "Nicolette Rhys," he mumbled to himself, "woman or witch, you have a great deal of explaining to do."

"Thank goodness you've come." Clea did not look at all surprised to see Gowan. As if standing sentry, watching for him, she nodded with satisfaction as he hurried up the path. She swung open the garden gate and stepped back to allow him inside. "You're just in time."

He didn't bother to ask what the devil she was talking about. He was not at all sure he cared. The bath that was intended to have refreshed Gowan only served to further heat his blood. The clean clothes that were meant to make him look more presentable and feel more like the gentleman he had always thought himself to be, only served as a reminder that he was woefully out of place in this strange country. The sight of one of the aunts meant that the other two were lurking somewhere nearby, and that only put him in mind of the fact that as strange as the country was, some of its inhabitants were stranger still, and the Rhys women, the strangest of them all.

Without giving Clea another look, Gowan marched through the garden. His gaze was trained on the closed cottage door and one, and only one, thought pounded through his head in just the way his footsteps hammered against the garden walk: he had to talk to Nick.

He was grateful he'd taken the time to have a bath and dress properly instead of running off at half-cock as he had been tempted to do. That had given him time to think, and the time he'd spent thinking had helped him put together the pieces of the puzzle of all that had happened the night before.

He was hardly calmer than when he'd found himself alone and half dressed in the clearing just two short hours before, but he was more sure of what he wanted to say. He was no longer going to have to ask Nick what happened. He remembered what happened.

Every look. Every taste. Every touch.

The only thing he wanted to know now was why.

Before Gowan ever got as far as the stoop with its intricate chalked designs, the cottage door swung open. In the pool of sunshine that trickled inside, he saw exactly what he expected to see: Belle and Tildy.

Belle hardly gave him a look. She was standing in front of the hearth, stirring something that bubbled like a volcano in the big black pot that hung over the fire. The mixture looked like mud and smelled like the Thames at low tide. His stomach lurching, Gowan turned away and found himself face to face with Tildy.

"She's upstairs," Tildy said, though he never had a chance to say why he was there. She turned in the direction of the narrow stairway that led up to the room that Gowan had occupied after the spring snowstorm. "You'd best hurry. I'm afraid she's going to need help this time. More help than we can give her."

With a mumbled oath and without another thought to the aunts, Gowan bounded up the stairs. He crossed the passage that led from the stairway to Nick's bedchamber. His hand raised to knock, he paused outside the door and reminded himself of the things he'd resolved on his way there.

He had resolved that no matter the provocation, his words would be reasonable and well thought out. He had resolved that no matter the difficulty, he would hold on to his temper and what was left of his pride. He had resolved that no matter what, he would never let Nick see how much their peculiar tryst had cost him, both mentally and emotionally.

He remembered the resolutions. Every single one of them. He simply couldn't keep them.

The explosion of anger that rocketed through him made Gowan forget everything he'd promised himself. It made him forget about knocking, as well. Punching open the door, he burst into Nick's room.

"What the hell's—?" The question caught in Gowan's throat at the same time surprise immobilized him. He stopped just inside the door, staring in wonder at the stranger who lay in Nick's bed.

It was a girl, a girl he'd never seen before. Gowan had no idea who she was just as he could not imagine where she had come from, but it took less than an instant and none of his medical training to see that there was something very wrong with her.

Like strips of wet paper, the girl's red hair was plastered to her head. Her face contorted with pain, she thrashed from side to side and clutched her swollen belly.

A small voice inside his head reminded Gowan that situations like this were precisely the reason he had kept himself to Harley Street and to the wealthy and never terribly ill people who were his patients there. He preferred his medicine predictable, impersonal, and paid for. It was a privileged type of medicine, and he had never made any apologies for it. It was a medicine that made no allowance for great quantities of blood, embarrassing amounts of pain, or babies.

No babies.

As if in response to the thoughts that pounded through Gowan's head, the girl in the bed writhed and moaned. There was little time between her contractions. Little time for her to relax and regain her strength and for her body, and the baby inside it, to ease into the birth process.

Still poised at the threshold of Nick's odd little room with its strange smells and peculiar contents, Gowan reminded himself that in his type of medicine, there was no place for the kind of panic that twisted through him and made sweat break out on his brow, just as there was no room for compassion or sensitivity.

He was walking into trouble. Years of medical training and experience told him that. He was taking the chance of baring his heart and his soul, and showing not only the world but himself, as well, that he was not a god who could relieve people's ills with a stroke of his pen against his prescription pad.

He was opening himself up to everything his type of medicine scorned—the compassion, yes, but the fear, as well. And the risk. He was walking into trouble. He knew it. He told himself that over and over. He was still telling himself that when he hurried over to the bed and consigned his type of medicine to hell.

Standing behind the open door where she could see but not be seen, Nick watched Gowan walk into the room and pull to a stop, his gaze riveted to her bed. She was not at all surprised to see him. Not after the aunts told her what they'd done. She felt as if she'd spent the morning holding her breath, waiting for this moment, and now that it was here—now that he was here—her heart started up again with a terrible thump that made her ribs ache and her throat tighten.

For the first time since last night when Mai Davies had stumbled to the doorstep, Nick was grateful that she had something to do with her hands and thankful she had more things to worry about than Gowan. They may not have been more important things, but there was no denying the fact that they were more urgent. Standing at her cabinet, she went on grinding a pestle into a wooden mortar, crushing a sprig of motherwort.

The scent that rose from the ground herb was bitter and aromatic and, catching it, Gowan turned to her.

"It is Mai Davies," she said, reading the question on his face. "She is in labor."

"I can see that." Gowan sounded no more pleased than he looked, though Nick was not at all sure if he was angry at her or at the situation he'd suddenly and unexpectedly found himself in. He laid one hand on Mai's brow while with the other, he felt for the girl's pulse. "How much longer?"

"By all rights, it should be weeks before the baby's born, but you know as well as I do, babies come when they will." There was a kettle of water boiling over the fire in the hearth and Nick went to retrieve it. She poured water into a cup and added the motherwort and a sprinkling of dried raspberry leaves to the herbs already in it.

"Mai's baby seems determined to come before the day is out," she told Gowan. Stirring the brew, she glanced at Mai and though she was convinced the girl was too lost in her own misery to pay any mind to their conversation, she lowered her voice.

"Things are not going well and I'm not sure why. I've done an examination and I can feel the baby's head well enough. But Mai is only sixteen, no more than a child herself. It is her first baby and she's frightened, poor thing. She's exhausted, and I can think of nothing else to do for her right now than give her this." Nick picked up the teacup and went over to the bed with it. "You'll help me?"

"Chloroform would be more useful." Gowan grunted and mumbled, but to Nick's relief, he didn't argue. Being careful not to disturb Mai any more than was necessary, he sat on the edge of the bed. He wrapped one arm around Mai's shoulders and lifted her so that she was sitting and when she was, he tucked her pillow behind her back.

"Nick's brought you some tea," Gowan told the girl, his voice as gentle as the reassuring pat Nick saw him give Mai's hand. "I'm sure it's delicious even if I don't know what it is." He looked past Mai to the cup in Nick's hands, sniffing the singular aroma that rose from the brew and his nose wrinkled. "What is it?"

"Motherwort to relieve the pain. Raspberry leaves to strengthen the womb. Wood betony and skullcap and valerian to calm her. She should be able to sleep when she's finished it. At least for a bit."

Nick didn't wait to see what Gowan's reaction might be. Without waiting for any more questions or the vehement objection she knew was sure to come, she sat on the bed opposite Gowan and spooned a bit of the brew between Mai's lips. "It will help ease the pain," she promised. "And the taste is not unpleasant." Nick watched, satisfied, as the girl swallowed.

Mai took another spoonful of the potion and sighed, the tension flowing from her body. Nick offered her another sip, and another, and before the cup was completely empty, Mai's eyes drifted shut and she slumped in Gowan's arm.

"What did you say was in that tea?" Settling Mai under

the covers, Gowan gave the cup in Nick's hands a curious look. "It works wonders."

"But it won't last long and there's only so much I can give her before there's a danger to her and the babe." A wave of anger washed over her and Nick bounded off the bed. "She should have sent for me instead of coming over the mountain by herself," she said, depositing the teacup on the table near the hearth. "There should have been someone to help her. But Mai's husband is a hard man and twice her age if he's a day. No doubt, he could not be bothered to move himself from his nice warm bed. I don't know how much longer her strength can hold out, poor child. She's been in agony for far too long. I found her on our doorstep well before midnight."

Nick caught herself just as the words left her mouth. She had not meant to bring up the subject of last night. Now, it was too late. Her back to Gowan, she cursed herself and rued her recklessness and busied herself cleaning out the teacup.

She might have known he would never be content to leave things at that.

Though she did not hear him approach, she knew Gowan had come up behind her. She felt the temperature in the room change, hot to cold to hot again, and before she could move away or brace herself, Gowan snatched her arm and spun her to face him. "What do you mean you found her before midnight? You couldn't have. You were with me at midnight."

The heat in Nick's body solidified like ice. For what seemed a lifetime, she could not make even a single word leave her mouth. Her blood pulsed so hard, it made her head throb. She ran her tongue over her lips and tried to prepare some kind of explanation that would clear his confusion and calm his anger at the same time. She prayed it would be enough.

She knew it would not.

"I'm sorry." The words lodged against the painful lump

in Nick's throat, and she tried clearing them with a cough. "They told me what happened," she said. "This morning. They admitted what they did. I would have come to see you then had Mai not been here. I would have come to explain everything and to say I'm sorry."

"They? They who? What are you talking about?"

Nick found herself entirely without the words to explain. Helpless, she shrugged. "The aunts," she said, her voice as hesitant as the glance she darted at him. "They told me what they did. They were . . . They were only trying to help."

"I don't give a damn about your aunts." Gowan may have been bewildered before, but it was clear now that her hesitancy had served only to turn his bewilderment to anger. His words echoed through the room and Mai moaned in her sleep.

Looking as blameworthy as he did worried, Gowan hurried over to the bed. Convinced Mai was as comfortable as she could be, he folded his arms over his chest and turned his stony gaze full on Nick. "It's you I want to talk about," he said. "You. Us. It's everything that happened last night."

The blood drained from Nick's face. Reluctant to discover exactly what he meant and sure that she had no choice but to ask, she swallowed hard. "What did happen?"

Gowan threw up his hands in frustration. He did his best to keep his voice down but there was no mistaking the edge of exasperation in it. "What happened? Devil take it, woman, you act as if you weren't there!"

Nick clutched her hands at her waist. She raised her chin and looked directly at him, vowing she would not lower her gaze no matter what he said or did.

She owed him that at least, she told herself. She owed him honesty. It was all she could give him now.

Nick took a deep breath. "I wasn't," she said.

If she thought the sting of Gowan's anger made her heart ache, it was nothing compared to the pain that shot through her at his look of complete disbelief. He let out a short, barking laugh. "What are you telling me? That it was one of your aunts?" He fought to keep his voice down and there was something in the half whispered words that made them sound all the more sarcastic. "I think not, Nick. I may have had a bit too much to drink, but I was not completely drunk. Don't try to tell me it was some other woman. The moon was up, don't forget. I saw you well enough. Every last delicious inch of you."

He crossed the room in three quick strides and grabbed for Nick's arm. His eyes were as cold as stone, his expression as hard as granite. "It was you, Nick. I'm sure of it. I think I know you well enough. I surely know you when I see you. And in the event I need to remind you, I did more than simply see you."

His fiery gaze touched her everywhere, her face and her throat and the place where her heart beat hard and fast against her dark gown. Hauling in a ragged breath, he tightened his grip. "I know your touch, Nick. I know the taste of you. And the smell. I know it was you."

Nick shook her head. She raised her chin. "No," she said. "It was not me. Nor was it one of the aunts. You were alone, Gowan. Completely alone."

Mai groaned and yanking her arm from Gowan's grasp, Nick took the opportunity to hurry to the bed. Gowan kept pace. By the time Nick got to the bed, he was standing on the other side of it. "You're mad," he said. "Every single one of you. I knew it the moment I woke up in this place."

Nick scrambled for something to say, anything that would make him understand, and believe. There was a bowl of cool water on the bedside table, and dipping a cloth into it, Nick wrung it out and held it to Mai's brow. She schooled her voice to a whisper. "You say what happened last night was real. You say I was there. But you can be sure, I was not. Ask Mai if you do not believe me. Ask the aunts. They will swear I was here every second of the night, just as they will swear to everything else. They have to, for they admitted the truth to me this morning. Now it is your turn to face that same truth. Tell me, Gowan, after I left you on the dance floor, you saw them, didn't you? You saw the aunts. You spoke to them."

"Yes. Yes. Of course I did." He waved away the significance of the confession with one hand.

"Tell me, did they give you something to drink?"

Gowan hauled in a sharp intake of breath. His cheeks ashen, he cast a glance to the other side of the room and the teacup Nick had used to administer the potion to Mai.

"Yes." The look that had started as anger on Gowan's face melted into shock. A single muscle at the base of his jaw twitched with the effort of control. "What exactly are you saying, Nick? Did they . . . did they drug me?"

Though she would have liked nothing better than to turn away, Nick forced herself to stay put. "They gave you a dreaming brew," she explained. "A wishing potion. The aunts cast a spell on you, Gowan and believe me, if I knew what they were about, I never would have let it happen. But I was gone. And it was a magic night. They wanted . . ." Blood rushed into her cheeks and because she could not bear to look at Gowan, Nick shifted her gaze to Mai.

"You mustn't be angry with them," she said, smoothing Mai's damp hair from her face. "They know what they did was wrong. And foolish. But they are fond of you, you see, and they took pity on you. Since I have refused to cooperate, as they so bluntly put it, they took it upon themselves to try and make you happy. They gave you a potion that would make you dream the thing you wanted more than anything in all the world. It doesn't take much to figure what that might be."

Nick felt as if she could touch the silence that fell in the little room. Her hands trembling far more than she liked, she dipped the cloth into the water again and soothed it over Mai's arms and neck. She did not dare to raise her gaze to Gowan for she was certain she would see disapproval burning in his eyes. It was the one response she knew she could not face.

The feel of Gowan's hand beneath her chin froze Nick's hands over Mai. He crooked a finger below her chin and raised her face to his.

"That explains it, then."

There was no condemnation in Gowan's eyes, only a look as soft as a kiss. It snatched at Nick's heart and left her breathless and sensing her amazement, Gowan offered her a lopsided smile. "That explains why I didn't get my wish."

It was Nick's turn to stare, shocked and speechless.

Gowan laughed. "It happened just as you said. The aunts did give me something to drink, though how they put one of their potions into my ale without my knowing is beyond me. I did dream, Nick. I dreamed of what I wished. I dreamed about you. Yet it wasn't you. Oh, she looked like you." Turning away from the bed, Gowan paced to the other side of the room and back again and by the time he came to stand in front of Nick, his mouth was tipped into a smile.

"At least she looked as I have always imagined you must look. But you . . . it . . . she . . . she didn't act like you. Not a bit. And no matter how much I told myself that this was my opportunity to make love to you as I have wanted to make love to you all this time, I simply couldn't do it."

Nick's mouth fell open. "You mean, you didn't—"

This time when Gowan laughed, the sound of it was warm and merry. "I didn't make love to her, Nick. I couldn't. It wasn't you and I do believe that somewhere deep inside of me, I realized that. She was some figment of my imagination. Some fantasy made up of the bits and pieces of every wild longing I've ever had." Gowan cocked his head.

"It seems," he said, "that the aunts were quite successful. They thought to give me my fondest dream, but even I didn't realize what that was. It seems my fondest dream was discovering that I will never be happy simply bedding you."

He laid one finger against Nick's brow. "I want your mind." He slid his finger along her throat. "As well as your body." He slipped it to her breast. "But I will never have all I truly want until I have your heart."

It would be so easy to lose herself in the look that brightened Gowan's expression, so simple to forget herself in the warmth of his touch. So unfair to them both.

Before he could see the hesitation in her eyes, Nick backed away. "I'd best get more motherwort," she said. "And water. We need more water. I'll go down and ask the aunts to get more water. And—"

Gowan would not hear of it. He snatched up her hand and when he spoke, his voice was as eager as the look in his eyes. "Don't be ridiculous. If you're upset about this whole, silly incident, you needn't be."

"It . . . it isn't that. It's—"

"Are you embarrassed?"

"Yes, I am embarrassed and sorely troubled by what the aunts did." Nick blinked back the tears that threatened to reveal her true emotions. She looked past Gowan to where Mai lay in her bed. "If I could have any wish in all the world, it would be that Mai did not need me. That I could leave. Now. Just as I ran from the dance floor last night." Holding tight to her emotions, she raised her eyes to Gowan's. "I would like nothing better than to leave this place and to leave you because . . . because I love you."

Of all the things she'd ever said to him, of all the things he'd seen since he'd come to Wales, this was obviously the most amazing, and the most splendid. A smile split Gowan's face. He pulled her into an embrace and dropped a kiss on her brow.

"That's wonderful!" He breathed the words against her ear and nuzzled his cheek into her hair. "Better than wonderful! It's incredible! The one thing that was missing from my wishing dream."

Before he could go on bewitching her with his words and with the promise of forever that shone through them as surely as it did in his eyes, Nick laid one finger against his lips. "No." She shook her head. "It is not wonderful. Not at all."

Hauling in a breath that was meant to steady her heart and did not even begin to work, she pulled away from him and crossed to the windows. Hoping the feel of the glass would damp the heat of passion that snaked through her at the same time it cooled the sting of regret, she laid her brow against the window glass.

It was little use. Nothing helped. She knew it never would. She could feel the tension. It hung in the air between them, unseen and unspoken, but so real, it made her feel as if all the air had been drawn from the room.

Her voice far calmer than the emotions that twisted through her, Nick tried her best to explain. "It will never work," she said. There was no easy way to wade into the story. Nothing to do but plunge headlong into it, and the only way to do that, to show him evidence of its truth.

Nick pointed through the glass to a place in the garden nestled against the stone wall. It was a tiny space shaded with oak trees, their barks shiny green with a tangle of mistletoe.

"My mother is buried there," she said.

It was not nearly the whole story, and certainly not enough to even begin to explain. Nick started again.

"She married when she was but nineteen. Her husband—my father—was a laborer. One of the young men who came to work the slate quarries here in the mountains. He was from the south. Nash Point, I think, or somewhere very near there. His work here was finished shortly after they were married and he took my mother home with him. By all accounts, my father was a great deal like Mai's husband.

Selfish, idle, and a good bit too proud for his own good. Once he was back with his own people, he lost interest in his wife quick enough. I was born less than a year later and already, he had left Mother to live with another woman."

Nick had no memory of her mother, no recollection of her voice or her touch, yet she swore that even after all the years, she could feel her pain. The emotion grabbed at Nick's heart and trembled in her voice.

"I believe Mother tried to keep the marriage together. At least that is how the aunts remember the thing. She tried everything she could and when it did not work, she had no choice. She came home and brought me with her. And then . . ." Her eyes clouded with tears, Nick stared down at the little place beneath the oaks. "And then she died."

Behind her, she heard Gowan move. Gently, he put a hand on her elbow and turned her to face him. The look in his eyes was as soft as a summer sunset. "It is a sad story, to be certain. But I am a different man. I would never treat you as poorly as your father treated your mother." He cast a glance to where Mai lay sleeping. "I would never treat you as that poor girl's husband has treated her. I hope you know that. I would never leave you, Nick, I swear it."

When Nick tried to speak, he hushed her with a look and offered a smile meant to dispel her troubles and dissolve her fears. "In any event, you are a very different woman, I think. You feel things with all your heart and all your soul, but I do not believe you are like your mother, Nick. You're a fighter. There's no doubt of that. You are not at all the kind of woman who would die of a broken heart."

"You don't understand," Nick said. "My mother did not die from the loss of her man. She died from the loss of her magic."

Eighteen

Nick did not have time to explain. Whether it was because her potion wore off or because the baby simply refused to be kept waiting, Mai woke with a start and let out a piercing scream.

At the first sign of Mai's distress, Nick curbed the powerful emotions that had so nearly overwhelmed her as she told her curious story. Without hesitation, she swung into action, her distress hidden behind a veneer of calm efficiency, her own anguish forgotten beneath her concern for Mai.

It cost her dearly.

Except for the deep spots of red that stained her cheeks, Nick's face was as white as chalk. Her eyes were filled with the same pain that had trembled through her voice only moments before, their usual clear color dappled with a smokey gray that betrayed her anxiety. Her hands curled into fists, her arms tight to her body, Nick hurried to Mai's side at the same time the door burst open.

After that, all was chaos.

The aunts scrambled into the room. Belle, naturally, led the way, her arms laden with clean bedding. She was followed by Tildy who was carrying a basin of water that sloshed onto the floor with every move she made. Clea came last of all, walking slowly and carefully, trying her best not to overturn the small metal dish in her hands. It looked like a brazier, and like a brazier, there was something burning in it. The smell reminded Gowan of the pine boughs his mother had always brought into the house at Christmas.

"Needles of the silver fir." One cautious step at a time, Clea walked past Gowan, offering the explanation at the same time she set the burning dish on the window ledge. "To protect the mother and baby."

Gowan glanced at the bed and at the girl in it. Another spasm racked her body, and Mai clutched the blankets and cried out, her sob so pitiful, it tore at Gowan's heart.

Protection, he thought, was exactly what Mai was going to need.

Stripping off his coat and rolling up his shirtsleeves, Gowan joined Nick where she stood at the foot of the bed. They spoke not a word, but exchanged worried glances, Nick's look confirming everything Gowan was already thinking.

It had been years since he'd assisted at a birth, years since he'd even seen one, but one thing was clear. The baby would come soon, and just as certainly, it was going to be a difficult delivery.

While Nick washed her hands in what was left of the water Tildy had brought into the room, Belle positioned Mai properly on the bed, her knees bent, her feet flat. Tildy took a jar of some oily substance out of her pocket. She anointed Mai's palms with the mixture while Clea lit two candles, one red and one silver. She placed the red one on the table next to the bed.

"Red for courage," she whispered to Gowan as she passed to the other side of the room to place the other candle there. "Silver as an offering to the female deities." Her eyes wide, she peeked at the bed as if she was afraid of what she might see there. "I think we will need all the help we can get."

For once, Gowan knew she was right.

Using the basin and the bar of coarse soap that was in it, Gowan washed to his elbows and dried his hands and arms on the towel Nick handed him. He stood back, watching as Nick conducted another examination.

She was quick and efficient, and far more considerate than any of the physicians Gowan had seen work while he was in medical school. When Mai sucked in a breath and her body tensed, Nick talked her through the contraction. She did not continue her probe until the pain ebbed. "I can feel the baby's head," she finally said. "That's good, Mai. That's very good."

It was good. Gowan knew it. But if it was, why did Nick look so alarmed?

When she was finished, Nick stepped aside, her expression thoughtful. "Will you have a look?"

It was not the question. It was the way she said it.

Something in the deceptively simple words told Gowan everything Nick did not want to say out loud. He nodded his agreement and conducted his own examination. He was not as gentle as Nick, not as skilled when it came to knowing just the right touch to use on a girl who was hurting as much as she was exhausted and as exhausted as she was frightened. When Mai winced, Gowan cursed himself.

He stepped back. "It shouldn't be long now."

"No." Nick glanced to the head of the bed. Tildy and Clea were standing on either side of the girl, each of them holding one of Mai's hands. Belle was adding more fir needles to the brazier. "But she hardly has the strength to push."

Even as Nick spoke, the baby's head crowned.

"Good!" The worry on Nick's face and in her voice disappeared. Smiling with relief, she rushed to take Gowan's place. "Good, Mai. Now push. It will be over soon. But you must push."

Mai tried as hard as she could and within another minute, the baby's head was out.

From the second they saw the child, its abnormal coloring

and eerily quiet face, both Gowan and Nick knew something was wrong. And they both knew what it was.

The cord was wrapped tight around the baby's neck.

Just as Nick obviously did, Gowan realized the situation was critical. Without the oxygen provided by its mother's blood supply, the baby would not live long. And with the cord tied the way it was, there was no way the child could get oxygen. Already, its skin was blue.

"It's a precious baby, Mai. A beautiful baby." How Nick was able to keep the worry that was etched on her face from spilling into her words, Gowan didn't know. She erased every trace of panic from her voice and talked to Mai as one might to a frightened child, each word resonating with calm certainty, each of her movements quick and sure. "We must get the baby's shoulders out so we can cut the cord, and you are going to have to help us, Mai. I know you are tired and I know it hurts, but you are going to have to try. You're going to have to push."

"Can't." Mai's voice was no stronger than the mewling of a kitten. "I can't do it. I'm tired. So tired."

"Yes. I know." One hand to either side of the baby's head, Nick tugged it gently. "But you're going to have to try, Mai."

She turned to Gowan, her eyes gleaming behind the tears that betrayed every emotion she refused to allow into her voice. "What can we do?"

Frustrated, Gowan cursed. If he could dream his wishing dream again, he knew what he would wish for. He would wish for his medical bag. He would wish for his office on Harley Street and his assistants and his equipment and a proper surgery where he could do a proper Caesar.

But he had none of those. Nothing but his own skill and the guidance of a woman who was brave enough not to let the horror of the situation panic her, and stubborn enough that he knew she would never stop fighting.

It was enough.

While Nick urged Mai to push, Gowan hurried to the side of the bed. Laying both his hands against Mai's abdomen, he pressed as hard as he could.

Mai shrieked and no amount of comforting from the aunts could make her stop. She writhed and flailed her arms, fighting off Gowan and the aunts with every last bit of her strength.

"Damn, but you're making this hard." Loath to make matters worse for Mai, Gowan grumbled to himself. His heart in his throat, his stomach tied in knots, he pressed her belly again, watching Nick from where he stood, waiting to see some expression on her face that would tell him the baby's shoulders had finally been delivered.

The instant he saw Nick catch her breath, Gowan hurried back to the foot of the bed. The baby's shoulders were out. He handed Nick the string that she'd left nearby and watched her tie off the pulsing cord, one piece near the child, another closer to Mai.

By the time Gowan looked up at Mai and back to Nick, she had the tiny boy cradled in both her hands. He was blue from head to toe.

Gowan snatched the child away from Nick and whacked it on the backside. When he got no response and no movement, he laid the baby over one arm, its head down, and thumped its back. There was no birth cry.

Though she could not easily see what was happening, Mai had enough of a mother's sense to know there was something wrong. Her moans of pain turned into a cry of grief.

Gowan passed one hand over his eyes. His shoulders slumped with what felt like the weight of the world. "Damn!"

Her expression blank, her cheeks wet with tears, Nick grabbed the towel that was lying on the bed. With vigorous strokes, she rubbed the child's body, its arms and its legs and its tiny torso. "No." Nick rubbed harder. Faster. She raised her eyes to Gowan and they were blazing, not with accusation or with reproach, but with determination. "I won't give up so easily. He's not dead. He cannot be. Try again. Do something. Do something, doctor."

"Nick . . ." Heaving a sigh, Gowan cast a glance to where Mai lay crying in Tildy's arms. "It won't help and it won't do Mai any good."

"No!" Nick refused to listen. Hurrying to her cabinet, she tore through the bottles and jars, filling her pockets with dried herbs and retrieving a white candle from its place on the highest shelf. She lit the candle at the hearth and brought it over to where Gowan stood with the baby in his arms.

The moment they saw what Nick was about, the aunts came to help. On a signal from Belle, they linked hands and closed a circle around Nick and Gowan and the child.

Before Gowan ever had a chance to protest or to beg Nick to remember Mai's pain and not offer her false hope, Nick sprinkled the baby's small, still body with a dried herb. Her face luminous with a glow that smoothed the lines of fear and fatigue from around her eyes and made her cheeks flame as red as holly berries, she passed the candle over the baby, her voice hushed, and when she spoke it was in a language so strange, Gowan knew it was not Welsh.

The aunts repeated Nick's words.

Nick spoke again, her words as ancient as the mountains, each syllable charged with power.

While the aunts echoed the chant, Nick took another herb from her pocket. Her hands trembling, she pressed it against the baby's brow and on its heart.

"Nick . . ." Gowan tried again. He could no more bear the look of blind determination on Nick's face than he could the sound of Mai's sobs. "Nick, you mustn't—"

He did not finish.

Every window in the room burst open. The fir needle

incense on the window ledge scattered in a cloud of ash and smoke. The candle flame blew out. So did the fire in the hearth. Though the sun still shone bright outside the walls of the cottage, inside, everything was as dark as midnight.

Gowan had no time to think on it or wonder what had happened. A tingling like lightning sizzled through the air. It fell over him like rain, prickling and pinning him. It snaked over his shoulders. It flowed through his hands. He felt himself wince, and then he felt something else.

The baby in his arms squirmed.

It cried.

"Mai is asleep and so is the baby."

Nick did not look up when Gowan approached. Her gaze fixed to the mound of earth beneath which her mother was buried, she drew in a deep breath of afternoon air and ran her hands through the grass where she was sitting. There was something about the feel of sunshine upon her face and the touch of the living earth under her fingers that helped slow the wild beating of her heart and relieved the ache inside her that was the remnant of her magic.

"Belle says you should get some rest, as well." Gowan dropped to the ground next to Nick. He wrapped one arm around her and drew her close. He smelled like soap and his skin was still warm from the water he'd used to wash up after the delivery. It was a wonderful scent, ordinary and comforting, and she sighed and laid her head upon his shoulder. "Tildy says you'll be tired for hours. And Clea . . . Clea said something about a nice cup of tea and how it would fix everything."

"Not everything." The truth flooded through Nick like ice water, chilling her to the bone, and she sat up. The last hours had been frenzied and frightening, but they had provided at least some respite from the task at hand. The birth of Mai's baby allowed her the chance to postpone telling Gowan about her mother and her magic, but the truth was far too clear: nothing could defer the responsibility forever. There was much to tell him and only one place to begin. At the beginning. Nick knew that well enough. She would have to begin with the earl.

She turned in Gowan's arms. "We Rhys women," she said, "we are cursed."

She expected Gowan to laugh, or to make some deprecating remark. He did not, and Nick laid her hand in Gowan's and his fingers closed over hers. She held fast to him and to the heart's ease he telegraphed through every pore. "It was the second earl who cast the curse," she said. "The second earl of Welshpool."

"My ancestor?" Gowan's dark brows dropped low over his eyes. He did not know the details, yet it hardly seemed to matter. He responded to the word "curse" the way most did. He knew the story was bound to be unhappy, and his inherent sense of justice and honor rebelled. A flash of anger lit his eyes. "What sort of curse? What—?"

Nick stopped his questions with a look that said it all: she would tell him, in her own way, in her own time, and she would not be hurried or pressed into a half-account. "His name was Rolph," she began.

As if anxious to get on with the story, Gowan twitched his shoulders. "I know about Rolph. Mrs. Pritchard told me."

"And did she tell you he was a vicious old tyrant? He treated the people of Rhyd Ddu cruelly. That is why—"

"That is why, even after so many hundreds of years, the villagers resented me so when I arrived. Yes. Mrs. Pritchard told me that, as well."

Nick let go a sigh of relief. At least she would not have to explain that much to him. "Rolph had a son named Giles who lived here with his father for a time." She paused, giving Gowan the chance to interrupt, and when he did not, she asked, "Did Mrs. Pritchard tell you about Giles?"

"She said there was a son, though I do not recall his name. She said he left one day and never set foot in Wales again. She did not say why."

"The why of it is easy enough," Nick told him. "Giles fell in love. With a local girl by the name of Enid. Enid Rhys."

Gowan's brows shot up and though there was no doubt of the answer, he asked his question nonetheless, as if hoping there had been some mistake. "One of your ancestors?"

Nick nodded, her gaze automatically traveling to the mound of earth between the oak trees. "One of my ancestors. And a witch. You see, our magic is handed down from one generation of Rhys women to the next. It has been for as long as anyone can remember."

As it did each time she recounted the story or thought on it over long, anger and despair washed over Nick. She pulled in a breath to steady herself.

"When Rolph learned that Enid and Giles wished to marry, he went into a rage. The prospect of Welsh blood running through the veins of his descendants was bad enough, it seems. But Rolph had had more than one quarrel with Enid. There was the problem of a serving girl who had been sorely abused and who Enid nursed on her deathbed. And a woman from the village had been left with a child by the earl." Nick managed a bittersweet smile.

"If you have not noticed, we Rhys women are an outspoken lot. We speak our minds and our hearts, and by all accounts, Enid was no exception. She took the earl to task more than once and he came to look on her as an enemy." As if the air around them still resonated with the emotions of those days long past, Nick's smile faded.

"But it wasn't so much Enid's temper that Rolph objected to. It was her magic. Imagine, he was afraid of our magic! He was afraid his granddaughters and their daughters after them would have powers he couldn't begin to understand. And because he was suspicious and greedy, he thought Enid might use her powers to somehow gain his fortune. He swore he would do everything he could to put a stop to Enid's and Giles's union. And he did. He put a curse on Enid and on every generation of Rhys women who would follow her. A curse we live with to this day."

Nick's cheeks flamed and her voice trembled far more than she would have liked, but she held tight to Gowan's hand. "If any one of us loses her virginity," she said, "she loses her powers as well. She loses all use and all memory of her magic."

In less than a heartbeat, Gowan's face paled. Just as quickly, it flooded with color. He cocked his head. "Then how—?"

She knew what he was going to ask and she gave him his answer before the words could ever leave his mouth. "Once each generation, one of the women must marry. How she is chosen is up to the women themselves. Belle tells me that the aunts and my mother drew straws. Mother lost."

Even a deep breath was not enough to calm Nick this time. She fought down the sour taste of despair that rose in her throat.

"It is thus every generation," she continued. "One Rhys woman must marry. She must produce the daughters who will carry on the magic. But the price she pays is high indeed. She knows that on her wedding night when she takes a man into her arms and accepts his love, she must surrender her magic."

As if even speaking about it was enough to bring the prospect all too close to reality, a shudder snaked up Nick's back and trembled over her shoulders. Though she tried her best to disguise it, Gowan couldn't help but notice. He pulled her into his arms.

Nick pressed her cheek to his chest, drawing peculiar comfort in the soft scrape of Gowan's linen shirt against her skin and the steady beating of his heart in her ear. "The women of the aunts' generation were very lucky in a way," she said. "There were four girls. Though my mother lost her magic, Belle, Tildy, and Clea kept theirs. Their duty was to pass it on to their nieces. To show them the healing ways. To teach them the secrets. But I've told you what happened. My mother died. Before she could have any other daughters." Nick leaned back far enough to look up at Gowan.

"I am the only one left," she said, her voice ringing with melancholy certainty. "If I die without daughters, the magic will be lost. Forever." She blinked back the tears that suddenly filled her eyes. "The aunts know I need to marry. They are no more pleased by the prospect than I am. Yet they know it is the only way. And I know they are right."

There was nothing Gowan could say to comfort her and he surely knew it. To his credit, he did not even try. He ran a hand through his hair and his eyes narrowed. "Why me?" He asked the question more of himself than of her, but Nick knew without a doubt she would have to answer it.

"You are the earl." Though she kept her voice down, the sound of it brought Gowan out of his musings. He looked at her with new interest.

"The earl, yes, but why me? Why the earl? Why not Hugh? He's a pleasant enough chap and would surely father healthy babies. Or even Iain? He's a widower. But me? What makes me so appealing to the aunts? It was clear from the start that they would like nothing better than to see the two of us fall in love. Why are they so anxious that we marry?"

Nick tried to explain as simply as she could. There was something reassuring in the repetition of facts with all emotion removed. She wrapped herself in the thought and in the small comfort it gave. "To understand, you must understand about curses," she said. "The words of a curse are powerful. When you cast one, the universe and the powers in it take the curse quite literally. You must be precise and very, very careful."

Gowan gave her a blank look.

"According to family history, when Rolph spoke the curse, he laughed." Nick shivered. "I know you'll think me foolish and fanciful for saying it, but I am sure it was a wicked laugh. An evil laugh. He was a scornful man, and though he was bold enough to cast a curse, he forgot to take care with the wording. I am sure he meant to be mocking. He said what he said because he thought there wasn't one chance in a million that it would ever happen. He told Enid that the curse could be broken. But only if one of his descendants married one of hers."

Instantly, Gowan's expression brightened. "Broken? The curse will be broken if we marry? You didn't tell me. You didn't—"

"You haven't let me finish!" She did not mean to snap at Gowan, yet that is exactly how her words came out. Unable to endure the spark of hope that brightened his expression, Nick turned away. "The curse would be broken for my daughters," she explained. "But not for me. If I marry the earl . . . if I make love to you, Gowan, I will surely lose my magic."

She felt Gowan move closer. Before he could take her into his arms and try to soothe her with the promise of a love that could never be fulfilled, she leapt to her feet.

As it always did when she had finished a strong spell, Nick's head spun. She braced one arm against the garden wall. Frustration spilled into her words. Anger sharpened her tongue. "I know what you are thinking. You are thinking that the aunts could tend to the magic. But you are wrong. They could not. Not the way I do. They could not supply the charms the village folk want and the cures they need. They would try. I know they would. But they are not skilled enough. And a daughter . . ." Nick shook her head.

The thought of a child of her own had always been a

wonderful dream. A child to play with and pamper and take for long strolls through the mountains. A child who could share all the wonderful things she had never been able to share with her own mother.

A wonderful dream. That's all it had ever been.

Until she met Gowan.

What had once been an unattainable dream was now more a hunger, a longing that tugged at her heart and threatened to shatter her determination. It taunted her day and night. The thought of sharing her love with him, and with that love, producing a wonderful and unique little person made up of the best of both of them. The thought of having a child. Gowan's child.

"It would be a good many years before any daughter of mine would be able to use her magic to help and to heal. And what are the people to do until then?" Her voice tight with the panic that twisted through her, she hurled the words at him, questioning him and herself and everything she had always been so certain of: her convictions and her beliefs. Even her magic.

"And what if we never had a daughter? What if we marry and have only sons? Or no children at all?" As if it might hold back the pain that shot through her, Nick pressed her fists to her stomach. "And my magic . . ."

"Your magic is as important to you as life itself." Gowan put one hand on Nick's shoulder. Gently, he turned her to face him, his gaze going from Nick to the window of the room where Mai lay resting with her child. "I have never been the kind of man who believes things he cannot see and touch. At least I never was before today. I do not know how your magic works, Nick. I do not know why. But I know what I saw today. It was something rare. Something wonderful. I could no more ask you to surrender your magic than I could ask the sun to stop shining."

Nick had not realized she'd been crying, but he brushed his thumbs over her cheeks, gently wiping away her tears.

"Your magic is vital to you, just as your mother's was to her."

She had expected an argument, there was no doubt of that. She had expected him to rant and rave and tell her all the reasons she was being foolish and impractical, and when she didn't get one, Nick stood and stared in silence.

Gowan offered her a lopsided smile. "I know, I can scarcely believe I'm saying it myself. But I know it's true. It's the damnedest thing, but I do believe it. I may never understand your magic as long as I live, but I know it is breath and air and life to you. I know it is all that matters."

Nick did not know how she could feel so wonderful at the same time she was so utterly miserable. Gowan's touch left her hot with desire at the same time she was chilled with the prospect of a future without him. She was filled with love one second and so empty the next that regret invaded every inch of her, tearing at her insides and sending her heart splintering into a million pieces.

"It is why I've done all I could to avoid you," she said, her view of Gowan clouded by the tears that stung her eyes.

"I know that now." He smiled down at her an instant before he squeezed her into an enormous embrace.

"It is why I wanted you to leave," she confessed. "Why I wanted you gone from the mountain and gone from Wales. You were too close. Too tempting. And my magic . . ."

"I know that, as well."

"And it's all so unfair!" Try as she might, Nick could not control her words. They escaped on the end of a sound that was between a sob and a hiccup. Before she could say anything else and make them both feel worse, she tried to pull away from Gowan, but he would have none of it. In as long as it took for him to wrap his fingers around her arms to hold her in place, the tenderness was gone from his voice, the laughter from his eyes.

"If you think I'm going to give up so easily, you don't know me nearly well enough. Damn it, Nick, we can't pretend the problem doesn't exist. We can't simply ignore each other. Not now when I know how you feel. Not when I feel the same way. It's absurd to think—"

It was the argument Nick had been expecting and she cut it short as quickly as she could, before he could beguile her into believing it. "Do we feel the same way?" It was a cruel question, but it needed to be asked. She yanked free of Gowan's grip. "You think you love me, but don't you see? They've bespelled you, surely, for it's what they've wanted since the day they learned you were the earl."

"The aunts?"

Nick did not bother to point out how ridiculous his question was. "Of course, the aunts. Have you not thought of it yourself? Do you not remember the day we met?"

Nick did. All too well. She remembered the heat that shot through her at the sight of Gowan's naked body. She remembered the bold touch of his hands and the tempting taste of his lips. She steered herself clear of the memory and all the disturbing places it might lead.

"As soon as they learned you were the earl, they gave you a love potion," she reminded him. "They wanted you to fall in love with me. They want the curse to be broken."

"No." Gowan did not even stop to consider what she said. He sliced his hand through the air, rejecting the suggestion instantly. "The first day we met, I will grant you that, they slipped something into the tea they made me. But aside from that, your aunts have been nowhere near me. Certainly not near enough to drug me as they did last night. I have had no contact with them. No strange incidents. Nothing at all except for those odd little gifts that—" Gowan's words ended in a kind of choking sound. His face went as pale as death.

Nick's own stomach went cold. "Gifts?"

"Gifts." Gowan repeated the word like a man in a trance. It was clear he was trying to think his way through to some logical explanation of the whole thing and just as clear, he would never be able to do it. "Delicious little seedcakes," he said, the truth of the situation emerging more certainly with each word. "Bottles of wine. Gifts but never any giver. They appeared at the Lodge like . . ." He swallowed so hard, Nick could hear it. "You don't suppose . . . ?"

"I do, indeed." Nick wasn't sure if the news made her feel better or worse. She had proved her point. The aunts almost certainly had something to do with the way Gowan felt about her. But if that was true . . .

Nick steadied herself against a feeling much like having the floor suddenly fall out from under her.

If it was true, it meant he didn't love her. Not really. It meant that though he thought his feelings genuine enough, they were nothing more than a deceit fabricated of magic and moonbeams. Like the distorted reflection in a broken mirror, his love was a mocking imitation of what she felt with all her heart.

"They wouldn't have done that to me or to you." Gowan's mouth twisted with disbelief and a note of anger edged its way into his voice. "They couldn't have. No one could be as cruel as all that."

"Cruel, indeed!" The cottage door flew open and Belle bustled into the garden. Tildy and Clea followed behind, tea trays in their hands.

Belle's cheeks were crimson with emotion. Her eyes glistened. "We did not mean it to be cruel," she said. "We simply had no choice. Nick would not cooperate. She would not listen to reason."

"Me?" Her voice filled with outrage, Nick rounded on her aunt. "Is it reasonable to manipulate a man's mind?" She waved a hand in Gowan's direction. "Is it right to play with his heart?"

Belle was not about to back down. She pulled back her shoulders. She was inches taller than Nick and she glared down at her, the fire of righteousness bright in her eyes.

"It hardly matters what's right or reasonable when things are so serious that—"

"Ladies." Gowan stepped between the two of them. He laid one hand on Belle's shoulder, the other on Nick's arm. "It will serve no purpose to argue, that's for certain. It hardly matters—"

"Hardly matters?" Nick's anger nearly choked her. Deprived of venting it at Belle, she turned it on Gowan. "She's spelled you and you say it hardly matters?"

"No. No. No." Belle interrupted with a crisp wave of one hand. "It was my idea. I will take credit for that much. But I will not be blamed for spelling the lad." She turned her head, directing a dragon's gaze toward where Tildy and Clea stood. "Tildy took care of the magic."

Tildy set down the tea tray she was carrying. "No." She shook her head so fiercely, her hair came loose. "No. No. No, indeed. I baked the seedcakes, but I did not cast the spell. Clea did."

Clearly confused, Clea fluffed her skirts, her face screwed into a pained expression that said she was trying to think her way through the thing. "Me? I delivered the cakes to the Lodge. Wasn't that what I was supposed to do?" Her face went white. She looked from Belle to Tildy. "Oh dear me, yes. I do remember now. Tildy, you did ask me to take care of the magic. I was so busy worrying about delivering the cakes without anyone seeing me that I quite forgot. Yes. Yes. Quite forgot."

A shocked silence fell over them all. Gowan was the first to break it. He threw back his head and laughed. "Do you know what this means?" He grabbed Nick's hands. "It means that for all our other troubles, there is one thing we can be sure of. Magic has nothing to do with the way I feel about you, Nick. At least no magic other than the magic of love."

Still laughing, Gowan spun Nick in a circle, faster and

faster until her head was as dizzy as her heart, and when he was done, he pressed her into an embrace.

"I still want her." He spoke to the aunts, and Nick did not have to look up to Gowan's face to know his smile was gone. In its place was a look of grim determination that echoed in every syllable he spoke. "You've tried to arrange our lives with your magic. Well, damn it, use your magic now. Use it to get us out of this. There must be something you can do."

Tildy's eyes filled with tears. Clea's were wide with worry. Belle's were pensive. They exchanged glances, then as one, slowly shook their heads.

"I'm afraid not." Belle gave voice to all their fears. "A curse is a curse, as I'm sure Nick has explained. It cannot be changed. It cannot be broken. And unless you marry and have a daughter . . ."

The implications of her words hung in the air like fog, chilling Nick to the bone.

It had been coming to this all along. In that one moment, Nick knew it certainly. All her life, she had been moving toward this moment, the moment of choice.

Holding tight to Gowan's hand, she turned to face him and opened her mouth, ready to speak the words.

"No, damn it." Gowan stopped her, one finger on her lips. "I won't let you do it, Nick. I won't let you give up your magic. And I won't lose you. There must be some other way. There has to be."

Nineteen

"There may be."

At the sound of the voice, Nick, Gowan, and the aunts turned as one. They had been so busy talking about the curse and worrying over its implications that they had not noticed Mrs. Pritchard come up the path. They found her standing just outside the garden gate, glancing at the bed of foxglove there as if she expected the devil himself to come leaping from behind it. She shifted from foot to foot and cleared her throat. "Not that I mean to pry, m'lord, or listen in on a conversation which is clearly none of my business, but—"

"Don't think a thing of it," Gowan told her. However unexpected the interruption and however unlikely the chance Mrs. Pritchard might know anything at all that could help them, Nick felt him tense with the same, sudden surge of hope that tightened through her. He left her side long enough to hurry to the gate and opening it, he stood back so that Mrs. Pritchard might enter.

Though she must certainly have been expecting the invitation, Mrs. Pritchard was clearly not ready for it. As if she was considering all the benefits of turning around and heading for the Lodge against all the dangers that might lie ahead in the garden of witches, she stood in place, her gaze going from the cottage in front of her to the path behind. Her mind was apparently far more resolute than her footsteps, which were decidedly reluctant. She inched her way into the garden, and Nick couldn't help but notice that all the while she did, she fingered something in her pocket.

Papur y Dewin, no doubt, Nick told herself.

Any other time, she would have let Mrs. Pritchard know exactly what she thought both of charms against witches and the people who carried them. This time, she bit her tongue and kept her criticism to herself, her hopes tangling around the promise that trailed, unspoken, from Mrs. Pritchard's words.

"I heard. About Mai and the baby," Mrs. Pritchard said. She stationed herself as close to the gate and as far from Nick and the aunts as she could. "Word has already come to the village that it is a strong, healthy boy. They say it was a difficult delivery and that the baby would not have lived if it had not been for—" She could not bring herself to finish, but continued on, her uneasiness hidden for the moment beneath her usual, brisk efficiency.

"There is something you should know, m'lord," she said, raising her eyes to Gowan. "Though it is not a family connection I am eager to acknowledge, Mai's husband is my grandnephew, and a sorry lot he is. Knowing something of what she endures, I have always felt for Mai. I . . . I am grateful." She turned to Nick and the aunts. "I am grateful to all of you. That is why I brought this." Fishing in her pocket, Mrs. Pritchard pulled out a folded piece of paper and held it up to Gowan.

The very sight of the paper made Belle, Tildy, and Clea suck in sharp breaths of horror. Their arms linked, their faces pallid, they retreated a step from Mrs. Pritchard and the paper in her hand.

Nick was not so easily frightened. One look at the paper told her it was not a wizard's charm. It was not any kind of charm she had ever seen.

Even before Gowan took it, Nick knew it was old. The paper was brittle and yellow and as he unfolded it, it cracked, bits of it fluttering to the ground like snowflakes.

What she couldn't explain was the way the paper made her feel.

Nick pressed one hand to her lips. The paper may not have frightened her as it did the aunts, but it did make her uncomfortable. Her uneasiness nibbled away at what was left of her composure and weighed against her heart like a stone. One excruciating second at a time, she watched Gowan smooth the paper between his fingers and when it was finally open, she leaned closer and let her gaze run over the dark, cramped script that filled the page.

It was nearly unintelligible.

Gowan must have thought the same. Squinting, he held the paper at arm's length. When that didn't work, he brought it up to his nose. That was no more successful than the first try and finally settling on some distance in between, he turned the paper so that it was full in the light and tried to read as much of the scrawl as he could. "I, Rolph, Second Earl of Welshpool, do curse ye—"

"Rolph!"

"Earl!"

"Curse!"

Their voices overlapping, the aunts scurried over, each of them vying for a place close enough to Gowan so that she might get ahold of the paper.

Gowan would have none of it. Keeping the paper above his head and out of their grasps, he silenced them with a look, and it was only after they were finally able to control all but their excited twittering that he turned his gaze on Mrs. Pritchard. "What is this?" he asked her.

"It is a curse, m'lord. The curse. Written in Rolph's own hand. According to family tradition, he wrote it down the day he cast it on Enid Rhys. That bit of paper's been kept in our bible for all the years my family has worked for yours. I never thought it important, m'lord. And it may not be. But when I heard what Little Nick did for the baby and

I thought about all she's done for you . . ." Flustered and embarrassed, Mrs. Pritchard straightened her skirts.

"Beggin' your pardon for saying it, m'lord, but it's clear to see you're a different man than you were when you came to the Lodge. And as much as I am loath to admit it, it would take a person as blind as Old Wallace to fail to see the reason. If that paper might somehow help you and Nick find happiness, then far be it from me to keep it from the two of you."

Mrs. Pritchard held out her hand and against the protests of the aunts who were anxious themselves to see and examine it, Gowan handed the curse back to her. "Here. See." Mrs. Pritchard ran her finger down the script, her skin looking paler than ever against the yellowed parchment. "I read it over carefully before I brought it here," she said. "Rolph does mention that the curse can be reversed if an issue of your family marries as issue of Nick's. But here . . ." Mrs. Pritchard slid her finger further along the paper. "Here, he says there is another way."

This time, Gowan, the aunts, and Nick all made a move for the paper at the same time. Nick got it first.

Her hands shaking with the same nervous drubbing as her heart, she read the words Rolph had written in anger so many hundreds of years before.

" 'My curse does stand and so to your descendants for all time unless there be such a man who is fearless enough to marry a Rhys woman or one who is fool enough to believe.' "

The message was meant for Gowan. There was no doubt of that.

The daunting certainty sunk into Nick's bones. "Mrs. Pritchard is right," she said, her own voice echoing in her ears. "You must believe."

"Believe?" When Nick handed the curse to him, Gowan accepted it and as if he might find the answer to his question written on it somewhere, he turned the paper over in his hands. "What the hell does that mean?"

The fact that he had to ask told Nick everything. Her heart sinking at the same time tears filled her eyes, she caught his hand in hers and held tight.

"Don't you see?" she asked. "You have the power within yourself to reverse the curse. But only if you believe in the magic."

He wanted to believe. More than anything.

Gowan wanted to believe in the magic, for in spite of the fact that he'd seen it with his own eyes, he needed some name to pin on the thing that happened three days earlier when Mai's baby was born. There was no logical explanation for it, and certainly no medical precedent, no reason that a child who had absolutely no chance of survival was, the last he'd seen it, thriving.

Magic seemed as good an explanation as any.

Besides, he wanted to believe in the magic.

He wanted to believe because he knew he had to do everything in his power to reverse the curse Rolph had been so cruel to cast. He owed it to the Rhys women, those of this generation, and the next, those of all the generations past. After so many years of heartache, it was the least he could do for them.

He wanted to believe in the magic. More than he'd ever wanted to believe in anyone. Or anything.

He wanted to believe in the magic because he wanted Nick.

God, how he wanted her.

He could feel his desire for her with every breath he took. He could smell it in the air. It tightened through him, a hand around his heart, and filled him with passion at the same time it left him empty, and tormented, and yearning.

He certainly wanted Nick more than he valued his pride.

Otherwise he wouldn't be standing here looking like such a silly ass.

Gowan twitched his shoulders and straightened the skirts of the long, white robe the aunts had thrown over his head.

"You look a perfect dewin," Belle said, adjusting the flowing sleeves of the robe.

"I don't want to be sorcerer, thank you very much." When Tildy dipped a clump of oak leaves into a liquid that smelled of moss and marigold and sprinkled it over him, Gowan winced. "I want only to get this over with." He looked past Tildy to where Clea was arranging objects on the table that was set in the center of the room. She lay a sword on it and lit a brazier. Its coals glowed like two cat's eyes through the dark. "Where did you say Nick was?"

"Nick is getting ready for the ceremony." Belle did not have to tell him to rein his impatience. The look she gave him told him all. "And you should be, as well. You must concentrate. And center yourself. Just as we've been trying to teach you these last three days. Nick will be here in time. You can be certain of that. I told her midnight exactly and your Mrs. Pritchard knows it. She promised she'd show Nick up herself."

"Mrs. Pritchard bring anyone here to the west wing?" Gowan might have laughed if Tildy hadn't picked the moment to motion him to bend down. She carried a gold headband in her hands and when Gowan leaned over, she set it upon his brow, its flaming sun symbol square in the center of his forehead. "Mrs. Pritchard hates this part of the Lodge," he continued as Tildy adjusted the headband until she was satisfied it looked just right. "She says it's infested and dangerous, and damned if she's not right. The walls are crumbling."

"Yes, there's no denying that." Belle looked around and Gowan followed her gaze. Most of the roof in this part of the house had long since rotted away. Above their heads, stars flickered like guttering candles. Small animals scrambled about in the deep shadows where what was left of the walls met all that remained of the ceiling, their claws chattering like nervous teeth against the worn floorboards.

"But you heard what else Mrs. Pritchard said," Belle reminded him. "This was once the library of the house. At least it was in Rolph's time. According to family tradition, this is where Enid came to him to berate him about the serving girl who died. He cast the curse here and this is where he wrote it down. This is where its echoes are the strongest. It is here it must be revoked."

"Yes, well . . ." Gowan waited until Tildy had finished fastening a gold band around his right upper arm. "I can but try. I—"

He did not finish. From where he stood, Gowan could see the doorway that led into the old library and from there, the passage beyond it. A pale glow lit the hall, an odd, skittish sort of light that danced against the worm-eaten paneling. The next thing he knew, Mrs. Pritchard came into the room.

Her hands trembling so that the candle she had clutched in them jumped, Mrs. Pritchard took one horrified look at the altar table set in the center of the room, another at Gowan's peculiar clothing.

One look was apparently quite enough.

Sputtering something that sounded very much like, "Really, m'lord!" she stepped back into the passageway and the last Gowan saw of her, she was heading back toward the habitable portion of the house as fast as she could.

Mrs. Pritchard took the candle with her.

At least Gowan supposed she had, yet he could have sworn there was some vestige of its glow out in the passage—a light that came and went like the twinkle of starshine, a glow that shimmered like the heated halo of air around a candle flame. It fused with the shadows, it melted them, until light and shadow swirled before his eyes. They coalesced, they crystallized, and when the world came back into focus, Gowan realized the shadow was really raven-dark hair, and the light, a white robe much like his.

As silent as a dream, Nick entered the room and every thought but those of her flew out of Gowan's head.

Like Gowan's, Nick's robe hung to her ankles and skimmed her bare toes. Like Gowan, she had a headband around her brow. Hers was silver, its color burnished by the light of the moon just rising over the mountains.

Nick's eyes looked silver tonight, as well. They glimmered at him through the shadows, bright with excitement, glowing with trust, luminous with the promise of a lifetime to come.

If he believed in the magic.

The thought sunk inside Gowan like a lead weight. Hoping to expel it, he allowed himself the pleasure of letting his gaze slide down Nick's body, from her eyes to her mouth and from there to where her breasts pressed against the soft folds of her linen robe, and when the moon climbed higher up the sky and lit the air behind her, he saw her body silhouetted through the fabric of her robe and realized she was naked beneath it.

Catching his breath, Gowan slid his gaze from Nick's waist to her hips. From her hips, he let it tease down her legs.

Damn, but he wanted to believe in the magic!

The thought crackled like fire through his blood and this time, he did nothing at all to damp it down.

He wanted to believe in the magic.

With his heart and with his soul. With every breath he took and every pulse of his heart.

He wanted to believe in the magic the way he already believed in Nick.

As if in response to some signal Gowan neither heard nor saw, Nick and the aunts moved as one. Nick went to stand before the table spread with its white cloth. The aunts closed ranks around Gowan: Tildy to his right, Belle to his left, Clea behind. They led him in slow procession to where Nick waited and once he was in position, the aunts stepped back and melted into the shadows.

Nick turned to him. Her eyes shimmered with moonlight. Her voice was low. Excitement and tension rippled through her words. "Are you ready?"

Gowan hauled in a breath. "I suppose so." He skimmed a hand along Nick's cheek. "Are you?"

Nick didn't answer. She stepped back and reaching for the sword that was laid upon the table, she handed it to Gowan.

Gowan wasn't sure what he expected. He supposed he thought the sword would be a plaything. He was wrong. It was strong and far heavier than he expected, and he balanced it in his hand and waited to see what he must do next.

Nick did not make him wait long. Closing her hand over his, she led him to the center of the room. "We must cast a circle," she said. "It will provide protection and concentrate our power. I can help you with that much but after the circle is cast, there is nothing more I can do. The magic must come from inside you, Gowan."

Inside him. It seemed unlikely. How could there be any room for magic when his worries and his desires and every damn carnal hunger he'd ever had were tied inside him like a Gordian knot?

"Begin with the east." Nick ignored his hesitation. She turned him to face the same direction as the table. "Train the sword toward the floor and slowly draw a wide circle all around us with it. Visualize a flame coming from the end of it. Silver-blue. Protecting. Clean, white light."

Gowan did as he was told. He pointed the sword toward the floor and with Nick's hand still over his, he completed a circle that enclosed both the altar table and them, a barrier that isolated them from the outside world, an invisible shield against the darkness.

Or was it?

Gowan squeezed his eyes shut and shook his head. When he opened his eyes again, it was still there. Light. Shimmering. Dancing. Light. Like will o' the wisps, it came and went, sparkling all around, ringing them with protection.

"Nick—?" Gowan wasn't sure if he was about to question his eyesight or his reason. It wasn't until he started to ask that he found Nick was no longer at his side. Standing in the part of the circle she had called the east, she passed her hand over a red candle. It flamed to life. She set the candle there, murmuring an incantation as she did. She did the same to the south with a white candle, and to the west with a gray one. She went to the north and set down a black candle and when she was done, she stepped up to the table.

She passed her hands above the brazier and like dust motes sparkling in the sunlight, something fell from them and hit the burning coals. A curl of smoke soared into the air and as if there were an invisible dome above them, it hung in an opalescent canopy above their heads. The room filled with a scent the likes of which Gowan had never experienced.

It was dusky, like old roses. And fresh, like the forest after rain. It was as potent as fine brandy, as heady as lusty lovemaking, as robust as the slap of an autumn wind.

It curled through Gowan, filling his lungs. It excited his mind at the same time it sharpened his senses. It roused some ability inside him he had not known existed.

Gowan wasn't sure where the notion came from. It was certainly not part nor parcel of any experience he'd ever had, yet suddenly, he knew exactly what to say. Exactly what to do. Clutching the sword in both hands he walked the circle anti-clockwise.

"I decrease Rolph's magic. I diminish his spell." Like a voice out of a dream, Gowan's own words drifted to his ears, a disembodied visitor from another world. "With heart and mind, with body and soul, I cancel the words he spoke in anger. I close the door on his power. I erase his curse."

He wasn't sure what he expected to happen next. Lightning, perhaps. Lightning would be dramatic. And appropriate. And very, very impressive.

But there was no lightning.

Thunder might have done the trick. Thunder answered by a little rumbling from the ground. Some sign that heaven and earth had heard him. Some indication that the magic had worked.

Instead, there was nothing.

Gowan's last words faded into the night. The candles winked out. The silver-blue flame around the circle vanished. The aunts were gone.

Not sure if it was safe to move, he looked at Nick. "That's it?"

"Only you can answer that." She moved from her place behind the altar table. "Is the curse broken?"

It was as impossible a question as he'd ever been asked.

Gowan set the sword back on the table and rubbed his chin. "That's the bally trouble, isn't it?" he asked. "There's no way for us to know."

The last thing he expected from Nick was a smile, but it was exactly what he got—a smile as suggestive as any he'd ever seen. And as alluring. A smile that traveled from her lips to her eyes and lit them with a spark that awakened an answering fire in him.

Taking Gowan's hand, Nick led him from the circle. "You're wrong," she said. "There is one way. And only one. There is one sure way to find out if your magic worked."

Twenty

Gowan couldn't help himself. It took him no time at all to realize exactly what Nick had in mind, and less time still to panic. He pulled to a stop, dragging Nick to a halt at his side. "Let's not be hasty."

"Hasty!" Like the sound of a waterfall, Nick's laughter sailed through the air. "It has taken us months to get even this far, and you call it hasty?"

"I call it foolish. Nick . . ." In his head, Gowan ran through all his reasons for resisting. He couldn't be sure of what had happened inside the circle he'd drawn with the sword. Was it magic or wishful thinking that had moved him to speak so confidently against Rolph's curse? Was it faith or simply the last hope of a man desperate enough to grasp at straws?

He'd told himself he wanted to believe in the magic. He still wanted to believe. But what would happen—to Nick, to him, to their love—if he didn't believe enough?

His head, he decided, knew all the reasons for resistance—well enough. If only he could make his body listen. The touch of Nick's hand was like fire on a cold day, warming him through and through. The whisper of her breath against his cheek sent desire surging through him. Still smiling that sly cat's smile of hers, she pulled him across the room and for the first time, he realized exactly where they were heading.

Where it came from, he had no idea, but on the far side

of the room was a bed. There was a cloth draped across it, a frothy sort of a confection of a thing. In the daylight, it may have been white or even light blue, but in the moonlight, it looked to be spun of pure silver.

The bed was tucked into a corner in a place where the walls were standing but the ceiling was completely gone. In hundreds of nooks and crannies spiders had woven their webs. They hung on all sides of the bed like a gossamer tent, sparkling with dew and moonbeams.

Next to the bed was a table and on it, a branched holder that contained three candles, red on the left, pink on the right, and green in between. Next to the candle holder was a single red rose.

Nick passed her hand over the red candle and it flamed to life.

Gowan couldn't help himself. He remembered what Clea had said about red candles during the birthing of Mai's baby. "Red for courage?" he asked, only half teasing.

Nick nodded. "Courage. And other things. Energy. Strength. Sexual vigor." She waved a hand above the pink candle. "And pink for love. Pink for healing the spirit. And for romance."

"And the last? What does the green candle signify?"

"Green is for marriage," she answered. "It is kindled from the flames of the other two. But not now. Not yet. Not until . . ." She dismissed the subject with one look at the bed and reaching for the flower, Nick stroked it against Gowan's cheek. "I think you'll agree," she said, "it is time to put our differences aside."

"Indeed." His head filled with the intoxicating scent of the rose, the single word trembled from Gowan's lips. The look in Nick's eyes was achingly sweet. It shot him through with longing at the same time it sent an icy finger of regret straight to his heart. He laid one hand over Nick's. "But we can't be sure—"

She stopped his protest with a kiss. "I have learned

something these last few months," she told him. "There is one thing we can be sure of. I always thought it was my magic. I was wrong. How can I depend on something that can dissolve so easily? How can I put my trust in powers that might disappear at any moment, simply because of the whim of a man like Rolph, a man who's been dead these hundreds of years?" Nick laughed. "I do believe the only thing we can ever depend on, Gowan, is each other. And our love."

Without another word, Nick stepped away from him. In a motion that was as fluid as the wind and as unaffected as it was innocent, she stripped off her white robe and stood before him naked.

Her skin was not as white as alabaster.

It was a foolish thing to think of at a time like this when his heart was in his throat and his body was tight with desire, yet Gowan could not help but smile at it.

She was not the Nick of his careless and wanton imaginings. She was not a figment of fancy, nor a personification of some ideal as impossible to attain as it was to possess.

She was a woman. A real woman. A woman whose body was not the body of some alabaster goddess. Nick's arms were bronzed from hours in the sun gathering her medicines. Her shoulders were sprinkled with freckles. Her breasts were not the voluptuous breasts of the Nick of his dreams. They were small and round and firm. Her legs were short and well-shaped, and when he glanced at the shadowy place between them she did not preen like the Nick of his wishing dream. She shivered and smiled, getting as much pleasure from his appreciative look as he did from the giving.

This was a woman. A real woman. A woman who was offering her body and so much more. She was making him a gift of herself. She was making him a gift of her magic. And all she was asking in return was his love.

As much as he would have liked to, Gowan could not tell her he knew full well what all this meant to her. He could not tell her anything. Not when his heart was so full. Not when his blood was rushing through his veins, liquid fire stoking the passion that throbbed inside.

He couldn't tell her so he didn't. He showed her.

Lifting Nick in his arms, Gowan carried her to the bed and laid her down.

Moonlight and candleglow washed over her. It touched her hair with silver and washed her skin with a color like pearls. The light brushed her shoulders. It grazed her breasts.

Gowan traced its path, first with his hand, then with his tongue. With his thumb and forefinger, he circled her breasts and watched, smiling, as her nipples hardened like jewels. He bent and drew one breast into his mouth, suckling her until she moaned.

Her fingers twisting round the bedclothes, Nick sucked in a quick, sharp breath. The thought of being intimate with a man had always been nothing more to her than the stuff of her wildest dreams. Now she found the reality was far more electrifying even than the dreams themselves.

With his hands and his lips and his tongue, Gowan laid a trail of fire across her skin and awakened an answering fire inside, a feeling that was much more a need than it was simply a craving, a hunger that surely started in the body but could only be fed by the soul.

Raising herself on her elbows, Nick slipped the headband from Gowan's head and laid it on the bed. She slid the armband from his arm. She might have helped him with his robe if it had not been such an awkward undertaking. Gowan realized it, as well. Smiling, he rose from the bed long enough to drag the robe over his head and discard it along with the rest of his clothes.

Men's clothing was as much of a mystery as men were themselves.

In the part of her that wasn't focused on watching, fascinated, as Gowan stripped, Nick was grateful that she wasn't expected to help him disrobe. At least not this time. There were too many twists and turns in the knot of his tie for her to fathom how it might be so easily loosened, too many buttons on shirt and pants and drawers for her nervous fingers to even begin to undo, and far too many splendid sights to keep her far too enthralled to help. When Gowan stood before her, naked in the moonlight, she let her eyes drink in every inch of him.

He was not the first naked man she had ever seen. In her healing, she'd treated many a man indeed, old and young, strong and frail. She had seen naked men aplenty, but there was never one who had this effect on her.

As if there was a hand around her heart, Nick felt her chest tighten and her eyes fill with tears of joy. Kneeling on the bed, she glided her hands over Gowan's broad shoulders. She slid her fingers through the silky mat of hair on his chest. She slipped them down even further, exploring and enjoying, and when Gowan caught his breath, Nick laughed.

"I think now, you do believe in the power of magic," she said.

"I believe in the power of love." Wrapping his arms around her, Gowan laid her on the bed and moved above her. "I think, perhaps, that is magic in itself."

It was.

There was magic in every slow and gentle movement of Gowan's lovemaking, magic in each kiss, each touch. There was magic in the rush of desire that shot through Nick when he entered her, and more magic still in the thrust of his body against hers.

There was magic in the breathtaking explosion of sensation that rocketed through her body, and in the sound of his voice calling her name against her ear, and in the spasm that coursed through him, signalling his satisfaction and his pleasure.

There was magic in the warmth of his embrace and in

the kisses he dropped against her brow and her cheeks and her lips, magic in the contentment and safety of the circle of his arms, and when he slid off her and laid at her side, one arm cocked beneath his head, there was magic in that as well, and in the smile he gave her.

With one finger, Nick traced his lips. "I do believe we can light the marriage candle now," she said. "I will take the red candle and you, the pink." She sat up and made a move toward the candelabra.

"No." Gowan stopped her, his hand on her arm. "It's time for a new tradition. Since old Rolph's time, there has been no other way for a Rhys woman to light the fire, not once she gave herself to her man. But I do believe we've changed that, Nick. We don't need to light the candle from the flames of the other two. You can do that yourself now. Just as you always have."

Nick knew he was right. There was no doubt, not anymore. There was only faith and trust. And love.

Nick passed her hand over the marriage candle. The magic that was inside her flooded her heart and tingled through her hands. The candle flamed to life.

With a smile, Gowan took her into his arms and kissed her.

And the real magic began again.